Enchanting Tales About
Affairs of the Heart
Signet Double Romances:

Her Heart's Desire
and
An Offer of Marriage

More Romance from SIGNET

Her Heart's Desire
and
An Offer of Marriage

by

Lynna Cooper

A SIGNET BOOK

NEW AMERICAN LIBRARY

TIMES MIRROR

NAL BOOKS ARE ALSO AVAILABLE AT DISCOUNTS IN BULK
QUANTITY FOR INDUSTRIAL OR SALES-PROMOTIONAL USE.
FOR DETAILS, WRITE TO PREMIUM MARKETING DIVISION,
NEW AMERICAN LIBRARY, INC., 1633 BROADWAY,
NEW YORK, NEW YORK 10019.

Originally appeared in paperback as separate volumes published by
The New American Library, Inc.

SIGNET TRADEMARK REG. U.S. PAT. OFF. AND FOREIGN COUNTRIES
REGISTERED TRADEMARK—MARCA REGISTRADA
HECHO EN CHICAGO, U.S.A.

SIGNET, SIGNET CLASSICS, MENTOR, PLUME AND MERIDIAN BOOKS
are published by The New American Library, Inc.,
1633 Broadway, New York, New York 10019

First Printing (Double Romance Edition), February, 1980

1 2 3 4 5 6 7 8 9

PRINTED IN THE UNITED STATES OF AMERICA

Her Heart's Desire

Chapter ONE

Judy Hunter sat with her knees close together under the plain black A-line, her hands clasping the small black handbag nervously. Her long brown hair was gathered severely against her head, fashioned into a bun at the nape of her neck. She wore owl glasses, dark-rimmed, that gave her the appearance of a prim old maid. From time to time she ran the tip of her tongue about her lips as her eyes took in her surroundings.

The walls were of wood, darkly stained, with here and there an oil painting to relieve their monotony. Above the paintings, tiny electric bulbs brought out the color of those pictures, their richness. A heavily upholstered leather divan was set against the far wall. End tables held twin Girard lamps, dimly glowing. Other chairs were scattered about in this reception room, of which she was the only occupant, saving the receptionist herself, a pretty blond with vivid coloring and clad in a shirt and sweater ensemble of pale blue. The blond girl ignored her, busily typing.

She was here on a legal matter; the letter in her handbag, which she had read a dozen times, assured her that it was to her advantage to come to the law offices of Parker, Perkins, Miller and Frentrup. Her Uncle Walter had died and left her his sole legatee, on a condition.

She remembered her uncle very well. She had not seen him for several years, he had lived in New Hampshire, had been retired a long time, and certainly had little enough to bequeath to her. The house, of course, and the land around it, and the letter had mentioned something about a bookstore; certainly, nothing else.

His pension and Social Security payments would have stopped on his death. Beyond this, he had nothing else.

Still, the sale of the house and its land, plus the bookstore, should net her a nice amount in these days of high real-estate values. And she could use any help she could get; the pay of a librarian wasn't all that wonderful. She did not let herself think of anything beyond this. It was inconceivable that Uncle Walter had been a rich man.

Judy sighed, knowing a stab of pain and grief deep inside her. If only Bill had lived, instead of drowning in that accident off Block Island. They could have been married, with this inheritance. Always they had held off, for one reason or another. Although they had been unofficially engaged, Bill had never given her a ring; he claimed he wanted it to be a big diamond, and he could not afford such luxury.

Dear Bill, with his gray eyes that could melt so tenderly or blaze with anger, so sloppy in his casual clothes. They had been so much in love! She thought of the little dinners they had had in her place or his, the bottles of wine they had shared, the candles lighted for a more romantic setting. Strange, though. He had never so much as kissed her as she felt a woman should be kissed by the man who loved her. Always it had been on the cheek, or a mere peck on the lips. "When we're married," he had said, "it will be different; it isn't fair to either of us, now."

He had been so thoughtful. So dear, so sweet.

Why, there was the time when . . .

"Miss Hunter."

. . . when it had been snowing so hard and she had begged him to stay overnight at her tiny apartment—he could sleep on the divan, she would make it up for him—and he had refused, saying that it would be better if he went home, snow or not, and . . .

"Miss Hunter! Miss Hunter!"

The blond girl was standing before her, smiling

down at her, though with a touch of impatience in her eyes. Judy started, jumped to her feet.

"I—I'm sorry. I was—"

"Daydreaming. Yes, I know. Mr. Miller will see you now, if you're ready."

"Of course."

She went behind the receptionist through a heavy oak door and along a narrow hall where doors opened onto small offices in which girls were busily typing. There was a faint hush in these offices; other than for the clicking of typewriter keys, there was no sound. The shag carpeting that had been in the reception room was continued here along this hallway, where their footfalls made no sound.

The blond turned to the right. The offices here, Judy saw, were larger and more luxuriously furnished than those others, and men were sitting behind desks, reading from law books or dictating to secretaries. A particularly large room, wood paneled, was shelved from floor to ceiling and filled with books. The law library. Two young men sat at a long table, dozens of books piled about them as they scribbled unceasingly.

The blond went through a doorway. "This is Miss Hunter, sir."

Judy found herself staring at a gray-haired man with horn-rimmed glasses, somewhere in his middle fifties. He rose to his feet and smiled at her, coming around the edge of his desk with hand outstretched. He wore a gray flannel suit, with striped tie and white shirt. Did all lawyers dress this drably? she wondered as she took his hand. But his smile was genuine as he welcomed her and gestured her to a chair.

"I must apologize for the delay, Miss Hunter. I've just received a phone call from Dave Carnegie. He'll be right over."

Judy stared. "Who's Dave Carnegie?"

The older man smiled. "He's mentioned in your uncle's will." A troubled look touched his face as he frowned very faintly. "Are you trying to tell me you don't know him?"

She shook her head. "I'm not trying to tell you, Mr. Miller, I am telling you. I've never heard of the man in my life."

Judy hesitated. David Carnegie, David Carnegie. Somewhere, recently, she had heard that name, or seen it. But where? She racked her brain, trying to remember. What was it about that name that had made such an impression on her? She could not recall. Still, she was perfectly sure she had never met or even seen this David Carnegie.

Mr. Miller sat down. He pursed his lips and shook his head slowly back and forth. "I'm surprised at this development, I must admit. I was under the impression you knew David. Though to be sure, he didn't say as much when we last spoke."

Judy drew a deep breath, her hands unconsciously tightening on her handbag. "I always thought that lawyers spoke clearly and lucidly, Mr. Miller. I must say you're not doing this at all. Or perhaps it's my own stupidity. But I'm not following you, not at all."

He laughed, then sobered. "I can't say I blame you. Lawyers don't always speak as lucidly as you seem to think, Miss Hunter. They talk gobbledygook quite often, sometimes even as a matter of course. However, I'll endeavor to clear up this difficulty just as soon as possible.

"It involves your uncle's will, first of all. In it, he—" He broke off as a knock sounded on the door.

The blond girl came in ahead of a tall man with tawny hair, wide shoulders, and dressed in a bold plaid suit with green vest, striped shirt, and solid green tie. He had an outdoorsy look about him, with his heavily tanned skin, and the look of faraway places in his blue eyes. He walked like an athlete, Judy thought.

Dave Carnegie? The man she ought to know and didn't?

He crossed the room and leaned over the desk,

shaking the older man's hand. Then he turned to Judy where she sat with stiff back, eyes wide behind her owl glasses.

"So you're Judy Hunter," he said softly, and smiled, showing very white teeth.

"And you're this mysterious Dave Carnegie."

He chuckled. "I'm not as mysterious as all that."

The older man interrupted. "What Miss Hunter is saying is that she's never met you, doesn't know who you are. It presents a difficulty, Dave."

Dave never took his eyes off her as he said, "No difficulty at all, Jim. Introduce us. Then she'll know me and I'll know her."

Mr. Miller said, "Miss Hunter, this is Mr. Carnegie. Mr. Carnegie, meet Miss Hunter. Dave, Judy."

Judy extended her hand. "Glad to know you," she said.

There was laughter in his blue eyes. "You're not glad at all," he accused. "And I can't say I blame you. You don't know the first thing about me. But I am glad to meet you. Very glad. Because I know something about you."

He turned, sat down in an easy chair that matched the one where Judy sat, and extended his long legs, crossing them at the ankles. For some reason she could not put a finger on, Judy resented his easy airs, his attitude of being completely at ease. She scowled at him, then turned away to look at James Miller.

"You sent me a letter asking me to come here to listen to my uncle's will, Mr. Miller. I gather that Mr. Carnegie plays a part in it. May I learn at long last what part that is?"

"Well spoken, Miss Hunter," agreed Dave Carnegie. "So let's get to the nitty-gritty, Jim. Bring out the will and let's hear it."

Judy arched her eyebrows. "You sound as though you know the will and its contents, Mr. Carnegie."

He looked surprised. "But of course I do. I read a copy of it years ago."

She stared at him blankly. Resentment surged inside her, so that she was forced to increase her grip on her handbag to keep from snapping at him. She would not see this arrogant young man after today—at least, she hoped not!—so she could well afford to be patient with him until she had heard just what it was her Uncle Walter had left her.

"Then I'm the only one in the dark," she said. Her eyes went from Dave Carnegie to the older man, who sat watching them both with the chagrin clear to see on his face.

"The will, Jim," Dave said gently.

"Ah, yes. Of course."

He opened a folder, drew out a will-back to which were stapled two sheets of typewritten legal paper. Judy saw the fancily scrolled *Last Will and Testament* on the will-back, and typewritten words beneath it.

James Miller began to read: "Know all men by these presents that I, Walter Kenneth Hunter, of the town of Morstead, County of Cheshire and State of New Hampshire, being of sound and disposing mind and memory, do make, publish and declare this to be my last will and testament, hereby revoking all wills by me at any time heretofore made.

"First, I direct my executor hereinafter named to pay all my funeral expenses, administration expenses of my estate, including inheritance and succession taxes, state or federal, which may be occasioned by the passage of or succession to any interest in my estate under the terms of this instrument, and all my just debts.

"Second, All the rest, residue and remainder of my estate, both real and personal, of whatsoever kind and character and wheresoever situated, I give, devise and bequeath to my beloved niece, Judith Ellen Hunter, to be hers absolutely and forever, upon the condition that she marry David Morgan Carnegie, the son of my very dear friend, Septimus Carnegie.

"Third—"

Judy leaped to her feet, staring from the lawyer to

David Carnegie where he sat relaxed and at ease in the leather easy chair. She opened her mouth, then closed it.

After a single glance at her angry face, the lawyer went on. "Third, in the event that my niece Judith Ellen Hunter refuse to marry the aforementioned David Morgan Carnegie, or in the event that she predecease me, then and in that event, I give, devise and bequeath all my property, both real and personal, to any charity designated by my executor.

"Fourth, in the event that David Morgan Carnegie predecease my niece, Judith Ellen Hunter, before this marriage takes place, I hereby give, devise and bequeath all my property, both real and personal, to my niece Judith Ellen Hunter, to be hers absolutely and forever.

"Fifth, I hereby appoint my lawyer and great personal friend, James Miller, to be Executor of this my last will and testament, and I direct that he shall not be required to post bond.

"In witness whereof, I have hereunto set my hand and seal et cetera, et cetera."

And Judy exploded. "This is the most ridiculous thing I—I've ever heard of! My uncle must have been out of his mind! Why, I never laid eyes on this—this man," and here her hand waved wildly at the smiling David Carnegie, "before today. It's absolutely unthinkable!"

"You can contest the probate, of course," Dave said gently. "Though I don't think you'd get very far. The condition doesn't violate any provisions of the Constitution, nor any local laws. Nor is the condition against any public policy."

His smile infuriated her. "I don't say it does any of those things, but I absolutely refuse to marry you. That's final. If I don't get my uncle's property, I'm not really out anything. I never expected him to leave me anything, anyhow."

"That's stupid," Dave said.

Her hands balled into fists. She wanted to hurl herself at him, to wipe that confident smile off his lips with a well-directed slap or blow. She fought down her anger, though her face was flushed and her eyes blazed furiously.

"St-stupid, am I?"

"I didn't say you were stupid. I was talking about your attitude."

"What's the difference?"

"Plenty. You can change your attitude."

"Well, I don't intend to."

The older man was making distressed sounds, rising to his feet and waving his hands at them placatingly. "Please, please. I must insist on more quiet. We can discuss this in a reasonable manner, I feel certain."

"I can," Dave said.

Judy snarled, "Oh, can you? Well, I can be just as easygoing as you, David Morgan Carnegie."

She sat down and crossed her legs. His eyes went to her legs; her skirt was up but she refused to pluck at it. Let him look, if he wanted. Little good it was going to do him. She even managed to plaster a smile on her lips.

"Now then," she stated firmly. "Is such a condition valid?"

"It has been held so," Miller told her. "It's a conditional will, of course, but the fact that a testator—someone who makes a will—intends a condition to take effect before disposing of his property has been upheld by our law courts. I refer you to the case of Barber versus Barber. Also, any condition calculated to induce a beneficiary to marry a certain person has been held not against public policy. I refer you here to the case of In re Liberman. This is New York law."

Judy was sobered, but she nodded.

"Very well, then. I can't fight the will. And I won't marry this—this fortune hunter! So I might as well go home."

Her lips quivered. She had not expected to inherit

anything from Uncle Walter, but to learn that her only relative would impose such a contingency on her was unbearable. The fact that Dave Carnegie was smiling at her in very friendly fashion didn't add to her peace of mind.

Dave said softly, "May I make a suggestion?"

She glowered at him. "What sort of suggestion?"

"Why don't we go down to the coffee shop and have a cup or two? Talk a little." He held up his hand as she opened her mouth. "In a friendly way, I mean. With no screaming, no insults, no losing of our tempers."

Oooooh! He was the most irritating, irrational man she had ever known. If he expected her to fall into his arms after he soft-soaped her, he had another think coming! He was probably out to get her inheritance, share in it.

"Just coffee, and maybe a cigarette or two, and talk," he went on, very gently. "I know this has been a shock to you. I'm sorry about that. But I didn't write your uncle's will."

She had to give him that, Judy reflected, she must try to be fair about all this. Drat Uncle Walter! What had the man been thinking of, to put her in such a position? But she would not cry. She refused to let the tears come, to take refuge behind them, as she was sure this fortune hunter expected.

She said, "I suppose we could do that."

"Good. There's no reason why we can't talk this over, just the two of us."

"It won't do you any good," she snapped.

His hand waved her remark aside. "Of course not. But try it. What do you have to lose?"

"All right, all right. I could use a cigarette and a cup of coffee right now."

"The treat's on me." He smiled.

"Oh, no. It's Dutch treat."

He shrugged and turned to Miller, who was watching them with his distress easy to read in his face.

His hand was toying with the will, lifting it and shifting it about on the desktop as though it were really the hot potato it seemed to be.

"Back in an hour, Jim? That OK?"

"Fine, fine. I have a bill of particulars to dictate, anyhow. It'll keep me busy." The older man looked at Judy. "We are your friends, my dear. Nobody is trying to rob you, or put one over on you. I've known your uncle a long time; he was a hardheaded businessman. I am sure he had a good reason for putting that condition in his will."

"Did he? I can't think of any."

Dave put his hand on her elbow, turning her gently. "Let's go get that coffee. And maybe a cheese Danish."

His mention of the pastry reminded Judy that she had not eaten breakfast today, she had been too anxious to get to these law offices and learn about that condition in Uncle Walter's will. Well, now she knew. And the man beside her, who was holding her elbow so gently as they strolled along the hall floor toward the elevator, was the cause of all her troubles.

Resentfully, she drew her arm from his clasp and walked beside him without so much as a glance in his direction. If it hadn't been for this—this David Carnegie, she would be an heiress in her own right. Not that she would inherit a vast fortune—that house in New Hampshire and the bookstore weren't worth very much. Still!

"Hey," he said.

Startled, she turned and met his blue eyes, seeing the smile and the friendliness in them. "There's no need to treat me like a pariah," he told her, "I'm not your enemy. On the contrary. Why don't you pretend we've just met, that I'm a customer at your library, or whatever it is you call the people who come to ask your advice? You wouldn't carry a chip on your shoulder where they're concerned, would you?"

She found that she was smiling. She could hardly help but smile, he seemed so perturbed by her attitude.

Judy discovered that she liked his sort of craggy face with its outdoors tan and the manner in which his tawny hair framed it. His lips were rather wide—didn't that indicate a generous nature?—and pleasant enough.

Her hand came up to touch her glasses, adjust them.

She blurted out, "You must think I'm some kind of nut."

"I think you're a very nice young lady who's had something of a shock."

"I'm not nice at all. I've been absolutely horrible!"

"Hey, now. Let's not quarrel about that."

How he did it, she wasn't quite sure, but he had both of her hands in his, and was holding them. For another reason she couldn't understand, her heart started thumping and her knees felt suddenly weak. But this was ridiculous. In another moment, she'd be blubbering on his shoulder.

She almost pulled away, but restrained the impulse. None of this was his fault; in a way he was only trying to help her out. *I must stop acting like a spoiled brat,* she scolded herself.

Aloud she murmured, "We won't quarrel. I'm not blaming you for any of this. It's all my uncle's fault."

He nodded. "That's better. Friends?"

"Friends."

They waited for the elevator in a cloud of unease. At least, she felt uneasy, though he seemed to be relaxed and comfortable.

David asked, "Do you like your work at the library?"

"Well enough. It's a job, and a good one. I'm a great reader, and it's a friendly place to be."

She chattered on about the books, the readers, the people who came into the library. She told him about one retired man whom she had come to know who had read every book in the library at least once, and was on the second go-round.

"The fiction books, that is. I'm sure he doesn't delve into psychology and higher mathematics."

By the time they were moving into the coffee shop, she felt very much more relaxed. She could laugh with him, even argue about some trades the Mets had made. He stood while she slid onto the booth seat, then sat across from her. When a waitress came with the menus, he waved them away and ordered two cheese Danish and two cups of coffee.

"Is that all right?" he asked.

"Of course. I think a cheese Danish would hit the spot right about now."

David talked about inconsequential things, the break in the weather, the prospect of a few sunny days after all the early summer rain, the possibility that oil prices might go up, and the latest bestseller on *The New York Times* book list.

When the cheese Danish came, Judy bit into it with gusto. It was fresh, delicious. And the coffee tasted super. *I ought not to be enjoying this so much*, she reflected. *This man across from me who makes me feel so comfortable is just after whatever money Uncle Walter left me.*

Glumly she reflected that the only way she could get that money—if there was any—was by marrying him. This she was not about to do.

"Another coffee?" he asked, reaching into a jacket pocket for cigarettes.

He offered her one, lighted it for her.

Then he said, "You'd be very silly not to marry me, you know." He held up his hand to forestall the burst of indignation that was shaping itself in her throat. "Wait, wait. Don't put that chip back on your shoulder. Just hear me out."

He smiled with his eyes as well as his lips, she noted. He was really a lot better looking than Bill had been. Poor Bill! She shivered, thinking on the manner of his death in Long Island Sound, how he must have struggled before going down. Tears came into her eyes.

"Hey, now. Don't cry, either. I'm not all that bad."

"It isn't you," she whispered.

"Love somebody else, do you?" His face became grave. "Ouch. I never thought of that angle. Stupid of me. A pretty girl like you, I should have known."

She shook her head, forcing herself to be calm. "There isn't anybody else. There was, but he's dead. And I'm not at all pretty."

Judy found herself telling him about Bill Evans, how they had met in the library when she first came to work there, how they had gone out to dinner and the movies, how an affection had grown between them.

"He wanted to marry me, but kept putting it off because he didn't have enough money. He wanted to get me a ring, but he claimed he couldn't afford it. But we were engaged. Unofficially, that is."

She was surprised to find herself saying this last bit of information almost defiantly, as though she didn't expect him to believe her. David Carnegie listened quietly, nodding sympathetically from time to time. His grave face encouraged her confidence, she found, and when she was done, he put his hand out to clasp hers.

"I'm sorry. No wonder you were disturbed when you learned about that condition in your uncle's will. Right now, nobody could replace your Bill. It was silly of me even to think of helping you."

Judy opened her eyes wide. "Helping me?"

"Well, of course. You can't get that inheritance without marrying me. I'm heart-free, always have been. I thought I'd be doing you a good turn."

She was speechless. "A good turn," she repeated.

"Wrong words, I can see that." He grinned. "How would you put it, then?"

"You're a fortune hunter," she exclaimed.

He sat up straighter, his smile fading. Anger touched his cheeks with a flush. Then he exhaled slowly, tilted his head sideways, and said, "So that's what's been eating at you."

He lighted another cigarette after offering Judy one, which she refused. He ordered another cup of coffee.

Then David said, "Look. There are agreements we

can enter into, whereby I relinquish all right to your money, while you're alive. I'm not sure whether I can relinquish all right to share in your estate should you die; I know you can't do it in New York. The surviving spouse gets it all—unless there are children, who get two-thirds and the spouse one-third—if you should die without making a will. I suppose New Hampshire law is something like that. Anyhow, that needn't bother you, if you don't intend to live in New Hampshire."

"It certainly won't bother me, because I don't intend to marry you."

David shook his head. "Why cut off your nose to spite your face, girl?" He lifted his hand, held it palm up, facing her indignant face. "Will you relax? You're a regular firecracker.

"Just listen to me a moment. You stand to inherit about thirty to fifty thousand dollars, as nearly as I can make out."

Judy said between her teeth, "So you checked up on the house and the bookstore? You know their value?"

David sighed. "I did some investigation for you." A mote of laughter came into his eyes. "After all, I felt I was doing it for my wife-to-be."

Judy scowled, but when she met those blue eyes with her own brown ones, she found she was beginning to giggle. If he were a rogue, he was a lighthearted one. She sighed and waved her hands.

"All right, all right. You did it for me."

"The house and grounds are worth maybe forty or forty-five thousand dollars, if you can find the right purchaser. The house is old but well-built, and there are about a hundred acres or so of good farmland." He made a face. "If you can get five thousand for the bookstore, grab it. It isn't worth that much, even."

Judy frowned thoughtfully. "I hadn't known Uncle Walter owned a bookstore. He didn't, last time I was up to spend a few days with him. The only bookstore I knew about was called—what was it now? The

Bookend, or some such thing. It was run by some old man who went about clad in rags, or so it seemed."

"That's the one. The Book Ends."

"And my uncle owned it?"

"The old man who owned it left it to him in his will. It's all legal and aboveboard."

Judy murmured, "Fifty thousand dollars."

"It isn't any fortune, but properly invested in bonds or even a well-paying stock it could bring you in an income of about four thousand a year. Isn't that worth some annoyance?" The laughter was in his eyes again.

July exclaimed, "But marriage! I—I just couldn't."

"It would be only a legal ceremony, over in a few minutes. Then you can go your way and I'll go mine."

She stared at him. Again, indignation flared in her. She found herself exclaiming, "Isn't anything sacred to you? But of course not! You're a huckster, that's all. Say 'I do' before a justice of the peace and have done with it."

Very gently, he said, "I'm not getting a penny out of all this, remember. I'll draw up a disclaimer and sign it for you. You can put it, together with the marriage license, in tissue paper and forget all about me."

His hand stopped the words she was framing in her mind. "Wouldn't an arrangement like that be worth fifty thousand dollars to you? After all, you aren't rich. You could use that money."

"I suppose you investigated me, along with the property?" she asked, the words like icicles dripping from her lips.

David shrugged. "I looked you up, I visited the library where you worked. I saw you were reasonably attractive."

"Oh! The nerve, the utter gall of—"

"I also did a little checking up on your financial status," he went on, ignoring her outburst, "and found that your salary and two thousand dollars in the bank are about the sum total of your worldly wealth."

Judy could only stare at him. *I am beyond words,* she

told herself. She was flushed with anger, her cheeks were burning, but she counseled restraint, even as every atom of her body told her to leap to her feet and march right out of the coffee shop and David Carnegie's life.

"Well?" he asked as she sat rigid, glaring at him. "There will be no ties between us. You can keep yourself sacrosanct for your Bill. I won't so much as put a finger on you. Unless, naturally, you decide you want your wifely privileges."

This time she did jump up, as much as she could in the booth, and reached for her handbag. Her lips were a thin line, her eyes were brilliant with fury. David leaned back in his bench and shook his head at her.

"Too impulsive. Much too impulsive. You must be one of these women to whom money is a dirty word. I've heard of them but, frankly, I've never yet met one. Fifty thousand dollars, properly invested. . . ." His words trailed off.

Judy sat down. With all her willpower, she sought to keep emotion out of her voice. "I won't deny that's a lot of money. It's a lot to me, anyhow. But marriage!"

"It's only a legal ceremony. As a matter of fact, you can divorce me after a time—if you really want to do such a foolish thing, that is—and go your way with four thousand dollars a year added to your income. Or you could take a trip to Europe. Or buy a new car. Or—"

"I know what I could do with the money," she exclaimed.

Her hand tightened on the handbag she still held. Very slowly she withdrew her fingers, folded her hands. She looked at him calculatingly. He was handsome enough, in that craggy way. He wore clothes well. He seemed well-to-do, but that was probably a pose. As a fortune hunter, he—but no. He said he would sign some sort of paper saying he would not claim any of her money. If he did that and all she had to do was say "I do" before a justice of the peace, for fifty thousand dollars ... well. It might not be treason to Bill Evans at all. There would be no love between them, of course. He had said as much.

"Did you really mean it?" she wondered. "About not wanting to—to act the part of husband?"

The flush was on her cheeks again. *What must he think of me, in this day and age, to ask such a question in this way? He sees me as a prim little librarian, half afraid of her own shadow.*

"Not even a kiss," he said solemnly, though that lurking laughter was deep in his eyes. "We shall be like strangers." He hesitated, then added, "Oh, there is one thing. I'm driving north tomorrow. If you'd like, I could drive you up to your farmhouse and leave you there to examine it and see a real-estate agent about selling it. And the bookstore as well."

"You're going to an awful lot of trouble for me," she burst out, "and I'm trying to find out the reason why."

"The goodness of my heart. No more."

The laughter was definitely back in his eyes, she realized, but for once she did not mind it. "I have some vacation time left. I suppose I could arrange to go up there for a few days, perhaps a week, to make those arrangements."

"Then it's a deal?"

Judy extended her hand slowly to clasp his. Turn it over in her mind as she would, she could see no ulterior motive behind his offer. If he meant everything he said, that is. And looking into those blue eyes, she felt assured that he did.

"Let's go tell Jim Miller about your decision," he said as they gripped hands. "He's rather worried about you, you know. He wants to see you get the property your uncle left you, but he sympathizes with your predicament."

James Miller was as delighted as David had foretold. He all but danced as he came around the edge of the desk to catch Judy's hands and hold them.

"I'll draw up the disclaimer myself, as your attorney," he told Judy. "And I'll be present as a witness at the ceremony to make sure everything goes like clockwork. You're doing the right thing, Judy. Be assured of that."

But am I? she asked herself glumly.

Chapter TWO

The ceremony was over. Judy stood a moment, looking up at this new husband of hers, half expecting and half dreading that he would kiss her. He was clad in a dark blue suit with pencil stripes, a blue tie, and white Hathaway shirt, looking every inch the successful businessman. He had been attentiveness itself, bringing her an orchid and watching her pin it to her own black silk georgette party dress. He had signed the disclaimer, and handed it to her as he had the orchid, with a faint smile.

Now she had spoken the words that made her his wife. James Miller came toward her, bent his head to kiss her cheek. He had brought his secretary, a rather plump, middle-aged woman who had dabbed at her eyes throughout the ceremony and explained, as she now pressed her cheek to Judy's, that weddings always made her weep.

Then a hand was at her elbow and David was turning her, leading her toward the door. He had the marriage license in his hand, which he gave her, telling her in a whisper to put it with the disclaimer.

They went down in the elevator together. Judy found that it seemed to make no difference in her life, now that she was Mrs. David Carnegie. She felt no breathlessness, no wild pounding of her heart as she would have done had she been Mrs. William Evans. It was all one great big letdown.

David said, "Your bags? They're back at your apartment, I suppose?" When she nodded, he said, "We'll pick them up and get started at once, if we want to be in New Hampshire before dark."

"Whatever you say," she agreed.

He gave her a quizzical look, but said nothing. On the sidewalk, James Miller and his secretary said their good-byes, Miller hailed a taxi, and they went off to his law office. Judy took a deep breath, staring around her at the hurrying crowds, the cars moving steadily along the street. She walked where David indicated by his pressure on her arm, and when she saw a battered Volkswagen she directed her feet toward it, only to be caught and held by his hand.

"Not that car," he said, amusement in his voice.

Embarrassment flushed her cheeks. "Oh! I thought—"

"I know what you thought. My car is farther on."

She saw a glittering maroon Jaguar V-12 parked near the curb. To her amazement, David was drawing her toward it. Her eyes ran over the chrome, the polished body, the luxurious interior, and she turned toward him, drawing a deep breath.

"Is this it?" she gasped.

"That's the one."

"Where can you rent a car like this?"

Patiently he murmured, "I didn't rent it. I own it." He opened the door, watched her slide in on the bucket seat. His grin was threatening to break into a laugh, as he stared down at her face.

Judy sat primly with her knees together, scarcely daring to breathe. Her eyes went across the dashboard, to the carpeting on the floor at her feet, to the bucket seat into which David Carnegie was resting his length.

And she had called him a fortune hunter!

He turned the ignition key, guided the car out into the traffic with an ease that told her more surely than any words that he was used to this Jaguar, that it was a part of him. Judy frowned, looking straight ahead.

"I don't even know what you do for a living," she said faintly.

"Does it make any difference? After all, we won't see each other after we get to Morstead. I'll drop you off at your uncle's place, and then go on to find a motel. You don't want it any other way, do you?"

They were stopped for a red light, and David was turning his head and smiling at her. *He smiles a lot,* she thought irritably. *Too much. It's as though he were being amused by a secret joke. Or by—me. Maybe I'm the joke.*

"No," she said slowly. "I don't want it any other way."

He nodded, eased the Jaguar forward into the traffic flow as the light changed. "Just the same, it isn't every day a girl marries," he said gently. "And it's perfectly natural to be curious about her husband."

"If you'd rather not tell me anything—"

"I'm not trying to hide anything, which is what you're thinking. I'm an only child. Or rather, was, since both my parents are dead. I was born and brought up in Pennsylvania. I went to Harvard and then to the Harvard law school. I'm a lawyer. I'm the Carnegie in Pierce, Carnegie and Mitchell."

Judy gaped at him. "But they're—"

"Corporation lawyers, yes. There's been a little in the papers about them recently. We defended a big lawsuit against that oil company—and won it. That's where you read about us, isn't it?"

She nodded, wanting to sink through the bucket seat and completely out of sight. The papers had been filled with the case—she had read them during her lunch break—and now it all came back to her, about the brilliance of a young trial attorney named ... Yes, yes! Of course! This was why his name had been so familiar to her! *He* was the David Carnegie who had been defense counsel for the oil company; it had been his brilliance at cross-examination that had turned the tide in the corporation's favor with the jury. The papers had predicted an even more brilliant future for young David Carnegie, likening him to James Bennett Williams and F. Lee Bailey.

She put her palms to her flaming cheeks. "I—I

called you a f-fortune hunter. What must you *think* of me?"

His laughter rang out. His foot braked the Jaguar to a stop in a line of traffic, then he turned and ran his blue eyes up and down her body, from her beige slippers to her brown hair. Judy reflected that she ought to have gone to a beauty parlor. She had despised the idea because this marriage ceremony was no more than a mere formality. It wasn't as if this man beside her had been Bill Evans. But now . . .

"I think you're far more attractive—or could be— than you'll permit. I think you're still carrying a torch for your Bill Evans. That's why you always wear black. Even that dress you're wearing now, for instance. It's almost fit for a funeral. I wonder how you'd look if you ever let go."

He sighed with theatrical heaviness. "It's a sight I'll never get to see, naturally."

She sat in silence, occupied with her thoughts. She found that she was resentful of his deception, to begin with; he could have told her he was *that* David Carnegie. It would have made things easier for her. Still, she wanted to be honest. He had been under no obligation to tell her anything. Especially after the way she had acted. She could scarcely blame him for the fact that Bill Evans had been drowned, and that she still clung to his memory. Nor for the fact that her uncle had put that contingency in his will.

She wouldn't have blamed him had he risen and walked out of her life completely, without talking her into marrying him and so getting her inheritance. She couldn't figure him at all. She slid her eyes sideways at him, studied his profile, admitting he had a good one, with a determined jaw and straight nose. His lips might be a shade too wide, but this would only be nit-picking. He was handsome; the girls at the library would goggle in awe and jealousy were she to stop by and parade him around as her groom.

Why had he gone to all this trouble to help her?

What did he get out of all this? He probably could have had his pick of a lot of society debutantes, she told herself morosely. He had no obligation to marry a nobody just to help her get her hands on fifty thousand dollars. He was a lawyer, he knew his own rights and duties. Why had he done it? Why?

She was still mulling over this when they came to a stop before the building in which she had a room and a half apartment. Judy wondered what his apartment was like. Filled with Saarinen furniture and tables by Luberto or Gordon, draperies by Kroll and lighting by Versen, most likely. She could picture it in her imagination and blushed at the idea that he was going to see her tiny little studio.

"No need for you to come up," she said hastily. "I can get the bags."

He gave her a glance that went right through her. Meekly she waited as he came around the side of the car and opened the door for her. His hand caught her arm and he walked with her across the sidewalk and into the lobby past Charley, the uniformed doorman. Charley raised his eyebrows and his mouth opened at the sight of her with a man. Especially a man like David Carnegie! Her eyes fell to the floor and she walked like a chastened child toward the elevators.

They did not speak on the trip up. David held out his hand, and when she looked at him questioningly, he said, "Your key, Mrs. Carnegie."

Mrs. Carnegie! It had a strange sound, it wasn't as though he were talking about her at all. She went on staring up at him, vaguely realizing that his hand was still patiently outstretched. She had opened her own door for so long that it took a moment for the idea to register. Flustered, she fumbled in her handbag, extracted the key, and handed it over.

"I could do it myself," she murmured weakly.

"You'll be on your own soon enough. Let me help you as much as I can. It will give me pleasure."

She walked beside him to the door, watched him fit

the key in and turn it. He threw the door open and stood aside for her to enter first. Like a zombi, she moved into the room and saw it with eyes that were still dazzled by her imagined construction of his apartment.

Everything was so worn! There was a hole in the carpet, too—she'd picked up the carpet at an auction; it was better than nothing underfoot on winter nights—and the couch that converted into a bed at night and the lamps seemed shabby and ravaged by time. She could not bear to look at him, but turned and bent to lift her valise.

His hand was there ahead of hers; the Ventura, thank goodness, was almost brand-new, and he lifted it easily. His blue eyes were on her face. She had the distinct feeling that he had taken in the apartment in one raking glance, and had dismissed it as of no account. Judy tilted up her chin.

"Some of us can't afford any better places than this," she declared.

"Why are you always running yourself down?"

There was no mockery in his face, only what appeared to be understanding and affection. She looked away from him, out the window at the brick wall of the next-door apartment building, at the frayed wallpaper of her room. To her horror, her lips began to quiver.

"Why did you do it?" she quavered.

"Do what?"

"Ma-marry me. You di-didn't have to. It can't make any difference to you whether I get my inheritance or not."

Oh, damn! Tears were blurring her eyes now and going to roll down her cheeks, and she wanted to play this so coolly!

He put down the valise very carefully and put his arms about her even more carefully, as though he expected she were about to pull away and lash out at his cheek with a palm. She went forward; she couldn't help it, really, his arms were so strong. She put her face against his chest and began to sob.

"You've been through too much." His voice came softly. "First with Bill Evans drowning and now this loveless marriage. Go ahead, cry. It will do you good."

He smelled of aftershave—Brut?—and tobacco, a man-smell she liked. She pulled away a little, trying to smile, fumbling for a handkerchief. His was there, suddenly, right before her. She took it, wiped her eyes and blew her nose.

"I must look utterly horrible," she muttered, not daring to raise her eyes to his. "My eyes will be swollen, my nose all red."

"Whatever will the doorman think?"

She looked up at him in surprise, saw the laughter on his mouth, and suddenly she began to giggle. "He'll think you've been beating me. Or worse. He's like a sheepdog with his flock, Charley is. Protects the virtue of the single girls who live here even better than they do themselves."

Judy sighed. Suddenly, she felt better. She handed him back his handkerchief, then snatched it back. "I'll launder it, send it to you," she gasped.

"Don't be silly. It's the only one I have on me. The others are in my bags."

He put it in his pocket, Judy decided, like a husband of long standing. Then he lifted the valise, guided her out into the hall, and walked beside her, and she found that she was enjoying the sensation. For too long, she had had to fend for herself in everything she did. Even Bill Evans had never been as solicitous as this. He let her precede him into the elevator, and out of it. He opened the big glass lobby door—ignoring the staring Charley—and escorted her to the Jaguar. He opened its door, watched as she seated herself inside, then closed the door. He placed her valise in the trunk.

Then he was back in the car with her, starting the motor, glancing at her and asking, "Are you hungry?"

"No. I ate breakfast this morning." She turned and

smiled at him, remembering the cheese Danishes they had enjoyed.

"I thought we'd stop for lunch in Holyoke, at a restaurant I know."

"Whatever you say."

They were on the Major Deegan Parkway when he spoke again. "How good a farmer are you?"

"Farmer? Why, I don't think I'm very good at it. I never have farmed."

"Then you'd better sell your uncle's place as soon as you can. Its fields need working. No sense in letting them lie fallow when they could be producing food for people to eat."

"Could I keep the house and rent the ground to farmers to produce extra crops?"

"I don't see why not. We could ask around about something like that, if you agree. I mean to stay on just long enough to handle these matters for you, with your permission, Judy."

It was the first time he had ever spoken her name. She liked the way it sounded on his tongue. She said, "I'd appreciate it, I really would."

When they were on the Cross County Parkway, Judy remembered the question she had asked him before she had started to cry.

"I'm not going to break out in tears again, but I would like to know why you married me. I really mean it. I just can't understand why. Here you are, successful, probably rich, too, and yet . . ."

He chuckled. "I could give you any number of reasons. Let's try them on for size. My father and mother knew your uncle; they wanted me to marry you just as your uncle wanted you to marry me. Or, how's this? As soon as I saw you, I fell heels over head in love with you."

"Please be serious!"

"OK, then. You don't like either of those. Well, I'm an altruist, I'm like a Boy Scout, I go around doing good deeds all the time."

"Honestly! I mean it. I really want to know."

"And I have no answer to give you."

She glanced at his profile. "Oh, come on. You're a very successful lawyer. Probably as clever as Machiavelli. People like you don't do things without a very good reason, especially something like getting married."

David Carnegie sighed. "I guess you deserve the truth, no matter how much I make myself out a heel."

Judy swung about as much as she could in the bucket seat. "A heel?"

He grinned. "Well, sort of. You see, there are two girls who wanted very much to marry me."

"Oh!"

His eyes touched her sober face. "I didn't and don't love either of them. Marriage to either would be a calamity, not only for me but for them as well. So I cast around for some way to get out of marrying one of them. Oh, they're great girls, full of fun, they love sports, the opera and fine arts, all the best things in life; they come from marvelous families; they're rich and will inherit millions."

Judy gaped at him. "And you didn't want to marry somebody like that?"

"Didn't love 'em."

"But you don't love me, either."

"Well, now. It's different with you."

She digested that as the Jaguar sped along the Hutchinson Parkway for a mile. Then she murmured, "It was a marriage of convenience, then?"

"Convenient for you, convenient for me. Right on. You get your inheritance, I get out from under. As a married man, I'm perfectly safe. I don't have to marry anybody. I'm already married."

"What if I divorce you? You said I was free to do it."

"Then I'll be so deeply sunk in gloom I won't see any females at all. My period of mourning for our shattered marriage will last years."

Judy began to laugh. She rocked back and forth, and continued even when he turned a startled face toward her; maybe she laughed even more because of his stark astonishment. She reached into her handbag for a bit of Irish linen and lace to wipe her eyes.

"You're terrible," she exclaimed happily. "You're absolutely awful."

His grin threatened to bisect his face. "You're not mad? I thought you—with all those prim and proper behavior patterns of yours—would be utterly horrified."

"I am, of course. Goes without saying. But oh! How it relieves me."

David frowned. "I don't get it."

"Here I am, worrying and worrying about you doing such a noble thing for me and me feeling so guilty because I've been abominable to you. But now that I know you have a very good reason for wanting to be a married man, I don't feel guilty at all."

"Friends?"

"Oh, yes, David. Friends."

He raised his eyebrows. "You know, that's the first time you've used my name. Say it again."

"David. David. David."

"It's beautiful the way you say it."

"Come off it. I'm Judy. Your wife, remember?"

Their laughter filled the Jaguar.

They filled the miles with idle chatter as a sense of camaraderie grew between them. The Merritt Parkway was lovely at this time of year, the leafy foliage of its trees and bushes seeming almost to reflect her own inner relief and delight. She stared at the scenery with contentment inside her, for the first time in months. Gone was her sorrow for Bill Evans; her memories of him seemed to fade the farther away from the city they went.

David Carnegie was not so much her husband as he was a fellow conspirator. True, he had helped her get that inheritance, but she had helped him out of the

clutches of those designing females. Judy was sure they
were designing, they had set their caps—to use that
old-fashioned expression—for him, and now they
would be disappointed. He was her husband. Judy's.
He was safely out of their claws.

She was a little surprised at her reactions. They were
probably very lovely girls; David had probably played
them as he might a trout in that stream behind Uncle
Walter's place, that ran right through his property.
Ooops. Her property now. She was glad he had escaped them, that he had married her. And this puzzled
her a little.

Actually, theirs was not a marriage at all, except in
the eyes of the law. But that made no difference. He
was her husband, she was his wife. The law did not examine into motives when a man and woman got themselves hitched.

As they were moving up U.S. 91, Judy said, head
tilted as she watched him drive, "Do you know, I don't
think I'll divorce you at all."

"Now what made you decide that?"

"What's safety for you is also safety for me. I never
wanted to get married, you know. Now I'll never have
to. Not really, that is—with all its implications."

"That makes two of us," he said.

"What a pair we are."

"Very levelheaded, extremely sensible, I agree."

Judy smoothed down her dark skirt. "You never
kissed me after the ceremony, you know. I appreciate
that."

"I can always amend that omission."

"No, that's all right," she said hastily. "It won't
make the actual ceremony illegal or anything, will it?"

"No fear of that. Everything was done in shipshape
order. You're my wife and I'm your husband. Trust
Jim Miller to see to that. After all, he's executor of the
estate."

They rode along, the Jaguar purring.

Judy asked, "What were you like, when you were

young? I mean, I ought to know something about my husband, oughtn't I, in case somebody ever asks me?"

"I was born a little over thirty years ago on a horse farm in Pennsylvania. My folks were rich. I was the only child. I was a brilliant scholar, I took prizes all over the place, I was a marvelous athlete, I scored seven touchdowns in one game, I—"

Judy laughed. "Good grief! I married the all-American boy. No, really. What were you like?"

There was a little silence.

Then David said, "I was very much a loner. There were no other children, though my parents were happily married. I went around with adults, for the most part, and was much on my own. I used to get into scrapes, like stealing pies and painting things red that never needed painting, especially red. I got whopped a couple of times by my father when I was especially wild. Looking back, I don't blame him in the slightest. If I'd been him, I'd have whopped me even harder.

"But somewhere over the years I learned something. You just can't go your own way in life, you have to think of other people, give something of yourself to them. I got rid of my excess energies in sports. And it's true that I scored seven touchdowns in a football game, in prep school." He added with a grin, "That feat got me a scholarship to Harvard to play flanker-back for them. I did all right in college, but I was no great shakes. I knew I'd never be drafted to play pro ball, so I went to law school.

"And here I am."

Judy said, "You've left out all mention of this wild love life of yours."

"Never had a steady girl, if that's what you mean. I always played the field." He made a wry face. "Maybe that was my trouble. Nobody ever really appealed to me. Except you, of course. When I saw you, I knew I had to marry you."

"Sure, sure."

He took his eyes off the road to glance at her. "Now what about you?"

"I thought you'd done some investigating?"

"It wasn't all that thorough."

Judy smiled faintly. She liked this husband of hers. Oh, not romantically. Anything but. Still, he seemed a good sort, thoughtful and friendly. There was a tiny warmth deep inside her, brought on when she heard that he'd never had a steady girl. Though why that should please her, she had no idea.

"I was an only child, too. I was sickly when I was young, I used to read and read. Clothes never meant as much to me as they do to most girls growing up. I wore just about anything that was at hand. I was my mother's despair. Poor Mom. She used to tell me I'd never catch a man, going around in jeans and a T-shirt all the time. She should see me now."

Judy gurgled laughter.

David turned the Jaguar off U.S. 91 toward Holyoke. Judy stared at the homes past which they moved, then found her attention caught and held by a large building that appeared to have been once a private home. It had been enlarged and added to over the years, there was plenty of parking space, and behind it was what had been a country store, but was now closed.

"The Yankee Pedlar." David smiled, seeing her interest. "It's one of my favorite stopping places when I head up into Vermont or New Hampshire."

They went into a lobby with little alcoves off it, with a dining area behind glass windowpanes to their left, and a curving hall lined with old lithographs that bypassed a bar and a number of tables to lead into a larger dining room. There were pots and pans hung on the walls and placed along a plate rail, together with an ancient musket or two with accompanying powderhorns.

Judy hugged herself. "I love it!"

"Wait'll you taste the food."

Over cocktails, David said, "I'll stay on in Morstead as long as you need me, Judy. I'll find a motel nearby and take up residence there. But I feel I ought to be with you when you look over your property and that bookstore, in case you have any questions."

She toyed with her glass, studying it. It didn't seem right to her that her own husband should go to a motel when there was so much room at Uncle Walter's place, but she certainly didn't want him under the same roof where she was sleeping. *I feel like a first-rate heel about it, but that's the way I am,* she told herself.

Aloud she murmured, "I'm grateful to you for your thoughtfulness, David. You must know that."

"Why? It was just a ceremony."

Was that coldness in his voice? She lifted her eyes to his, startled, saw that he was staring out the window beside which they were seated. Her heart beat a little faster. Surely he wasn't expecting her to invite him into her bed, now that they were married? No, no. Of course not. She was no glamor girl, she wasn't even attractive. He certainly couldn't be hankering after her when he'd had his pick of really gorgeous girls in the city. She was being stupid.

Judy licked her lips. With an effort she made herself say, "If you'd like to stay at the house . . ."

His eyes came back to hers. His lips widened into a grin. "God forbid. But it was nice of you to ask." After a moment he added wryly, "No matter how much it hurt you."

Judy stiffened. He didn't have to act as though she had the plague! She wasn't all *that* unattractive. On the other hand, she was the one who was denying him the shelter of her house. And she was his wife. But in name only. In name only!

"We had a bargain," she breathed.

"Easy, there. Don't get on your high horse. I have no intention of intruding on your privacy. That's why I'm going to a motel. But I do want to stay around for a day or two, to make sure you'll be all right, before I head on up north for a few days of fishing."

"Fishing?" she asked.

"I deserve a vacation after that trial I just went through. Do you have any idea how much work it was? Oh, not the actual trial, though that was tough enough. But the preliminary work, the reports to read, the statistics to absorb, the witnesses to meet and question. I told myself, halfway through the trial, that I needed a vacation. This is it."

"Oh!" She had wondered how a busy lawyer could afford to go traipsing over the countryside with her. "Then I'm not putting you out—too much."

"Not a bit of it. I'm having fun."

She eyed him warily. "Are you?"

"It isn't every day a guy gets married." He laughed and covered her hand with his. "Relax, relax. You're like a sister to me. Right? And I'm like a brother to you, right? Now here comes our food. Enjoy."

There was a seafood platter for her, a rather large slab of roast beef for him. Big rolls, a small tub of butter, and a green salad made her mouth water. Judy hadn't realized just how hungry she was. She reached for her knife and fork with a keen sense of appreciation.

They ate in silence, though she flashed glances at him from time to time, seeing how much he was enjoying the meal. For some reason, this pleased her. She liked a man who ate his meals with relish. It indicated that he would enjoy other things in life just as well. She flushed faintly and told herself it didn't matter a tinker's dam—whatever that was—to her, what David Carnegie enjoyed or did not enjoy.

They had a deal. Nothing more.

Over coffee and cigarettes, David said. "We have about an hour's ride ahead of us. Maybe a little more. We'll be in Morstead long before dark, give us plenty of time to have a look at the house, make sure it's in working order for you."

For the first time she wondered what it would be

like to live alone in that big, old house. It had everything she needed: propane gas in tanks for cooking, an oil burner to take the chill off the rooms if the nights turned cold, and a big fireplace in which Uncle Walter used to burn logs. Were there any logs in the shed attached to the kitchen? She would have to go see.

"How long will you be away fishing?" she asked.

"A couple of weeks, at least." He hesitated, then asked, "What about that library of yours? When do you have to be back?"

Judy took a sip of coffee. "I'm not even sure I am going back. If I can think of some way to make a living in Morstead, I definitely won't. I love the country."

"Well, I'll stop by on my way back, just to see how you're getting along. And if you've decided by that time you want to return with me, you're welcome."

She sighed. "It's such a sudden change. I'm not used to it, yet. I can't make up my mind about anything, it seems."

"You will. You'll have plenty of time to think during the next couple of weeks."

He was right about that, Judy knew, preceding him along the hallway to the lobby. It was going to be very lonely, at first, all by herself in that big house. There would be a lot of work outside, gardening, and maybe in the house, too, cleaning. She could not work the farm part, not without help, and she was not about to hire laborers. The best thing for her might be to sell the place.

In the car and going north on U.S. 91, Judy wondered out loud about that. "I do love it, but I don't know whether I can manage it, alone."

"Once you sell it, it's gone. There's no hurry in making up your mind. Just do some thinking."

Judy nodded and turned her gaze to the side of the road. This was lovely country all around them, with the sun glinting on distant water, with the deep green leaves of the trees soothing to her eyes. *I'll sleep well tonight,* she reflected.

They went through Hadley, Deerfield, Bernardston, and then they were in Vermont, easing along at a steady sixty miles an hour. Judy felt that she was being spoiled by this husband of hers, in this car, eating at such places as the Yankee Pedlar. She made a wry face. It would not be easy, after this, to return to her little studio apartment and her desk at the library.

But forget that. Take in this moment, hold it to her heart, and let her pleasure become a memory to cherish when she had to return. If she ever went back, that is. There must be something she could do, in Morstead, to earn her bread.

Brattleboro was off to their left, and the signs announced that Bellows Falls was next. "We turn off there for Morstead," David mentioned.

The nearer they came to Morstead, the more nervous Judy found herself. It was all very well for her to claim she could live alone in the country and like it, but could she? There would be no super to complain to about heat, to make repairs, to put in new light bulbs when the old ones burned out. She would have to do all this herself.

Her eyes slid sideways. She wouldn't even have David to help her. He would be at a motel, getting waited on. Judy scowled, imagining a pretty waitress hovering over him, eager to leap to fulfill his slightest whim.

They crossed the Connecticut River and turned left.

David said, "You'd better direct me here. I'm familiar with this section, but I don't know all the turns."

Judy sat up straighter, murmuring, "Up that hill ahead and turn right. You have to make another right turn, but I'll tell you when."

It seemed no time at all before she was saying, "There it is, to the left, the house."

She leaned forward, staring.

It was as she remembered it from her last visit: white clapboard with windowsills and trim painted blue, the shed to the left—it had been a blacksmith

shop in the last century—and the house spreading outward to the right, with the trees all around it to give it
shade. The porch beside the shed led up to the kitchen,
and a main entrance was another thirty feet or so to
the right, leading into a small hall between the dining
room and living room.

David turned off the ignition and stretched.

Judy said, "It hasn't changed, not at all."

"Seems your uncle kept it in good repair. It looks
neat and well cared for. Shouldn't be too much for you
to do."

He opened his door and got out. Judy did the same,
raising her arms high above her head and stretching.
She moved about, eyeing the house, then went to
where David was opening the car trunk. He bent to
reach into the trunk and lift out her bags. Judy went to
join him.

Suddenly something struck her shoulder and she
toppled forward onto David. He whirled, his face white
with shock, hearing the echo of that gunshot, seeing
Judy limp and lifeless beside him, blood staining the
back of her dress.

Chapter THREE

Judy opened her eyes.

David was holding her in his arms, his eyes glazed with shock and worry. There was a sharp pain in her arm; it made her gasp and throw back her head.

David breathed. "This can't have happened. It just can't!"

She tried to move. There was a blinding stab of agony, and she fainted, but only for a few seconds. When she recovered, she found that he was running down the zipper at the back of her dress.

"Hey now," she protested weakly.

He looked at her. "I've got to stop that bleeding until I can get you to a doctor! You're not all that modest, are you?"

"You're certainly not going to undress me!"

David sighed. "Deliver me. All right, have it your own way."

His hand yanked up the zipper. Then he put that same hand to her sleeve, and ripped. The sleeve came off. David said, "I know I'm hurting you, but I tried not to. If you insist on my not seeing your body, it's this or not at all."

He threw the sleeve onto the grass, put a towel around the wound. Then he was removing his belt, putting it around her upper arm and tightening it. "Keep it that way, but loosen it every once in a while," he told her.

He slid his arms under her, lifted her against his chest. When she made some sort of mumbled protest, he said, "I'm not about to carry you over the threshold, if that's what's worrying you. I'm going to put you in the car and find a doctor."

She subsided. It was good to be cradled this way, to be babied. The pain had lessened a little, she felt giddy and weak, but when he slid her into the bucket seat, she found she could move without too much effort.

He ran around the car and slammed the trunk lid closed. Then he was beside her, turning the ignition key, backing out into the road. "Where's the doctor?" he wanted to know.

"There's Dr. Adams over in Walpole."

"OK, then. Hang on."

She sat with her back against the rest, eyes closed, vaguely aware and not caring that the Jaguar was probably breaking every speed limit in the world. She remembered to loosen the belt, then tighten it, and found she could do it well enough, even with one hand.

The Jaguar braked to a halt. Judy lifted her eyelids, saw the big stone house where Doc Adams had his office. She sat there while David came around to open her door, but when he would have carried her into the office, she refused.

"I can walk, I can walk. Just—just let me lean on you."

The nurse took one look at her, let out a little cry, and ran to put an arm about her waist. "The doctor has a patient, but I'll take you in right away, honey. What in the world happened?"

She gave David a quizzical look. He shook his head and said, "I didn't do it. It must have been a hunter."

"It isn't the hunting season," the nurse snapped.

Dr. Adams came to see her almost at once, walking ahead of the nurse into the room, his face grave, furrowed with worry. The kindly old eyes behind his glasses lighted up at sight of her.

"I've seen you before. Don't tell me, I'll remember where in a little while. My, my. What happened, young lady?"

"Somebody shot me," she murmured.

"I'll have to report this to the police, you know. But never mind that right now. Come into the other room."

The nurse aided her, an arm about her middle. Judy
was still weak from shock and some loss of blood. The
nurse brought her to the table and assisted her to lie
flat.

Dr. Adams approached with a hypodermic, which he
injected into her arm, saying, "This is a local; it will relieve the pain." His eyes smiled down at her. "You can
watch or not, as you please."

Judy preferred not to watch; she closed her eyes and
knew from the sounds about her that the doctor and
the nurse were working on her wound. Thoughts ran
around in her head like frightened mice. If it weren't
the hunting season, who could have shot at her? Probably an illegal hunter, no matter what the nurse had
said.

But—

There had been no animals around the Hunter
homestead. She was reasonably certain of that. Even if
there had been, for a hunter to have missed by so wide
a margin seemed unbelievable. She was with David at
the car trunk. No. The bullet had been aimed at her,
all right. There was no doubt about it.

This brought even more amazement to her mind.
Who in the world wanted to kill her? It wasn't as if
Uncle Walter had left any other relatives who might be
out to dispose of her to get his estate. She was his only
living relation, there was nobody else.

It made no sense, none at all.

Her eyelids were very heavy. She wanted nothing so
much as sleep right now. She dozed for what seemed
an instant, then Dr. Adams was putting an arm under
her, raising her to a sitting position. She glanced at her
arm, swathed in a bandage. The nurse came and fitted
her forearm into a sling.

The doctor said, "It's a clean wound, no bones broken. The bullet went right through. You'll be all right
in two weeks or so. Until then, I don't want you using
that arm. Are you left-handed?"

When she shook her head, he nodded. "Good. Your husband can undress and dress you."

Judy felt her heart flop over.

She said weakly, "You mean I'll be that—that helpless?"

She could hardly come out and say that David Carnegie was her husband in name only, and that they both intended it to remain that way. She was certain that she didn't want him taking off her clothes!

Dr. Adams grinned. "I know. Husbands are helpless when it comes to anything like that, but you'll wear comfortable things, easy to get it and out of, for the next week or so. I want to see you day after tomorrow, to change your bandage. Same time, same place."

The nurse smiled. "We'll go in the outer office, Mrs. Carnegie, to fill out the necessary forms. You have medical insurance?"

She nodded. As a librarian, she belonged to a Blue Cross-Blue Shield group. She wondered whether David had any such insurance. He must have—he was a lawyer, he would know about these things.

She found she walked more firmly, the pain was gone. Before she left, Dr. Adams pressed a vial into her fingers. "In case the pain gets too much for you, take one of these tablets. It will ease it."

David was pacing in the reception room. At sight of her, he came to put an arm about her shoulders. "Was it very bad?" he said, worried.

"She was a regular Trojan." The nurse smiled, and sat down at the small desk and reached for a card and a pen. She looked at David. "You've already told me Judy is your wife, Mr. Carnegie. But I'd like a little more information, addresses, medical insurance, if any. That sort of thing."

Judy murmured. "My Blue Cross card's in my wallet."

She waited while the questions were asked and answered. David did all the talking, and Judy heard him give an address on East 86th Street for their residence.

Probably his apartment, she realized. Under the circumstances, there wasn't much else he could do, of course. He wasn't about to blurt out the fact that they didn't live together, and didn't intend doing so.

He came to her, assisted her to her feet, helped her from the office and toward the car. He said, "This changes a lot of things, doesn't it?"

She glanced at him. "What things?"

He waited until she was seated before he said cheerfully, "I can't run off and leave you like this. I'll have to stay at the house, whether you like it or not."

Judy sighed. The man was right, of course. She wasn't able to do very much, with only one arm. At first, that is. In a couple of days, he could go on to his fishing trip. But right now all she wanted was to climb into a bed and go to sleep. She flushed faintly, wondering how she was going to manage to remove her clothes without assistance.

He was not about to undress her. She knew that much.

David drove in silence all the way back to the house. When he braked the Jaguar and turned off the motor, he looked at her.

"Does the arm hurt?"

She shook her head. "No. I can feel it, naturally, but it isn't too bad." She held up the vial of pills that she found she was still clutching in her right hand. "If it gets bad, I'm to take one of these."

David nodded. "All right. My first duty is to get you to bed." He smiled faintly. "Do you want to sleep in that dress? Or how shall we arrange this?"

Judy said weakly, "I—I don't know."

"All right. Leave it to me, then."

He removed the house key from her purse, went and opened the door, then returned for her. She found she could negotiate very well without assistance, and she made a great show of being independent.

The house was cool, but the air was stagnant from being shut up so long. She walked through the kitchen and the dining room into the little front hall. David glanced up at the stairs.

"Can you make them on your own?"

She nodded, but noted that he was right behind her in case she should falter. At the top of the stairs she turned left into the master bedroom. To her surprise, the bed was made, with a quilt folded neatly at its foot. Judy sat down and bent to remove her shoes. She felt giddy suddenly and almost toppled over.

David said, "Here, let me."

"I can do it. Just wait a second."

"Oh, don't be a little idiot!"

He knelt, removed her shoes, then lifted her legs and swung them onto the bed. He reached for the quilt, drew it up over her.

"There, how's that?"

She nodded, smiling faintly. "It's just fine. And, David . . . thanks."

His eyes were tender as he stared down at her. "All right if I open the windows to give you some fresh air? I'll pull down the shades, if you want." He opened the windows, drew the shades to darken the room. He came back to stand beside the bed.

"It'll do for now. But later, you're going to have to forget this false modesty of yours."

No way, she thought silently. *I wouldn't even let Bill Evans undress me, and I loved him. Somehow or other I have to do this for myself. I must force myself to do it, even if it hurts like blue blazes.*

He stood a moment longer, then went out of the room, closing the door. She could hear him going down the stairs, walking across the dining-room floor. He would bring in their bags, probably select a bedroom for himself, and see to dinner.

Dinner! There was probably nothing in the house to eat.

She would have to do something about that. But not now, not just yet. She was so tired, so tired. . . . She let her eyes close. . . .

Judy woke to complete darkness. She lay quietly, remembering. Her arm had begun to ache, and she thought about the pills. They were on the night table beside the bed, with her purse. She reached for them. *I'll need water, I could never swallow a pill with a dry throat.* She threw back the quilt, swung her legs off the bed, and leaned to turn on the bedside lamp.

Dizziness washed over her. She sat a moment, swaying. *I won't call out to David, I just won't! I can do this by myself.* But she was suddenly afraid to try it. Suppose she collapsed, lay helpless on the floor? David would hear her fall, come running upstairs. He would undress her, slip a nightgown over her, and put her back in bed again.

Oh, dear Lord! What will I do?

Then she heard him on the stairs. The door opened and he was looking in at her. "Awake, are you? Good. Oh, I see you have the pills. You'll want a glass of water."

"Is the water turned on? I mean . . ."

"Everything's in good working order, I saw to that. Your uncle never stopped the electricity, and the propane tanks are almost full. I've been out shopping, bought us some much needed supplies. You've been asleep for three or four hours."

"What time is it?"

"A little after nine."

"You must be starved."

"And so I am. But I waited for you."

She shook her head. "I'll never be able to eat. You go ahead. Forget about me."

"Nonsense, you have to keep your strength up. The nurse said so."

Judy had no recollection of Nurse Duffy saying any such thing, but she wasn't about to argue. She watched David cross the room and enter the small bathroom, then heard running water. He came back with a glass and handed it to her.

"Take your pill, then lie down. Rest a little more.

I'll go start dinner, and be up to get you." His head tilted slightly as his eyes searched her face. "No. I think I'll prop you up with some pillows; tonight you can eat in bed."

"I really don't want to eat, David."

"I know, I know. But you have to."

He was being entirely too dictatorial, Judy thought. But then, he meant it only for her own good. He was probably thinking that the sooner he was rid of her, the sooner he could be out in some trout stream casting for a fish.

She nodded, trying to smile. "All right. Whatever you say."

She lay back, and he pulled up the quilt and left her. She dozed.

In no time at all, he was back again. The tray in his hands held a bowl of steaming chicken soup, a glass of milk, and a plate of crackers. He put down the tray, put three pillows behind her, then drew her up into a sitting position.

"What about your dinner?" she asked.

"I'll eat it later. Go on, I want to make sure you finish that soup and milk."

"David, I couldn't. Really."

He sighed and sat on the edge of the bed. "Do you want me to feed you?"

"Of course not."

"Then eat."

He put the tray on her thighs, moved to draw a chair close to the bed. He sat down and watched her. Judy scowled down at the soup. If she didn't eat it, he would make her, she knew. She sighed and reached for the spoon.

To her infinite surprise, the soup was delicious. She ate half the broth before she spoke again. "It's really good. You're quite a cook."

David grinned. "That's Mrs. Polanski's soup, not mine."

"Mrs. Polanski?"

"She and her husband run the general store in town. When she heard what had happened to you, she insisted on giving me a container filled with soup of her own making; she wouldn't hear of my not taking it. Of course, I'd already bought a lot of meat and groceries—"

I can imagine, Judy thought. *Men!*

"—so she figured I was a good customer, I suppose."

"Word will be all over the countryside by tomorrow morning," Judy moaned.

"And why not? No reason to hide what happened, is there? The doctor will have made the report to the police. As a matter of fact, a state policeman stopped by a little while ago, to get my version. There's no police force in Morstead, as you must know."

Judy frowned. "What did you tell him?"

"The truth; what else? I said a hunter was probably out shooting and winged you."

"But that can't be, David. There weren't any animals around to shoot."

"I know, but it's what I told him," he commented wryly.

Their eyes locked. Judy asked faintly, "Do you know what this means? Someone must have been trying to kill me!"

"The state policeman agreed. He's doing some investigative work on the matter. What puzzles me is why anyone should want to kill you. How would your death benefit anyone?"

Judy licked her lips. "Maybe Uncle Walter had some enemies."

"Your uncle's dead. If he were alive, I could see shooting you, to make him grieve. But not now. No. Someone around these parts wants you dead, Judy. I mean to find out why."

There was a grimness in his voice that startled her. She had seen only one side of this David Carnegie, she realized. He had been polite, solicitous, friendly, even tender toward her. Now she was seeing a different David, alert and angry, filled with a grim purposefulness that almost shocked her.

"Finish your soup," he said softly.

She did, and then drank the milk. She felt warmed, and a lassitude slid over her. Her eyelids drooped. David took away the tray, turned back to her, helped her slide down under the quilt, and removed two of the pillows.

"You'd be more comfortable in pajamas," he said.

"I'm fine as I am, thank you."

"Yes, Mrs. Carnegie."

Judy opened one eyelid, squinted up at him. "Are you trying to remind me that I'm your wife?"

"I'm trying to tell you that I want you to get better as fast as possible. I think you need your proper rest for that, not just to cower all dressed under a quilt. Suppose somebody comes to see you, like a policeman? You're going to look mighty silly. And you aren't going to go back to the doctor in that same dress, are you?"

Judy felt miserable. She knew she couldn't undress herself and dress herself without help. But she wasn't going to let David Carnegie do it. Oh, no. She would do it herself. Somehow.

She said, "I'll think of something."

"OK, then. Sleep well. If you need me at any time, just yell."

He went out and closed the door. She was asleep almost at once, and dreamed of being caught in a stampede of wild animals with hunters and gun-bearers all firing high-powered rifles at her. She ran and ran, but the animals ran faster, though she seemed to outrace the bullets. Right ahead of her was a huge chasm, like the Grand Canyon. The animals didn't seem to mind it, they just jumped over it. But she couldn't do that! Still, she must try. She leaped and began to fall, turning over and over, screaming. . . .

She woke gasping, covered with perspiration.

She lay there, staring around her at the room with

its bureau and leather easy chair, book rack and curtained windows. Uncle Walter's room. She had been shot yesterday. Wonderingly, she lifted her right hand, ran her fingertips very gently over the bandages. The pain had subsided, and she felt much stronger.

But would exercise of any kind, even getting dressed, bring back that pain? She dreaded it, but she dreaded even more the idea of David removing her clothes. It was early, very early in the day, just a little past dawn. She listened; it seemed that David was sleeping soundly for there was no sound in the house.

She slid from the bed, stood up. She was much stronger, she could stand without that dizziness, she could walk about. She rearranged the sling to a more comfortable position.

Her bags were on the floor. She would not lift them, she would kneel down, take out what garments she might need, and get out of her soiled dress.

It took her half an hour, but she finally contrived to slip into pajamas—the jacket of which she had to sling over her left shoulder, she just couldn't manage the left sleeve—and put a robe across the foot of the bed.

She would dearly have loved to take a bath, but this would have to wait. Tomorrow, maybe she could accomplish that.

Judy got back into bed, tired from the effort. She slept some more. When she woke, David was in the room, clad in slacks and a sleeveless shirt. He grinned at sight of her.

"So. You did it." His hand waved at the heap of her discarded clothes. "I'm glad to see you're feeling better. Are you well enough to come downstairs for breakfast?"

She was hungry, she discovered, which was a good sign. She nodded, saying, "I'll be down directly."

David handed her the robe, his face sober. But his eyes were laughing at her, she saw. "You can put this on after I'm gone. Your slippers are by the side of the bed. I put them there. I'll go and start the bacon and coffee."

He went down the stairs, and Judy sat up. It was easy to slip her feet into the fluffy bedroom slippers, thrust her right arm into the robe. The sling was in the way, but she pulled the sash around her middle, and then stared down at it helplessly.

David would have to tie it. She just couldn't see any way to do it. Pulling the robe tighter about her, she moved from the room and down the stairs, pausing to glance to her left into the big living room. Everything was as it had always been when Uncle Walter had lived here: the massive furniture, the overstuffed divan, the heavy chairs. Sighing, Judy moved through the dining room and into the large kitchen.

David was at the stove, turning the bacon in a skillet. Judy smelled perking coffee. He turned, grinned at her, and said, "Need help? Sure you do. Here, let me."

His hands deftly tied the sash. "There now. You're quite presentable."

She smiled up at him. "You're very good to me. I appreciate it, David."

He waved a hand. "Always take good care of my wives."

Her eyebrows arched. "Oh? Didn't know you had so many of them."

His hand touched her elbow, turned her toward the breakfast table covered with a cheery red and yellow cloth, eased her into a chair. There were plates, cups, and saucers on the cloth, as well as glasses and place settings.

"You're a regular jewel," she said, laughing, then caught her left arm as pain touched her.

"You all right?"

"I shouldn't have laughed. If I move carefully, I'm fine. Remind me not to try skipping rope."

He studied her face, then nodded. "After breakfast, upstairs you go and back to bed."

"But there are so many things to do!"

"I can handle them all. You just relax and get better."

She stared out the big bay window at the forested slopes across the road. It was pleasant country, this, so different from the crowded city. Some people might not like this quiet, but it soothed her, made her relax. If only she could find some way of making a living here, she would certainly throw over that library job and take up residence in this big old house.

She sniffed. Frying bacon and toasting bread. Her mouth began to water. She turned and watched David lift out the bacon, set it on a paper towel to drain off the fat, then saw him break two eggs and drop them into the skillet. He seemed quite competent, well able to care for himself. No wonder he didn't need a wife! He was probably used to doing quite well on his own.

"I ought to be doing that," she murmured.

"Nobody can manage bacon and eggs as I do. I'm a past master at it. Ooops. Time to butter the toast."

He poured cold milk into their glasses, then reached for a spatula. In moments her bacon and egg, sunnyside up, was before her, with buttered toast. Coffee perked off to one side of the big iron stove.

"I'll cut it for you," David offered.

It was easy enough to eat with her right hand once the cutting was done. Judy discovered that her appetite was ravenous. She finished every last bit, and reached gratefully for the coffee cup that he had filled.

He lit a cigarette, handed it to her, then lighted his own. As he blew smoke, he said, "There are things I have to do today. No sense putting them off. I'll bundle you back in bed, then go to look at that bookstore. I . . ."

Judy was not looking at him. Her attention had been caught by a sleek red Cadillac that was easing in off the road, on the other side of the white picket fence. A woman was behind the wheel. David, seeing where she stared, turned to look, too.

The woman got out, stood a moment regarding the

house and the maroon Jaguar. She came around the end of the fence and up the path toward the house.

"Who's that?" David wondered.

"Never saw her before in my life."

"I'll go see what she wants. Probably a real-estate dealer, wanting to know if you want to sell the place, and how much you're asking."

The woman was slim and much too nicely curved, Judy thought, staring at her. Red hair hung down to her shoulders and was set off beautifully by a white cashmere sweater and plaid skirt. She had good legs, too. She was about Judy's age. Her face was absolutely beautiful.

David was at the front door, opening it.

"Hi," said a cheerful feminine voice, "I'm Melanie Rodgers."

"Sort of a one-woman welcome wagon, I assume."

Her laughter rang out, full throated and sultry. "Well, not quite. But almost."

"Come on in, we were just about to have our second cup of coffee. Won't you join us?"

"Glad to. I came to say hello to the new neighbors. You are the new neighbors, aren't you?"

"You might say that, yes. I'm David Carnegie. Come in and meet my wife."

Judy waited, staring down into her nearly empty coffee cup. She always felt a little at a loss when confronted by one of these glamor girls, so outgoing and self-assured. Melanie Rodgers was entirely too beautiful, too lovely. The brief glimpse she'd had of her through the bay window told her that she wore her clothes well, was probably very rich, and likely as not was accustomed to getting just about everything she wanted out of life. Judy wondered if she might come to want David Carnegie.

Then she smelled perfume, and raised her eyes as the redhead came into the kitchen. The smile on that lovely face seemed to freeze at the sight of her.

"Oh! You've hurt your arm. I am sorry."

David said, "My wife was shot yesterday. This is Melanie Rodgers, Judy. My wife Judy, Melanie."

Melanie turned her expressive green eyes up to David. Even her eyes were gorgeous, Judy thought. "Shot? But how? Where?"

"Right out in the front yard. We'd just stopped and were about to take our bags into the house when—bango! Somebody put a bullet through her arm."

Horrified green eyes stared down at Judy. They made her seem small and insignificant. "But how awful for you! Who did it?"

"We don't know," David exclaimed grimly. "But we're trying to find out."

"You poor dear. This must be dreadful for you."

David pushed a chair forward. Melanie sank into it very gracefully and crossed her legs. She didn't seem at all the sort of person who would live in Morstead, Judy reflected. Big city was written all over her.

Judy asked, "Do you come from around here?"

"We have the house on the other side of the brook." She waved a carefully manicured hand. "Actually, we live in Boston; this is our summer home. Daddy takes the summer off, and I come with him."

Judy could not resist asking, "Aren't you bored?"

Melanie laughed. "We belong to the country club, we play golf and swim, and there are dances to attend. We have house parties just about every weekend, people up from Boston and Cambridge, you know. It keeps us busy."

Melanie sprang to her feet as David approached with a third cup and saucer. "Here, let me help you with those."

"David's very efficient around the kitchen. He cooked our breakfasts. He also made the coffee."

Melanie looked up into David's eyes. "An unusual husband, my dear." The green eyes glanced at her arm in its sling. "Especially handy to have around at such a time."

David grinned. "I have my uses. But it's put rather a crimp in our honeymoon."

Drat! Judy thought. *Why'd he have to bring* that *up?*

Melanie bubbled, "Honeymoon? How exciting! And are you going to live here in Morstead?"

"We're not sure," he said. "Judy's inherited this old house and a bookstore in town. We came up here to look over the property, try to decide what to do."

Melanie sat up straighter. "The Book Ends! Of course. This is the Hunter place, and Walter Hunter owned the bookstore. My father's interested in it."

Judy stared at her. "Your father wants to buy The Book Ends?"

"I'm sure he does. I've heard him speak of it, again and again."

Judy glanced at David, but he was watching Melanie. Eating her with his gaze, Judy thought irritably. After all, he was her husband. He was on their honeymoon. Must he show his male interest in so obvious a fashion?

She said, "Do you know how much he'd pay for it?"

"It seems to me he said it would be a bargain at fifty thousand dollars."

Judy almost dropped the cup she had been holding. "Fifty thousand? Dollars?"

Melanie nodded. "I overheard him telling a friend of his. Frankly, it doesn't seem worth all that much money—I hope you don't mind my being so frank, my dear—but I really don't. Have you seen that store?"

Judy shook her head. "Not for a long time. Not since Johnny Edmonds owned it. My uncle must have bought it from him. Why, I can't imagine."

David was still gawking at Melanie, Judy noted. She finished her coffee in one gulp and thrust the cup and saucer at him. "May I have some more, *dear?*"

With reluctance, he looked at her. "What? Oh, yes. Coffee. Of course."

Melanie said, "But you'll have to discuss all those

business matters with him. I haven't any head for such details."

I'll bet, Judy told herself.

David poured more coffee for everyone, then said to Melanie, "I'll have to drop in and see your father, if he's in the market for that bookstore."

"Why not come over with me and see him now? He'd be happy to meet you, talk over the sale with you."

David glanced at Judy. *Nice of him,* she reflected. *I'd begun to think he'd forgotten all about me. And I really can't blame him. I must look a frump alongside Melanie Rodgers. My hair isn't done, this bathrobe I'm wearing is five years old, and these pajamas are right out of a bargain basement.*

"I'd prefer Judy to be there when I spoke to him," he said slowly. "After all, the bookstore is hers. She'd be the one who'd have to say whether or not she wanted to sell it."

He was looking right at her, but Judy would have bet twenty dollars he wasn't seeing her. He seemed sunk in thought, vaguely troubled about something. Was he regretting the quixotic notion that had made him marry her? Now that he'd met the glamorous Melanie Rodgers—who had a wealthy father, obviously—he was having second thoughts. She felt resentment stir in her.

Judy said, "I've been thinking of running that bookstore myself. It would give me something to do."

Melanie opened her green eyes wide in surprise. "That old place? It's dust and cobwebs all over." She flushed faintly, and exclaimed, "Oh, forgive me. I didn't mean to sound—to sound disparaging."

Judy made herself smile. "You were just speaking the truth. It's how I remember The Book Ends, too. Dusty and cobwebby. Exactly. But it would still give me something to do."

David said, "It will need an overhaul, a thorough

cleaning and repainting. But it might be made worthwhile. That's what your father probably intended."

Melanie shrugged. "Perhaps. I had the idea that he would turn it into a warehouse of some sort. He has a few bookstores, among other things. His business interests are widely diversified, and he keeps those bookstores he owns as a sort of tax shelter. At least, I think he does."

You aren't as addle-pated as you might want us to believe, Melanie Rodgers, Judy thought. *I'll bet you have a mind as sharp as a steel trap under that mop of red hair.*

The redhead was saying, "You must come to the country club, David. And you too, of course, Judy—just as soon as your arm heals. There's golf and tennis, and we have a fine pool. You can eat there, too. And there are the summer dances. Oh, you'll love it."

She was staring at David as she spoke, and he was gazing right back into those green eyes. Judy cleared her throat, but neither of them noticed. *They wouldn't see me if I stood on my head,* she decided morosely. *It isn't that I'm jealous—oh, no?—but they could remember I'm here. At least, David could.*

But then, why should he? They had a deal, no more. He was her husband in name only as she was his wife. He owed her nothing, really. Just the same, he could be a little less enthusiastic in his admiration of this woman. Especially since she was sitting right here with them. He could spare her this humiliation!

Melanie was rising. David got to his feet too, saying, "I'll see you to your car."

The redhead turned to Judy. "I do hope your arm will be better in just a little while. It must be terrible to be so incapacitated." Her sultry laugh was low, insinuating. "I'm sure I would hate it myself. Not to be able to play golf or do—other things."

Judy forced herself to be pleasant. "It'll heal in time. And with the good care David gives me. He's quite solicitous, really."

Melanie blinked, smiled, said, "I'm sure he is. But I must be running now." She put her hand on David's arm. "But we'll be seeing you, won't we? Just run over any time. If I'm not home, Daddy will be there. He's very hospitable."

Then she was walking out the porch door, with David at her heels. Judy watched glumly from the bay window as he took her elbow as if to aid her to walk down the flagstoned path. He walked very close to her, and she seemed almost to lean upon him, as though she were the one with the wounded arm. Judy scowled. She was discovering that she resented Melanie Rodgers very much, and this surprised her. After all, she and David were not in love. He was her husband, but that didn't mean a thing.

Or did it?

She found she was tapping her fingernails on the tablecloth, and balled her hand into a fist. But she went on watching as David opened the car door for the redhead and stood there, after she was inside the car, talking to her in a most friendly fashion.

As the car pulled away, he stood staring after it, lifting an arm to wave. He turned and came back to the house almost grudgingly, head bent and frowning slightly. Was he remembering at last that he was a married man? That he had a frump for a wife?

Judy bit her lip. Oh, she wouldn't interfere with any romance he might be contemplating with Melanie Rodgers. But she wished he might have the good sense not to conduct it in front of her.

He closed the door and came to the breakfast table, still with that frown on his face. He said slowly, "Fifty thousand dollars for the bookstore. Could it be worth that much?"

Judy shrugged. "How would I know?"

She was being irritable, she knew, but did not care. Resentment at his conduct was still strong inside her. Maybe it showed on her face, for he seemed vaguely surprised.

"You've seen the store; I haven't."

"What difference does it make?"

He sat down and rested his elbows on the table, his eyes always on her. "It makes this difference. If a smart businessman like Emmett Rodgers is willing to lay out fifty thousand dollars for a piece of junky real estate, there's something wrong somewhere."

"He may want it as a tax shelter. Your girl friend seemed to think so."

David arched his eyebrows. "My girl friend? You give me too much credit, Judy. I wasn't interested in her as a woman——"

Oh, no? Ha!

"——but as her father's daughter. She stopped by to look us over, to report back to him about that offer. You didn't leap at it, and I think it disturbed her in some way."

"The only thing that disturbed her, as far as I could see, was little old me in my frayed bathrobe and old pajamas. Not that I'm much competition for a girl like that. But still, I'm your wife. Not," she added hastily, at his quizzical look, "that I am, other than in name, but she doesn't know that."

"Yes, I think she interests me very much, though not in the way you seem to think. We'll cultivate her friendship, you and I, and that of her father."

"Oh, will we? You may, for all I care, but——"

"I'm only doing it for you," he said gently. "If I can get Emmett Rodgers to up his offer, I'll know I'm right."

"Doing it for me?"

"To get you more money as your inheritance."

She fumbled with her spoon, eyes lowered. "I don't mind if you see her, David. I know I'm not much of a wife. You're free to do as you please. What do they call marriages like that? Open marriages? Yes."

"Will you shut up?" he said grimly.

Startled, she stared at him. He rarely used that tone of voice to her, and it brought her up short. He said, more gently, "I'm intrigued. I want to see how high Rodgers will go for The Book Ends. Even more than that, I want to know why he's offering so much money. Doesn't that fact interest you at all, since you own The Book Ends?"

"I suppose so."

It didn't, really, she found. What interested her far more was Melanie Rodgers and what David thought of her. *Really* thought. Not just words about her, trying to put her off by saying Melanie was here only because of her father.

"You suppose so?" he asked in astonishment.

"Yes, then. Yes, yes, yes. Is that the answer you want?"

"It is. We'll go have a look at that place just as soon as you can move about without pain. I very much want to inspect it. It can't be worth fifty thousand. What troubles me is why Emmett Rodgers thinks so."

Judy had no answer to that.

Chapter FOUR

Judy watched David as he gathered up the plates and cups and saucers and carried them to the sink. She scowled, realizing that this should be her chore and not being able to help him. He was very efficient, she discovered, using the dishpan and some powdered soap, rinsing the dishes under cold water. Vaguely, this annoyed her.

"I'll do those," she offered once, halfheartedly.

"Nonsense," he replied, looking over his shoulder and grinning. "I want you to save your strength."

"What for?" she asked suspiciously.

"You're going to have to help me when we go over your uncle's papers. And we want to do that as soon as possible, to know where we stand."

He did the last dish, wiped his hands, and turned to her with that friendly smile on his lips. Judy eyed the neatly stacked dishes, the sink which he had just washed clean, and the dishcloth he had hung up so carefully.

"Are you sure you've never been married?" she wondered.

His eyebrows rose. "Just because I can do dishes and leave them neatly to drain? No, no. I've never been married before."

He advanced on her, caught her by her good arm, and raised her to her feet. "Exercise," he murmured. "I don't want you to turn into a lazy harridan."

Judy scowled darkly. "A harridan is something like a fishwife, isn't it?"

"A vixenish old lady. Right."

She would have pulled free of him except that she saw the mirth in his eyes. She stared up at him, only too aware of his animal magnetism that made her knees go all watery under her.

She smiled faintly. "All right, maybe I deserved that. It's just that——"

"This whole situation is a little much for you. I know. But things have a way of evening out, with a little help from the people involved. So now I'm going to put you to work."

"Doing what?"

"Find your uncle's strongbox, or wherever it is he kept his personal papers, his deed, his bankbooks, anything like that. We'll want to go over them together."

"But I don't know where . . . No, wait. Maybe I do. Come on."

Her hand drew him after her, out of the kitchen and through the dining room into the den where Uncle Walter had kept a desk and chair, an easy chair where he read so much, and a bookcase filled with his old favorites. There was a rather large closet, too, that backed on the kitchen pantry.

A small safe lay on the floor of the closet. Judy stood and stared down at it. "Once he was showing me his collection of coins—oh, they didn't amount to very much—and I remember he stored them in here. But how do we get it open?"

"Try pulling the door."

The door was locked. Judy sighed, glanced at the desk. Maybe her uncle kept the combination in there. She went to the desk, opened drawers, searched among old calendars, empty pads of papers, old pipe cleaners, some very old three-cent stamps, until she finally produced a matchbook cover which she opened.

"There! I knew I'd seen this before. Right there. Three numbers. Twenty. Eleven. Fifteen."

David stepped back, gestured her toward the closet. When her eyes questioned him, he grinned. "I like a reliant, self-sufficient wife. You open the safe."

"You're impossible," she said, smiling, but she knelt and began to turn the dial.

After a few mistakes, she heard the tumblers click and she yanked open the heavy door. There were his coins, kept helter-skelter in a wooden box—the sight of them made her eyes blur for an instant—and a big brown envelope frayed and worn, bulging with its contents. Judy drew it out and passed it up to her husband.

David studied it a moment, turning it over and over in his hands. He bent and looked inside the safe which, other than for the box of coins, was now empty.

"All right, let's go have a look."

When Judy was seated across the dining-room table from him, he opened the envelope, brought out the papers inside it. "The deed," he said, and read it swiftly, eyes moving back and forth.

He was in his element here, Judy thought, dealing with legal matters, and a sense of warmth and vast security came over her. She sat staring at him until he looked up and caught her gaze.

For a moment, David did not speak but looked as deeply into her own eyes. Finally he sighed and nodded. "The deed's been executed properly, and recorded. The next thing on the agenda is to go to the county hall of records and make certain that Uncle Walter didn't sell the place."

"But that's impossible!"

"Nothing is impossible. I'm sure your uncle still has title to this house and the land around it, but I want to be positive." He held up another paper. "This is his title guarantee, which shows that he owned the house when he bought it. If no other deed has been recorded, you're home free."

Judy sighed. "I would never have thought of anything like that."

"As I say, I want to make sure. I'm nit-picking. But I've learned that it's wisest to nit-pick when something important is at stake." He showed his teeth in a grin. "Besides, it will give us something to do with you until that arm heals."

David was paying no attention to her, he was lifting a bankbook, extracting it from its plastic envelope, flipping open the pages. His eyes ran down the columns of figures and his face subtly changed.

"What in the world would your uncle pay out fifty thousand dollars for?" he rasped.

"Fi-fifty thousand dollars?" she gasped.

He showed her where the withdrawal had been made some years before. Uncle Walter had had seventy-seven thousand dollars in his savings account at that time. The withdrawal had been made a little more than seven years ago.

Judy raised her eyes, stared at David. "But—why? What could he have bought?"

"Don't know and won't guess. Let's try to find out."

David spread papers before him, began selecting them carefully, reading them, putting them to one side. Finally he sat back, frowning.

"It wasn't to buy this house, at any rate. He paid for that a long, long time ago. This has to be the answer."

He held up a legal paper. Judy eyed it narrowly. "It looks like a deed."

"It is a deed—to The Book Ends. Dated the same day as that on which your uncle withdrew the fifty thousand."

Judy gaped. "But—he wouldn't pay that much money for that old store! I've seen it, David. It's all cobwebby and dirty, just like—just as that redhead said."

"Melanie Rodgers? Yes, she was rather disparaging about the place, wasn't she? Still, her father seems willing to buy it, and for fifty thousand dollars. Why is that?"

"Why did my uncle pay so much for it?"

"We're going to have to visit that store before long and try to find out the answer ourselves."

Judy half rose from her chair, but his hand stopped her. "Oh, not right now. Let's say in a day or two. I want you to be stronger, in case there's any work to be done."

She ignored the humor in his voice to protest, "But these matters are so important."

"Not more important than your health. And speaking of your health, I think it's time for a walk."

"A walk?"

"To look over your property. If you don't want to see it, I do, to get an idea of how much arable land you have and whether it can be rented out to some farmer nearby who can till it."

"I'd rather go see the bookstore."

"Of course you would. But not yet." When he saw the anger flare in her eyes, he said, "You just aren't strong enough. I'm not going to have you have some sort of relapse on me. Remember, I'm on vacation, and I do want to get in some fishing."

"Oh! Of course. How selfish of me."

"Now don't get on your high horse, for Pete's sake. I'm doing the best I can for you."

The fury left her abruptly. The man was right. She was being very selfish. They had been so close here, like a real wife and her husband going over their affairs together, that she had momentarily forgotten that theirs was only a marriage of convenience.

"I'm sorry," she muttered, eyes downcast.

To her amazement, he leaned over and kissed her cheek, murmuring, "You're forgiven. Now go upstairs and change into something like slacks and a pullover so you can go outside."

Judy gaped at him. It was the first time he had ever kissed her. The thought came into her mind that her cheek was a hell of a place to kiss a girl. Almost as if she were his sister. Still, it was what they had agreed on, wasn't it?

As she sat there bemused, he asked, "Is there anything I can do to help? Get you out of that robe or the pajamas? Or even—"

Judy jumped to her feet. "No, thanks. I—I can manage."

She fled with the faint feeling that he was laughing at her. When she was in her room, she turned and stared at her reflection in the mirror, seeing the high color in her cheeks, her sparkling eyes. She seemed different, somehow, and touched her cheek where he had kissed it.

Why should she feel so giddy, so excited? She certainly didn't love David—though she did admit to liking him—and he most certainly was not in love with her! The way he had mooned over Melanie Rodgers was answer enough for that! The kiss he had given her was nothing more than a friendly gesture.

She put it out of her mind, or sought to, as she struggled with slacks and pullover. She managed the slacks rather neatly, she felt, but the sweater was a little beyond her. It meant taking her arm out of the sling, and this she could not do, not without pain. She stared at the sweater in mingled frustration and self-pity. She was going to manage. She was!

Her lips a thin line, wincing against the pain, she slid her arm out from the sling and inserted it into the sweater sleeve. Sweat beads came out on her forehead. Once she thought she was going to faint, and she leaned against the night table and closed her eyes, trembling.

But she succeeded. When she put the sling back on, the pain eased. She took a pill from the container, poured a glass of water, and swallowed it. After a little time, the pain went away.

She came down the stairs slowly so as not to renew the pain. David was waiting in the dining room. He had gathered all the legal documents and papers together and was slipping them back inside the brown envelope.

His eyes lighted up at sight of her. "Hurt, didn't it?" he murmured sympathetically. When she nodded, he said, "You could have saved yourself a lot of pain if only you'd asked for help."

"I—couldn't."

He sighed and handed her the envelope. "Put it back in the safe and lock it. I think it might be a good idea for you to find a safe-deposit box in some local bank and store the deeds away, together with the title search." He shrugged. "Just a precaution, it isn't absolutely necessary."

They went out into morning sunlight and a cool wind blowing from the woods across the road. A stand of poplars hid part of the road, so that, except for the white picket fence and the barn-garage at the far end of the property, the house seemed surrounded by trees.

David brought her past the little garden—untended now, given over to weeds, but that once had bloomed with flowers when Uncle Walter had been alive—and the shed that had been a blacksmith house, long ago, along a stretch of long-uncut grass.

"Either I'll have to mow this, or you'll have to hire some local help. Until your arm gets better and you can do it yourself." David waved an arm, indicating the lawn that lay on the other side of the house, where the barn-garage stood, and the grass between the back of the house and the brook, which bore the local name of Cool River. "There's a lot of it."

Judy sighed. "If I decide to live up here, I'll do it myself."

She breathed deeply of the clean, fresh air. Often enough her uncle had told her that there was no air like New Hampshire air. It was cool and fragrant with the nearness of the woods and growing things. The sun was warm on her shoulders and felt good.

She enjoyed the sight of white baby's breath and blue verbena, and the blackberry bushes that edged a stand of wild grass caught her eyes. She must bake a blackberry pie, or several of them, when those huge blackberries were in season. Long ago she had done this for Uncle Walter; he had teased her by saying it was her one real talent.

They moved between the trees—it was cool in their shade—and heard the gurgling of the brook where it made a bend and ran between stony banks until it curved and slid away to the north. Now Judy could see the rail fences that divided the house and its lawns from the farmlands.

"Good water for irrigation," David said, nodding at the stream. "If a man dug himself a well and laid down pipes, a generator might give him all the water he'd need to raise fine vegetables."

Judy glanced at him sideways. "Thinking of becoming a farmer?"

"Not when there's a farmer here already."

A man in overalls and sweat-stained shirt was ambling toward them, on the other side of the fence. His face was bronzed, deeply seamed, and when he nodded at them, it seemed to Judy that he winced a little, as though it hurt his neck. When he spoke, it was with a decided New England twang.

" 'Morning. You'll be Walt's niece, I'm thinking."

Judy smiled at him as David leaned his elbows on the fence. "I am. I've just driven up from New York."

"Ayow." His eyes touched her arm. "Seems I've heard about you, that shooting and all."

"Know anything about it?" David asked.

"Can't say I do. But 'tweren't no hunter."

"What makes you say that?" Judy asked.

His eyes touched her face, looked away. "Nothing to shoot on your front lawn. Man'd have to be a pretty bad shot to miss so badly. Nothing in these woods, neither, 'ceptin' maybe for a few deer now and then."

David said, "That's it. He was after a deer."

The man locked eyes with him a moment, then shrugged. It was no skin off his nose, he seemed to say, if they wanted to fool themselves that way.

He looked off across the field. "Rented this place

from your uncle in the past. Planted here, got good crops. Paid your uncle—"

"Two hundred dollars for its use," David said, smiling.

The man cleared his throat. "Well, yes." He smiled faintly. "Willing to pay as much this year, late as it is in the season. Couldn't do anything until I'd seen you, of course. No sense putting down seed and have you claim it for your own."

Judy exclaimed, "Why, of course. I'll be happy to let you plant there, Mr. . . ."

"Judkins. Abel Judkins."

He did not offer to shake hands, but Judy put out hers, impulsively. Abel Judkins clasped her fingers gently, as though by the act they were sealing a bargain. His dark eyes looked sideways at David.

"Always gave Walt a share of the crops," he muttered. "Reckon there's no sense to changing that."

He looked faintly embarrassed when Judy thanked him effusively. "Been waitin' for you, as a matter of fact. Want to get my crops in just as fast as I can. Didn't think you were ever comin' up."

"Will probate takes a little time," David said. "We've been moving pretty fast, actually, since Walter Hunter died only a couple of months ago." He hesitated, then asked, "Wouldn't want to buy a bookstore, would you?"

Abel Judkins regarded him soberly. "Ought to be askin' Emmett Rodgers 'bout that. Heard tell he might buy it, leastways he's been askin' questions."

"So I understand." David leaned across the rail, offering his hand to the farmer. "I'm very glad to have met you, Judkins. If there's anything we can do for you, don't hesitate to ask."

He took Judy by the arm and led her away from the fence, toward the woods and the little stream meandering over its bottom stones. Abel Judkins stood with his thumbs hooked into his overalls under his armpits and watched them go.

Judy exclaimed, "Of all the silly ideas! Whatever made you think that man would be interested in The Book Ends?"

"I didn't expect him to be. But they hear things in these small towns. Witness the fact that he was there to meet us when we went for our walk. He'd heard we were back, he knew you'd been shot. I figured it wouldn't hurt to ask about Emmett Rodgers."

"So now you know he really is interested in that store."

"And I'm more puzzled than ever. At first I thought Melanie had made a mistake, but now I guess she was telling the truth."

Judy felt excitement leap inside her. "David, let's go have a look at it right now."

"Right now you're going to take a rest. You've tramped enough."

"I don't want to take a rest. I want to go to the bookstore."

"Tomorrow, maybe. If you're stronger."

He would hear no argument, nor was he moved by her cajolings—as when she offered to bake him a pie if he'd take her. His hand on her good arm was firm as he walked her between the trees and out across the lawn toward the house.

"A garden lounge, and some iced tea. I'll make the tea and then sit with you." After they had walked for a time, he asked, "Can you really bake a pie?"

She swung on him indignantly, only to discover the smile on his lips. Judy sighed. He was always teasing her, getting her on the edge of an outburst, then grinning at her like a silly ape.

Judy realized suddenly that he was doing it to keep her mind off her arm. It did not throb anymore, it actually felt pretty good.

She said slowly, "I'm going to bake you a pie such as you've never tasted, husband mine, just as soon as the blackberries get ripe."

"That won't be for some time now."

"You can drive up here later on. The pie will be ready when you are."

"It's a date. We'll have a second honeymoon."

The laughter was in his eyes again. Judy found herself giggling and leaning against him with her uninjured arm. David put his arm about her and held her against him as they strode along. Just as he might have done if she had been his sister, she found herself thinking.

He would not let her go in the house, and he brought out the garden lounge and a chair for himself. Then he went indoors and made iced tea and carried it out on a tray. She sipped it, found it delicious.

It was so pleasant and peaceful here! The air was balmy, touched with the fragrance of honeysuckle and roses. Judy lay back in the lounge, settling herself comfortably, telling herself this was the way life was meant to be lived. The city and her job as librarian were far away, she had no worries with David here to see to everything. Even the fact that someone wanted her dead was like a bad dream, forgotten for the moment.

She murmured deep in her throat with happy contentment, smiling in friendly fashion at David, "I could take a lot of this."

"No reason why you shouldn't. If you—"

"Hi, down there!"

Judy jerked upright, spilling the iced tea on her wrist.

Melanie Rodgers was coming down the far slope at the west end of the house, smiling and waving. She wore a brief sunsuit that clung to her body as wet nylon might.

Even Eden had its snake.

"Surprised to see me so soon again? I went home and told my father all about you, and he wants to meet you. Isn't that wonderful?"

She addressed herself to David, who had come to his feet and was standing, smiling down at her. *Look how he eats her up with his eyes,* Judy thought. *Like a lovesick schoolboy! The mere sight of it makes me nauseated.*

"He says there's no better way to do business than over a dinner table. Or a golf course."

Melanie swung about to Judy, smiling sympathetically. "The golf course would let you out, with that bad arm of yours, wouldn't it? So it will be dinner. Shall we say this coming Sunday night at our house? At five for cocktails?"

She had turned, was again speaking to David. Judy opened her mouth to protest; she would still have the sling on this Sunday, she would appear not only as a frump, but as a wounded frump.

"I'm afraid this Sunday is out," she found herself saying. "We have so many things to do. Perhaps the following week, if that suits"—she almost came out with, "your royal highness," but amended it (rather weakly, she felt) to a mere—"you."

Melanie arched her eyebrows, let her disappointment be seen. David frowned, parted his lips, then closed them.

"If you can't, you can't." The redhead smiled. "Daddy will be very sorry. He's looking forward to meeting you so much."

I'll bet, after you've been prodding him, Judy thought.

Melanie put a red fingernail on David's chest, drew it up and down as she stared up at him. "But we don't have to be so formal as to wait for dinner parties, do we? I want you—and your wife, naturally—to come over to the country club for a swim in the pool. These warm days of early summer makes the water feel especially invigorating."

Judy ran her eyes up and down Melanie Rodgers. She would be absolutely breathtaking in a bikini. It would be a tiny one, no doubt, so that male eyes (especially David's) could get the full effect of her natural assets.

"Why not sit down and share some iced tea with

us?" David invited. "The pool sounds like a great idea. But right now we're so busy, doing one thing and another, that we're going to have to take a rain check."

Melanie puckered up her lips, showing how kissable they were. Judy kicked at the inoffensive lounge. Neither of them noticed, of course.

"I do have to run right now. Maybe next time?"

"Any time at all."

David walked with her to the road. Judy stared off across the back lawn at the brook babbling inanely as it ran over its bottom stones. A dinner party! She would need a summer formal for that, and she had none. She didn't even have a party dress, outside the one in which she had been married. She'd bet Melanie had summer formals. Plenty of them. Plunging this way and that, too.

When David returned, after what seemed a long time, Judy eyed him ferociously. "It must be annoying to have a wounded wife who can't go to parties with you. I'll bet that one wouldn't let a bullet wound stop her!"

"Then why do you?"

Judy glared at him. "You know very well I don't have any clothes to wear to a party such as that one's going to be. I'm a librarian, remember? I don't have money to squander on such luxuries as a summer formal."

"Don't be a ninny."

David stretched out his legs, resting them on the lounge and crossing them at the ankles. He lifted his iced tea and sipped it, his eyes studying her over the rim of the glass.

"Jim Miller will have sent the death certificate and a copy of the will, together with a copy of the surrogate's decree, to your bank here. I don't think there'd be any objection to your taking out a couple of hundred dollars and spending it for frills."

She sat up. "Oh! I—I forgot about the money in his savings account."

David shrugged. "If the bank hasn't received any papers yet, then I'll give you the money. As a little wedding present, let's say."

It was on the tip of her tongue to snap out that she couldn't possibly accept money from him, but the look in his eyes held her silent. She wriggled her toes, staring down at her slippered foot.

"That's very kind of you, David. But I'm not in a partying mood, really I'm not."

"You will be, by next Sunday."

"Oh, will I? And why?"

"Because Emmett Rodgers wants to buy The Book Ends. And by that time, we'll have visited the bookstore and got an idea as to its worth."

"If you say so."

She tried to recapture those moments of peace and serenity she had known before Melanie Rodgers had come traipsing down the slope. The day was just as warm, the breezes as cool and as filled with fragrance, but it was not the same. Life and its problems had a way of intruding, even into moments like these. She wondered if David felt the same way she did, and glanced at him from the corners of her eyes.

He was looking toward the brook, his eyes dreaming. Thinking of Melanie? He was very handsome, she realized, with his tawny blond hair and those very blue eyes, with his outdoors tan and athletic build. No wonder the redhead was so taken with him. She herself . . .

Well, Judy? You yourself—what?

She kicked at the lounge again. She liked him. She would admit to that but to nothing more, because there was nothing more. If it had not been for Bill Evans, she might even have come to love this David Carnegie in time. But not now. No way.

But if she did not love him, why did she become so concerned when Melanie made sheep's eyes at him and pursed those red lips? She had always despised dog-in-the-manger tactics.

She was about to speak, when David turned and looked at her.

"It's unreal, this place. So beautiful, so peaceful. I almost envy your Uncle Walter for all the years he spent here."

She had been about to tell him to go to the party without her. It was only fair to him. Now she nodded and said, "I was thinking the same thing, before Mel—a little while ago."

"It could be absolute heaven, you know."

She regarded him suspiciously. "It isn't heaven now?"

He studied her slyly. "Well, it's almost."

She knew what he meant, she wasn't dumb. If he had a loving woman by his side, it would be bliss. Not a wounded frump who wouldn't even let him get close to her.

Judy got off the lounge. "I'll get us some more iced tea."

"Oh, no. That's my job. You just sit there, and don't walk around without me."

She stared at him. "Why ever not? It's my property. I ought to be able to go where I want without—"

Judy caught her breath, remembering the gunshot that had put the bullet wound in her arm. But who would want to kill her? Who? Certainly that book store wasn't worth all that much, to justify murder!

David gently took the glass from her, and waited until she had slipped back onto the lounge. He walked across the lawn with his easy stride and Judy realized suddenly that he was here only as her protector, a sort of guardian.

Her life had been threatened.

He didn't want her to be killed.

Chapter FIVE

They ate lunch in that same spot on the back lawn, out of sight of the road, with David carrying down a small table, then using the grill that was set in a clump of flowering bloodroot. He cooked hamburgers, fetched cold root beer from the refrigerator, and then sliced onions and placed them on a plate.

Judy watched with a critical eye.

After a time, she murmured, "You know, you make me feel absolutely useless."

He grinned. "Isn't often I have anyone to fuss over. Makes me feel important. Besides, if I didn't have something to do, I'd go stark, raving mad. Now eat up and get your strength back."

She eyed the hamburger he placed in her good hand. It was like a picture out of *Good Housekeeping,* and she found she was actually hungry. She bit deeply into it and chewed. David came to join her, also munching.

When they were done, David said, "We'll take a ride this afternoon, sort of mosey past the bookstore. But we won't stop," he added as Judy sat up straighter. "Maybe in a couple of days."

The Jaguar purred along smoothly over the roads, between the farmlands, through shady woodlands where the sun did not reach and a coolness lay around them. A tiny stream, half hidden behind banks filled with ferns and purple dogbane, caught her eye. Once they trundled over a covered bridge.

It was pleasant to be here, to be driven about, to be handed out of the car when they came to an especially lovely spot which David wanted to absorb before going on. He was very solicitous of her, holding her good

arm when there were stones to be stepped over, or
fallen trees to avoid.

Sometimes they sat on flat stones and watched
brook-water flow past, not speaking, just letting the
quiet of the countryside seep into their pores. Judy realized that she was happy, happier than she had been
in a long time. If only her days could always be like
this, lazing and eating and riding about, with nothing
on her mind.

Once she said, as she dropped a tiny twig in a
stream and watched it float under an arch of drooping
fern, "Where are you going fishing, when you leave?"

"Up north, at Umbagog Lake. There's a brook there
that abounds in trout." He reached in his pocket for a
pack of cigarettes, offered Judy one, then lighted them
both. "There's nothing like fishing at early dawn, with
your fly rod whipping and a big fish waiting."

He chuckled. "Man I know has a cabin. Gave me
the keys. I'll stock it with beans and bread and cheese,
depend on my fishing for the rest."

"You make it sound like fun."

"I'll take you along sometime. You'd love it."

"What's the name of the trout stream, or does it
have one?"

"Mollidgewock. An old Indian name. It's quite long,
too. More like a river."

She sighed. "If it's so far north, it must be even
more rustic than it is here."

He laughed. "It's primitive. I go for days without
seeing a single person."

"And you like that?"

"It's a change. I get enough of people in the city.
They're everywhere. Up there, it's out of bed before
dawn, into the stream or out onto the lake by canoe,
and to bed at night when the shadows grow long."

They walked along the edge of the brook for a little
while, side by side, not speaking. *I don't have to talk
with him,* Judy thought; *there's no need to chatter and
chatter as if to fill a vacuum. We get along quite well,*

as a matter of fact. If it were not too much like treason, she reflected, she would have to admit that David was easier to be with than Bill had been.

The Jaguar moved along the miles with easy power, and Judy sat with her head against the headrest, idly watching the land move by. *I don't want this day to end,* she told herself. It had been so lovely, so tranquil. Even Melanie Rodgers was like something out of a dream.

She turned her head and smiled at David. "Talk about the life of Riley! I never realized I could have so much fun."

"Fun? Just riding around and looking at scenery?"

"It's very soothing. You're soothing too. Did you know that?"

He frowned. "I'm not sure how to take that, nor whether it's a compliment."

She bubbled with laughter. "It's meant as a compliment. There aren't any men I know about whom I could say the same."

"What about this Bill Evans?"

"No. I was never as easy with Bill. It's odd, now that I think back on it. I was happy, yes. But never as relaxed."

David grunted.

He did not speak for another few minutes. Then: "We're coming into Morstead proper. Use your eyes, now. The Book Ends ought to be somewhere around here."

Judy pushed away from the seatback to stare out the window. She saw storefronts and cars parked before them, recognizing a few of the stores from long ago. Up ahead would be The Book Ends, as she remembered, a white clapboard building with twin bay windows and a sign hanging in front that . . .

"There it is," she exclaimed.

David slowed the car, peering to his right.

The sign was dirty, the bay windows grimy. The clapboards, which Johnny Edmonds had always kept freshly painted, were absolutely filthy. The building needed a painting, the sign a redoing, and those windows a good washing.

And she hadn't even seen the inside.

In dismay she looked at David. He shook his head, saying, "Work is indicated, young lady. Much work."

Judy wailed, "Why would anybody pay fifty dollars for that place, let alone fifty thousand?"

"There's a good reason," he muttered grimly. "A damned good reason."

He stepped on the accelerator, eased the maroon car at a faster speed, as though he wanted to put The Book Ends far behind him. He was frowning, Judy saw, as though deep in thought.

Finally he said, "Tomorrow we go to see Doc Adams. After that a trip to Brattleboro is indicated."

"Why Brattleboro?"

"To get my wife some clothes."

Judy stared at him. "I can wear my party dress, the one I was married in. It will do."

It wouldn't, of course, not with Melanie Rodgers around. But she could never hope to compete with the redhead, and it was no use even to try.

David must have sensed her thoughts, for he turned to her with a smile. "You aren't Miss Hunter the librarian anymore, you know. You're Mrs. David Morgan Carnegie."

"Well, yes, but—"

"And Mrs. David Morgan Carnegie will dress accordingly." He hesitated, then muttered, "Maybe we ought to drive down to New York. I'm not at all sure about feminine fashions in Brattleboro."

"Brattleboro will have all we need." Judy smiled.

She sat in a warm glow of delight all the way home. She had forgotten that she was Mrs. Carnegie, to tell the truth. She was still thinking of herself as Judy Hunter, librarian. Certainly David would want her to look her best; it would be a reflection on him if she didn't. But she was secretly happy to think that it was important to him how she looked.

Maybe she'd get to show Melanie Rodgers, after all.

That night a cool wind from Canada came down to brush away the heat of the day, so they ate indoors, after David had grilled the steaks over charcoal briquettes. Judy made toast and a salad; she insisted on that, she could manage that very well even with only one working hand.

She found candles in a sideboard drawer and lighted two, setting them on the dining-room table so that the atmosphere, at least, was romantic. She could not do up her hair, she let it hang, but she did manage to give it a good brushing so the candle flames would pick out highlights in its brown tints.

Afterward they sat in the living room, enjoying cups of coffee and cigarettes.

When she went upstairs to bed, Judy told herself she could take a lot more of days like this one. Her arm did not bother her as much when she undressed, and she felt that in a few days she might be able to discard the sling.

Dr. Adams confirmed this next morning when David drove her to visit him. He was very pleased, nodding and smiling, telling her that the wound was healing very nicely; it had been more painful than serious; by the end of the week she could discard the sling, but she must see him before she did so.

Then they went shopping in Brattleboro.

There were no stores to compare with those in New York, but Judy discovered a stylish boutique that carried a few designer clothes. She was particularly taken by a summer formal designed by David Crystal, of silk chiffon in a frosted coffee color. The lace showed the flesh of her arms and shoulders and, to Judy's mind, a little too much of her bosom.

As she pirouetted in front of him and the three-way mirror, David nodded. "It's perfect for you. It compliments your hair and coloring."

It did flatter her, she realized, as she stared at her reflection. Still, it was a bit too low-cut, and made her vaguely uncomfortable. When she said as much to David, he stared at her.

"Can you imagine what sort of dress Melanie Rodgers will be wearing?"

She considered that, frowning slightly. She certainly didn't want to be thought prudish, but she wasn't going to display her body so obviously. Judy sighed and shook her head.

"I could never wear it," she told him.

"Certainly you can." To the hovering salesgirl, he added, "We'll take it."

Before Judy could open her mouth, he smiled at her. "If it makes you feel any better, select another. We'll take both of them."

Again, Judy stared at her reflection. David was right, she knew; he had an instinctive appreciation of line and coloring. And besides, Melanie Rodgers would be wearing a strapless, backless number, showing herself off the way Judy could never do. She didn't want to be eclipsed too much. Defiantly, her lower lip protruded.

"No," she said firmly. "This one will be fine."

She flushed a little as David raised his eyebrows, and muttered, "After all, I am your wife. I want to make a good showing."

"Good girl. Now for the rest of the things."

"Rest of what things?"

He caught her by an elbow, brought her in the frosted coffee gown to look at casual wear, at sports clothes, at bathing suits. It was David who insisted, almost to her horror, that she outfit herself with A-lines and shirtdresses, with slacks and shorts, blouses, sweaters, and half a dozen different shoes.

"I'll never be able to wear all these things. Never!" she protested.

"Don't be silly. You'll be back here within a couple of weeks, buying more."

She stared at him. "Have you lost your mind? All I want to do is loaf around the house, maybe garden a little when I can . . ."

"No way. You have social obligations. And I can't have you going to the country club in blue jeans and a pullover."

"Oh, can't you?"

He held up a forefinger. "Remember our bargain. I'll be gone in a few days, but until then, you're my wife."

Judy began to giggle. "I must be the only wife in civilization who fights her husband when he wants to buy her clothes. All right. Buy away."

She offered no further objections except when it came time to select a bathing suit. There Judy stood firm. No bikini. Absolutely. No two ways about it.

"You'd look great in one." He grinned, letting his eyes slide up and down her body.

"No deal."

He sighed exaggeratedly, but gave in when she chose a skintight Cole of California in an imitation tigerskin. It had been so long since she had worn a bathing suit of any description that she wondered whether or not she should forget the whole idea.

The bill came close to a thousand dollars, and Judy nearly fainted. "How can you be so extravagant?" she demanded under her breath as delighted salesgirls were gathering up the many boxes and carrying them out to the Jaguar.

"Consider it as a trousseau," he said, grinning.

Her head went back. "I will not. I'll pay for it myself."

"Now, that you will not do." He chuckled, taking her by the elbow and leading her to the car. "It isn't very often I get to spend money on anyone besides myself. I find it's fun."

"I don't know whether I ought to go see a headshrink or send you to one. I know most girls would think me absolutely crazy to protest what you've done. They'd take all this with gleeful yelps."

"That's why it's so much fun. You should have seen your face when I ordered those two cocktail gowns and then that sunsuit. I think the salesladies firmly believed you'd just come out of a mental hospital."

"Or that you had."

He nodded judiciously. "Yes, that thought touched my mind. However, my money was good and so they didn't bother to ask."

When they were on their way, Judy frowned. "How come you had so much cash with you? Do you always carry so much?"

"Only on vacation. Oh, and that reminds me, I have to stop off and cash some traveler's checks."

At the bank, they learned that James Miller had not yet sent on the death certificate nor the probate papers that would clear Walter Hunter's account to Judy's name. David insisted on opening an account in Judy's name and deposited a thousand dollars for her.

She said, "You throw money around like water, you know that?"

"I have an expensive wife."

Judy glared, but could think of nothing to say.

During the next few days, they remained at the house, Judy doing some light gardening at David's insistence, to keep busy. He mowed the lawn himself with an old-fashioned mower he found in the barn. When they were finished with their chores, Judy made iced coffee and carried it to the brook, where they sat on flat stones dipping their bare feet in the brook and letting the cold water cool them.

Gradually, her wounded arm got better. It was only a flesh wound, as Dr. Adams had told her, more painful than anything else, and when the bandage finally came off, Judy was relieved to see only a very faint scar. She was even more relieved to be able to dress and undress without discomfort.

So far, she had refused to wear any of the clothes

David had bought at the Brattleboro boutique. He said nothing, but she caught him looking at her from time to time with a quizzical expression.

She had tried them on in the privacy of her room, had been horrified at how much of her legs the mini-skirted sunsuit showed, at how revealing the cocktail dresses were, with their lace inserts and low-cut bodices. Her old blue jeans and that ragged pullover were perfectly fine for gardening chores and sitting on the back lawn.

Then one morning he said, "I'm glad you're wearing those old things today. We have work to do."

"What sort of work?" she asked suspiciously.

"We visit The Book Ends this morning and try to straighten it up. It's time we did. Your arm is better; you can sweep and mop."

"Oh? And while I'm sweeping and mopping, what'll you be doing?"

"Checking on the inventory. Trying to find out what makes that place so valuable."

Her heart leaped. "You think you can?"

"I can try."

They drove to town with the Jaguar loaded down with mops and pails and brooms. David parked behind the store, then walked around it, Judy beside him, studying the outside.

It was a good-sized building, two stories high. Johnny Edmonds had lived on the top floor so as to be close to his business, and when he had been alive, he had maintained the premises in apple-pie order. But he had been dead for two years now, and signs of neglect were apparent. Uncle Walter hadn't been up to taking care of his house and the store—he had been an old man—and so had let it go to seed.

David lifted the key he had found in the den desk and inserted it. The door opened and a musty smell came out. Judy followed him in, went to the side windows, opened them, then moved to the back of the store, where a fan was set in a rear window. She flicked the switch, glad to find the electricity was still turned on, then swung around to study the place.

There were some cobwebs, and dust on the floor, but all in all, it wasn't as bad as she had expected. There were shelves along both walls, and several long tables in the middle. David was standing at one of the tables, lifting books and examining them, then putting them down.

Judy went to the nearest shelf, ran her finger along the books. Dust. Each book would have to be taken down and cleaned, the shelves themselves would have to be washed, maybe even painted. She sighed. It was a large order, and one she didn't have any special desire to fill.

David walked back to her.

"It certainly isn't for the stock in trade that Rogers wants this place. Most of the books, even the so-called new ones, are a couple of years old. That figures when you consider the fact that Edmonds died a couple of years ago and nobody's paid any attention to the store since then."

Judy made a face. "Is it worthwhile cleaning up?"

"All depends. What are you going to do with it?"

"I know, I know. If I decide to stay on in Morstead, it will give me something to do, running it. If I want to sell, there's no sense in killing myself to make it spick-and-span."

Her shoulders lifted, fell. "I might as well get to work. I have nothing else to do and it will make a better impression if it's clean."

She went out to the Jaguar and brought back mops and pail and broom, also several dust rags. She ran water in the pail, adding a cleaning liquid. David reached for a dust rag.

They worked unceasingly for two hours. Judy swung her mop, rinsed it out, used fresh water, emptied that. She worked steadily, moving from the back of The Book Ends to the front. When she went down one aisle, David was in the other, dusting off books, dusting the shelves, replacing the books.

Occasionally passersby would peer in through the grimy front windows at them or stand a moment in the open doorway, but no one spoke to them. Typical New England reserve, Judy thought. Or maybe it was that way everywhere. In New York, it wasn't any better.

Finally David called a halt.

"Enough for today," he told her, as she paused over the mop, brushing at her fallen hair with a wrist. "We've made a good start. I don't want the place to get to be too much for you."

"It is already," she muttered glumly.

But when her eyes took in the clean floor, the books that seemed almost new compared to what they had been, she felt better. Her eyes slid uneasily to the bay window. The panes really ought to be cleaned, it would improve the appearance of the store tremendously. Judy sighed and reached for the pail of dirty water.

A shadow touched her. She glanced up, saw a balding man with horn-rimmed glasses and a large belly beaming at her from the doorway. He was wearing a shirt and tie, but carrying his jacket, and he looked vaguely like a traveling salesman to her.

"Hi, there," he beamed. "I'm Charley Underwood."

"Hello." Judy smiled, wondering just how filthy she looked. "I'm sorry but the store isn't open. What I mean is, there's nothing for sale yet. You see—"

David was at her elbow, smiling, waving a hand invitingly. "Pay no attention to my wife, she doesn't understand book people. If there's anything you see that you want, we'll be glad to sell it to you."

Not understand book people? She was a librarian! She opened her mouth, closed it as the stranger laughed and said, "No, no. I'm not after books. But I am interested in buying this place."

There was a little silence.

Then David asked, "How much are you willing to pay?"

The stout man considered, lips pursed, his eyes, sharp behind his glasses, going up and down the shelves of books. Judy amended her earlier estimate of him. This one was no traveling salesman.

"Stock's worth maybe three, four thousand at tops. Store's in reasonably good condition, you have a fair piece of ground here, with plenty of space out back for parking. I might go as high as twenty-five thousand. All cash, mind you."

His eyes touched David, slid sideways at Judy. Disappointment was easy to read in them at their reaction.

"Doesn't appeal to you? No, I see it doesn't. Thought you'd leap at my offer, that's why I made it so high." He paused a moment, then smiled broadly. "I see, I see. Thinking of opening the store yourselves, making a livelihood from it. Give you a living, eh?"

"To tell the truth, Mr. Underwood," David said slowly, "we've already received a far better offer. From Emmett Rodgers."

The man's face became very bland. A shrewd trader, Judy thought. "Have you now? And how high did he go, if you don't mind telling me?"

"He's willing to give fifty thousand for it."

The man beamed. "Went as high as that, did he? Well, now. I know Emmett Rodgers and his reputation. Not a man to buy a pig in a poke. If he can go fifty, I'd be willing to up my own offer to sixty thousand dollars. All in good, hard Uncle Sam dollars. Now what do you think of that?"

David said, "It's most generous of you, I'm sure. However, my wife," and here he turned to Judy where she stood leaning on the mop-handle, "will want time to consider each offer. You can understand that, surely?"

"But of course, of course." The fat man nodded, smiling happily. "No sense rushing into anything, I always say. Still, I want to impress on you that my offer stands. I'll be most happy to pay you sixty thousand, or even—perhaps—slightly more.

"Just don't do anything about selling the place until you see me. If Rodgers tops my offer, give me a chance to top him in turn. Like an auction, eh? With the little lady standing by to take a fine profit."

He beamed and smiled some more, waved a hand, and walked off down the sidewalk. Slowly, David turned to look at Judy.

"Well? What do you have to say now?"

"I think they're all crazy."

She gestured at the store, at the grimy windows. "This place isn't worth any more than twenty thousand, at its best."

David rested against a table, nodding. "The stock is about three thousand, give or take a few hundred. The site, the goodwill, the building . . . add, say, fifteen thousand. At most. That gives us eighteen thousand. And Charley Underwood offers sixty."

"Maybe there's oil underneath it." Judy giggled.

"All this proffered wealth is too much for you, my dear," David mock-frowned. "It's gone to your head."

"But there has to be *some* reason," she wailed. "It isn't books, it isn't the store building. What is it?"

"We're going to find out." David nodded grimly.

He walked down the aisle to a door, opened it. There were stairs there, leading upward, Judy saw as she ran after him. They went up the treads into a three-room apartment consisting of a small living room in the front, a bedroom at the back, and a tiny kitchen with a bathroom beside it, in the middle.

They examined each room. The living room held a worn sofa, a very worn easy chair, a portable Admiral television set, a table piled with dusty books and magazines, a small bureau, and a straight-backed chair. Cheap reproductions of the works of Andrew Wyeth and Eric Sloan added color to the drably papered walls.

"Nothing," muttered Judy.

David began turning the pictures, lifting the cushions of the chair and sofa, feeling the material. Judy exclaimed, "Do you think he hid his money in here? Is that it? Was Johnny Edmonds some sort of miser?"

David shrugged but went on with what he was doing. Judy came to help him, wildly excited. Uncle Walter had taken fifty thousand dollars from his bank account, and in return, apparently, had received a deed to this store from Johnny Edmonds. If Johnny Edmonds had not spent the money, it might be hidden here.

But if it were, why was it hidden here instead of being deposited in a bank, gaining interest? Why had her uncle given the money to Edmonds in the first place? Certainly not so he could have put it in a chair cushion, like a squirrel burying nuts against an oncoming winter!

David opened the bureau drawers, searched them. Judy lifted the frayed rug, peered under it. They went over every inch of the room without discovering a thing, other than the fact that this room, like the store below, needed a good cleaning.

They worked over the bedroom, the kitchen, the bathroom. They found nothing that was at all helpful.

"The cellar," said David.

They went down into a musty, airless cellar, found old crates, piles of old papers, neatly tied and stacked, an oil burner, and a snow shovel. Tools were placed neatly on or alongside a workbench, pushed back against the stone wall. Judy stared at the stone floor, the stone walls, the tiled ceiling.

"Beats me," she murmured.

From the look on David's face, he was beaten, too.

Chapter SIX

"I was sure we'd find something," he told her as they went up the stairs and into the store. "Something, a paper or papers that would give us a clue."

"Maybe there isn't anything."

"But that makes no sense. Look around you. Is this place worth even close to fifty thousand dollars? Or sixty?"

Judy shook her head. He was right. Property values in Morstead, though far greater than they had been when her uncle bought his house and Johnny Edmonds opened his bookstore, were nowhere near those figures. She might expect—with luck—to get about twenty-five thousand for this property. Certainly, no more.

Not unless there was a hidden asset that neither she nor David had discovered. "We'll just have to keep on searching."

"But not today."

He smiled at her. Something about his look made her glance sideways at a dusty mirror hanging over a small sink in this office part of the store. She had dirt on the tip of her nose, down one cheek. Her hair was matted with perspiration and stuck to her temples. A cobweb had somehow managed to adhere to her pullover.

Judy gave her reflection a rueful smile. "A bath is indicated." She nodded. "And these old things are going to be dry-cleaned."

She picked up her shoulderbag and slipped it over her shoulder by its wide strap. Her eyes rested resentfully on the pail, the mop, the broom.

"You," she exclaimed to them, "can stay right here."

She walked toward the front of the store, with David following. As she put a hand on the doorknob, she saw a red Cadillac ease by, with Melanie Rodgers at the wheel. Her heart came close to stopping.

"I can't let her see me like this," she wailed. "I just can't!"

David grinned. "OK, scoot out and run around back and hop in the Jag. I'll be right on your heels."

Judy ran, not looking at anything but the ground before her. She heard David ease the door shut, lock it, and then she was in the parking lot, sliding into the Jaguar. She slumped down and closed her eyes.

If that redhead sees David and walks over here, I'm going to die! she thought. *She'll be in some sort of gorgeous creation and here I am like a carefree scrubwoman.*

He was in the car then, chuckling at her.

"I think she saw us, I know she slowed the Caddy as she went past. So we've got to make a run for it."

"Drive fast, David. Drive very fast," she breathed.

He started the motor, swung about. Judy eased upward in her seat, relaxing a little. They were going to get away. Melanie Rodgers would not see her in this disreputable state.

And then the Cadillac came into the parking lot, slid to a stop in front of them. David sighed and braked. Judy moaned.

Melanie Rodgers stepped out, waving gaily. She was impeccable in an Anne Fogarty creation of pink linen.

"Be brave," David whispered.

"I could kill her," Judy breathed through clenched teeth.

"I thought I saw you two in the store," the girl caroled as she came up beside David. "Working hard, were you?"

Her eyes merely flicked at Judy, but they took her in, from grimy cobweb to smudged nose. Her face did not change expression, but Judy knew she was laughing at her. She'd bet Melanie Rodgers never got a fingertip dusty from one end of the week to the other.

"You'll be in the mood for a swim. That's why I stopped you, to invite you. Come on over to the country club, David. Just tell the gateman that you're my guests. I'll leave word."

She put a gloved hand on David's arm, leaned closer so she could get a better view of Judy. "I'm ever so glad to see your wound is better, Judy. But you mustn't over do. So be sure to come along with David and relax."

Melanie wriggled her fingers and was gone in a hip-swinging walk that made Judy grit her teeth. Melanie eased into the Cadillac, gunned the motor, and was off.

David said, "That was kind of her, to invite us. I can't think of anything I'd rather do this afternoon than go for a swim in a cool pool."

"You go. I'll stay home and take a nap."

"You will come," announced David, "and wear that new swimsuit."

She fidgeted, squirming angrily. It was on the tip of her tongue to refuse, but instead of replying, she thought about all that David was doing for her—very unselfishly, really—and was silent. If he wanted her to appear at that pool as Mrs. David Carnegie, then she would. In a sense, she guessed she owed it to him. But not until she'd had that bath!

She ran into the house and up the stairs to her bedroom. She heard David enter, mount the stairs. For a moment she thought he was going to knock on her door, but he passed it by after a moment of hesitation and went into his own room. Judy shucked out of the pullover, dropped it into a hamper. She went into the bathroom, ran the water in the tub.

If her husband wanted her to go to the country club with him, she would. What did she have to lose? After all, in a few more days, he would be gone to that trout stream up north.

She took pains with her hair, doing it in an upsweep,

after she had luxuriated in the bathtub for almost an hour. She slid into the tigerskin swimsuit and stared at herself in the standing mirror. Her color was high, her brown eyes seemed enormous in her flushed face. Her brunette hair set off the oval of her face, and a love-lock had dropped beside her cheek where it had escaped a pin.

She was vaguely surprised at her appearance. She seemed almost a different person. Maybe it was the swimsuit, it certainly showed enough of her body, and hinted at the rest. Or it might be her face; it seemed softer, somehow, and fuller. Her lower lip protruded slightly in reaction to her defiant thoughts.

If this was what David wanted, this was what David was going to get. As her husband, he wanted her to wear this outfit, so she would. If he didn't object to her body's exposure, why should she? She could go back to her jeans and pullover after he'd left for his fishing.

When she came downstairs, the matching tigerskin robe thrown about her shoulders, David was in the living room glancing through one of her uncle's books. At sight of her his eyebrows raised, his lips pursed in a soundless whistle.

Something in his eyes made Judy flush, but she lifted her chin and turned about as might a model. Excitement surged inside her. She had never felt quite this way: provocative, desirable. For almost the first time in her life, she realized what it was like to be a woman.

And that was strange, for she had been in love with Bill Evans. Yet he had never put this tiny fire in her, this breathlessness, this feeling of—yes, power. She looked at David sideways, with a downward tilt of her lashes, as though seeing him as an entirely different person.

He was grinning at her, the ape.

"There. It didn't hurt, now, did it?"

Didn't the big idiot feel the way she did? Apparently not. But just how did she feel? She wanted him to cross the intervening few feet and take her in his arms.

Didn't she? No, of course she didn't! But she did feel a little funny, she admitted that to herself.

"Time to go, I guess. Mustn't keep the pool waiting."

Nor Melanie Rodgers, either, she thought savagely. And was vaguely frightened at her feelings. Well, for once she didn't feel inferior to that redhead.

David was wearing a pair of mid-thigh trunks, broadly striped in white and black, with a terrycloth robe open in front. Judy caught a glimpse of his wide chest, powerfully muscled legs. For some reason she couldn't quite put a name to, the sight of him like this made her understand that this man was her legal husband.

To cover her thoughts, she swung around and made for the front door, picking up her bag on the way. She had brought big bath towels from upstairs, but when she would have lifted them, he was there before her.

"You're a lady of leisure now." He smiled. "I'll do all the heavy work."

Heavy work, indeed. If he'd been swinging that mop earlier, he would be in no mood to do anything but lie down on a bed and sleep. Still, it made her feel good that he should pamper her, even in this small way.

The country club was set back in rolling meadowlands, with a fringe of trees here and there hiding it from the road, and Judy could see the golf course off to the right as they swung up the graveled drive and around into the parking lot behind the graystone building that was the clubhouse. Poplars bordered the parking lot, which was filled with cars, and where the ground was raised a little in the middle, an old well stood, bowered in ivy.

"Probably part of a farmhouse that stood here at one time," David guessed as they walked past it and around the side of the clubhouse where a sign directed them toward the pool.

Melanie came to meet them, attired in a bikini that showed off her suntanned body. Judy felt misgivings as her eyes ran up and down that perfect figure. There was no way she was able to compete with her.

"The water's fine," the redhead said, laughing. "Do you want a swim first or would you prefer a drink?"

"A dip first." David grinned, helping Judy off with her robe.

Melanie glanced at her, and her face seemed to harden.

So then. I was right! This suit does *do things for me.* She guessed she'd have to thank David for that, for he had insisted over her objections that she buy it. She tucked stray hairs into her bathing cap with a sense of satisfaction.

David caught her hand, ran with her to the edge of the pool. They dived in and swam side by side down its length, then came back. Judy was like a seal in the water; she had been swimming ever since she could remember. She kept pace with David for a while, but then he surged ahead a little, fell back when he realized it, and stroke for stroke they went up the pool and down. Her arm troubled her not at all.

Melanie had ordered drinks for them, Tom Collinses with a sprig of mint and cherries. Judy sipped hers gratefully as she sank back in a lounge chair and surveyed the people at the pool.

They were young mothers with their children, for the most part, with a sprinkling of young single women like Melanie, together with a few older men who were coming off the golf course for a dip before they went home. It was pleasant here, the sunlight was warm on her water-chilled skin, and the Tom Collins was delicious.

If she and David ever lived here, she would want to belong to this club. It would be so pleasant to come to on hot summer afternoons. Did David play golf? Probably. Well, she could learn, she would play around the course with him and . . .

Judy came up short. Whatever was she thinking of? She and David living here? What nonsense. They were

just like ships passing in the night, really. He was going
to leave her in a week or maybe two, to finish his vacation fishing up north. She would probably never see
him again after that.

She stared down into her glass.

She didn't want to think about that, nor admit even
in her own mind that she would miss him very much.
He had grown to be almost a part of her. She could
lean on him, let him make the important decisions,
count on him in a pinch.

A hand touched her arm.

Startled, she stared into his eyes, found them gently
smiling at her. "Sorry to bring you back from wherever
you were, but Melanie would like to know what kind
of sandwich you want for lunch. Roast beef? Club?
Bacon and tomato?"

"I'm s-sorry," she stammered. "I was thinking."

She settled on tunafish salad, with iced tea. She was
ravenously hungry, she decided. That exercise in The
Book Ends was showing itself. She watched David rise
and walk away with the redhead.

They belonged here, those two, Judy told herself
morosely. They fitted in here, they were a part of this
sort of life. Her and her dreams! What nonsense. Nobody wanted a mousy librarian as part of a country
club. She wasn't even David's wife. Not really. He had
just done her a favor, marrying her so she could get
her inheritance from Uncle Walter.

No wonder he was so anxious to run off with Melanie. They both were an integral part of this sort of
life. They belonged where she didn't. She took another
swallow of the Tom Collins. He'd be free of her,
though, in a little while; he could do what he wanted
then. He wouldn't have her around his neck all the
time like a millstone.

They returned in a little while, David carrying the
big tray that was heaped with three sandwiches and tall
glasses of iced tea. *He pampers her just the way he did*

me, by carrying those beach towels. He'd do the same for any girl. Judy scowled.

"Here, this will make you feel better," he was saying, handing her the plate with the tunafish sandwich.

"I feel all right," she muttered.

"I know, you're just tired."

She bit into the toast and tunafish. Certainly she was tired, and upset for some reason she couldn't name. But she watched David and Melanie as they ate and chatted and laughed. The redhead sat entirely too close to him, Judy felt, ignoring the chairs and lounges, choosing instead the tiled edge of the pool.

From time to time she would put her bare shoulder to his and nudge him with it as she chatted. Judy tried to catch what they were saying but they were a little distance away and she could get only an occasional word. She wished she could interest David in that way, talking animatedly, giggling at something he would say and glancing sideways at him flirtatiously.

She just didn't have it in her, she might as well admit it.

When she had finished her sandwich and iced tea she leaned back and closed her eyes. She might as well get a suntan while she was at it, and reached in her handbag for the suntan lotion.

She dozed for a time. When she woke, David and Melanie were in the pool, very close, and the redhead was pouting, looking very little-girlish and helpless. Then David caught hold of her by the waist and eased her farther into the water.

The idiot! He was going to give her a swimming lesson. And she could swim like a female Mark Spitz, Judy would bet. She watched them carefully, taking note of the fact that David's hands touched Melanie a lot more than seemed necessary.

"Don't you swim?"

Startled, Judy looked up into a pair of slate-gray eyes set in a heavily tanned face under a mane of thick black hair. The man was in his early thirties, she would

guess, and had a muscular build just as good as
David's. He was smiling down at her in friendly fashion
as water dripped from his swimtrunks to the tiles.

"I'm Ed Malone," he introduced himself. "I've been
watching you lying here in the sun. You must be bak-
ing. A dip would really cool you off, you know. But if
you don't swim, I'd be glad to teach you."

His even white teeth flashed to his grin.

Judy said promptly, "I think you're absolutely right.
A swim is indicated."

She rose to her feet, seeing David glance at her and
the man beside her in startled fashion. *Did you think
you could tuck away your wife in a chair and forget
about her, Mr. Carnegie?* she thought. *Not on your tin-
type, to borrow an old phrase.*

She paraded to the edge of the pool, poised a moment, then dived in. A moment later, Ed Malone was
beside her and they churned water as they Australian-
crawled up and down the pool twice.

When they hung on the edge together, with Judy a
little winded, Ed Malone said, "I knew it. You're a
regular fish in the water."

"You knew no such thing. You wanted to give me a
lesson."

He smiled ruefully, meeting her laughing eyes.
"Well, you may have something there. I haven't seen
you around before, and I always like to get acquainted
with all the pretty girls."

"Even if they're married?"

"Oh, especially if they're married. No danger of
complications then."

She laughed with him, chatted as if she had known
him all her life. There was something boyish, friendly,
almost puppydoggish about Ed Malone; he seemed to
laugh at life and its problems and let some of this spill
over into his attitudes toward people. He was an insurance salesman and real-estate agent, he said. He had
come up here from Boston some years back to found
his own business.

"I don't get rich, but I make a buck here, a buck there. And you can't beat the life."

"You chase girls instead of dollars."

"One might say that. Not that I'm having too much luck at the moment."

"Well, after all, I've only been married about a week and a half. Really, now."

He made a face. "If I'd known that, I'd have waited a few more days."

Judy erupted laughter. It was pleasant to linger here in the pool and bandy words with this handsome man. She was very much at ease with him; it wasn't at all the way it was with David. She didn't mind when he hooked her middle with his arm and toppled her back into the water, yelling, "Race you to the other end." Nor did she object to his hand that touched her a little too much as he helped her up out of the pool.

Now why was that? she asked herself. Because she knew that Ed Malone was just idly flirting? And that she was responding to it in appreciation of the compliment he was paying her by his attention? No. It had to be something more than that.

David and Melanie were watching them approach, Melanie eyeing her with suspicion, David with something like surprise. She pulled off her bathing cap and introduced Ed and David.

"You're a lucky guy," Ed said. "Your wife is a real stunner."

David nodded. "Wouldn't have married her otherwise."

When she went to introduce Melanie to Ed, the redhead murmured coldly. "We've already met." There was a curious tone to her voice that made Judy raise her eyebrows. These two knew each other, and Melanie didn't care for the big Irishman.

"Ed's in real estate," she commented to David, watching Melanie stare off across the pool, too obviously ignoring her new companion.

"That's very interesting," David said. "Judy here has

inherited some property in Morstead. A big house, a lot of land, that bookstore in town."

Ed apparently scented business in the offing, for he looked at Judy more seriously than before. "Interested in selling?"

"She isn't sure. She may want to sell the bookstore, certainly, but even then, her mind isn't made up. Judy thinks it would be fun to run it for a while."

Melanie brought her eyes back from the pool to glance up sharply at her, Judy noticed. There was cold calculation in that gaze, and a hidden hardness.

Judy spread her hands. "David is often so busy at his law work that I'm left very much a widow. Sort of like a golf widow. Times like that, I'd like to have something to keep me occupied."

"You won't make money," the redhead pointed out.

"Oh, David has lots of money. It would be a fun trip, that's all. Besides, I'm not at all sure I'm going to. It's just talk, and that's easy enough."

Ed murmured, "You could get twenty thousand for the store. Maybe even twenty-five, with any kind of luck."

So, then. Ed Malone didn't know about the store's real worth. For some odd reason, it made Judy like him all the more.

David looked glum. "I thought differently, somewhere in the neighborhood of fifty, even sixty thousand."

The Irishman shook his head. "Maybe in the heart of the city. But not up here in the hinterlands. No way."

David smiled. "It might interest you to know that we were offered sixty thousand only this morning."

Melanie swung around, exclaiming, "Sixty thousand?"

"That's right. Somebody named—what was it, Judy?—oh, yes. His name was Underwood. Charley Underwood."

Malone goggled at him.

The redheaded girl looked as if she'd bitten into a lemon. Judy smiled down at her, idly running a towel over her arms.

She said sweetly, "It would be hard to turn down an offer like that."

"Grab it," Ed Malone said huskily. "You'll never do any better."

David glanced at Melanie. "Oh, I don't know. We might."

"Look, Carnegie. Take my word for it. You can't do any better than that, not for The Book Ends. I know the property. There are homes around here that will sell for a hundred, two hundred thousand dollars. But those are estates overlooking a lake or the river, or with a terrific view. With stables and such, and perhaps working farms to go with them. But that bookstore? Never."

"Oh, well. It's just a lot of talk. Judy isn't sure she knows what she wants to do yet."

As if by common consent, they abandoned all talk of The Book Ends, and chatted about the weather, the golf course, the state of the economy, the trouble in the Middle East. From time to time, Melanie Rodgers would frown off into space as though worrying; neither of the men noticed, but Judy did.

Melanie would report back to her father about Charley Underwood, Judy felt. How would Emmett Rodgers take that offer? With a shrug and a smile? Or would he feel obliged to top it? For the first time, Judy felt a desire to attend that party the Rodgers were having, after all.

They wandered from the pool to the car lot, and David spread towels on the bucket seats. Ed held out his hand, telling David not to sell to anybody until he had come to see him. Melanie, who kept as far from the Irishman as possible, seemed almost to sneer at his words.

After they were in the car, Judy saw Melanie go off

in one direction, Ed Malone another. "I wonder what the trouble is between them."

"She's probably jealous of you."

"Of *me?*"

"You were pretty buddy-buddy with him."

"Well! This from you. You, who were all over that redhead playing at teaching her to swim."

David grinned. "She really isn't a very good swimmer. I'm surprised. I thought a girl like that could do just about anything."

"I'll bet."

He eased the Jaguar along the road, sitting relaxed at the wheel as was his habit. "I'll ignore the innuendo and point out that I was only playing up to her for business reasons."

"Funny business."

"You know, you sound exactly like a jealous wife. But that can't be, because we're only partners in a little game. It can't matter to you how I carry on with Melanie."

"Certainly not."

"It isn't as if you were in love with me."

"Exactly."

"For that matter, you were having a lot of fun with Malone. Never saw you so animated. He's very good-looking, of course, and has a certain way about him. Pushy, but friendly."

Judy considered that. "I suppose an insurance salesman or real-estate agent has to be pushy, don't you?"

"Not around you. Oh, I saw the way he just walked over to you and started talking."

"And why not? They're all friends at that pool."

"You aren't part of the crowd. You were a stranger."

Judy slithered around as best she could in the bucket seat so as to watch his face. "You know, David Carnegie, if I didn't know better, I'd say you sound a little jealous yourself."

"I just don't want you to make a fool of yourself, that's all."

"Why . . . why . . ." She sat bolt upright, anger flaring in her. "How—how can you begin to talk to me about me making a fool of myself when you—when you've been carrying on like a lovestruck calf with that redhead!"

She bounced around in the bucket seat as much as the seatbelt would let her, flushed and indignant. "I've never been so insulted. I was just being friendly. I talked and laughed and had a swim with Ed. What was I supposed to do, turn away from him when he spoke to me?"

She thought a moment, then added sweetly—too sweetly—which might be considered a danger sign, "I was doing exactly what you were doing. He's a real-estate agent. I figured it might be a good idea to get his opinion on the bookstore. Just as you play up to Melanie to find out more about her father's offer for the place."

"You didn't know he was a real-estate agent when you spoke to him."

"And I never would have if I hadn't."

She sat back, crossed her legs, and stared straight ahead.

The car reeled off the miles, past farmlands and roadside stretches covered with fairybells and buttercups. The mountains in the distance were purple with haze, remote, tranquil. It was a peaceful scene, in direct contrast to the storm of injured innocence that raged in Judy.

The utter gall of the man! He could do as he pleased, laugh and talk with Melanie Rodgers, but if she so much as exchanged a pleasant word with another man, he was up in arms.

She was out of the car almost before he had braked it, marching herself up to the house, fumbling in her shoulderbag for the key. She inserted it, turned it, stalked inside. David Morgan Carnegie was a boor! He was not at all the nice, friendly person she had imagined him to be. Now she was finally seeing him in all his true colors.

He was at her heels as she moved through the kitchen and into the dining room on her way to the stairs. His hand caught her, swung her around.

She glared up at him.

"We really don't have anything to say to each other, do we?" she asked coolly. "You've made it very plain what you think of me. What's fine for Jack is not so good for Jill, is it? I thought you were so levelheaded, but I'm finding out that you're really only a—"

That was when he took her in his arms. Judy fought against him, beating his chest with her fists, but she was no match for his male strength. Inexorably, despite the little cries and pleas that she was voicing, he brought her up against him.

And then he kissed her.

Judy felt his lips, soft and gentle against her own. She had expected a savage kiss, was quite surprised at the reality. And she could not deny that she enjoyed it. Something happened to her right then, her heart exploded and her legs got rubbery.

If he hadn't been holding her, she would have fallen.

For an instant she returned that kiss. She knew that he felt that pressure and raged at herself. She pushed away, and knew a sudden fury at him for letting her go.

She must play this cool, she told herself. This was no time to lash out, to let him know how deeply she had been stirred. If he ever realized that, there would be no living with him. Not the way they had been, anyhow.

"I suppose you're quite proud of yourself?" she said coolly.

David eyed her calmly. "You are the most exasperating female I have ever known. I suppose you want me to pack and get out of your life now."

She considered that, head tilted to one side. "No, I don't think so. I rather imagine you were just trying to assert your so-called male supremacy, to prove you could kiss me any time you wanted, or something like it."

"It wasn't like that at all."

"Then how was it?"

He shook his head, pushed past her. At the foot of the staircase he turned and said, rather bitterly, Judy thought, "You wouldn't understand. You wouldn't understand at all."

He clomped upstairs, leaving her thoughtful.

When she came up to remove her bathing suit, he was at the door of his bedroom, still wearing his terry-cloth robe.

"Look, Judy. Let's go out to eat tonight. There's a place Melanie was telling me about, the Black Lantern or some such name, just outside of Keene."

"Why not?" she said. At least, it would give her a chance to see other people, to see new surroundings. She wouldn't be faced only by the man who had just kissed her.

The more she thought of the idea, as she slipped into one of the dresses he had bought her, the better she liked it. She did up her hair and slipped a few bangles on her wrist. In the ice-blue dress, she felt cool as an Arctic breeze. And this was just the way she wanted it. There must be no more emotion between them, no quarrels that might fuel the male vanity of David Carnegie.

They were silent in the Jaguar as it moved along the miles between Morstead and Keene. David paid strict attention to the road and to his driving. Judy was satisfied to scan the countryside, hazy in the early dusk of evening, reflecting that there was no reason why she could not just ignore that kiss and what it had done to her.

David had stirred her, she admitted to herself, and she was surprised at the fact. She had always felt herself a little above any such weakness. She was vaguely troubled, as though she had glimpsed an unsuspected facet of her character that displeased her.

As they moved out of Keene, past the college, he said, "I suppose you're waiting for an apology."

"Whatever for?"

Oh, she knew what he was talking about, and she suspected that he was aware that she knew; it annoyed her a little.

He ignored her words to say, somewhat grimly, "All right, I apologize. I shouldn't have done it. I won't say I'm sorry—because I'm not. But I do apologize. I broke our agreement."

"But why did you do it?" Judy pressed. "You know there can't be—anything like that between us."

To her surprise, he chuckled. "If I told you, you'd get angry again, and I don't want that."

"No, please. I promise I won't get mad. Why did you?"

"Ever the woman. Can't let well enough alone."

"It's just that we had such a wonderful relationship, before you went and spoiled it."

"Chalk it up to the fact that you were very kissable at the moment."

Judy frowned. "I've never been kissable in my life."

Even as she said it, she felt there was something vaguely wrong. No woman should ever admit she was not kissable! It was like a denial of her very femininity.

"Because you've always fought against it." He waited, but when she did not answer he added, "You were very much a tomboy in your early years. You never liked clothes, you used to drive your mother wild. Remember you told me that on our drive up here?"

She remembered. It was the truth. She had always scorned the typical female traits, choosing rather to subordinate them to the necessities. It had been so much a part of her that she never gave it a second thought. Yet now, sitting at ease in the powerful

Jaguar beside this man who was her husband, she knew she had been living a lie.

She was just as feminine as Melanie Rodgers. Yet why had she hidden that femaleness in blue jeans or dowdy dresses? Because she was afraid? But that was nonsense! Of what was there to be afraid? Deep down inside her, the answer lurked, but she could not summon up courage to search for it.

David was holding out his hand.

As he had done once before, so he asked again, "Friends?"

She laughed, gripped his hand. "Friends. Yes, David. As we were before."

"And no more kisses."

She hesitated before murmuring, "No, of course not."

A hidden part of her almost wished he would kiss her again. It had been so—well, so pleasantly disturbing. She had never felt quite that way before. But she could not tell him that! It would ruin everything.

But the air had been cleared between them. David appeared to relax more as he drove, and she put her head against the headrest and smiled at the world around her. Life was once again worth the living.

The Black Lantern was crowded, as it always was, according to a woman waiting in the anteroom beside them. Even with a reservation, which David had made by telephone before they left, there was half an hour to spend over a cocktail before their name was called.

Dinner was perfect. There was roast beef, Yorkshire pudding, and afterward, pie a la mode for David while Judy contented herself with a sherbet. David was an amusing, solicitous companion; he made her laugh with stories about his early years as a lawyer, he regaled her with tales from his football years at Harvard. She felt she knew him even better as they lazed over cigarettes and coffee, and felt more keenly the subtle bond that had sprung up between them.

There was no hint of trouble as they cruised through

the soft New England night. Not until they came in sight of the house and saw the Highway Patrol car before it, its flashing lights heralding bad news, did the reality of the outside world move in to jar them.

A state trooper was waiting at the picket fence.

Chapter SEVEN

He was a big man in a gray uniform with slouch hat low over his eyes and a big gun holstered at his hip. He came away from the fence as David braked the car, and strolled toward them almost casually.

Judy sat upright, heart thumping. Even David seemed grave, she decided after a swift glance at his face.

"Something wrong, officer?" he called.

The man bent down, looked inside at them. "You own The Book Ends in town?"

David nodded. "My wife does."

"Someone broke in there tonight, vandalized it. I came over here just as soon as I learned you were the owner. Man named Malone told me. He's at the store now, watching over it. You want to follow me?"

"We do. And thanks, officer."

The patrolman went back to his car, got in. He drove off with David following. In the car, Judy discovered that her hands were clenched into fists.

"Why, David? Why'd anyone do it?"

"Must've been kids."

She eyed him sideways. His lips were tight, his scowl was savage. In a small voice she asked, "Do you really believe that?"

"No, I don't suppose I do. The store's been there for years, has never been touched. Now all of a sudden when you show up as owner and refuse to sell, someone breaks in. It's too much of a coincidence."

"But why would anyone do it? To force me to sell?"

"I think they were looking for something."

"But there's nothing there, outside of a lot of books.

Nothing of real value. We looked ourselves and didn't find anything."

"Whoever did the breaking in didn't know that. Or if they did, they felt they could find what we didn't."

She sat back, worried, fretful. "Do you think they did? Find anything, that is?"

"Not unless they knew where to look, and what they were looking for." He thought for a moment, then asked, "Did your uncle ever hint about something valuable that might be in that store? Think hard now. He probably wouldn't come right out and name it, but he might have tried to give you some clue."

Judy thought. Her uncle had always been so amiable, so relaxed, so easygoing; she always remembered him as a jovial person. She hadn't even believed him to be a very good businessman, he never seemed interested in making money.

"Not a thing," she said at last. "When we were together, we were always going off somewhere to see the sights, or so he could fish from the boat he made me row. He never said anything at all about money."

"Too bad. It would've been a help."

Ed Malone was standing in the open doorway of The Book Ends. The store was dark, unlighted. Judy saw him first as a dark shadow in which a red dot glowed as he drew in on a cigarette. When the Jaguar pulled to the curb he threw away the butt and came across the sidewalk toward them.

"Mighty sorry about this, Judy, David," he announced. "I was working late in my place down the street. When I started home, I saw the door here was open. I stopped, took a look in, and phoned the police."

The trooper had come up, stood listening.

"Is it—very bad?" Judy asked.

"Have a look for yourself."

David came around to open the door for her but Judy could not wait for that. She got out, ran toward the dark store, hesitated in the open doorway, then reached for the light switch.

The long room was a shambles. Books were scattered in the aisles, apparently pulled down from the shelves and searched, then tossed aside. Even the books on the table had been examined, thrown aside. Remembering the work she had done here earlier, Judy groaned.

"Oh, no! No."

David was at her elbow, gripping her arm and squeezing. Malone had stood aside from them and for the patrolman. She turned, glanced at both of them, her despair easy to read in her strained face.

"I suppose it's too early to ask if anything's missing," asked the highway officer.

David said slowly, "We didn't make an inventory. But I can't believe someone was in here looking for reading material."

The officer's gaze sharpened. "Was there any money in the cash register? Could robbery have been the motive?"

"Well, if it was, I don't know what they hoped to get. The store hasn't been open for business during the past couple of years. We were in here earlier, cleaning it. I took a look at the books. As far as I could tell, none of them was at all valuable."

"Then it was just vandalism."

When David hesitated, Judy snapped, "It was more than that. No young people did this for kicks. It was something else."

"What would that be, do you imagine?"

"They want me to sell this place. They hired somebody to come in and mess it up, hoping I'd be so frightened, or maybe so disgusted, I'd accept their offers."

The patrolman brought out a notebook. "Who are these people, ma'am?"

David interposed smoothly, "My wife is upset, officer. She can't give you any names."

Judy glanced at him, saw his warning glance. A stubborn conviction clawed its way up into her throat. "Well, maybe I can't prove anything, but I can have my suspicions."

David smiled at the trooper. "We'll have to have a look around, naturally, discover if there is anything missing. We haven't gone over the inventory; frankly we don't know just what sort of stock is in the store."

The officer folded his book, nodded. "My name is Trent. Jim Trent. If you find something's missing, I'd like you to get in touch with me. In the meantime, we'll treat it as vandalism. I'll ask around to find out if anyone saw any kids in the store, entering it or leaving it."

Judy would have spoken but David forestalled her. "That would be best, I feel, under the circumstances. I'll contact you when we have anything that can be used as evidence."

He drew an engraved card from his wallet, passed it over. He said, "We're staying at the Hunter house, for the next week at least. If you learn anything, I'm sure you'll get in touch."

Trent eyed Judy, whose rebellious face mirrored her anger. She shrugged, began to walk up an aisle, stepping between the books, lifting a few and putting them on the shelves.

The action gave her something to do, ease the fury simmering inside her. She had not expected anything like this, not in a sleepy little town like Morstead. She was more convinced than ever that there really was something valuable in The Book Ends, something so valuable that someone would commit a crime for it.

But who?

Emmett Rodgers? That fat man, Charley Underwood?

It did not make sense. At least, as far as Emmett Rodgers went. He was a wealthy man, he would not stoop to such tactics. She knew nothing at all about Underwood. But she meant to learn. Somehow, in some way.

She paid no attention to David or Ed Malone or the highway patrolman. They were behind her, grouped at the door, talking in low tones as she busied herself with the books. Not until David came up to her and caught her by the hand did she stop from lifting books and putting them back on their shelves.

"They've gone," he said softly. "It's time we left, too."

"But this is such a mess. We ought to straighten it up at least."

"Tomorrow, yes. It's almost midnight."

She sighed and looked around her. "I just can't believe it. Who'd do such a thing? Why, David? Why?"

"You said it yourself. Either to try to make you sell. Or to find whatever it is in this store that's so valuable. Now come along. It's time you hit the sack."

She followed him out into the night, which had suddenly lost all its charm despite the overhead stars and the blue velvet sky and the slash of silver moon. For a moment she leaned against him, gathering strength from his hardness, enjoying the feel of his sympathetic arm about her.

"A month ago, I was just a librarian without any problems. Now look at me."

"You're a lot better off than you were. You're a married woman, you're an heiress, you stand to become even richer." His voice made gentle fun of her. "Isn't that worth a little trouble?"

"I suppose so." She let her head rest against him, found his arm propelling her across the sidewalk toward the Jaguar. "Who do you think did it? Melanie's father? That man Underwood?"

He saw her seated in the bucket seat before he made any answer. "I didn't want you spouting out about them in front of Malone or that policeman. If you made any wild accusations, you could find yourself facing a slander suit, perhaps. As a lawyer's wife, you have to be careful about things like that."

Judy protested, "But you must have thought about them!"

He got in beside her, hooked his seatbelt. "Sure I did. But I didn't go around accusing anyone."

"All right, I stand rebuked. But just between ourselves?"

He shook his head. "I can't believe Rodgers would do such a thing. Not that he's above any such shenanigans, maybe, but it would have to be an awfully big haul to make him act this way. And he wouldn't do the searching himself, naturally."

"Drugs? Do you think it's something like that? But no! Uncle Walter would never have been involved in anything like that."

The Jaguar moved slowly along the road. "What concerns me even more than what it is, is—where is it hidden? We went all over that building. We didn't break down any walls, of course, but short of doing that, we covered every inch of the place."

"Tomorrow," Judy said firmly, "we will search again."

Next day they were in The Book Ends before nine, Judy in her jeans and pullover, David in disreputable slacks that he claimed were his good-luck fishing pants, and a shirt that had seen better days. They attacked the books first, putting them in order on the shelves after dusting them off and opening them, rifling through them in case some paper or note from her uncle or Johnny Edmonds might be in one.

They worked steadily, without a halt until midday, when David insisted they stop for cigarettes and iced coffee, which he would provide by going to the general store. Judy slumped against a counter, blowing a strand of hair from her eyes. Iced coffee and a cigarette sounded like a slice of heaven at that moment.

It was while Judy was alone, still lifting and stacking books, that Charley Underwood walked in, beaming with good nature. He took a look around him, puffed out his cheeks and gave a low whistle.

"I heard about the vandalism," he said, with sympathy in his voice. "I'm mighty sorry about that. Seems these kids of today will do just about anything."

Judy regarded him from under lowered brows, half a dozen books in her arms. "If it was kids," she muttered.

Underwood raised bushy eyebrows. "You suspect someone else, then?" He thought about that for a moment, staring at the floor. "Hey, now," he blurted. "I hope you don't think I had anything to do with this! I can see how you might, what with me making my offer to buy this store. But I assure you, Charley Underwood doesn't resort to any such underhanded tactics as this."

Judy smiled faintly. "I'm sure you don't. Reasonably sure, anyhow. Still," she added with twinkling eyes, "the thought did cross my mind."

"And Emmett Rodgers, eh?" he guessed shrewdly. "You thought he might have hired someone to mess up the place."

This man, plump and faintly perspiring, was not the simple individual he appeared, with that beaming smile and innocent look. There was a shrewd brain behind his broad forehead, Judy realized.

"Rodgers wouldn't do such a thing," Underwood went on slowly, shaking his head. "I've locked horns with him over a deal or two, always found him to be honest and aboveboard."

He held up a hand, palm toward her. "Not that he won't skin you alive in a deal, if you're stupid enough to let him. But out and out skulduggery—no. He wouldn't stoop to it. No reason why he should, with his money. He can get just about everything he wants legally."

Unless there was something illegal about it, she told

herself. Then he might. She sighed. It was all too much
for her wits.

David came in then, carrying cardboard containers
of iced coffee. He was surprised to see Underwood, but
greeted him cordially, passing a container to Judy and
offering his own to the stout man. Underwood declined
with a shake of his head, but watched as Judy sipped
and David took a long swallow.

"Just stopped by to repeat my offer," he explained
genially as David lighted two cigarettes and passed one
to Judy. "Sixty thousand, all cash, for the store as she
is. Even upset."

"It won't be upset much longer." Judy smiled.
"We're going to straighten everything out. Aren't we,
David?"

He looked around him, sighed and nodded. "Even if
it breaks my back."

"Save yourself the trouble. Leave her as she is and
sell out to me. I can have the money in your hands in
an hour."

Judy sighed, glancing around her. "You tempt me
very strongly, Mr. Underwood. But the answer is still
no. At least, for the moment."

The stout man laughed. "I can wait. Half my
business consists of waiting, anyhow."

He waved a hand, turned, and walked out.

David lingered over his cigarette and iced coffee,
staring out the front window and frowning every so often. Judy watched him as she sat on a little stool and
tapped ashes off her own cigarette. Over the past two
weeks she had come to know him rather well, she felt;
he was deep in thought at the moment, so she remained very still.

"The lawyer," he said finally, turning to look at her.

"What lawyer?" Judy asked blankly.

"The lawyer who drew up the deed to The Book
Ends, the one man who ought to know all about this
place."

Judy jumped up. "David! Why haven't you thought of him before? Certainly, he's the man we want to see."

He looked vaguely shamefaced. "I've been meaning to see him. It was in the back of my mind, in New York. I wanted to learn more about this bookstore in which your uncle acquired such an interest, so late in life. It didn't make sense to me.

"And the day we were going over his papers, after you'd taken them out of the safe, the idea came to me again. All I can say is, things have moved at such a fast pace, they drove it right out of my mind."

"Some lawyer you are," she commented darkly, with a hint of laughter in her throat.

"I'm on vacation," he said loftily, then caught her by the arm. "Come on, we'll go home and dress, have lunch out, and call on the man this afternoon."

Judy stared around her, her housewifely instincts clamoring, but she sighed and nodded. The store could wait. Charley Underwood said he would take it as is, she was sure Emmett Rodgers would do the same, so there was really no need to kill herself. And David wasn't really much help. Manlike, he started in with a lot of gusto, but that tapered off soon enough. She guessed this cleaning up didn't really hold his interest.

He said now, "I should have liked to do a little more searching, but right at the moment, I think it's more important to find out what we're looking for. I hope that lawyer can tell me."

As they came out on the sidewalk, a little old woman hastened her steps toward Judy. She was wearing a long blue dress, with a straw hat perched on snowy white hair. Behind steel-rimmed glasses her eyes were sharp, birdlike.

"Oh, dear. Are you the new owners?" she called.

Judy smiled, "That's right."

"And are you going to open the store for business?"

She sighed. "I read a great deal, it's almost my only pleasure now. And I do miss The Book Ends."

"Well, I'm not sure. We've had some trouble, someone broke in and messed things up a good deal. We're trying to straighten things out."

"And you will, dear. You will. Johnny Edmonds always kept a very neat store; he would get any book for me I asked for. I do hope you'll do the same." She sighed and seemed thoughtful.

"Though he would go off from time to time, in those two or three years before he died. He'd lock up the store and pay no attention to business at all." She smiled happily. "He always said he was after new stock, but if you ask me, he was only taking time off for fishing. I never saw any new books when he came back from those trips. None at all. Still, maybe you'll do better."

Judy got into the Jaguar, giggling. "Our first customer. I might even have made a sale."

"So Johnny Edmonds went on trips, did he? Now, I wonder where. And why."

"Probably what the lady said. He goofed off, went fishing."

Judy donned a print shift with matching sandals, adding summer jewelry, for the afternoon. Excitement flared in her from time to time; she had caught it from David, she knew, for he was so certain they would really discover something important from the lawyer.

When she came downstairs he was slipping the deed to the bookstore into his lightweight sports jacket. He glanced up, took her in with a stare, smiled, and nodded his approval. It came to Judy that lately she was more interested in clothes than she had ever been in her life. Was this because of David? He so obviously appreciated seeing her well turned out.

They lunched at Winding Brook Lodge, in its hushed atmosphere, over brook trout and eggplant. The butter sauce was especially flavorful, she noted, and wondered what else, besides butter, the chef had put into it.

Then they were on their way to Walpole where Andrew McAndrew had his legal offices in a white clapboard building which had, originally, Judy was sure, been a small private house. It was situated on a little triangle of land between two country roads, and shaded by huge elms.

David paused to look around him when he emerged from the car. "I sort of envy this man," he muttered. "Imagine having this as an office. It's a far cry from Park Avenue."

An old man was puttering about some files as they entered. He turned and glanced at them over horn-rimmed glasses which he wore low on his nose. Gray hair rose up around his head, haloed by sunlight. Judy thought he needed a haircut, and possibly a shave. He put down the file he was holding and slowly straightened.

"Anything I can do for you folks?"

David smiled at him as he pulled the deed from his jacket and handed it over. "You made this out for Johnny Edmonds, or for Walter Hunter, I'm not quite sure which. I'd like to ask you some questions."

Andrew McAndrew limped toward at battered desk, seated himself in an equally battered chair. He opened the deed, examined it, nodded.

"Wrote this up for them both," he admitted. "Anything wrong with it?"

"No, no," David hastened to assure him. "We would like to know why Walter Hunter was interested in acquiring a bookstore at his time of life."

"Wouldn't know about that. I did all his legal work, such as it was. Same for Johnny Edmonds. Used to go fishing with them both."

David smiled faintly. "Is that your usual habit, appearing for both sides on a legal matter?"

Andrew McAndrew looked over his glasses warily. "You a lawyer?"

"I am." David held up his hand. "I'm not criticizing you, I'm just curious."

"Well, as I say, I did legal work for both of them. They came to me one day couple of years ago. Johnny wanted to make over his bookstore to Walt. Seemed they had some kind of agreement, they were plenty excited about it. Didn't tell me anything, I didn't ask, though I sort of hinted around."

He stared out the window at the lawn, a faraway look in his eyes. "They were thick as thieves, like little boys with a great big secret. Oh, I knew they had some sort of deal cooking, no reason for Johnny to deed his store over to Walt if they hadn't. But they never told me what it was."

"Walter Hunter took out fifty thousand dollars from his bank on the same day this deed was made out. There has to be a connection."

"I would have to agree with you. But—fifty thousand dollars? The Book Ends isn't worth more than twenty."

David smiled thinly. "My wife has been offered sixty for it."

Andrew McAndrew removed his glasses slowly, reached into a hip pocket for a handkerchief and began to polish them, very carefully. He said softly. "My, my. Sixty thousand dollars. It doesn't ring true, sir. There is something out of whack, there. Have you any idea what it might be?"

"I was hoping you might tell me."

"This interests me very much. Very, very much." He put his glasses back on the tip of his nose and stared at David, then at Judy. "Might I inquire who made you this offer?"

"A rather stout man named Charley Underwood. Do you know him?"

"Underwood. Underwood. Hmmm. If it's the man I think he is, he's very shrewd, an excellent businessman. If he made you such an offer, it means he must expect to make a good profit, yes."

Judy interposed her voice between theirs, saying, "And Emmett Rodgers offered me fifty thousand."

"Rodgers and Underwood. My, my. I would search that store very carefully if I were you, Mrs. Carnegie."

"We already have. And we've found nothing."

She looked so helpless, she guessed, that Andrew McAndrew said soothingly, "Now, now. I'm sure it will turn out all right." He hesitated, then murmured, "There is one person you might see who could help you. I don't know whether she know any more than I do, however."

"And who is that?" David asked.

"Nellie Edmonds, Johnny's sister. He didn't live with her, he lived over his bookstore, but he ate a lot of his meals with her. He shared a garden with her back of her house here in Walpole."

Judy sat forward on the edge of her chair. "We'll go see her at once. This afternoon."

McAndrew held up a cautioning hand. "I must warn you. She's rather closemouthed, like Johnny himself. Doesn't blab very much. As a matter of fact, she may not even let you in. She keeps pretty much to herself. Old New England stock, her family's been here since the days when there were Indians behind every bush and tree.

"People like that don't take kindly to strangers."

"You know her," Judy pressed. "Perhaps you would come with us, to ease the way." She added, "We'll gladly pay you for your time."

Andrew McAndrew was embarrassed. He shuffled some papers about on his desk, staring down at them. He cleared his throat, stared out the window.

"I would be happy to come with you, except for one thing," he said slowly. "Nellie feels that her brother and I—and your Uncle Walter—cheated her in some manner. She feels the bookstore should have been hers. By deeding it to Walter, her brother did her a wrong turn. I'm sorry, but that's the way it is."

David frowned. "Then, even if she did know some-thing, the chances are she wouldn't tell us, anyhow."

"I'm afraid not."

Judy stared at the old man helplessly.

Chapter EIGHT

A stray sunbeam touched her hand where it lay on the desk. Judy felt its warmth, though the rest of her was cold. Was she never to solve this riddle, this puzzle of the bookstore? She moved her hand and put it around her handbag, which she squeezed hard.

"Did Johnny Edmonds cut off his sister, then, in his will?" she asked weakly.

"By no means. He left her everything but the bookstore, a sum in the neighborhood of eleven thousand dollars. I handled the estate, I made sure she was given the money. Nevertheless, she did feel let down."

David looked grim. "We probably won't get very far, but we'll go see her, anyhow. All she can do is refuse to talk to us."

Andrew McAndrew nodded, scratched an address on a slip of paper, handed it over. "That's where she lives. You take the main road out of town, on the way to Keene. It's a big house with shingles, a slate roof, that has an enclosed porch three-quarters of the way around it. There's a sign with her name on it; it's on the right, going south."

Once away from the air-conditioned office, Judy felt the heat of the summer sun, even through her light dress. It warmed her only slightly. She told herself that even if this Nellie Edmonds refused to see them, they really wouldn't have lost anything. They would be back where they had started, that was all.

David drove slowly, as much to enjoy the view of the distant mountains and the fields as because he was unsure of just where the woman lived. Judy looked at him from time to time, thinking that he didn't seem at all troubled. She relaxed against the seat, deciding she would take her cues from him.

The house was as the lawyer had described it, large and spreading, shaded by big trees and set in a vast lawn. There was a big garden behind it, which Judy could see by peeping past an old stone well. Evidently the Edmonds had lived here for a long time. Perhaps long ago there had been farmland attached to this house, which had been sold over the years for new homes.

They walked up a flagstoned path. David rang the bell.

A woman clad in slacks and white blouse came to the door. She was tall, gaunt, and her face, heavily seamed, was the color of mahogany. She scowled at them as she opened the porch door.

"You must have lost your way," she announced angrily. "You'll be wanting directions."

David smiled. When he wanted, he could charm the dew off grass, Judy thought. It probably stood him in good stead with juries during his trials.

"We came to see you, actually. You are Nellie Edmonds, aren't you?"

The woman eyed him sharply, hesitated, then finally admitted it. "Not that I can believe you came to see me—nobody ever does. I don't have anything anybody wants."

"Now there's where we differ. You have information."

She stared at him. "Information? About what?"

"Your brother Johnny."

She drew in her breath sharply, peered at them more closely. "You aren't relatives of mine, are you?"

David smiled. "Unfortunately, no. But we would like to talk about him."

"Nothing to talk about, far's I can see. He's dead."

"Exactly—and his secrets with him."

He had caught her attention, with that last bit, Judy

realized. The woman nibbled her lower lip, frowning. "What sort of secrets?" she asked at last.

"Secrets we don't want the whole world to know about, do we?"

She considered that, then opened the door a little. Grudgingly, of course, Judy felt. It seemed almost to pain her to move out of the way so they could enter.

"We'd best talk in the parlor," she muttered slowly.

They walked ahead of her into a room right out of the Victorian era. Judy doubted that, outside of dusting and cleaning, anything had been moved in the past hundred years. The woodwork was painted a dark brown, and the wallpaper, still retaining some of its youthful colors, was dark green with yellow flocking. The chimneypiece was of carved mahogany with a mirror above it. The drapes were dull maroon.

The furniture was massive, heavily upholstered, including a grand pianoforte and jardiniere, sofa and large armchairs. The shades had been pulled, allowing little or no sunlight to penetrate here. Nellie Edmonds gestured them toward the sofa. She herself sat bolt upright in one of the wing chairs.

"Now what's this about my brother's secrets?" she asked.

"Well, you know that he and Walter Hunter had some sort of deal worked out between them."

She shook her head and her lips thinned. "I know no such thing. I do know that Walter Hunter cheated me of my inheritance, with the help of Andy McAndrew."

David smiled with genial charm. Even Judy, at whom the smile was not directed, felt its force. Nellie Edmonds blinked, drew a deep breath, and her lips twitched in what was probably meant for a return smile.

"I don't blame you for feeling that way, not in the least. It must have been a disappointment to you not to have taken over The Book Ends."

"I'd have sold it just as fast as I looked at it," she

snapped. "No sense holding on to a white elephant like that." Her dark eyes swiveled sideways, took in Judy and the rather short print shift she was wearing. Her look as good as told Judy she was an immodest hussy to be showing off so much of her legs. Judy repressed an insane desire to giggle.

"Of course you realize Walter Hunter paid your brother fifty thousand dollars for that store?"

Nellie Edmonds opened her lips, closed them. She turned a pasty shade of white and seemed about to faint.

"Fi—fifty thousand dollars!" she gasped. "I don't believe it!"

David was nothing if not earnest. "Neither do I, actually."

Judy started to say something, thought better of it. Instinctively she understood that David was actually cross-examining a witness, in a manner of speaking, leading her on, doing his cleverest to elicit information from her. His face was filled with concern for her, for Nellie Edmonds, and the woman seemed to sense it.

"You don't?" she exclaimed eagerly.

"I think the money was given to your brother for another reason."

The woman shook herself. "There was no such amount in his bank," she declared firmly. "I'd know, wouldn't I? I was his executor."

"Executrix, for a woman," David said gently.

"Yes, executrix. I meant that. But there wasn't any money like that. Would you like to see his bankbook? I can show it to you, I have it in a drawer in the chiffonier. It's the canceled one, of course. The money's in my name now—what there was of it."

Without waiting for a reply she crossed the room, opened a drawer, brought out a bankbook, and carried it to David. He opened it, making room for her on the sofa beside him. Judy moved over slightly, entranced by the manner in which David was making himself so palsy-walsy with this gnarled old woman.

"You're absolutely correct." He nodded, flipping the pages of the bankbook. "There are no large amounts of money placed on deposit. This means, of course, that he has a secret bank account somewhere else. Possibly, that is. Or else—he may have spent it."

The woman snorted. "On what?"

"There is that." David smiled. "Not many places around here where a man can squander such a fortune. No wine, women, and song, if you'll pardon the allusion."

Her eyes glinted. "Johnny was a good boy. He had no vices." She thought a moment. "Outside the fact that he liked to go fishing so much, that is. And a man can't spend all that much money on fishing gear, can he?"

"Not around these parts, ma'am."

"Then what'd he do with it?" she asked triumphantly.

David tapped the bankbook on a palm. His eyes narrowed as he asked, "Do you suppose he was blackmailing Walter Hunter?"

Judy didn't know who was the more surprised, she or Nellie Edmonds. The older woman stiffened, head back, gazing at David in something like horror.

"My brother? Blackmail anyone? Don't be daft!"

David was apologetic. "I am sorry. I really am. I meant no offense. But you see, we have all that money to account for. If it was blackmail money—oh, I'm sure it wasn't!—but if it were, your brother would have kept it in a hidden place, wouldn't he? For fear Walter Hunter might go to the police?"

"You're on the wrong track completely," Nellie Edmonds announced firmly. "In the first place, Johnny would never lift a finger to blackmail. In the second, what could that old man Walter Hunter have done that would be worth that much money to keep quiet? They were good friends, Johnny and Walter." She added darkly, "And that lawyer man, Andrew McAndrew, as well. Thick as thieves, the three of them. No, it wasn't blackmail."

She hesitated, drawing a sudden breath as though an idea had just come to her. She seemed vaguely embarrassed, looking down at the hands with which she was pleating a fold of her dress.

It seemed painful for her to talk, but she whispered, "Of course, Johnny went off for weeks at a time all by himself."

When David seemed interested, she went on in a somewhat stronger voice, "He wouldn't tell anyone where. At least, he wouldn't tell me. He got in his old jalopy and went driving somewhere. Stayed away two, three weeks. When he came back, he was as closemouthed as a clam. Not a word, never a hint about where he'd gone."

"A woman?" David guessed.

Nellie Edmonds snorted, "Not likely. I'd have known if it were something like that. A woman can always tell." Her eyes slid sideways at Judy. "No, it was a different sort of thing. Johnny was very elated, very excited."

She thought a moment. "Now that I think back, it seems to me that Walter Hunter was also very excited at the end of each of Johnny's trips. I never could understand why. He didn't go along with him, stayed close to home on that farm of his. But it was almost as if he and Johnny shared some sort of secret."

"But you don't know what that secret could be?"

Nellie Edmonds shook her head slowly. She retreated within herself, staring off across the room but not seeing it. Then she seemed suddenly to wake up.

"My goodness, what kind of hostess am I? I've never even offered you a thing to eat or drink." She stood up suddenly. "Iced tea and cookies." She commented, almost shyly, "They're my own cookies, you understand. Oatmeal."

Judy said they would be delighted, and offered to help. Nellie Edmonds looked at her, paused, then smiled weakly. "Come along, child. You can get the glasses down for me, and the tray, while I make the tea."

The kitchen was just as old-fashioned as the parlor. It seemed all brown wood to Judy at first, the dresser, cupboards, doors, and chimneypiece all of that same, monotonous dark brown. A huge iron stove had been set into a false hearth, framed by a coal scuttle and shovel, poker and coal hod. A rather large kitchen table held a rolling pin and some scattered bits of flour, together with half a dozen cookie tins heaped with cookies set out to cool.

This place could be made into a showcase with a little ingenuity and some money, Judy thought. She stood admiring it, was roused when the woman touched her elbow.

"This was the way it was when I was a little girl," she said softly. "I've often thought of having it modernized, but it wouldn't be as charming, would it?"

"It would not," Judy declared stoutly. "I wouldn't change a thing. Except maybe—"

"Go on."

"If the woodwork weren't so dark . . ."

Nellie Edmonds laughed. "Yes. White. Wouldn't it be cheerier with white paint? And perhaps yellow curtains?"

"It would be perfect. If I could, I'd like to come and help you."

They chatted as they prepared the iced tea and the cookies on a porcelain tray which, to Judy's stunned amazement was real Rockingham. When she commented on it, Nellie Edmonds shrugged.

"There are a lot of old treasures like that in these New England homes. The old ones, that is. People keep them as heirlooms from a grandmother or a grandfather, even from a great-grandmother. You just have to know where to look, I guess."

The cookies were delicious, Judy found, munching away, sipping the iced tea. She had come to like this old woman with the indomitable spirit, the crusty exterior under which was lonely shyness. She and Nellie chatted on as David sat listening, eating cookies himself.

Judy called his attention to the tray, pointing out that it was Rockingham. Nellie Edmonds added that her grandfather had brought down a complete set from Canada when he had once gone there on business. It had been her grandmother's proudest possession.

When the cookies and the tea were gone, Nellie seemed apologetic. "I wish there was more to give you. Or to tell you. But Johnny was so closemouthed, he never blabbed his secrets.

"He was never much of a talker. Always liked to be by himself, for the most part. Working on things. He built my bed, did I tell you? In his workshop in the bookstore, some years back. He could do just about anything when it came to carpentry. It was a birthday present. Lands! I was never so surprised in my life."

She insisted that they come upstairs with her to admire it. It was a magnificent piece of work, Judy realized. Excellent for an amateur, being of solid walnut, stained and polished to a high gloss. There was a bureau, too, and a small writing desk and chair.

"Johnny made them all, gave them to me at different times. He loved working with wood. I've tried to decorate it as it should be."

The chintz curtains and bedspread were of a flower design, and stood out with startling beauty against the darker wood.

"It's a lovely room, lovely," Judy enthused.

Nellie Edmonds nodded. "I come here to sit sometimes and knit, and remember all the old times, the sleigh rides in winter, the times we used to sneak off to the pond to go swimming, the apples we ate during the autumn."

She sighed, then turned on David almost fiercely. "The mere idea of Johnny being a blackmailer is ridic-

ulous. He wouldn't do a mean thing. Not ever. Besides,
he liked Walter too much to hurt him."

"I know," David said gently. "I know."

She walked with them to the Jaguar, insistent that
they visit her again, that they come to dinner. "I'll bake
an apple pie, and have chicken and dumplings." She
laughed. "It'll be a little bit like old times."

She sighed. "Maybe I'll even invite Andy. I guess it
isn't his fault Johnny didn't leave me more than he did.
Not that he wasn't good to me," she pointed out hastily.
"He left me all that cash, so that I get along very
nicely."

There was a lump in Judy's throat as the car pulled
out of the driveway and away from the side of the road
to make its turn. Nellie Edmonds waved to them,
smiling happily. She was a lonely old woman, severed
from all reality but her old house and the garden behind it, the Victorian furniture and her memories. Judy
thought it would be nice to see her again, and this
time, just out of friendliness.

David said, "It wasn't exactly wasted, our visit."

Indignantly, she snapped, "I should hope not!"

"Got to you, did she?"

"Didn't she—to you?"

"Oh, yes. But she also told me a lot. Quite a lot, as
a matter of fact. Without realizing she was doing it. Or
meaning to, I suppose."

Judy stared at him. "I didn't think she told you anything. You aren't any the wiser, are you, about what
happened to that fifty thousand dollars, or why Johnny
Edmonds gave or sold his bookstore to my uncle?"

"Let me put it this way. What I heard confirms my
suspicions."

"Which are?" she hinted.

David grinned. "That today is Saturday and tomorrow is Sunday."

"Are you out of your mind?"

"Sunday. Doesn't it ring a bell?"

Something unpleasant, Judy felt. She snuggled back

into the seat and let her thoughts slide around. Sunday was—Sunday. She was thinking like Gertrude Stein. *A rose is a—*

She jerked upright. "Sunday! Of course. That party at the Rodgers'." Her eyes glanced sideways at him, suspiciously. "I suppose you can't wait to go?"

"I want to have a talk with Emmett Rodgers."

"And to dance with his daughter, maybe?"

"That too, naturally."

Despite her inner hesitancies, Judy found an eagerness in herself to attend the Rodgers' party. She found herself thinking as she went about her chores next day—dusting, sweeping, doing a little gardening with David—that Emmett Rodgers himself might well answer the question that disturbed both David and herself. Certainly the man would be willing enough to explain why he would offer fifty thousand dollars for a little country bookstore.

And she desperately needed to know that answer; it was troubling her far more than she let David know. The mere hint that Uncle Walter may have been blackmailed was enough to make her fretful, uneasy.

Her memories of him were so good. He had been kind, gentle, he loved growing things like these phlox, these zinnias which she tended now herself on hands and knees. It was inconceivable to her that he could have been mixed up in anything for which he would have to pay hush money.

David, of course, was no help at all.

She relaxed in the sunlight, scowling down at a lovely Mary Helen dahlia. What was it he had said, last night at dinner when she had pestered him so much? Yes. . . . "We really don't know very much about your uncle, do we?"

It was true. She hadn't seen him for several years, she had been too busy at her job to get away. Still, she could not believe it of him. When she had expressed her convictions about her uncle's moral standards, David had merely shrugged.

"He spent a fortune on something, we know that. To keep Johnny Edmonds quiet? It could be, Judy. It could be."

Judy kicked a clump of dirt. The worst of it was, he was absolutely right. It *could* be. . . .

She spent a long time over her dressing. The frosted coffee gown was magnificent, with its lace over her shoulders and arms. She seemed almost ethereal in it, with the skirt rustling faintly to her steps as she moved about her bedroom. She had done her hair in an upsweep, had added rhinestone earrings and a bracelet (which she had purchased a long time ago and never worn), so that when she studied herself in her mirror, she admitted that she had never appeared more elegant.

David walked around her twice, when she made her appearance. "Perfect," he said softly, at last. She could have hugged him.

They were very much the prosperous young couple as they drove up the Rodgers' drive, the maroon Jaguar newly cleaned—David had worked over it that afternoon with soap and warm water and the hose—and glistening. It stood out even beside the Cadillac and the Thunderbird that were also parked nearby.

Melanie met them at the door, exquisite in a lime gown that was like a pale green mist clinging to her body. Her eyes clouded over when she saw Judy, and Judy understood suddenly that until this moment the redhead had never considered her much of a rival. If she had wanted to make a determined play for David, that is.

Melanie enthused over them, caught David by the hand and tucked his arm in hers as she led the way through a tile foyer that held half a dozen oil paintings. Judy trailed after them, feeling vaguely like the odd one out in a threesome.

The room into which Judy stepped was all white and gold, the walls and furniture seeming to blend together in a harmony that suggested an interior decorator. A gold rug was underfoot, in which she seemed to sink to her ankles as she trailed after David and Melanie. Her husband could have turned, waited for her, but no, he seemed much too taken with the redhead's good looks.

They moved toward a big armchair in which a tall, thin man wearing an impeccably tailored white suit was comfortably ensconced, a martini in his hand. He was engaged in a conversation with a stout man on his right, but he broke it off as Melanie stopped before him.

Judy saw his eyes sharpen as they raked David over, as if sizing him up. They slid sidewise at her, and widened slightly. Was it in admiration? Or because his daughter had led him to expect some sort of dowdy frump?

"Dad, I'd like you to meet David Carnegie." Melanie turned, seemed to be searching, then added, "And his wife, Judy."

Emmett Rodgers came to his feet, hand extended. "David Carnegie. David Carnegie? Don't I know that name from somewhere?"

"You ought to," grunted the stout man. "He made you a lot of money."

Rodgers never took his eyes from David, but he said to the other man, "Is that right, Hadden? Now, how did he do that?"

"He's David Morgan Carnegie, the lawyer. Defense counsel in that Consolidated Oil trial. Broke the back of the government's antitrust action. Your stock went up ten points after the verdict came in, and is still climbing."

Emmett Rodgers grinned. "I should be shot, Carnegie. Of course! And I followed that trial every day in the Boston papers."

David smiled. "I was lucky."

Rodgers snorted, "No such thing. It was work and attention to details, as well as a knowledge of the law. I'm very happy to meet you and your very lovely wife."

David reached back, caught Judy by the hand and drew her up beside him. "She is lovely, sir. I'm a very fortunate man." He hesitated a moment, then added, "She's an heiress."

Rodgers glanced at her, his eyes keen. "Yes. The bookstore in town as well as the Hunter holdings."

"The store was broken into the other night. Ransacked."

The other man nodded. "Heard about that. Too bad. These youngsters of today are not to be believed."

He didn't look at all like a guilty man, Judy thought. If he had hired someone to make that search of The Book Ends, it certainly never showed on his carefully shaved face. He seemed sympathetic, concerned, vaguely bothered.

"We can talk more about that later. I have a rather attractive offer to make you for that store." He smiled as he gave his full attention to Judy. "An offer which I hope you can't refuse, to borrow a phrase."

Then he dismissed all this as he turned to his daughter. "Mel, see that the Carnegies are well cared for. I'll leave you in their hands."

Judy still had her hand inside David's. She was not about to relinquish it, as the redhead turned to them. Rather, her fingers tightened, were given an answering squeeze.

They moved across the room, began the introductions to the other guests. Judy was never very good at names, though it was not often that she forgot a face. These were the society bluebloods of Morstead and the surrounding communities, she gathered. People of some importance, for one reason or another, or they would scarcely be invited. They were pampered, well-dressed, some of the women even overdressed, and they all could manufacture mechanical smiles at will.

Melanie brought them to a bar, where David requested a gin and tonic and Judy settled for a tall Tom Collins. They found chairs in a corner of the room beside a couple who, Melanie offered, were very excellent golfers. They were also members of the country club. Judy noted that Ed Malone was nowhere in evidence.

Almost casually, Judy managed to bring his name into the conversation, explaining how she had met him at the country club, but that there seemed to be a coolness between Melanie and him. The other woman, Rhonda Turcott, leaned closer, conspiratorially.

"They really did like each other, you know. But her father objected to him. Malone doesn't have enough money, it seems."

"And Melanie accepts that?"

Rhonda shrugged. "She likes the easy life. I can't say I blame her."

"But they ought to be friendly when they meet. They acted almost like cat and dog."

"Ed had a confrontation with Emmett. Words were said. Shouted, rather, I daresay. Melanie took her father's side."

"It seems too bad."

David said softly, "Judy's a romantic. She thinks there's nothing to equal love."

He was regarding her thoughtfully, and she knew instinctively that he was remembering Bill Evans. It was Bill Evans and his memory that stood between them, he felt. Which gave Judy pause. Was it? After all, they had agreed on a marriage that was to be no marriage. He certainly didn't expect her to play the part of loving wife, did he?

Still, they had come to know each other so much better over the past two weeks, and they got along so well. Could he be changing his mind about matters as they stood between them? Judy hoped not. She liked David, but she did not love him. And she knew that he didn't love her.

More drinks were served, and she and David mingled with the other guests, came to know them. From time to time Judy felt eyes on her, turned, saw that Emmett Rodgers was regarding her intently, much as he might size up a business rival.

The dinner table was set superbly, she found as they went into the big dining room. There was Wedgewood china, crystal goblets, candles glowing in the early dusk. Their first course was shrimps flambes coated with cognac, served on bamboo sticks. As she devoured them she thought fleetingly of the meal she had served David last night, which had consisted of grilled hamburgers, baked beans, and potato salad.

The duck in red wine sauce, served with buttered wild rice, was so mouth-watering that for a little time Judy forgot all about the bookstore and her marriage. She wondered vaguely who the chef might be, and when one of the other diners complimented Emmett Rodgers, he admitted he took Chin Lee with him everywhere.

"He can cook in Italian, French, Swedish, or Chinese." Rodgers laughed. "All I do is furnish him with the ingredients he needs. Then I settle back and let him take over."

Judy was sitting on Rodgers' right, David to his left, obviously because he wanted to have them close at hand when he decided to bring up the subject of the bookstore. She added her compliments to those of the others.

"Every bride should have a Chin Lee in the background," she murmured with a glance at Melanie at the far end of the table. "That way, she could be certain she'd never lose her husband."

Rodgers patted her hand, giving her a big smile. "You have no need to worry, my dear. A bowl of soup with you would be the equal of the finest dinner the Caesars ever gave."

David agreed that this was true enough, the guests laughed obligingly, and the talk slid off from food to servants and then to general subjects. During the conversation, Judy noted that Emmett Rodgers could discourse on almost any subject at all.

"Melanie never did tell me what your own business is," Judy said, glancing at her dinner companion. "Frankly, I wondered why on earth someone like you should be interested in The Book Ends."

He smiled at her, but his eyes were still sharp. "I have many business interests, my dear. I'm a stockbroker, first of all. I'm the Rodgers in Rodgers and Quincy in Boston. But I vary my interests. I'm the president of a publishing house, and of a flourishing line of shoe stores. I'm chairman of the board of a number of corporations. I like to have my fingers in several pies at once."

"The publishing house, of course," she murmured. "That's why you want the store."

"I've wanted it for some time now. I've had the thought of establishing a number of small-town stores, to bring the product directly to the consumer."

David interposed, "But is there sufficient business to warrant it?"

Rodgers gestured. "At worst, they'd serve as cheap warehouses. You know how valuable city property is, how high the taxes are. In small towns like Morstead, taxes are a mere pittance by comparison. I could extend onto it, use the living quarters as extra space. It would be well worth it."

Judy let the matter drop, and David followed her example. She saw approval in his eyes, however, and felt a warm glow inside her. She had broken the ice; now he could follow up their little talk with something more direct.

At the moment, their attention was on a maid wheeling in a dessert trolley laden with chocolate Annatorte, nut-slabbed Kaffeetorte, Truffeltorte, and Nuss-Weichseltorte, tipped by brandied cherries. A low sound of appreciation went up around the table, with some of the women complaining that they would put on too much poundage by succumbing to such temptations.

Everyone had helpings, however, Judy noted, deciding on an Annatorte for herself. With the rich black coffee, platters of whipped cream were handed out, to be spooned onto the coffee in great gobs.

It was such a meal as she had never seen, she knew, and realized that only a man with a lot of money could afford to squander it in such quantities. But to Emmett Rodgers, this was a way of life. Whatever he wanted, he could get. All he needed was money, and he had plenty of that. He wanted The Book Ends, he was prepared to pay for it.

They had no chance to talk about the store until much later, however. A room had been cleared to one side of the dining room, and a small orchestra that had been playing dinner music now would switch over to tunes to which the guests could dance.

David led Judy out onto the floor, where she was swept into the stately measures of a waltz. Judy had never been a dancer; she had always avoided occasions when someone would lead her around a waxed floor, but she found herself following David quite easily. She was not quite sure that she enjoyed this feeling of his male body touching her own, and she tried to keep as far from him as possible.

Yet as the music continued, as the rhythm of the dance seeped into her, she was more and more relaxed. Odd that he should have this effect on her. She had never danced with Bill Evans, she remembered. And that was a little strange. But Bill had never cared for dancing; a waste of time, he called it.

Yet when Melanie and a handsome young man with long black hair cut in, Judy was disturbed. She could not follow this stranger as she had David, and she saw, out of the corners of her eyes, that the redhead was plastered up against David, her head on his chest, as she blended perfectly with his dance steps.

She was not jealous, she knew that. It made no difference to her what David did. Just the same, he didn't have to hold her so close, dancing with his eyes half closed, as though he and Melanie were communing in a way that she, Judy, could never do.

And so she welcomed the intermission to thank her partner and move across the room to seat herself, expecting David to follow and join her. He did nothing of the kind. He stayed talking with Melanie until the orchestra began again, a lively rock number, into which the two flung themselves with laughter and a sense of easy camaraderie. Judy sat and watched, seething.

Somewhat to her surprise, it was Emmett Rodgers who rescued her from her wallflower status. His hand caught hers and he lifted her to her feet and invited her to join him. He was a magnificent dancer, with a natural sense of rhythm, and Judy tried to throw herself into the spirit of the occasion.

If she were to lead this sort of life, she told herself darkly, she was going to have to learn how to dance. It was a necessary social adjunct. For the first time, she regretted the fact that she had been a tomboy in her formative years.

Then Rodgers was leading her to a punchbowl, pouring her a drink in a crystal goblet, and guiding her out onto a large, flagstoned patio that gave a view of mountains in the distance and a stretch of rolling farmland silvered by a brilliant moon.

"This is great country," Rodgers said. "I could be quite happy to live here year around."

"Then why don't you?" Judy wondered. "You certainly have enough money to indulge your wishes."

He smiled down at her. "Business is my lifeblood. Without it I think I'd wither away as a flower might without water. No, no. I enjoy all this, it gives me a rest, it clears my head for business when it's time to go back to Boston."

He sipped the punch, smiled down at her. "And while I'm resting and relaxing, I like to keep my hand in. That's why I'm so interested in acquiring The Book Ends. What do you say? Shall we strike a deal between us and agree to it with the slapping of the hands, as do Irish horse dealers?"

Judy looked into her goblet. "I'd be happy to, but I'm really not sure that I want to sell. You see, I may give up my library job and stay on in Morstead. Having the bookstore would give me something with which to occupy my time."

"I understand that, naturally. But fifty thousand dollars, properly invested, would bring you in about forty-five hundred dollars a year. More than you could clear from The Book Ends in a year, when you consider you'd have to pay taxes on the property, insurance costs, and all the rest."

"Sixty thousand at nine percent would bring in even more," said David, appearing suddenly beside them, and smiling faintly.

Emmett Rodgers turned to him, eyebrows raised. Anger flashed in his gray eyes, Judy was sure, and she had the feeling that Emmett Rodgers might be a very dangerous man when crossed.

Chapter NINE

David was smiling gently as he faced the older man, and Judy felt suddenly at ease. For some reason, he always had this effect on her; she knew that he would handle everything quite capably.

He said now, "We've already been offered sixty thousand, Rodgers. Man by the name of Charley Underwood is willing to take the bookstore off Judy's hands for us."

Emmett Rodgers finished off the last of his punch and put the goblet down very carefully on a patio table. "Charley Underwood. Of course. I should have expected it."

"A business rival?" Judy asked.

"Something of the sort, yes. It's amazing how that man discovers my interests and cuts himself in on them."

He glowered at the distant mountains, tipped with moonlight-silver. For an instant, Judy was afraid he was going to thrust past them and leave them standing together on the patio, alone. But he sighed, brought his eyes back to David, and gave a brief nod.

"Very well, then. Underwood's offering sixty. I'll up my own offer to seventy-five thousand. See if Charley Underwood will want to top that!"

He went away then, back stiff and rigid. David gave Judy a brief little smile, even as he stepped closer to her. Through the open patio doors the music came swelling, inviting to the feet. David drew her into his arms, began to dance.

It may have been the moonlight, the romantic setting, or perhaps just the memory of the way Melanie had danced with him that made Judy put her own body up against him and let her head rest against his chest. She found it surprisingly easy to follow him, his hand at her back guided her, made her seem to know instinctively which way to turn, how to place her feet.

She relaxed and let the sound roll over her, knew the man-scent of her husband, sensed his strength and affection. Her eyes closed and she floated as in a dream, scarcely conscious of what she was doing or where she was.

When the music stopped, David still held her pressed against him. And David kissed her.

She clung to him, returning his kiss, still under the spell of the moonlight and the dance. Her heart thumped crazily, her legs went watery, and she let herself sink against him. The kiss went on, and Judy realized vaguely that at this moment, in this wild tumult of her senses, David could have done anything to her that he wanted, and that she would have welcomed his every move with delighted enthusiasm.

"Oh! I'm sorry to interrupt you lovebirds."

Melanie Rodgers' voice was like icewater over her. Judy stepped back, flushing, flustered. David did not move for a moment, then turned slowly to face the redhead.

"Blame the moonlight and this patio," he said lightly, "as well as my wife's attractiveness."

Was it her imagination, or did Melanie make a face, there in the shadows? No matter. She felt warm and friendly to David for his words. Even if they were husband and wife in name only, it was pleasant to hear him refer to her as attractive.

Melanie said, "I thought we might have this dance, David."

They could hear the sound of a car motor starting, and people calling out their good-byes from the front steps. A little breeze came up from the meadows, carrying the sweet scent of evening primrose.

David smiled. "I really think we ought to be getting

along. We have a lot of work tomorrow at the book-store, putting things to rights."

Melanie gave him a long, searching look, then shrugged. David expressed his gratitude for the evening, remarked that he must go and find her father and, with Judy, thank him as well. He reached for her hand, caught it, drew Judy with him.

She was still in that dreamlike state as she went with him to say her farewells to Emmett Rodgers. The older man was rather grim, she felt; apparently it hadn't pleased him to learn that Charley Underwood was after The Book Ends, too. Still, he seemed pleasant enough, waving away their thanks and inviting them to be frequent visitors.

Yet when she was alone in the Jaguar with David, Judy felt some of that dreaminess fade out of her. Almost warily she glanced at her husband. Was that moment on the patio a mere impulse? Or had he decided that they should now live as husband and wife? Nervously she clasped her tiny evening handbag, telling herself that it had been only the moonlight and the sweet smells of summer that had caused her riotous reaction to his kiss.

"I'm a little tired," she ventured in a small voice. "Are you?"

He glanced at her, and Judy knew he was following her thoughts. "It's been a long day. We have an even longer one tomorrow. I think we both need a good night's sleep." He hesitated and then asked, "Don't you agree?"

"Oh, yes. Yes, I do."

When they came to the house, David got out and opened her door for her, walked with her toward the front door. Judy waited until he unlocked it, then slipped past him, almost running toward the stairs. Only when she was in her bedroom, with the door closed and leaning against it, did she relax.

If David had taken her in his arms downstairs, if he had ignored her protests, she knew very well that she would have fallen into his embrace almost with exuberance. What was the matter with her? Where was the rather prim librarian who had looked so suspiciously at David Morgan Carnegie when James Miller had read the terms of her uncle's will?

Judy moved to a lamp, switched it on. She turned to stare at herself in a mirror. She was flushed, she had never been so excited. Her lips appeared almost beestung. The result of that long kiss? She touched them shyly with her fingertips.

"Watch yourself, Judy," she whispered. "This marriage isn't going at all the way you wanted it."

Lightly, she did a few dance steps around the room. No, she was not the prim librarian, not any longer. She was an entirely different person. She liked wearing lovely dresses, she liked dancing with David, she liked —yes, she did!—she actually liked David kissing her.

"You be careful," she scolded her reflection.

David wouldn't need much hinting to understand that her feelings had changed. He was a man who was used to girls. He would understand that she wanted him to kiss her again, unless she were on her guard.

As she tumbled into bed, she told herself she would cook him an especially delicious breakfast, first thing in the morning, as a reward for not having followed that patio kiss to its logical conclusion. Even as she told herself this, she frowned. He could have made *some* effort to kiss her again, once they were in the house. She hadn't run all that fast from him, had she?

Judy sighed . . . and slept.

She woke early, lay a moment enjoying the sunlight pouring in the bedroom windows. The house was very quiet; David was still sleeping. She slid from the bed, showered, slipped into a sunsuit, one of the gifts David had all but forced on her at that boutique. It was pale blue with white polka dots, leaving her arms and legs quite bare. A couple of weeks ago, she wouldn't have been found dead in such a garment.

But she reveled in it as she ran downstairs and into

the kitchen, where she busied herself in putting coffee on to perk, in frying sausage patties, in whipping up batter for griddle cakes. She sang to herself as she worked, moving deftly from the big iron cookstove to the walk-in pantry where the dishes were so neatly stacked, to the refrigerator for maple syrup and butter.

When she felt eyes on her, she turned. David was standing in the doorway, staring. Something in that stare made her flush.

"Just getting your breakfast," she sang out hurriedly. "I hope you like griddle cakes and sausages. We have a lot of work to do, so you'd better eat up."

He ate as if food were going out of style, keeping Judy hopping to make enough pancakes to feed his appetite. Judy loved it. She sat and watched him eat, almost forgetting to eat, herself. It was a completely new experience for her, she found, this catering to the appetite of a man.

Was it part of that dreaminess that had come over her last night? Was she still under the spell of the moonlight and David's arms about her? It must be something like that, she guessed; all she knew was that she was taking great enjoyment out of seeing him finish off the griddle cakes.

And later, when they were in the bookstore, it was fun to work beside him, to see his hands and face dirty, to know that they were laboring together on a joint project. She herself was as grimy as he—the floor needed another mopping—but she didn't care a hoot about her appearance because she had caught David giving admiring glances at her legs.

Her heart sang and she worked without any sensation of work. It was enough to be with David, to share these hours with him. When he called for a moment of respite, to share a cigarette and some hot coffee she had put into a thermos earlier, she leaned her shoulder against him and sighed happily.

It was almost two o'clock when David finally straightened up and announced that it was time to eat.

Judy said, "I'll drive over to the deli, get some sandwiches and potato salad. Won't take me a sec."

She washed her hands and face, caught up her shoulderbag and moved toward the door. David sat on a small chair and lighted another cigarette. "Iced coffee," he called after her. "Don't forget that."

Judy slid into the Jaguar, started the engine. In the rear-view mirror she caught sight of two men getting into a black Volkswagen, but paid them no attention. She drove carefully, taking the corners easily, and noticed the black car once more, following her.

There was a straightaway up ahead; she would make better time along there, on this country road. But when she speeded up, the black car spurted forward and turned out to pass her. Judy muttered under her breath, eased up on the gas pedal.

The black Volkswagen turned inward, cutting her off.

Judy yelled, braked.

The other car slid to a halt, the two men got out, came back toward her. She stared at them unbelievingly. Were they angry at her? But why? It had been their fault, the near accident.

"Come on, lady—out!"

They were on a deserted stretch of road, there wasn't another car in sight. Judy felt her heart leap, knew the tightening of her middle that told her better than anything that she was scared.

"What—what do you mean, get out?"

"Just what we say."

A hand reached for her door handle. The door opened. Two hands came in to catch her arms, yank her sideways out of the car. The hands let go of her suddenly so that she fell into the dirt.

"Are you crazy?" she shrieked, shaking.

One of them grinned at her. It was a twisted, cruel grin, and she remembered the vandalized bookstore. Certainly Emmett Rodgers hadn't sent these men, as he hadn't sent anyone to ransack The Book Ends. Had he?

"What—what do you want?" she cried as hands lifted her, set her on her feet. One of the men backhanded her across the cheek, knocking her against the Jag. Her cheek smarted, her head reeled, pain erupted inside her.

The other man watched, grinning. He caught her arm and twisted it up behind her back, holding her helpless. The one who had hit her across her face advanced, making a big fist. He held the fist up to her, drew it back slowly.

Judy closed her eyes. He was going to strike her, she knew it was going to hurt. She would be knocked unconscious.

And then—

A horn blared, far away.

She opened her eyes. The one who had made the fist turned his head, stood watching. The pressure on her twisted arm eased up. Judy drew a deep breath, screamed.

Surely the person in the car would hear her, help her!

The two men turned, ran for their own car. Now Judy could see a Ford Maverick racing down the road toward them. The men leaped into their car, slammed the doors. An instant later, it took off, dust rolling up behind it.

Judy began to shake.

This could not have happened. She was unused to violence of any kind. She closed her eyes, opened them, was aware that tears were running down her cheeks. If only David were here to put his arms around her, to soothe her, to comfort her!

The Maverick slowed, stopped. A man opened the door, got out, and came walking toward her. He was lean but with good shoulders, he had black hair, and he was wearing a turtleneck sweater and blue jeans. His face was tanned, and—vaguely familiar.

Judy stared, catching her breath.

It could not be! She was delirious, out of her head. She began to shake even more, backing up slowly until she felt the hard body of the Jaguar against her bottom.

"It is you, isn't it, Judy?" the man said.

Judy tried to speak. Twice she opened her lips, but no sound would come out. The man was walking toward her, both hands outstretched. He reached out, caught her hands, held them.

"I've come back, you see," he said gently.

"Bill? But it can't be you. You're—dead!"

Bill Evans threw back his head and laughed. His gray eyes were filled with amusement as he looked down at Judy; then he stepped back and took her all in, the sunsuit and her tanned skin. He nodded happily.

"You're different," he told her.

Then he glanced down the road in the direction that the black Volkswagen had gone. "What was that all about?"

Words still would not come to her. All she could do was stare at him, at his familiar face with its high cheekbones and the firm chin, the long-lashed gray eyes. Yes, this was her Bill. Come back to life, just in time to rescue her from those men.

"There's been some trouble," she said in a rush. "It's about Uncle Walter's bookstore. You remember my Uncle Walter, the one who lived in New Hampshire? He died, Bill, and left me his property."

"Lucky you." Bill laughed.

She shook her head, strangely reluctant to tell him about David. She exclaimed, "But never mind me. What about you? I just can't believe this. I thought you'd drowned off Block Island."

"I lost my memory; that's why I haven't been in touch before." He stared off across the fields toward the mountains, hazed purple with distance. "The boat I'd rented turned over, and something hit my head."

He put fingers to his temple, touching it lightly. "The scar's gone now, but for a time I had quite a welt. I swam and swam. I never will forget that swim, Judy. It was awful. Just water everywhere. Not a sign of land."

His face showed he was reliving those hours. Judy put her hands on his, squeezed sympathetically. Bill smiled down at her as he had in those old, almost-forgotten days.

"I finally reached shore and lay there like a dead man, I guess. First thing I knew some fishermen found me, took me to a local hospital. I was there a couple of days, getting my strength back. But my memory wouldn't return. I didn't know who I was, didn't know anything about myself.

"Amnesia, the doctors call it. Said my memory might come back, might not." He shrugged. "I got a job at a gas station to buy my food and a rented room. When I could, I tried to find out about myself. No luck. My wallet must have gone into the sea, with all my identification on it."

Judy suddenly remembered David. He was hungry, he would be waiting in the bookstore for her and the sandwiches. She said to Bill, "Oh, I forgot. David! He'll be ravenous. I've got to get some food. Follow me, Bill. I'll introduce you."

"Who's David?" he asked softly.

"Oh! You—you don't know him. He—he's my husband."

Bill seemed to draw away from her, a hurt look in his eyes. "Your husband. Oh, yes. I remember something about that, from the inquiries I made about you—after my memory came back."

Judy asked, "You inquired about me?"

"Well, certainly. Just as soon as I remembered who I was, I—but never mind that now. You were going to get this David some food. You go ahead, I'll follow to see you aren't set on by any other toughs."

She nodded, moved to enter the Jaguar, aware that Bill was scanning the sleek lines of the car with keen eyes. She wondered what he was thinking, miserably aware that he must be reasoning that no sooner was he dead and out of the way than she had run right to some rich man and got herself wedded. But it wasn't that way at all.

Judy drove slowly, carefully, lost in her thoughts. What was she going to do now that Bill had come back, literally from the grave in which she had buried him? There was David to consider, too. She could not abandon David just because Bill had showed up; they had too much in common now.

Her chin firmed. Bill must be made to understand that things were not as they had been those long months ago. She was married now, she wasn't alone in the world. He could not pick up his life with her as it had been. And yet the sight of his face when she had mentioned her husband was like a stab wound in her heart. She had felt so sorry for him!

Poor Bill. None of this was his fault, but he was the one who was suffering. She imagined that the time lapse when he had lost his memory was like a split second. As far as he was concerned, their relationship was as it had always been. He just couldn't understand the fact that she was a wife now. She had to be very diplomatic about all this.

At the delicatessen, she ordered roast beef and turkey sandwiches, containers of ice-cold coffee and root beer, pickles and potato salad. Bill was beside her, telling her how hungry he was, that a little more salad and a couple extra sandwiches would not be wasted.

He was like the old Bill, teasing and cajoling until he got his way. He insisted she buy David some cold beer instead of the coffee he had intended, he chided her for not being an understanding wife, he added a few packs of cigarettes to the packages and watched as Judy fumbled in her handbag for a twenty-dollar bill.

Bill carried the bags out and put them in his car. "In case you have an accident." He grinned. "Or in case some more men come to bang you around. We don't want anything to happen to the food, do we?"

Judy laughed, as he did. He was the same old Bill who had meant so much to her, always teasing, always making a joke out of things. It had seemed so wonderful, his attitude toward her, when she had been going with him. And it still pleased her, it made her realize that they could pick up as they had been before the accident that had taken his memory.

Just the same . . .

Judy sighed as she started the Jag and eased it out into the road. Just the same, it wasn't like the old times. How could it be? She was married, she and David had worked together, lived together (well, sort of), and had come to an understanding which she held close to her heart.

Bill was an intruder.

Judy scowled at her thoughts. What was the matter with her, to think this way about Bill? She loved the guy! She let her mind run back in memory to the good times they had enjoyed, to the laughter they had shared, to their intimate little dinners in her apartment. They could pick up where they had left off in time.

Time! Yes, that was the answer. She had to be fair to David. And to Bill, too. She mustn't let herself be stampeded into a wrong move, just because her head was still whirling from what had happened.

David would go north to his fishing in a day or two. Bill would stay on, she supposed. He would stay at the house with them, there was plenty of room. Instead of just herself and David, there would be the three of them. When David was gone, she and Bill could make their plans.

She would get a divorce. David had as good as said she could do this, that he wouldn't fight it. Then she and Bill could get married and live here in Morstead. Bill could get a job somewhere around here, maybe over in Keene. It would all work itself out, if she had enough time.

Judy braked the Jaguar to a halt, saw Bill ease his Ford Maverick up beside her in the bookstore parking lot. He got out, caught hold of the packages, gave her a friendly grin.

"Lead the way, princess. The faithful dog follows."

Judy turned and started toward The Book Ends. Her feet dragged, though, and her heart seemed to weigh a ton. This was not going to be easy, introducing David to Bill. She hoped they wouldn't get into a fight.

Chapter TEN

David was dusting books as she came into the store with Bill right behind her. David glanced up, gave her a big smile, then froze with his dust rag just touching the book he had been cleaning. His eyes went beyond her to the grinning Bill, and his face hardened.

Almost instantly that cold look was gone, he was lowering the rag, putting down the book, and moving forward. Had she only imagined that momentary hardness, that suspicion in his eyes? He was friendly enough, greeting her with a smile and looking beyond her expectantly at Bill, who was placing the packages on the book counter and starting to hold out his hand.

"David, this is Bill. Bill Evans," she exclaimed breathlessly. "He isn't dead, after all."

"So I see." David nodded, taking the hand Bill offered and gripping it. "There must have been a mix-up somewhere."

"I lost my memory in the boating accident; I spent a lot of time not knowing who I was."

Judy let her eyes run over them. Bill was lean, hard as whipcord, almost devil-may-care in his confidence. David was slightly taller, huskier, with wider shoulders, deeper in the chest. Bill was dark, with black hair, David was fair, his tawny blond hair almost golden. And her heart went out to both of them.

"How did you find out who you were?" David asked.

Bill chuckled. "Got a bop on the head during a fight at a bar." He made a face, looking sideways at Judy. "I was a different sort of person, I suppose, during those days when I didn't know who I was. Pumped gas, drank beer at night in a local joint with truck-drivers and farmers. One night . . ."

He paused, frowning. "I had too much to drink, I guess. I got quarrelsome, picked a fight with a big truckdriver." Bill made a face. "He beat the hell out of me. But he did me a good turn, at that.

"He socked me one so hard I fell back off my feet and my head banged into a tree bole. We were fighting outside the gin mill, you see. I didn't know where I was, because I was Bill Evans again, going down with the boat on top of me.

"I asked, 'What am I doing here?' and the truck-driver saw that something funny had happened. I told him what I'd gone through, and we ended up by treating each other to drinks."

Bill shrugged. "After that I quit my job, went back to the city, looked for Judy, found she was gone. Some old lady in the apartment house said she was married recently. . . . That was quite a jolt, I assure you."

He looked almost apologetically at David, at Judy. He spread out his hands. "I figured I'd find out where she lived, see her, tell her I was still alive, wish her good luck, and walk out of her life."

"And now?" David asked quietly.

Bill's eyes sharpened. "What do you mean, 'And now?' "

"Now that you've discovered she's come into some money, are you still going to walk out of her life?"

Judy burst out, "David! How could you?"

"No, no, Judy," Bill said swiftly, holding up his hand. "I don't blame David at all. I'd ask the same question if I were in his shoes." He turned to David very seriously.

"I went to the marriage license bureau, found out the witness was that lawyer named Miller, heard a little something about Uncle Walter's will. Well, said I to myself, maybe Judy had to get married, after all, in or-der to inherit. I decided to come up here to see how you were making out."

His grin was very friendly. "Now that I see you're in good hands, I can relax."

He reached for one of the packages, began taking out sandwiches, paper containers filled with pickles and potato salad. "I'm starved, even if you aren't. Come on, give me a hand."

For a few moments David stood quietly, studying the man before him. Then he shrugged almost imperceptibly, and went to help him. Judy watched them eating side by side, knowing a surge of relief that went all through her. She smiled happily and moved to join them.

To her delight, David and Bill got on fairly well; they talked and chatted about sports, about economic conditions, about the bookstore. Bill was very interested in the mystery surrounding it, could hardly wait to help them make their search.

"But we've been over it ourselves," Judy told him. "We didn't find a thing."

"Can't see the forest for the trees." Bill nodded. "I'm a new pair of eyes. I may be able to spot something you didn't."

They spent the rest of the afternoon searching. For all his confidence, even Bill had to admit he was beaten. "If it's in here," he said at last, coming out of the cellar, as dusty as themselves, "it's hidden so well it can't be found."

David said, "I'm beginning to think there's nothing at all here. Whatever your uncle invested in, Judy, could be anywhere."

He was thinking about blackmail once again, Judy knew with swift intuition. She felt a stab of anger, but told herself morosely that he might be right. It didn't seem possible, but then it hadn't seemed possible that Bill Evans was alive. In this world, anything could happen.

They were coming out of The Book Ends when the red Cadillac pulled in against the curb. Melanie Rodgers waved to David, got out, and came to meet him. She wore a tight-fitting jumpsuit that blended perfectly with her coloring and the long red hair that touched her shoulders with scarlet flame.

Judy became very conscious of her casual clothes, of the dirt and grime on her hands and face.

"Hi, there," Melanie said gaily. "I've come to invite you to the country club dance this Saturday night." Her eyes took in Bill, smiled vaguely in his direction, then focused on David.

"You will come, won't you?" she pleaded.

"Wouldn't miss it for the world. The only trouble is, we have a house guest."

"Well, bring him along. There's always room for one more."

She tucked her arm in David's and walked with him toward the Caddy. Judy watched them go, side by side, and her lips drooped at the corners. A nudge on her arm made her turn and look up at an unsmiling Bill Evans.

"Your jealousy is showing," he muttered.

Judy stared at him. "Jealousy? You're wrong, Bill. I'm not jealous of David. We have an understanding."

He shrugged. "If you say so."

Yet she waited for him and walked with David to the Jaguar, leaving Bill to follow in the Maverick. As she buckled the seat belt she said, "I had some trouble on the road, David."

He glanced at her. She could not read his expression—he was withdrawn, remote. Now that Bill Evans had come back into her life, was David about to relinquish his role as husband?

"Two men attacked me."

Ah, that touched him. He straightened, his face white, as he reached out for her hand. "What happened? Are you all right?"

She told him about it, staring down at her hand which he was holding. "I can't understand it. Why would anyone want to hurt me? They didn't ask for anything, it was just—just as though they were there to have some fun."

"Not on your life. They were there because they had been sent. By Emmett Rodgers? Or by Charley Underwood?"

He drove slowly, occasionally glancing in the rear-view mirror. "I owe your friend Bill a vote of thanks for his action in rescuing you. Funny he didn't mention it."

"Bill's no braggart. Besides, he was so busy explaining how he had found me that I guess he forgot."

"How could you forget a thing like that? And what about you? Weren't you frightened?"

"Well, of course I was."

She had been so busy watching Bill and David, worrying how they would get along, that it had driven all thoughts about her being waylaid from her mind. She could scarcely admit this; David would never understand it.

"This changes things a little," he murmured.

Something in his voice made Judy jerk around to face him. "What do you mean? How does it change things?"

"I was going to leave you in a day or two, now that Bill Evans is here. I was going up north, to get in that fishing."

She stared at him. "David, you can't!" she burst out impulsively. Her fingers tightened on the hand that David still held. "You wouldn't go off and leave me!"

Fear come into her throat, suddenly and inexplicably. She had realized, of course, how she depended on David, but not until this instant had she understood how much. The idea of never seeing him again left an empty feeling inside her.

She added weakly, "You just told Melanie you'd go to that country club dance. I heard you say so."

"That was only to avoid an argument. She would have insisted, and I wasn't up to telling her about you and Bill. Surely you can understand that?"

She nodded glumly, watching the roadside landscape as it rolled by. She didn't want David to go, she wanted him to stay on, at least until this problem of the store was settled. She had come to depend so much on him. She didn't know what she would do without him.

She said softly, "Bill won't know how to cope with these matters. You're a lawyer, you can understand them."

"Oh, don't worry about Bill. He'll look after your interests. Maybe even better than I."

Judy was not happy. She would carry on; there was nothing else for her to do. Still, David could have planned to remain until The Book Ends was disposed of. She felt a vague resentment toward him, as though he were running off and abandoning her.

To her surprise, David was quite affable to Bill once they were at the house. They prepared the charcoal briquette fire, chatting and laughing; they cooked the steaks together; and David mixed the drinks and brought them out onto the screened-in porch where they would eat. He even insisted that Bill accompany them to the dance, when Bill demurred.

"Plenty of pretty girls to dance with there. You'll have the time of your life." He went on. "If you don't have the right clothes, we can always fit you out."

Bill looked at her. "What about it, Judy? Do you think I should go?"

It was David who answered. "Of course you should. Judy'll have a partner when I get too tired."

In the end, Bill came with them, riding in the back of the Jaguar, clad in plaid slacks and a white dinner jacket which he had purchased in Keene, admitting that he hadn't expected to need such formal attire. He looked handsome, Judy thought; he would be right at home with the country club crowd.

She herself wore a slit-to-the-knee powder blue silk gown, with summer jewelry to match. Her hair was in an upsweep, as usual, but she had added a jeweled

ivory comb that David had bought, and which she
secretly admitted gave her rather an air of elegance.

Melanie Rodgers waved to them as they entered.
"I've put you at our table," she told Judy. "You really
don't know anyone else here, and I thought it would
help break the ice."

She linked her arm in David's and led him off, leaving Bill to escort Judy. Bill murmured, "I'd watch out
for that one if I were you. She has designs on Dave."

"He can take care of himself," she said as lightly as
she could, but she could not keep the bite from her
tone. Bill gave her a long, slow look.

Everyone was in a party mood, there was much
laughter all around them, but Judy could not enter into
the spirit of the evening. For one thing, Melanie was
wearing a white jersey gown, cut low in front and back,
that showed off her figure to anyone who cared to look.
Then again, she had appropriated David, dancing with
him in that manner which Judy found so repulsive, absolutely plastered up against him.

She was left with Bill. She should have been delighted, she supposed, but she could not rid herself of
the feeling that if Bill hadn't been there she would have
played the role of onlooker.

"Do you realize this is the first time we've ever
danced together?" Bill asked, as they swept around the
floor.

"Yes, it is, isn't it?"

She really wasn't paying too much attention to what
Bill was saying; her whole attention was on David and
Melanie. They fitted so beautifully together! They
came from the same social strata, they had the same
interests, they were the beautiful people of whom Judy
had read. She had no business being there; David and
Melanie belonged in this country club set, she didn't.

"Hey," Bill said. "I know you love the guy, but stop
showing it so plainly."

Surprised, Judy exclaimed, "We don't love each
other, Bill. Not in the slightest."

"Come on, Judy."

"No, it's true. I only married him to get my inheritance."

He looked down at her, his gray eyes thoughtful. "Are you trying to tell me you don't love him?"

"That's the way it is."

He jeered, "I don't believe you."

The music stopped, the dancers applauded. Judy caught Bill by the hand, drew him after her. "Let's take a walk in the gardens, Bill. I—I'll tell you all about it."

The night air was soft and balmy. Judy paced between rows of flowering begonias, past rose bushes and rock gardens. Overhead the moon was brilliant in its setting of blue sky and stars. A soft wind moved past them.

And Judy talked. She spoke of that day when she had met David Morgan Carnegie for the very first time, of how she had been repelled by the idea of marrying him, of how he had talked her into it. Bill listened quietly, without speaking, head bent slightly. She explained why David had married her, to avoid marriage with a couple of girls in the city.

She touched on the fact that someone had shot her, that David had cared for her—he couldn't very well have left her to fend for herself with only one usable arm—and how they had learned how much money Emmett Rodgers and Charley Underwood would pay for The Book Ends.

When she was done, Bill looked off across the golf course. His face was cold, hard. He said at last, "Then you're free to divorce him?"

"Certainly. We agreed to that right in the beginning."

His eyes came down to meet hers. "And will you?"

Judy opened her lips, then closed them.

Almost hesitantly she said, "I suppose I will. Yes. In a few months. Not right away. I don't want it to appear that I just married him to get Uncle Walter's property."

"Why not?"

Judy moved her hands helplessly. She had no answer to that one, she realized, beyond a vague feeling that the marriage might not be legal if she rushed into a divorce court right away.

Bill said, "You've fallen in love with him. You don't realize it, maybe, but you have."

She moved away from him indignantly. "I've done no such thing. He's never laid a finger on me."

Bill grinned. Angry, Judy snapped, "He hasn't!"

"With the two of you under one roof? Being man and wife?"

It was weak, she knew, but she murmured, "He's always respected my wishes." Better not tell Bill about those kisses, then he'd surely never believe her!

"OK, OK. If you say so. You always told me the truth in the past. I can't see any reason why you should lie to me now. I guess I just can't understand it."

They went back to the table to find David and Melanie with their heads together, chatting. David stood up as Judy approached, but it was Bill who held her chair for her.

"Melanie has been telling me I shouldn't run off and go fishing as I'd planned," David told her.

Bill looked interested. "Where do you fish, Dave?"

"Umbagog Lake. I use a cabin on the west bank."

"Sounds like fun."

David glanced at Judy. "Oh, it is. I can't think of anything I'd rather do more."

"The honeymoon is over." Melanie laughed.

Judy looked at her nearly empty glass, twirling it. She said, "David and I have an understanding. I'm not the sort of wife who tries to cramp his style. I feel he needs a vacation, not only from his law work, but also from me, every so often."

Melanie said, "Oh."

The evening went very slowly. David danced with her, but Judy held herself aloof from him. She would not put her body up against his, as Melanie had done. She was hurt, she supposed, that David had danced first with the redhead rather than with her. He could have made the effort to act the part of husband. Or maybe he figured that with Bill Evans here, Judy didn't want to have anything to do with him.

That was why he had intended going fishing, until he learned of the attack on her. He was odd man out, with Bill here. The ninny! Didn't he realize how much she had come to need him? She felt miserable.

Just before the next dance, Ed Malone came over to say hello. He kept looking at Melanie, Judy realized, but the redhead would not glance his way. When the music started, he came around to stand beside her.

"How about it, Mel?" he asked gently. "Care to dance with me?"

Indecision wrote itself across Melanie's lovely face. Judy sensed that the girl wanted to be held in Ed Malone's arms, but that sheer pride was keeping her back.

Judy said, "Go on, Melanie. If you don't dance with Ed, I will."

The redhead locked eyes with Judy. Judy smiled. Slowly, Melanie's lips curved upward and she nodded. "You have two men to entertain you. I think I will."

She rose and went into Ed Malone's arms.

"What was that all about?" Bill asked.

"You wouldn't understand." Judy smiled.

For some reason she couldn't put a finger on, the evening brightened suddenly for Judy. David caught her hand, led her out onto the floor, and now she let herself rest against him as she followed his lead perfectly. Out of the corners of her eyes, she saw Bill staring at them thoughtfully.

In the middle of a dance step, David asked, "Do you want to divorce me, Judy? If you do, I won't stand in your way."

She was so surprised, she was speechless. She drew back away from him, staring up into his eyes. Did she want to divorce David? Unbidden, a part of her screamed "No!"

"Do you want a divorce, David?" she murmured.

Surprised, he missed a step, caught himself quickly. "I thought now that Bill Evans had showed up alive and well that you would."

"I don't know. I'll have to think about it."

"I can't stay on here forever," he growled.

By which he meant that he couldn't go on living with her, seeing her every day, and not wanting to take her in his arms, to kiss and caress her. Judy was thrilled. She wanted David to kiss her. Yes, she did. She didn't know what was happening to her, but she reveled in this feeling.

She put her head against his chest, let her body sink against his, invitingly, temptingly. Again David went tense, for a moment. Then his arm tightened around her, pressing her to him.

Bill Evans was still watching them, but this time he was frowning.

Melanie did not return to their table, and no matter where Judy looked, she could not see Ed Malone. She smiled to herself.

Bill and she were alone for a few minutes as David went to get the Jaguar. Bill drew her into a corner, said, "I don't think I'd better stay on with you and David any longer, Judy. It isn't working out the way I thought it might."

"Don't be silly, Bill. Everything's fine."

"Sure it is, with you and him. I love you, you know that. But you've gone and fallen for Dave. I'm only in the way."

"Don't be like that, Bill. You know how I feel about you."

"Will you divorce him and marry me?" he asked bluntly.

She was silent a little while, then said, "I can't, Bill. Not yet. You have to be patient."

"That's what I thought."

As they drove homeward, Bill announced his plans to take off that very night and drive back to the city. Nothing David or Judy could say would persuade him to change his mind. He packed his bag, shook hands with David, gave Judy a faint smile, and drove off into the night.

"That was sudden," Judy said.

"It's surprising," David agreed. "What brought it on?"

"He wanted me to divorce you. When I said I wouldn't, he must have made up his mind."

David caught her arms, started to draw her to him.

"No, David," she said, pushing away.

His hands fell away and he gave her a long, searching look, then he turned and moved toward the staircase. Judy watched him go, misery in her heart. Why had she pushed him away? Why couldn't she have let him kiss her, caress her, as she wanted to be kissed and caressed? She bit her lower lip, tears coming into her eyes.

What was the *matter* with her?

She ran toward the stairs. The light was on in David's room; she heard sounds that indicated he was walking around. She ran to the doorway, staring in at him.

His bags were open and he was moving from drawer to bags, hands filled with shirts and underwear. Judy stared, wide-eyed, her heart sinking.

"I'm packing," he answered her unspoken question. "I should have had the guts Bill Evans had. I'm not wanted here, so why stay?"

Judy opened her mouth to reply.

In the distance, a siren sounded.

Chapter ELEVEN

David swung around toward the window. The siren wailed like a lost soul, Judy thought, its sound rising and falling. For the first time, she saw redness in the night sky, and went to stand beside him at the window.

"It's something in town," he muttered. "It looks as if . . ."

"Never mind that," Judy said softly. "About us, David. I want to tell you that—"

A car came racing along the road, horn blaring. They could hear the squeal of brakes, the screech of rubber on asphalt. The horn went on sounding.

David flung open the window.

"It's the bookstore, it's on fire," Ed Malone yelled up.

David turned to stare at her. "That does it," he whispered softly, and caught her by the arm, drawing her to the door and down the stairs.

Melanie was in the car with Ed Malone, Judy saw as she followed David out into the night. She was leaning against Ed, who was talking to David. Judy caught a few of their words.

". . . Driving Melanie home when . . . everything's going, no chance to save it . . . sorry, Dave, but that's the way it is. The volunteer fire department doesn't stand the ghost of a chance."

David turned, put an arm around her. "We'll drive down, meet you there."

They could see the flames quite clearly now, like living scarlet tongues against the night sky. An emptiness lay in Judy. Her uncle had paid a fortune for that store. Now it was worth absolutely nothing. She sat tense as David drove as close to the fire as he dared.

She sat in the car as he got out and went to stand beside Ed Malone.

There were other men here, too, members of the volunteer fire department, she guessed. They had a hose out and were playing streams of water over the flames. But it would do no good. The fire had too firm a start, and the whole building was going to burn to the ground.

Judy stared wide-eyed. This was all that was needed. Bill had gone, David was going out of her life. Even her uncle's inheritance—or a good part of it—was lost to her. She could not cry, she was beyond tears.

After a time David came to lean on the car window-sill. "It can't be saved. I'm sorry, Judy. There'll be nothing left but ashes. I'll take you home to bed, then come back."

She was numb. She could not protest against going home, she could only sit there as David drove. Once she asked, "Do you think Melanie's father did it?"

"Of course not. Nor Charley Underwood. Doesn't stand to reason. They wanted the store, or what was in it. They wouldn't have burned it. It's probably an accident. Faulty electrical wiring or something like that."

She got out and walked like a zombi to the door. David let her in, saw her upstairs before he turned and went back to the car. Judy flung herself across her bed, fully dressed. She was utterly miserable. Her life was shattered about her . . . she had lost everything. She turned over, buried her face in her arms, and wept.

She cried herself to sleep. . . .

The smell of frying bacon woke her. She pushed herself up, sat on the edge of the bed, memory coming to her in a rush. David! David must still be here. No one else would be cooking. Excited, forgetful of the fact that she was still in her evening gown, she ran down the stairs.

"David! You're still here!" she cried happily.

He turned from the iron stove with a grin. "I had to come back, to show you what we found."

His hand gestured at two metal boxes, scorched by fire but intact. "They were in the debris this morning when a state trooper and I went over the place. The trooper said the fire looked suspicious. There was a smell of kerosene all over the store.

"And in the cellar, we found those boxes. They're locked. I don't know who has the key. But they belong to you, along with whatever's in them."

She looked at the metal boxes.

"What's in them?"

"We'll take them to a locksmith and find out, just as soon as you change and have had breakfast. Go on, take a shower, get into some slacks. I'll change myself later, after we eat."

He had stayed at the fire all night. He was still protecting her, looking out for her interests, Judy realized, and felt warmth inside her. She turned and ran for the stairs, to do what David had said.

They found a locksmith in Bellows Falls, an old man who walked with a limp as he came around the back of his narrow little store to examine the metal boxes that David set on his counter. It took him only a few minutes to open them.

Judy waited, scarcely able to breathe. What could be inside them? Oh, this was what Uncle Walter had paid out all that money for, there was no doubt of that. David had told her that the state trooper guessed the boxes had been hidden in the false ceiling of the cellar. No wonder they had not been able to find them!

Judy remembered that his sister had told her Johnny Edmonds had been very good with his hands. He had made her bed, other articles of furniture. How easy it would have been for him to drop the ceiling to hold those boxes so no one could ever have found them!

She stared as the lids went up, and disappointment grew in her. All there were inside those boxes were a number of books and a couple of envelopes. She sagged against the counter.

David reached for one of the books, lifted it, stared.

He gave a slow whistle. He put the book down, picked up a second. His rather drawn face relaxed, as he turned to her.

"You're a rich young woman, Judy," he said gently. "I don't know how rich as yet, you'll have to get some advice, but I'll bet a cookie it will be at least a quarter of a million."

The locksmith gawked. "Just for some old books?"

David grinned. His hand lifted the first book. "This is a mint copy of Edgar Allan Poe's *Tamerlane*. His name doesn't appear on it; it's signed 'A Bostonian.' It was printed in 1827 by a printer named Calvin F. S. Thomas, in Boston. This book alone is worth at least twenty-five thousand dollars."

The locksmith muttered under his breath.

"Take this one," David went on, lifting another tome. "This is the Bay Psalm book, published in 1640 in Cambridge, Massachusetts. There are—or were—only eleven copies known to exist. Each one is worth roughly twenty-five thousand dollars. Probably a bit more in these days of inflated prices."

He touched an envelope, opened it, peered inside. "There's a stamp in here." He brought it out and Judy stared at the tiny thing, colored blue and with the words *Hawaiian Postage* on it, and below the numeral 2 the words *Two Cents*. David took a long, slow look at it, very reverently placed the stamp back in the envelope and placed the envelope carefully in the metal box.

"A Hawaiian Missionary," he murmured in a dazed way. "The Christian missionaries in Hawaii used this stamp a lot in the old days, writing home; that's why it has that name."

He drew out a handkerchief and touched his forehead. "That stamp is worth about half as much as the British Guiana stamp that's worth a hundred thousand. I'd say this Hawaiian blue alone will get you fifty thousand dollars, Judy."

The locksmith had turned a pale green.

David closed the lids, paid the locksmith his fee, and carried the boxes out to the car. "We're going to put all these things in a safe-deposit box, or a couple of them."

He closed the trunk, turned, and looked at Judy, who was just coming out of shock, she realized. He grinned at her. "Hello, rich girl. Your uncle wasn't such a dingbat after all, was he? No wonder Emmett Rodgers was willing to go to seventy-five thousand for that store. He would have pulled it down to the ground in order to find these boxes. Somehow, he had an idea of what was in them."

"Those trips Johnny Edmonds made," Judy murmured. "He used to go into the backwoods and visit people, looking for books he could buy for his second-hand trade. He knew of terrific buys he could make, but he needed cash. Uncle Walter had the cash. They were partners, I suppose. To protect his investment, Uncle Walter had Johnny Edmonds deed over the bookstore—and what it contained—to him, in case Johnny died before my uncle. If my uncle died first— well, maybe those books would have belonged to Johnny alone."

As they were driving through Bellows Falls, David said, "You'll have to go see a rare book expert, and then a stamp expert, Judy. They'll advise you as to what to do: sell them at auction or to some avid collector who'd give his shirt for any one of those items. They'll know the rich collectors; they do business with them all the time."

"I'd like you to be with me when I do," she said in a small voice.

He was silent for a few seconds. "Anytime, Judy. You know that."

She wanted to ask him to stay on, to unpack his bags, to forego his fishing trip. But the words stuck in her throat. Judy wanted David to be the one to say that he didn't want to leave her. She was being stubborn, she knew, but that was the way she was.

They parked in the Morstead bank lot, went in and asked for two large safe-deposit boxes. Judy signed the necessary forms, and paid the fee. Then with David looking on, she transferred the contents of the metal boxes.

They walked out into the sunlight, David carrying the fire-scorched metal boxes. "These you can throw away, whenever you want."

"I think I'll keep them in memory of Uncle Walter."

"You can always sell the bookstore property, you know. Might pick up a few thousand dollars by doing that. No sense in rebuilding the store."

She nodded glumly. *Forget the bookstore, forget money,* she felt like yelling at him. *Think about me, about us. Tell me you don't want to go away, that you want to stay on with me and be—be my husband! Really my husband.*

Judy flushed at her thoughts, sitting quietly in the Jaguar as he drove back home. If only he would stop the car, pull her into his arms, and kiss her the way he had. She would break down then, she would tell him that she loved him, that she wanted him as a loving woman wanted her man. But he just kept driving, with his eyes on the road ahead.

It took an effort to open the door, to follow him up the path to the house door. Her feet dragged, and she felt abandoned. She would willingly have thrown away those rare books, the rare stamp, if only he would turn around and tell her he couldn't leave her, that he needed her to be a part of his life.

"May I help you pack?" she asked weakly, when they were going up the stairs.

"No need, I'm just about done," he answered cheerfully.

She sat on a chair and watched him fill his luggage, her hands clasped, fingers working. *Don't go!* she pleaded mentally. *Please stay, David! I'm confused. I need time. I love you but I'm too proud to beg.*

When the two bags were locked, David turned and

smiled at her. I'll be out of your way now, Judy. I'll be up at Umbagog Lake, in case you need me."

He lifted his luggage. Judy trailed him down the stairs and out to the Jaguar. When the bags were in the car trunk David turned and held out his hand.

"Still friends?" he asked.

She nodded, swallowing hard, and took his hand. She watched, misery in her eyes, as he got into the car, started the motor, backed out onto the highway. Judy waved, and David waved back. Then the Jaguar was gone in a spurt of power that took it around the bend and out of sight.

Judy stood a long time, staring after it.

Well, she had what she had wanted from the very beginning, now. She was alone and unencumbered; she was fairly rich, or would be. David had done what he had agreed to do, right from the start. He had gone out of her life. She had no husband, he had no wife. It was as simple as that.

She turned and stared at the house. It was big, rambling. She would rattle around in it like a pea in a pod. There would be nobody to talk to, no more frying bacon to wake up to in the morning. There wouldn't be anyone who might grab and kiss her unexpectedly, no one to take her into his arms and tell her he loved her.

Tears came into her eyes. Angrily, she brushed them away as she walked toward the house. *Judy Hunter— oops! better make that Judy Carnegie—you're a fool. You didn't know how happy you were, with David in the house. And now he's gone.*

She tried to occupy her mind by working in the garden, weeding and clipping. She got out the mower and walked up and down, exhausting herself while making sure the grounds looked neat and orderly. In the late afternoon, she put on her bathing suit and went down to the brook, cooling off in the moving waters.

She ate a lonely dinner of baked beans and a hamburger. It tasted like cardboard.

She found a mystery novel in her uncle's library and read herself to sleep.

When she woke next morning, she stared at the ceiling a long time. Was this what her life was going to be like from now on? Working around the house, eating lonely meals, taking a book to bed with her at night? She would die, she would just die here, withering like the last leaf on a tree.

Judy made herself get up, pull on blue jeans and a blouse. She brushed her hair loose, scowling as it fell down below her shoulders. There was no sense in fixing it neatly, there was no one to see her. Glumly she told herself she would become a regular old witch after a few months of this sort of life.

In the kitchen she perked coffee and stared at what was left of the pancake batter. If David had been here, she would have jumped at the chance to eat griddle cakes, to consume three cups of coffee and talk over the coming day with him.

She put the batter back in the refrigerator and settled for coffee.

She was on her second cup, swallowing it as one might medicine, when a red Cadillac pulled in close to the picket fence. Judy frowned at Melanie Rodgers as the redhead got out and began her walk up toward the front door.

You're too late, sister. David's gone! He's left us both.

To her amazement, when she opened the door and looked at Melanie, she saw tears running down the girl's cheeks. Impulsively, her heart went out to her.

"Melanie! You poor dear. What's wrong? Come on in."

"I'm absolutely miserable," the redhead sobbed. "I want to talk to somebody. Where's David?"

"He's gone."

"Gone?" Something in her face must have betrayed her, Judy realized, because the redhead put a sympathetic hand on her arm. "Don't tell me you two love-birds are having trouble, too?"

Judy tried to smile. "We've never had anything but trouble. We only got married so I could get this house."

Melanie looked shocked. She groped her way to a chair and sat down. "But you're in love. I couldn't be mistaken. That's the only reason I sort of—well, tried to latch on to David. I knew you two were secure, and I—I wanted to make Ed Malone jealous."

Judy smiled, this time. "And did you?"

Melanie scowled. "He liked David too much. I think he saw through me. We had a long talk the other night, after the country club dance, when we discovered that fire. I'm sorry about that."

Judy poured hot coffee, pushed cream and sugar toward the redheaded girl. "It turned out all right," she said, and explained about the two metal boxes.

Melanie laughed delightedly. "I'm so happy for you. Daddy heard rumors about Johnny Edmonds' trips, he knew Johnny knew a lot of people, suspected that he was buying up some rare things, that he kept them in the bookstore. But I'm glad he didn't buy the store. I'm glad you got all those goodies." She sighed. "I just wish I could get one goodie myself."

"Why can't you?"

"Daddy doesn't approve of Ed Malone. He—he isn't rich enough to suit him. As if money were the only thing in the world!"

Judy drew a deep breath. "I'm a fine one to be giving advice, but if I were you I'd run to Ed Malone and tell your father to go jump in the lake. Or words to that effect."

Melanie lighted a cigarette, drew in smoke. She wore a white turtleneck top and a culotte skirt of huge white flowers on a green background. She looked startlingly beautiful, but Judy realized she was as unhappy as Judy herself.

"I may do just that," she said at last, thoughtfully.

"All this summer I've been absolutely miserable inside. The only times I've been happy were when I was with Ed."

"Good girl," Judy approved.

"Ed makes a good living, I don't need Daddy's millions. Let him keep them."

Judy smiled faintly. "You'd be surprised how much fun you can have just eating pancakes with the man you love." She straightened. "And speaking of pancakes, how about some? I have the batter all made. I wasn't hungry, but now I'm starved."

"I am too. Let's do it." Almost shyly, Melanie added, "You'd better show me how; in case Ed likes griddle cakes I'll have to be able to make them."

Judy brought out the griddle, showed Melanie how to pour, explaining how to mix flour, eggs, and milk. She carried the maple syrup and butter to the table, put on more coffee to perk.

After they had eaten, Melanie asked, "What about you? I take it David's gone fishing, but he'll be back soon, won't he?"

Judy shook her head. Then under Melanie's sympathetic gaze, she poured out her whole story. The redhead sat quietly, not saying a word until she was done.

Then she said, "You don't love this Bill Evans, you never did. You had nobody else to cling to at the time, so he became the one man in your life. You magnified him in your own mind, especially when you thought he was dead by drowning. You made a martyr out of him, Judy—but you didn't love him."

Judy nodded. "I know that now, when it's too late."

Melanie grinned. "What's too late? All you have to do is go up to Umbagog Lake and get into bed with him. He is your husband, isn't he? So tell him you love him."

"Maybe he doesn't love me."

Melanie hooted. "The man adores you! Weren't you aware of how he looked at you when you weren't looking? That's why I picked him to make Ed jealous. I knew I was safe enough with David."

Judy stared at her, "Well, I was jealous of you!"

Melanie laughed, then sobered. "There was no need to be, believe me. That man of yours is just that. Your man . . . if you want him badly enough to let him know. He probably thinks you still love Bill Evans."

Judy leaped to her feet. Of course! That was it. David had asked her if she wanted a divorce at the dance. He probably felt she was too shy to tell him.

"The big idiot!" she screamed.

"You're the idiot," Melanie said dryly. "And so am I. But it's not too late for either of us, is it?"

"I'll need a car."

"I have a little Pinto you can borrow. Daddy keeps it as a spare, in case something goes wrong with the others."

"Give me ten minutes to pack."

"I'll do the dishes. Time I learned how."

Judy raced upstairs, her heart singing.

Chapter TWELVE

The day was warm, the Pinto easy to handle as Judy sat at the wheel and moved northward along Route 9 to Concord. She was filled with determination, with a realization that at long last she had come to terms with her life, that she knew exactly what she wanted, and was out to get it.

She had been a little idiot, but that was all behind her. She was a wife now, on her way to join her husband. A wife in every sense of the word. Yes, yes, yes, her heart told her. She belonged in David's arms, her lips were made for his kisses, and nothing was going to stop her.

Judy had no eyes for the beauties of the world around her, except in a vague way. Even the scenic route from Concord along 93 was only a vague perception, a background to the happiness inside her. Besides, she was traveling too fast to admire the rolling countryside, the distant mountains, the Old Man of the Mountains. All she could think about was David, and falling into his arms.

At Errol, late in the afternoon, she had to stop and ask directions. Umbagog Lake lay half in New Hampshire, half in northern Maine. It was very remote from any town—that was probably why David liked it as a vacation spot—and it was heavily forested.

The sun was setting as she eased the Pinto along the narrow dirt road which swept the lake borders. The blue sheen of the water caught her eyes, its beauty touched her mind. Rocks lay like misshapen bundles along the shore, which was dotted with ferns and leaves that dipped their ends into their vivid reflections. A cool wind stalked the trees, rustling the branches.

In time, and after several mistakes, she saw the cabin, recognizing it from David's description. She went past a car parked under the trees, and when she saw the Jaguar, she knew she had come home.

Judy leaped from the car and ran. She threw open the door and called his name. Silence came about her, holding her still.

Of course! He'd be out fishing.

Where was it he had said he fished for trout? Some stream or other, with an Indian name. Mollidgewock. Yes. Judy had no idea of where the trout stream might be. She would wait here for him, surprise him when he opened the door.

She spared a glance around the big room, seeing the Navaho rugs on the floor, the mounted moosehead above the big brick fireplace, the heavy furniture that struck her as being so masculine. Crossed sabers on a wall, a small bar behind which were dozens of liquor bottles, a few pictures of outdoor scenes, told her that this cabin was a male retreat, that had probably known very few females.

Judy grinned. It would know one now!

She moved toward a back door, stepped out onto a balcony girded by logs that served as a balustrade. There were chairs here, a redwood lounge covered by worn cushions, a standing ashtray filled with cigarette butts. Judy turned toward the lake.

A canoe was making its way in toward shore, heading for the rocks that extended outward into the lake. She took a long look and her heart leaped when she recognized David. He was not at the trout stream, after all. She started to raise her arm, then dropped it. David would expect a lonely cabin, instead he would have a wife who would leap into his arms, who would shower him with kisses.

She hoped he had made a good catch. She had skipped lunch and was ravenous. From the window she could see him approaching the shore, angling his canoe toward three flat-topped boulders that made a natural quay.

Just as the canoe ran in against the rock, Judy saw movement to one side, out of the corners of her eyes. She turned and watched a man in a lumber jacket, carrying a rifle, move toward the canoe. His back was to her, but there was something menacing about him that struck a chill into her.

David had not seen the waiting man, as he was hidden from view by some trees. David ran the canoe in close to the rocks, reached out to catch one, steady the rocking craft. He tossed some fish out onto the huge boulder, then stepped nimbly ashore.

At the same moment, the rifle came up, aimed right at David's heart. Judy tried to cry out, but could not. Her throat worked with the fear inside her. She had to reach them, to interfere, to defend David in some way. Heart thumping, she looked wildly around her, saw the stairs leading down from the balcony. She ran, slipping and sliding in her haste.

The man with the rifle was facing David. His finger was on the trigger. He meant to shoot David, to kill him, to murder him in cold blood! Judy sobbed, moaned as she ran past a berry bush and between two tree boles.

"No! Wait! You can't. I won't let you!"

Only the wind heard her voice.

She stumbled, sprawled headlong, not twenty feet from the two men. Her hands went into the soil, caught at leaves and fallen pine needles. She must push herself to her feet, run between that rifle barrel and David. She got to her knees.

And then she froze.

The rifleman was speaking, and she recognized his voice.

"Sure, I came up here. You don't think I was going to let you live, do you?"

It was Bill. Bill Evans!

Judy stared, shocked into immobility. He had said

he was going back to New York, that he was stepping out of her life.

"I tried to kill you once before. Yeah, that's right. When you and Judy arrived at the house, your first day up here. I missed you and hit Judy when she bent over to help you. I damn near died myself then."

"So it was you," David said quietly.

"Yeah, yeah. You didn't swallow that line about my losing my memory, did you? I wondered about that. Judy took it, hook, line, and sinker. But then she's always been a little fool, where I was concerned. She thought I loved her. That was a laugh.

"She wasn't even fun to be with, she was so damn prim and proper. I was never going to show up again in her life, but when I heard from her neighbor that she was getting married, I beat it down to the marriage license bureau, then hotfooted it over to that lawyer, Miller.

"I made up a yarn about being a cousin of hers, learned where you had gone. I drove up here like a bat out of hell. I didn't stop or anything. I made it just in time, just as you arrived. I figured I'd make her a widow and then show up myself in a few days to console her. It wouldn't have taken her long to fall into my arms and to marry me.

"Then her inheritance would be mine."

His chuckle was thick, oily. Judy stared at his back as though he were a stranger. This was not the Bill Evans she had known. It could not be! And yet the hard truth of the matter was that—yes, this was Bill Evans. But he was a different person, someone out of a nightmare.

David said. "You nosed around, learned about the bookstore and the money being offered for it, and you decided to play your cards differently."

"Smart of you. I did. It was me who ransacked that store, hunting for whatever was inside it that made it so valuable. Not kids, not vandals. Me. I didn't find a damn thing.

"So I figured it might be a good idea to show up, to learn the lay of the land between you and Judy. My God! I never realized you hadn't put a hand on her. I hired those two thugs to stop her car, to scare her. When I showed up to rescue her, I figured she'd drop into my arms like a ripe peach.

"So I made up that story about being hit over the head when my boat turned over—I'd had a friend phone and tell her much the same thing a few months ago when I wanted to be rid of her, so it was easy to add to it. It was all hogwash, but she bit.

"I thought I could talk the little fool into divorcing you and marrying me. That way would be safer than killing you. But she had to go and fall in love with you."

David started, moving forward. The rifle barrel came up, aimed straight at his heart. David snarled, "She doesn't care for me. Man, I know."

"She worships you. Toward the end there, all you had to do was crook your finger and she'd have fallen into your arms. But you kept thinking she loved me; you were too much of a gentleman, I guess, to push. But I knew how matters stood between you, even if you didn't.

"So I set fire to the bookstore, that night I left you. If I wasn't going to have what was in it, I was going to make sure neither of you were either."

There was a little silence. Judy gathered her strength, rose up onto her feet, moved forward cautiously, setting one foot down carefully without a sound, then the other. She must make no noise, she musn't startle Bill into shooting David before she could act.

Bill said slowly, "I hung around out of sight. I saw that state trooper and you bring out those metal boxes. I followed the two of you to Bellows Falls the next day. I went into that locksmith's store after you'd left. He was still in shock from what you'd found in those boxes, and he couldn't wait to tell about it."

Again came that thick, oily chuckle. "So then. Judy's a rich little girl, I told myself. Well, now. I had to do something about that. If I could get rid of you, I figured I could come back up here and console the sorrowful widow. Sooner or later, I could have conned her into marrying me."

Judy was close behind Bill now. She was sure David had seen her, but he hadn't let on. She crept closer, taking care to avoid brushing against any branches or underbrush. Bill did not suspect—his back was to her, his entire attention was on David. Judy drew a deep breath.

In another moment she would leap, throw her arms about Bill, try to wrestle him off balance. She tensed, crouched down, hands balled into fists.

She jumped—

As she did, her ankle turned and she fell sideways.

She landed hard, and Bill swung around, the rifle muzzle within inches of her face. Out of the corners of her eyes she saw David spring forward. He slammed into Bill Evans, drove him sideways off his feet. The rifle exploded, and Judy heard a bullet scream as it whistled through leaves and buried itself in a tree trunk.

She sprang up. David was astride the fallen man, driving fists down into his face. But Bill was tough, and he fought back, arching his spine and lifting David upward.

As he went, David caught the rifle, tore it from Bill's grasp, hurled it to one side. Judy sprang for it, grabbed it, held it in shaking hands.

Now David and Bill were on their feet, circling. David was saying, "You might as well turn around and get out of here. Judy's here. She heard you. You'll never marry her now, no matter what happens to me."

Judy was shocked at Bill Evans' expression. It was feral, wolfish, as he bared his teeth. There was a coldness, a cruelty, about the narrowed eyes and hard face that sent fright deep inside her. This was a Bill Evans she had never known.

He snarled, "Then I'll kill you both. I'll find some way of getting those books and stamps out of that bank vault, even if I have to forge her name."

"Bill! This isn't you!" Judy cried.

"You were too much in love with me to bother about what I was. I never loved you, Judy. You weren't even fun to be with. You'd never have seen me again if your uncle hadn't left you all that loot."

Bill threw himself forward, fists flailing. David stepped back, warded off the blows with his left arm, drove in with his right, catching Bill in the midsection. Again he drove forward, then slammed his left into Bill's jaw. Bill rocked back, gasping for breath.

David gave him no rest. He was on him, pummeling, using his arms like pistons, his fists like piledrivers. Bill reeled back. His heel hit a root and he fell heavily.

He lay a moment, panting. David had stepped back, waiting, fists still clenched. Bill came up on an elbow, then rose slowly to his feet. His face was marked where David had hit him. He labored for breath, but there was a savagery deep inside him that told the terrified Judy that he would never quit, that David would have to kill him.

Bill moved sideways. Too late, Judy realized he was not moving toward David but toward her. Bill lunged, his hands stabbed out, and he yanked the rifle from her grasp. Judy fell against him, knocking him sideways. Bill dropped and the rifle barrel went deep into the soft loam of the ground.

David was springing forward but Bill was rising to a knee, rifle coming up and aimed at David. A twisted grin gleamed on Bill's face. "I got you both now. There's nothing you can do."

He rose to his feet, shaking with fury. Judy felt David move toward her, put an arm about her, seek to thrust her behind him. Bill barked laughter.

"It won't do any good to try to protect her, Carnegie. I get you first, then her."

The gun came up. Judy closed her eyes.

There was a stunning report, a thick scream from Bill. Judy stared, saw Bill falling backward, in among the boulders. David reached for her, swung her around, held her close against him.

"The gun barrel was clogged," David was whispering. "It happened as he fell, when the gun went into the ground. It exploded."

He put her aside, went to kneel and look down at Bill Evans. David turned a sober face. "I don't know whether the explosion killed him or he died when he hit those rocks. His head—well, it isn't a pretty sight. Come up to the cabin. We'll call the police, tell them what happened."

Judy moved with him in a daze. She could not believe what she had heard and seen; it would take a long time for it to sink in. Meanwhile she was quiet, watching as David made his phone call, sitting on the edge of the divan, hands clasped and working.

When the police came she answered their questions, watched as David walked with them to where the body lay. It seemed to take forever but at length the body was gone, the police went away, and she was alone with David.

It was very dark by this time. David had turned on the lights and was standing, looking down at her.

"You saved my life, you know," he murmured gently. "I'll be forever grateful." He ran fingers through his tawny hair and a puzzled expression touched his face. "What I can't understand is what you're doing here at all."

How was she going to tell him what she and Melanie had decided, back at the house? Suppose he didn't want her as she wanted him, as a wife wants her husband? Maybe he didn't love her, after all. Still, both Melanie and Bill had seemed certain that he did.

Judy licked her lips. "I came up here to be—to be with my husband."

His eyebrows rose. There was disbelief in his eyes, and Judy told herself miserably that she didn't blame him. She sighed and came to her feet, moved toward him, put her arms about him and lifted her face.

David closed his arms around her, held her soft body close to his. For a long moment he stared down into her eyes. Then his lips were on hers, pressing, demanding. And Judy answered that pressure; she tightened her arms where they hung about his neck.

It was a long time before he let her go, to whisper, "I don't know whether I'm dreaming all this or not, but if I am, I don't want to wake up."

Judy urged herself even closer, murmuring, "I've been an idiot, Dave. I think I've been in love with you right from the very beginning. I was too dumb to know it. Melanie and I had a little talk. She's gone off with Ed. I came up here to you. We didn't want either one of you to get away."

David drew her toward a big easy chair. He sat down and pulled her onto his lap. Judy cuddled into his embrace with a deep sigh. He began to kiss her lips, her eyes, her forehead, her throat. And Judy almost purred.

He whispered into her ear, "I fell in love with you when I saw you in the library, long before you ever met me. That's why I wanted to marry you. I hoped I could make you love me—but for a time there, I was about ready to give up. Especially when Bill Evans showed up."

David looked over her head. "This isn't much of a place."

Judy smiled. "I think it's heaven."

"What I mean is, there's only one bed."

"Good."

David pushed her back so he could look down into her face. "It's a big bed, of course. King-size."

"Wonderful. You sleep on your side and I'll sleep on your side."

David laughed and hugged her. "I just can't believe this."

Judy sprang to her feet, caught him by the hand, and now it was her turn to draw him after her. "Let's go make sure you do believe it, David. For all the rest of our lives."

An Offer
of Marriage

Chapter One

The night was one of the most beautiful that Beth Sheldon could remember. The stars were brilliant in the blue velvet sky, the moon was like a huge silver ball, and the wind, filled with the fragrance of honeysuckle and hyacinths, seemed like a caress as it brushed her face. She walked slowly, breathing in the cool spring air, forcing herself to this casual pace when her every instinct clamored for her to run. To run and run and run!

Beth Sheldon was terrified.

From time to time she paused, standing very still, letting her eyes turn this way and that, as if expecting to see some shadowy shape hurtling out upon her. There was a formlessness to this shape she awaited, a facelessness that added to her fright. She had no way of knowing who or what was her enemy. All she understood was that someone or something wanted her dead.

Movement among the dead leaves off to one side of the woods startled her into an outcry, and she stood frozen, unable to move a muscle, until a rabbit bounded across the road ten paces away, hopping madly through the moonlight.

Beth let the air out of her lungs as she sighed with relief. Her right hand tightened on the heavy blackthorn walking stick she carried. Ever since that day, a week ago tomorrow, when she had almost died in the turbulent waters off Capstone Rocks, when someone had caught at her ankle and tried to keep her underwater, she had been filled with nameless dread.

She put away that memory, using all her willpower. Yet it persisted, with a remembrance of that instant when iron fingers had closed on her ankle, when a dead weight had dragged her down. And down. And down, until her lungs had come close to bursting, until she had wrenched free and—

Beth shook a little, standing there, whimpering.

There was no reason anyone should want to kill her. She had never harmed anyone. She led a quiet life, living in the cottage that was her home and studio, where she wrote the books for children that had given her, she liked to feel, something of a reputation in the field. She never troubled anyone; she was too deep in her work to bother much about the life that went on around her.

And yet—

Someone beneath the surface there near Capstone Rock *had* tried to drown her, had sought to keep her there forever, perhaps pushing her lifeless body into a rock crevice so that no one would ever find her. *Why* had he done it? *Who* had it been?

How often lately had she lain awake at night, listening to the nighttime sounds around her cottage, puzzling over these questions without result! The more thought she gave to the incident, the more confused she became. It was hopeless, trying to make sense out of the inexplicable.

Her hand loosed its frenzied grip on the blackthorn stick. She looked around her at the country road, at the trees and underbrush hemming her in. Sometimes she thought she was stupid to leave the security of her house and go strolling like this, but she needed the exercise. She had to wipe away the cobwebs from her mind.

Beth walked on.

She must conquer this fear. It had all been a mistake, what had happened off Capstone Rock. Nobody wanted Beth Sheldon dead. It had been a mischievous teen-ager who had grabbed her ankle and yanked her downward. It had to be. Just the same, some womanly intuition told her there was something more to it than that. Unless it was her imagination, a prowler had been keeping her under surveillance recently, after dark at her cottage. Twice she had caught glimpses of someone or something out there under the trees, just watching.

She kept eyeing the woods on either side. Was someone here now, coming after her? She caught little sounds, the breaking of a twig, the brush of—a foot?—in the dead leaves on the woodland floor, the harsh sound of someone breathing.

Her chin firmed as her head lifted. She would not panic. She was a sensible woman in her middle twenties; she had made her own way in life for the past five years. If anyone were to attack her, she would use the blackthorn stick to smash and batter him. She was not a helpless child. She had taken care of herself too long to get hysterical over this wild flight of imagination.

The road straightened as she went around a curve. Beth walked with longer strides, using the walking stick firmly, keeping to the center of the road. If anyone were to jump out at her, she would see him in plenty of time to defend herself.

Above the night sounds she heard a deeper noise. A car was coming, moving fast. She turned, catching the twinkle of headlights in the distance.

"The fool," she whispered. "He must be doing eighty."

Casually, she strode to the bushes that rimmed the straightaway, her eyes on the twin beams of light that were touching the bend now. Then they straightened, illuminating the dirt road, the bushes, and the hanging tree branches. It was a powerful car—the deep throb of its motor told her that much. And it was coming fast. Very fast.

She shrank back. In an instant it would be past her.

Something hit the middle of her back. Whatever it was shoved her forward, viciously. Right into the path of that hurtling machine.

Beth tried to cry out, but her tongue was frozen.

There was a searing white brilliance in her eyes. The blackthorn stick fell from her numb hand as she put those hands before her, to try and push away from that dark monster that was right on top of her.

Something hit her.

She was lifted, flung aside like a rag doll, as her whole world reeled around her. She had the sensation of flying, of soaring through the air. In that same instant she caught the shriek of brakes, the skidding slide of the big car. There was an explosion. . . .

She heard voices, as in a dream.

"The girl's alive. I'm not so sure about the man."

"He must have been barreling along. Will you look at these skid marks?"

"You know who he is, don't you?"

"I do. So be easy with him. Can we get him out?"

Beth Sheldon felt momentarily annoyed. What was so important about the driver? How about her, the victim? It was the man who had been speeding on this narrow back-country lane. The accident had been his fault. She—

She knew sudden fear.

No! The accident had not been his fault. Someone had been behind her, had pushed her into the path of that car.

She lost consciousness a second time.

There was a smell in her nose. Ammonia. Irritated, she moved her head from side to side, then heard a chuckle.

"She's coming around."

"Who is she, anybody we know?"

A deeper voice, that of an older man, said, "Name's Sheldon. Lives alone over on the Hollow Road. Has a cottage there."

Beth opened her eyes.

Two young men wearing the austere whites of ambulance interns were bending over her. One of them was smiling down at her. In the bright light that came from a car's headlights, she saw he had long blond hair and a moustache. The other intern was dark and clean-shaven, with crisp, black hair.

The blond man said, "You're a lucky girl. I don't think you have any broken bones. Still, we'll have to make a more thorough examination."

Beth found her mouth was very dry, so dry that her tongue seemed to stick to the roof of her mouth. She asked weakly, "Could I have some water?"

It was the dark young man who put an arm under her back and lifted her very gently. His eyes were on her face, sharp and intent. Probably wants to see if anything hurts me, she thought. To her surprise, nothing did.

Ooops. She winced as pain stabbed into her shoulder.

"Your shoulder," the dark-haired man said. "Got a black and blue mark on it. You must have fallen into the fender or the bumper."

"S-somebody p-pushed me."

His dark eyebrows lifted. "Out here? In this godforsaken spot?"

She nodded weakly. "Yes. I heard the car coming. He was going awfully fast, so I got over to the side of the road. Then, just as he was about to pass me—somebody shoved me."

The man with the deep voice came into view, leaning down to stare at her. Beth recognized him as Abe Boldin, owner of the general store over in Rocky Cove, where she shopped occasionally. Her lips twitched as she tried to give him a smile.

"Shoved you?" Boldin asked disbelievingly. "Who'd do a thing like that?"

It was too long a story to tell them here and now. The disbelief in his voice was echoed in the eyes of the others. Beth sighed, "Never mind. But I did feel hands against my back, pushing me."

"Maybe a tree branch hit you, or you stepped back into it. It bent and appeared to push you . . ."

The blond man broke off his explanation when his eyes met Beth's. He shrugged. "All right. Have it your own way. Somebody hates you and pushed you into the car. Fortunately, it didn't do too much harm. Can you stand?"

He held her hands in his and pulled. The other intern was supporting her back and neck. Beth made it to her feet, swayed a little, and then realized that, outside of her aching shoulder, she was quite all right.

She realized also that her sweater was disarranged, that her bra was undone, and that the intern had given her a thorough examination while she had been unconscious. Well, they'd have to do that, so they could check that no bones had been broken.

Somebody handed her a glass of water. She drank it gratefully, then handed back the empty glass. As she did so, her eyes saw the crumpled car, wrapped halfway around a thick tree bole, and she gasped.

"The man, the one who drove the car," she cried, her words spilling out. "What about him? You've been working over me, but he may need you more than I do."

"He's on his way to Memorial Hospital," the blond intern said.

"But is he badly hurt?"

His face grew grave. "He's unconscious. I don't know if he'll live. There might be internal injuries, as well as a broken arm, along with some ribs. But the doctors will work on him at the hospital. If they can save him, they will." In an awed voice, he muttered, "They'll probably have Donovan up from Boston to look at him."

The name meant nothing to Beth.

She practiced walking a few feet, then came back. Her shoulder still hurt, but other than that, she seemed healthy enough. When she saw her blackthorn stick lying on the ground a few feet away, she went and picked it up.

"Can I go home now?" she asked.

The dark-haired intern said, "You ought to have a more thorough examination. We have an ambulance here—come back to the hospital with us."

"There's no need for that," she said slowly. "Really, I feel fine. Except for the shoulder, that is. Besides, I'd rather see my own doctor."

The interns looked at each other. It was the blond who said, "I guess that'll be all right. You're a lucky girl. But get in the ambulance, anyhow. We'll drive you home."

Abe Boldin muttered, "I can take her. I know the way."

Beth Sheldon felt relief wash over her. To have to walk home after what had happened was unthinkable. The man who had shoved her in front of the car might still be waiting somewhere in the woods. She realized without caring that all her bravery had suddenly oozed right out of her.

"If it wouldn't be putting you out of your way, Mr. Boldin, I really would appreciate it."

She thanked the two interns, then went with Abraham Boldin to his pickup truck. His gnarled hand caught her elbow, and he assisted her into the cab. Beth sank back against the cushions with a grateful sigh.

Boldin started his engine, backed, and turned.

He said, "Lucky thing for you and him that I worked late

tonight. Might be nobody else'd be traveling this road this time of night."

"Oh, I am grateful, so grateful."

He pooh-poohed her gratitude, but nonetheless he was pleased. "Heard the crash from about a mile away. Got here just as soon as I could. When I saw what had happened, I ran through the woods to the Cantrell place and made a phone call. Ambulance got here pretty fast."

"A lucky thing for that driver. And for me."

Boldin drove in silence for a few moments. Then he asked, "You said something about feeling somebody push you, back there. Did you really mean that?"

"I did. It was two hands. I couldn't be mistaken about that. I felt them distinctly."

No need to tell him about the hand that had caught her ankle a week ago, that had sought to drown her. Glancing at him out of the corners of her eyes, she could read the disbelief in his face. Beth felt resentment stir inside her.

"It wasn't any tree branch, as that intern said, Mr. Boldin. I guess I can tell the difference between a branch and a pair of hands."

"But why would anybody want to hurt you? Doesn't make sense."

"Just the same, it happened."

He gave her an odd look from under his bushy eyebrows. Beth Sheldon had lived for the past five years in this little backwater part of the country. She knew the clannishness of the local residents, whose grandparents, for the most part, had lived in the same houses they now inhabited. They had a news grapevine, too, and she had no doubts but that her story would be all over Rocky Cove before tomorrow noon.

She could imagine the pitying looks she would get. The old-maid writer, the one who keeps to herself so much, back there in the woods along Hollow Road, is finally cracking up, they would say. Maybe she was, at that, she reflected ruefully.

Beth tightened her lips. She had felt those hands, just as she had felt fingers around her ankle. Someone wanted her dead. She was convinced of that, but she knew well enough she would never convince Abraham Boldin—or any of the local people—of this fact. They lived their lives in a calm little circle which shut out a lot of what went on in the world. Well, as a writer, she herself lived in an even tighter little circle.

The headlights picked out a white picket fence and a mailbox, and Boldin put a foot on the brake. He pulled up before the gate and turned to look at her.

"Here you are. I'd advise you to get a good night's sleep. You'll feel better about all this in the morning."

The voice of common sense. She nodded, giving him a brief smile, and reached for the door handle. "I want to thank you for everything, Mr. Boldin. You've been a real hero."

He chuckled. "Wife'll be on my neck soon's I get home. I'm way past my proper time. She'll have me dead by the side of the road if I don't hurry."

She hesitated as she stepped to the ground. "Should I call her, tell her you're on the way?"

He grinned, shaking his head. "Doubt there's any need for that. 'Less I miss my guess, Ada Cantrell's been talking to her already. She heard me phone the hospital and the police to report the accident."

"The police," Beth repeated.

"Hank Layne was there and gone by the time you came to. He had your name and address, I gave it to him. He'll likely stop by to see you tomorrow."

Beth frowned. "Shouldn't he have stayed to make sure I was all right before he left?"

"He went off with the ambulance that held the driver. Had to get him on an operating table fast." Boldin gave a grim smile. "Only one police car in these parts, anyhow. Not as if we were a big city."

One police car, yes. And one police officer—Big Hank Layne in his khaki uniform with the broad leather belt around his stout middle and the gun butt protruding from his holster. Hank drove that lone car along the country roads every so often, when he wasn't sleeping with his feet propped up on his desk in the town jailhouse office. Beth smiled. What need had Rocky Cove for more police cars or more police officers?

She wondered vaguely who the driver of the car had been, that he was considered so important they would bring a specialist up from Boston, and need the services of Hank Layne to get him onto a hospital operating table as fast as possible. She opened her mouth to ask Abraham Boldin, but he put his pickup truck in gear just at that moment, and the meshing of the ancient gears drowned out her voice. She watched the truck move off into the dark night.

Beth lifted the gate-latch as she entered the flagstone path that wound between the tulip borders toward the front door. She moved up the path at a fast walk, not wanting to stay outside in the darkness longer than she must. She would have to rearrange her schedule so she could walk during the daylight hours, instead of after the moon had risen.

She had liked the starlit nights and the big ball of moon that hung above the treetops, however. These spring nights were so calm and peaceful, she had reveled in them. But that was before tonight.

The door opened to her key, and her hand reached for the switch. The light was warm and comforting, showing her the hooked rug, the couch and easy chair, the two big bookcases, the hanging baskets holding her Swedish ivy, the grape ivy, and fuschia. She glanced around the room as if to reassure herself of her own safety, then closed and locked the door, sliding home the bolt.

She moved from the enclosed porch into the living room, and through it into her bedroom. She wanted hot cocoa and a cigarette, but before these, she needed to get out of her clothes and into a warm, woolly bathrobe. As she walked, she hit all the light switches until the cottage blazed.

Pulling down the shades, she slid out of her clothes and examined her bruised shoulder in the bathroom mirror. The flesh was black and blue, and felt sore, but she could move the shoulder without too much difficulty. She noted also that her left arm was also turning dark here and there.

As she had been shoved forward, her left arm and shoulder must have struck the right fender or bumper of the car. It had been only a glancing blow—she remembered the shriek of brakes as the driver had tried to avoid her—or she might not be standing here. She made a face at herself, reaching for the flannel pajamas and woollen bathrobe she had placed on the clothes hamper.

"You're no threat to anyone," she told her reflection. "So why should anyone want you dead?"

There was no answer to that, or if there was one, she couldn't think of it.

She went on staring into the mirror, seeing a face framed by rich brown hair, dominated by large brown eyes and an overgenerous mouth. Her lashes were very long—they seemed almost like tiny fans to her—and with the rich brown of her eyebrows and her thick hair, gave her the appearance of a woods dryad, or what she imagined a woods dryad might look like. A man had once told her there was an elfin quality to her features, but Beth thought them rather plain and ordinary.

Sighing, she eased into her flannel pajamas and bathrobe.

The hot cocoa tasted so delicious, she had two cups. Vaguely Beth understood that it was not the cocoa so much as it was the peace and serenity of her own kitchen, where she was quite safe, that induced this warm, cozy feeling inside her. She sipped slowly, letting herself relax, trying to think of the book on which she was working, planning out her next day of work.

When her eyelids began to droop, she said, "Enough. It's time to hit the sack."

She gathered up the cup and saucer, and put them in the sink. She would clean them tomorrow, with the breakfast dishes. Half asleep, she trudged through the cottage, switching off the lights until only her bedtable lamp still glowed.

Sliding out of the heavy robe, she eased herself between the sheets and pulled the covers up over her ears. She sighed, nestled herself more comfortably, and was asleep. She dreamed of cars endlessly chasing her through an eerie woodland, of stumbling and falling, of hands shoving her this way and that, but always in front of the oncoming cars.

Twice she woke in the night, sitting up and staring around her, realizing that these were only dreams. Then she settled back to slumber. When a stray sunbeam touched her eyes she woke, stretched lazily, and lay a moment, contemplating the ceiling.

As always, her mind went to the book she had almost completed. Another few weeks and it should be ready for her publisher. Usually, she mailed out her manuscripts to her agent, but she rather thought that this time she would drive them to New York, to present it in person.

It would give her a chance to get away from whoever wanted to kill her.

She threw back the bedclothes and ran for the shower, dropping the flannel pajamas on the way. Warm water and soap and a brisk toweling gave her a sense of well-being.

"Bacon and eggs today, my girl," she told herself. "I find that I am ravenous."

The bacon was frying crisply when the doorbell rang. Wondering who could be calling on her at such an early hour, she turned off the gas, wiped her hands on a towel, and walked toward the front door.

A tall man with graying hair, clad in an impeccably tailored corduroy suit with a print tie against a solid pink shirt, stood on the tiny stoop. Beth stared at him, realizing that she had never seen him before. Her hands went to the lock to open the door, when she realized that her life was still in danger.

"That's nonsense," she muttered in vexation. "A man like this isn't going to hurt me."

His smile was broad and friendly as the door swung open. "Miss Beth Sheldon?"

"I'm Beth Sheldon. But I don't know you."

He took out his wallet, extracted a card, and handed it to her. It read: Bertram K. Lambkin, Attorney-at-Law. His office was located in Boston. From the card, Beth's eyes lifted toward the man himself.

"This is going to be very sudden, Miss Sheldon. I represent Neal Harper and—he wants to marry you."

Chapter Two

Beth stared at him, not believing what she had heard. Suddenly she felt that his eyes were reading her thoughts. They were sharp and inquiring as he held up a hand to forestall anything she might say.

"This is very sudden, quite mad, perhaps, from your point of view. But believe me, my client makes the offer in utter seriousness."

"You *are* mad," Beth declared. "I don't know any Neal Harper, and I'm not in the least interested in getting married. Especially not to a kook."

Lambkin chuckled. "I can't say I blame you. I protested his decision as best I could, not from any doubts as to your eligibility of being his wife—since I had never met you—but solely from the point of view of my client's welfare."

Beth shook herself. "Won't you come in? After all, we can't talk about marriage on my doorstep, as if you were selling—well, soap or brushes."

She felt an insane desire to giggle. This was ridiculous! It was like that dream last night, when cars had been chasing her all over the place. Maybe she was still dreaming. She stepped back and moved her hand invitingly.

Bertram Lambkin stepped into the porch, running his gaze

over the furnishings with approval. He seated himself in the easy chair, leaving her the couch.

Beth said, "Who is Neal Harper, to begin with? And why does he want to marry me?"

"He was the driver of the car that knocked you down last night."

Beth exclaimed, "Oh! Oh my goodness. How—how is he?"

Lambkin looked grim. "He's dying, I'm sorry to say. Oh, they're going to operate on him—Donovan's there already, he flew in early this morning with me—but there's little or no hope."

Beth stared at the man. He seemed sane, in full possession of his faculties. She shook her head hopelessly.

"If he's so badly off, why would he even think about marriage?"

"He wants to make last night up to you. It's the only way he knows how. Yes, yes. It's sudden, quixotic. Mad, even, as I suggested. But that's the way Neal is."

He frowned, then went on. "Neal was conscious when I was allowed to see him, about an hour ago. They're going to operate on him this morning, of course. That's why he insisted I come over to see you right away. He didn't know whether you were married or not. I made inquiries and discovered you aren't."

He gave Beth a big, charming smile, to which she responded with a faint quirk of her own lips. She said slowly, "This is the silliest thing I've ever heard of. It's completely out of the question. I have no desire to marry anybody. I'm quite happy as I am."

"You would be even happier as his widow. Neal Harper is a disgustingly rich young man. He's one of *the* Harpers."

He spoke as if she should know the Harpers. Well, Beth reflected, she didn't and had no desire to—no, wait. There was a Harper House a few miles away, up on the ridge that overlooked all of Rocky Cove, the surrounding countryside, and the sea.

"Harper House," she murmured slowly.

"That's the family residence, yes. Neal runs the family businesses, which are many and varied. He's a bachelor, a very eligible bachelor, I might add, and something of a—well, I suppose the term is playboy."

"And you want me to marry him."

"I don't. He does."

Beth shook her head. This whole business was too fantastic for words. It was out of the question, naturally. She had never loved any man, had never even thought of marrying. She had been on her own for so long that she felt quite independent, quite capable of taking care of herself. She had absolutely no wish to take care of a man.

She was about to stand and declare this little talk at an end, when Lambkin spoke again. "Please. Don't rush into any hasty decisions."

Beth stared at him. "You can't be serious. Look, Mr. Lambkin. You seem to be a sensible man in full possession of your faculties. If some woman had knocked you down with her auto and had crashed it, was in danger of dying and wanted to marry you, would you say yes?"

The lawyer chuckled. "If I weren't married and the woman was as rich as Neal Harper, I'd give it some thought."

"Suppose this Neal Harper gets better?" she asked suspiciously.

Lambkin looked grim. "Unfortunately, there's not much chance of that, unless Donovan can pull off a medical miracle."

"Somebody mentioned this Donovan last night. Just who is he?"

"One of the greatest surgeons ever born. His scalpel, some men have said, is a magic one. He would do anything for the Harpers. Grandfather Harper put Augustus Donovan through medical school, when he was just a poor Irish orphan. He has never forgotten."

"And if he saves Neal Harper?"

Lambkin smiled. "Then you can get a divorce. Free of charge. Neal will pay for it, and will settle a very handsome sum on you. Half a million, at the least."

"He's a nut. An utter idiot."

The lawyer frowned. "Actually, he's a brilliant man. Oh, he has his eccentric moments—this is one of them—but don't get the wrong impression of Neal Harper. He always knows just what he's doing."

"Except now."

"He was completely sane when I left him. Dying, yes. But

his mind was very clear. He gave me instructions about a number of deals I am to handle for him in his absence. And then he mentioned you.

" 'I want to make it up to her,' he said, and waved aside all my objections. I did object, Miss Sheldon—strenuously."

Beth laughed. "Good. You're on my side."

Lambkin chuckled. "Neal said he'd never done anything for anyone except himself all his life. Before he died, he wanted to do one good deed."

"If he's afraid of a lawsuit, tell him to forget it. My shoulder and arm are bruised, but other than those injuries, I'm really fine. It was only a glancing blow."

"Neal's thoroughly covered by insurance. He isn't worried about any lawsuit. This is something special, for him. It's his way of making up for all the silly things he's done in the past."

"This isn't silly?" Beth yelped.

"Not to him. He's determined to marry you. If you had been there and seen him, talked to him, you'd have understood."

Beth shook her head. "Well, I wasn't and there's no sense in talking about it anymore. Tell the man I'm flattered and grateful, but it's no go. I won't marry him."

She stood up. After a moment, during which he scanned her features very closely, Bertram Lambkin also rose. She read the sympathy and understanding in his face, and also a stubborn determination.

"Think about it," he said quietly. "It won't be much of a sacrifice, you know. It isn't as if the man's going to live. You will be a wealthy widow, accountable to no one."

She was indignant. "I'd be benefiting because of a man's death. How can you ask me to do such a thing?"

"On the contrary, you'd be doing Neal a favor. You'd be letting him die with the knowledge that he's done at least one good deed in his life."

"You make him out to be a monster."

"I don't mean to. Neal Harper has two sides to his character. On one side, he is—well, the complete businessman, sharp, clever, with a knowledge of finance that few of us possess. On the other, perhaps it's just that he needs relaxation, but he does the most outlandish things.

"For instance, he takes over girls, when they interest him, as though he had created them. He plies them with furs, with diamonds, with cars. And then he drops them suddenly, without a word of explanation."

"If you think that endears him to me, you're mistaken," Beth said dryly.

"He also races cars in the Indianapolis 500, and he races boats, too. He seems to have an almost reckless disregard for his own life."

"He was doing eighty along that country road last night."

"You see? Sometimes I think he has a death wish. His family has tried to make him marry and settle down. Always, until now, he has avoided marriage like the plague."

"He's still avoiding it, because I'm not about to marry him. Tell him that, if you'll be so good. Now I must go back to my breakfast. I have to finish a book, and I have no more time for Neal Harper."

Lambkin sighed, looked grim, then shrugged. "I've done what I could. Neal doesn't like failure. I don't know how he'll take this."

"Then don't tell him."

She stood and watched the lawyer walk toward the glistening Mark Continental parked in front of her gate. She waited until he pulled away before she went back to the kitchen and turned the gas on under the half-cooked bacon.

What an odd man this Neal Harper must be! To ask a perfect stranger to marry him, without having so much as seen her. He couldn't have had more than a glimpse of her flying body as she had been thrust toward his car last night. Marry her, indeed. The man really was a kook.

She scrambled two eggs, made toast, then feasted slowly. She enjoyed two cups of coffee, smoking two cigarettes with them. She had been eager to get to her book, but she found her mind wandering to the man in the hospital bed and the lawyer who had come to ask her to marry him.

She was sorry for him, but she could never marry him. It was too insane even to consider. Of course, if she married him and he died, she would become very rich and would never have to depend on her writings to earn a livelihood. It was a nice thought, but a foolish one.

Determinedly she washed the dishes, dried them, put them

away, then went into the little room off the living room that was her den, her workshop.

Her desk was set before a large bay window that gave her golden sunlight in the morning and enough light in the afternoon, except on gray days, so that she didn't have to turn on the electrics. Her typewriter was placed on an angle of the desk, within easy reach of her fingers. Her notes and research books stood on a small table on the other side of the desk.

There were bookshelves along all the walls, Eric Sloane and Andrew Wyeth prints above them, and an easy chair where she read at night. It was not a large room, but it was pleasant and comfortable. She had written well in this room. Inside it, she felt cut off from the world. She lived only in the pages she was typing, amid the characters she was creating.

She sat now and examined her notes. After a few minutes, she swung around to her Remington and began to type.

Two hours later she rose, poured coffee for herself from the morning pot, and smoked a cigarette as she read over what she had written. She made corrections, then began to type again.

It was a little past one when she was finished. She pushed back from the desk, rose, and stretched, telling herself she needed a good, long walk. She was not going out at night anymore, so she would slip into her Hush Puppies now and wander up near the cliffs.

She was still wearing the slacks and pullover she had donned after her shower, thinking then that they would be fine for hiking. She reached for the blackthorn stick and locked the front door behind her.

It was one of those beautiful spring afternoons, with the sky a cerulean blue without a speck of cloud in it. The air had lost its winter bite but was still cool, though the sun on her back warmed her as she tramped along.

After a time, she regretted having skipped lunch.

When she came to the clifftop, she sat on a flat stone and let her eyes run over the sea. Her gaze was drawn to Capstone Rock, perhaps five hundred yards out. It was one of a number of jagged stone giants that thrust a path into the ocean, and was reputed to be an excellent spot to avoid, either in a motorboat or sailboat. The tricky currents had smashed more than one hull there in the past.

She herself, when she did scuba diving, had used a rowboat rented from the Johnson marina. She had wanted to verify an underwater sensation for the book she was doing, and it had been a sensation all right, her experience there.

After a time the cool seawind bit through her sweater. She rose and began the long walk back to the cottage. As she came in sight of it, she saw a man standing in a copse of trees, studying the cottage.

Beth froze.

Was this the one who had pushed her into Neal Harper's car last night? Terror ran along her veins, making her shiver and dart sideways behind a tall oak tree. After a few moments, the man moved off, cutting between tree boles and out of her view.

He had been tall, very husky, with long brown hair and, she thought, a beard. As far as she knew, she had never seen him before. But there had been something very menacing, very dangerous in the way he had stood so quietly, never removing his stare from her little house.

Beth half ran the rest of the way back, and did not relax until she had closed and locked the cottage door behind her. She leaned against the wooden panelings, eyes closed, and tried to control her hurried breathing.

This was intolerable. She could not go on living like this, on the edge of disaster every day, and night. She must do something, anything, that would guarantee her safety.

She walked to the kitchen, took out a cooked chicken from the refrigerator, and made herself a sandwich. As she was eating, she thought of Neal Harper.

He would have been operated on by this time. Either Augustus Donovan and his magic scalpel would have cured him or would have failed. Beth scowled. She supposed she ought to phone the hospital to find out whether the operation was a success or not. After all, the man had proposed to her.

She began to giggle. It was all so nonsensical!

After she had eaten and put away the dishes, she lifted the phone and dialed the hospital. "I'm calling about Neal Harper. He was operated on this morning. I was wondering if the operation was a success."

"I'm sorry," a crisp voice replied. "I'm not at liberty to

give out any information except that Neal Harper is in intensive care."

She thanked the voice and hung up. She had made an effort, at least, and felt better for it.

She spent the remainder of the afternoon in the easy chair in the den, reading. Twice she was startled by sounds from the woods around the cottage, and once she went to a window and looked out, thinking she had seen movement.

"I'm like a prisoner here," she told herself. "I don't dare go out, and even when I'm inside the house, I think I see things."

In a sober mood, she prepared supper. Tomorrow she would have to drive into town and replenish her supplies. She was running short of eggs, bread, and canned soups. The prospect of going into town did not please her, as it usually did. What was to prevent that man who had pushed her, who had spied on her cottage, from causing a serious accident tomorrow? An accident in which she might be killed.

At nine o'clock, her phone rang.

It was Bertram Lambkin on the other end. He said, "Neal's dying, Miss Sheldon. Won't you please reconsider your decision? He can't possibly last through tomorrow."

"Oh, really, Mr. Lambkin."

Did he sense the strain in her? The uncertainty? Suddenly he was murmuring, "I'm coming right over to see you. Please let me in. We can talk, and this time I think I can convince you that you'll do well to let Neal marry you."

Before she could reply, he hung up.

Beth scowled angrily, staring at the phone in her hand. She wasn't going to marry the guy, that lawyer was just wasting his time. She was of half a mind to get undressed, get into the tub, and not answer the doorbell.

Still, if Lambkin were here, nobody would make any attempt to break into the house and kill her. Beth felt a little better about his calling, and she even sang as she went to the cupboard where she kept a few bottles of wine and a fifth of Scotch for occasional callers. She wondered if Bertram Lambkin were a drinking man. Or Neal Harper, for that matter.

When the doorbell rang, she was almost cheerful.

"Come in, come in," she exclaimed, glancing past the lawyer at the darkness beyond him. "What will you have to drink?"

"Nothing, thank you."

He was in a subdued mood. There was none of that charm with which he had plied her earlier in the day. He sat rather heavily in the same chair he had occupied earlier, and put his hands on his thighs.

"I've been a busy man, Miss Sheldon," he stated. "I've been drawing up legal papers, I've been pulling strings, I've been at my wits' end, frankly, trying to get things done. I'm tired, I'm not a young man any more, and all I can think about is bed."

Beth smiled faintly. "Yet you're here."

The lawyer sighed. "It's my last port of call. I'm here to tell you that Neal Harper will settle a hundred thousand dollars in your name as soon as you marry him. No matter what happens. The hundred thousand is yours. All you have to do to earn it is go through the legal ceremony of marriage."

Beth could not breathe. She sat up, taking gulps of air. Her thoughts were all tangled up, and she just couldn't straighten them out.

"Tax-free, naturally. It will be a once-in-a-lifetime gift. Invested properly, it will bring you in a yearly income of nine thousand dollars, or close to it. Perhaps more."

Beth felt her throat constrict. "I could go away from here," she said softly. "I could live anywhere."

And under any name she chose. She would be able to escape the threat that hovered over her. That man could go on watching the cottage until his hair turned white and he would never lay eyes on her again.

Lambkin smiled. "You seem to be a thrifty young woman. Living here, eight or nine thousand dollars a year would be all the money you'd ever need."

"You make it very tempting."

"Good. But not tempting enough?"

She shook her head. "Give me a chance, please," she exclaimed, and laughed, clasping her hands. Her eyes glowed, and there was color in her cheeks. Then she hesitated. "Isn't there some sort of law about waiting a few days before getting married? I'm not up on this, I admit, but—"

"Everything's been taken care of. I have a judge's order permitting the marriage. I told you I was busy."

Money can accomplish anything, she thought. It could even save her life. There would be no need for her to cower here in fear any longer, no need to be frightened of long walks, of men watching her house.

"Let me get you a drink. Please," she exclaimed.

He smiled, settled back, nodded his head. "If you have it, Scotch on the rocks. I could use a drink now, I believe."

She ran into the kitchen, her heart pounding. A hundred thousand, all hers. Eight thousand dollars a year income. Just by saying a few words before a justice of the peace. It was ridiculous, but she would be stupid to turn down such an offer.

Her hand shook as she poured Black and White over ice cubes in an old-fashioned glass, but she did not spill a drop. She would permit herself a glass of burgundy at the same time, to celebrate. She lifted the tray and carried it out to the porch.

"To your happiness," Lambkin murmured, lifting his glass.

"And to my future husband," she found herself saying.

Her future husband, poor guy, was going to die tomorrow. Beth felt suddenly sad. She had never met Neal Harper, but no matter what he was like, or what he had been, he deserved something better than a loveless marriage.

She sipped the wine, feeling very much like a heartless opportunist. "It isn't right, my doing this," she said slowly. "Oh, I don't mean marrying this man. I have nobody to answer to, what I do is my own business. But taking money for it smacks so much of—of commercialism, of greed, that . . ."

Her words trailed off. Lambkin smiled at her above his glass. "You're doing the man a favor, believe me. He can die in peace, knowing you'll be well cared for."

"All right," she muttered. "I'll do it. I don't like the idea, but—oh, damn it. I'll tell the truth. I can use that money to get away from here and never come back."

The lawyer said, "I spoke to the ambulance people this morning. They said you claimed somebody pushed you into the car." He drew a deep breath. "Are you afraid, Miss Sheldon? Will the money help you run away from that danger?"

Beth nodded miserably. Hers would be a marriage between a man who was dying and a woman who was going to die unless she married him. She wondered if any other marriage had been arranged under such circumstances.

Chapter Three

He lay like a dead man, swathed in bandages. His face was partially covered, and his features were bruised and swollen, so that it was hard for Beth to get any indication of what he looked like. A ripple of pity ran through her, so sharp that she almost turned and fled. It seemed so heartless, so macabre, this marriage which was to take place.

In a whisper, she asked Bertram Lambkin, "Are you sure he wants to go through with this? I—I feel as if I'm taking unfair advantage of him."

"Please . . ."

It was the man in the bed who spoke, barely above a murmur. Beth turned and stared down at him. Was it her fancy, or were his lips smiling, under all the bandages and bruises?

"It will make me happy, very happy."

Tears came into her eyes. The poor thing! No matter if he was a kook, or mad. It was his dying wish to marry her, to make her his wife. She could only respect his desire, see it through.

She had spent last night tossing sleeplessly in her bed, wondering if she were doing the right thing. Even after she made the decision to do as the lawyer asked, she was still filled with doubts and foreboding. If her life had not been in danger, she

27

would never have consented. But that hundred thousand dollars—it meant so much to her! Actually, it meant her life.

"You're a heartless, greedy woman, Beth Sheldon," she had muttered as she turned over and drew the covers closer.

But right now she did not feel that way. She was doing what this poor wreck of a man wanted. What did it matter, a few words before the justice of the peace, who was talking in low tones to a doctor in the background? So she would be a widow in a few days. At least, Neal Harper would die happy.

She reached out a hand to him, then drew it back as if afraid she might hurt him. She nodded vigorously, not trusting herself to speak. Twice she swallowed before she said, "Yes, yes. Of course. Don't worry about a thing."

The doctor came forward with the justice; there was also a nurse there, who would be a witness. As the doctor nodded, Beth reached down and caught Neal Harper by his fingers. She was surprised at how warm they were, and how strong. They tightened on her hand, gripping it hard.

She answered the questions the justice of the peace put to her, then listened as Neal Harper gave his replies. It was the lawyer who produced the wedding ring—a circlet of pure white diamonds—and slipped it onto her finger.

"I now pronounce you man and wife."

It was done, over with. There would be no more soul-searching, no more doubts. She was Mrs. Neal Harper. It was an accomplished fact.

Beth hesitated, then bent forward. Her eyes met his eyes, hidden in the shadow of bandages and bruises. He was staring up at her quizzically, and his fingers gripped her hand even harder.

As she straightened up, flushing faintly, the doctor was saying, "I think that will be enough. I would have forbidden this marriage except for the fact that the patient insisted on it so vehemently that I thought it might be best to humor him."

The bandaged man muttered, "I'm going to die anyhow, doc. What's a few hours, more or less?"

The doctor and the nurse moved them out of the room, together with the justice of the peace. Lambkin paid the justice, then brought back the marriage certificate to Beth.

"You might as well have it. It won't do Neal any good."

She nodded, putting it into her handbag. She had dressed very carefully for the wedding, choosing a satin silk crepe in white with navy blue bodice and matching accessories. Something told her that Neal Harper had approved of this. It really didn't matter, but after all, he was marrying her, so she had felt obliged to look her best.

"The check will be along in a few days."

Beth lifted her head and looked up at the lawyer. "The check? Oh!"

The hundred thousand dollars.

She said slowly, "I wouldn't take the money, you understand, if—well, if I didn't need it so much."

The lawyer smiled gently and patted her hand. "You'll have more use for it than Neal."

They said a few more words, then Beth walked out into the sunshine, looking around her at the parked cars, the white walls of Memorial Hospital, telling herself she didn't feel any different than she had an hour ago, when she hadn't had a husband.

Actually, she supposed, she still didn't have one.

Except in name. And he was going to die soon. In a few days, a week. Certainly he couldn't live any longer than that. Again, she felt pity stab deep inside her, and tears came up into her eyes.

She walked toward her maroon Ford Pinto, which she had insisted on driving over to the hospital this morning, when Bertram Lambkin had come to call for her. He was a busy man, she had pointed out; he had better things to do than drive the bride back home.

She drove home slowly, feeling vaguely let down. There should have been *some* sort of celebration, a wedding breakfast or at least a bottle of champagne to drink the health of bride and groom.

Beth made a face. How stupid could she be? It would have been more than slightly gauche to drink Neal Harper's health. Still, she had an empty sensation in the pit of her stomach. Something was missing.

"You're hungry," she announced to herself. "It's past eleven o'clock and you haven't eaten, and you miss your food."

On an impulse she pulled in to the Fife and Drum, a local

restaurant on the road to Rocky Cove. She had come here before when she had felt the need to get out of the house, to taste a meal cooked by someone other than herself. There would be a marriage breakfast after all, even if the only one there was the bride herself.

Ooops. She still wore the white lace bridal veil that she had made this morning, when the mirror had told her silently that something was missing. She removed it, slid it into the glove compartment, and fluffed up her hair.

Nancy, the waitress who usually served her, widened her eyes at the sight of her. "Well, we're dressed up today. What's the occasion?"

She wanted to say that she had just been married, that she was about to receive a check for a hundred thousand dollars, but she had grave doubts as to how Nancy would receive such news. With whoops of uncontrollable laughter, no doubt.

"Nothing special," she announced. "I just wanted to doll up and get away from the house."

Nancy nodded soberly. "I get that feeling myself every so often."

She lingered over melon, scrambled eggs and bacon, then several cups of coffee. She didn't want the breakfast to end. Her eyes caught the diamond circlet on her finger, and she studied it, wondering how much it had cost. A pretty penny, no doubt. She had the feeling that Neal Harper never did anything by halves. Fortunately, Nancy hadn't noticed it, or if she had, thought it was some dime store gewgaw.

Just the same, Beth tucked it away in her handbag.

She drove home slowly, wanting to stretch out the hours. There was work waiting for her at the cottage, a book to finish. She had wasted enough time already. It was time she forgot Neal Harper.

For the next few weeks, Beth threw herself into a frenzy of production. Her fingers flew across the typewriter keys as she all but locked herself in her den from nine in the morning until one in the afternoon. She had lunch, forcing herself to eat in the kitchen or, on warm days, on the flagstone patio that looked out across a stretch of woodland toward the sea.

After lunch she walked up and down the road for close to an hour, carrying her blackthorn stick. She was wary on these walks, eying the woods on either side of her, poised to flee as fast as she could run if she caught a glimpse of that long-haired, bearded man she had seen watching the cottage.

Yet nothing happened. It was as if her marriage had dispelled the threat that hung over her. Still, she didn't lower her caution. In another week the book would be done, and she would be off to New York.

Time slid by very swiftly. One morning Beth woke, remembered that she was a married woman, and wondered if her husband were still alive. After breakfast she telephoned the hospital. Neal Harper was still alive. No, there was nothing else the informant could add.

Beth wondered if she should go to see him.

She decided against that, after much thought. After all, she wasn't a loving wife, she had only married the guy because he had insisted on it, as a sort of death wish. If she showed up at the hospital, his family might begin to think she was after more than the hundred thousand dollars. Beth didn't want that, not at all. As for that money, she had deposited the check in the local bank, explaining to the manager that she was going to invest it after seeking financial help in New York.

Strange, she didn't feel like a rich woman. The money was there, that was all. Oh, she daydreamed about it from time to time—she wouldn't have been human if she didn't. But the book was taking so much of her time and thought these days, she hadn't much time even for daydreaming.

As she worked, she had the uneasy feeling that Neal Harper was taking a long time dying. Even as she did, she scolded herself for being heartless. The doctor had said he would die in a week. Well, he was still alive after several weeks.

Was he going to live?

She wanted him to live. Didn't she?

"Of course I do," she exclaimed aloud.

Just the same . . .

She had to put him out of her mind and finish this book. Only one chapter left, another few days. She reached for her pile of notes and forced herself to concentrate on them.

On the day she finally finished her manuscript, she packed her two Ventura valises, phoned the hospital again to be told Neal Harper was still alive, and drove into town to cash a check for a thousand dollars. She was going to be in New York for two whole months, and she had decided to buy herself some new clothes for the trip around the world she would take to escape the menace to her life. And she wanted to get financial advice, on what to do with her hundred thousand dollars.

She drove down U.S. 95 on a glorious day. The sun was out, the flowers in the fields were blossoming brilliantly, and she was at peace with the world. In two months she would come back and settle her affairs.

She lunched at the Publick House in Sturbridge, and arrived in New York around six. She drove to her hotel, gave the car to an attendant and her bags to a bellboy, and walked into the St. Moritz. She would have a shower, dress for dinner, enjoy a lazy meal, and then climb into bed around ten. She ought to be bright-eyed and bushy-tailed, come morning, after such a sleep.

The months that followed were like living in a fairy tale. She turned over her manuscript to her agent and worked on revisions with her. She was recommended to a financial analyst at Merrill Lynch, who took her to dinner and showed her around town as soon as he learned she had a hundred thousand dollars to invest. And in between times, she haunted Saks Fifth Avenue, Bergdorf Goodman, and Bonwit Teller, establishing charge accounts at each store.

She spent over three thousand dollars on clothes.

Alone in her room, Beth Sheldon told herself she must be crazy. Three thousand dollars! Still, those evening gowns and casual skirts, the blouses and pants suits had really made her lose her normal cool. She would be able to hold her own with any traveler, now.

Of course, such garments would be wasted in Rocky Cove. Who knew or cared that this suede coat and this handbag were Gucci's, that this cocktail gown was by Valentino, and that plaid skirt with solid brown blouse had been created by Pierre Cardin?

"I'll know," she muttered mutinously, lower lip protruding.

She also picked up circulars from travel agencies, to study in her hotel room. Beth wasn't sure just where she wanted to go. She had always wanted to visit England, because some of her novels for children were placed there. And Ireland, of course. She had a vague idea of green fields overlaid with mist and little stone houses seen like playthings in the distance whenever she thought of Ireland. And Italy. Yes, most definitely, Italy.

But she needed time to think, to make up her itinerary.

The two months went by all too fast. At breakfast on the morning of her departure, she could not believe that her holiday was over. At least she didn't have to worry about another plot, another book. She had plenty of money now. It was a warm feeling.

In that same mood she walked out to her car, tipped the bellboy who placed her bags in the trunk and the attendant who had fetched the car, and eased the Pinto out into traffic. She drove carefully, disliking the city traffic, breathing with relief once she was on the Major Deegan Expressway. She decided to avoid the New England Thruway; she would take the more scenic Merritt Parkway and U.S. 95.

She let the cars go by her, since she was in no hurry. She would be home soon enough, faced by the man or men who had sought to kill her. She had put all thoughts of them out of her head in New York. He or they had seemed far away, almost nonexistent, while she had been so busy with her agent, her financial analyst, and her shopping trips. Now she was on her way back to danger.

But she wouldn't stay long at the cottage—just for a day or two. Long enough to make up her mind where she wanted to travel to, and to make the necessary arrangements. Maybe she'd even put the cottage up for sale.

It was dusk when she arrived home.

The cottage seemed very much the same, but there was something odd about it. Beth paused with her bags halfway out of the car trunk to stare and stare again. The grass had been mowed, her flowerbeds neatly weeded.

Beth put down the bags, frowning. What good neighbor had done this for her? Abe Boldin? Hardly. Nor any of the other people she knew in Rocky Cove. Puzzled, she went into the cottage, turned on lights, and caught her breath.

There was no dust anywhere. Her plants had been watered, too.

"I don't like this," she told the living room.

Fear touched her for an instant. Had that bearded man

made himself free in here? But no. Certainly not. Besides, he wouldn't mow the lawn and water her ivy and fuschia for her. Not when he was expecting to kill her.

She closed the door carefully and locked it.

There now. She was home again, back with all the fright and uncertainty that had come so recently into her life. She put away her things, took a long, lazy shower, and slipped into a nylon tricot mini-gown that was little more than a wisp of black fluff, almost transparent. It had cost her plenty, but she had been unable to refuse it.

She pivoted before the bedroom mirror, saying, "You're a shameless hussy, Elizabeth Sheldon."

She was all alone, so there was nobody to see her in this excuse for a nightgown. Still, she reached for the matching robe that covered her a little more, but not much. She pranced into the kitchen, made herself a sandwich of the bread and cold cuts she had bought at the local delly, and brewed a pot of coffee.

She had just finished half the sandwich when the front doorbell rang.

Beth yelped and dropped the sandwich. Who could that be, coming here at this hour? She jumped up, ran into the living room.

"Who is it?" she called.

"Come on, open up."

Her heart thudded. It was that prowler, the bearded man who had watched the cottage, who had probably pushed her in front of Neal Harper's car.

"Go away or I'll call the police!"

She was reaching for the telephone when she saw the door opening slowly. She was so shocked that she stood motionless, staring, forgetting the phone in her hand, unable to do anything but concentrate on that slowly moving door.

A man stood there, smiling at her.

He was handsome, with black hair and sideburns, and gray eyes that seemed to take her in with one slow, almost lazy glance. His lips were wide and rather full. He was dressed in a blue, pin-stripe suit with a shirt of raised satin and jacquard stripes, fronted by a Givenchy tie. He was not the man who wanted to kill her, Beth thought dully.

But she had never seen him before.

"Go away," she whispered.

Her hand waved the phone at him, as though the sight of it might frighten him. She backed away, carrying the phone as he advanced into the living room.

"What do you want?" she whispered.

"Just to have a look at you. You're rather pretty, you know." His head tilted and he smiled again. It was a friendly grin, and it eased a little of her panic. "As a matter of fact, you're more than pretty. You're almost beautiful."

"Oh, am I? *Almost* beautiful?"

What was the matter with her? What was she waiting for? She had the phone in her hand—all she had to do was dial Big Hank Layne. Instead, she stood here like a ninny, eyes fastened on this tall stranger who was so much at ease.

He spread his hands and looked apologetic. "Very well, then. Very beautiful. Does that make you feel any happier?"

Her chin tilted. "I think you'd better get out of here. This farce has gone on long enough. If you don't, I really will call the police."

"Why?" he asked, obviously curious.

"Because this is my house and you don't belong in it. Oh, why am I making explanations to you?"

He sat down in the leather chair to one side of the fire-place and crossed his legs at the ankles. His eyes went around the room, from the big sofa to the flower stands, to the coffee table, to the bookshelves built into the wall on either side of the mantel.

"Yes, I'm going to like this cottage. Very much. It's quite homey, quite comfortable."

Beth gaped at him. Then, determinedly, she pulled her stare away from him and glanced at the phone. Carefully she inserted her finger and began to dial.

"I wouldn't, if I were you," he said conversationally.

"And why not?"

"What are you going to tell the police?"

"That you're trespassing."

"I don't think Hank will agree with you."

Suspiciously she asked, "Oh? And why not?"

"Because I have every right to be here. I'm your husband. Neal Harper."

The phone fell from her nerveless fingers as she backed up

two paces until the edge of the sofa was behind her knees. She sat down abruptly.

"You're Neal Ha-Harper?"

He grinned good-naturedly, "I forgot. Last time you saw me, I had bandages all over my face. No wonder you didn't recognize me."

"But—you're supposed to be dead. I mean—that is, the doctor said—said you weren't going to live."

"Gus Donovan is magic with a scalpel and some thread. He sewed me up inside, fixed my busted ribs and such, and—*voilà!*"

She could not breathe. It was as if someone had her around the windpipe and was slowly choking her. This was not believable, what was happening. This man before her had no right to be alive. He should be dead. In some vague way, she felt cheated.

Yet she had to be sensible about this. She was happy that he was alive. Yes, she was. She remembered her tears of pity in the hospital on her wedding day. Her wedding day. What a joke.

"I'm glad for you," she said slowly, taking her time with each word. "It must have been awful, thinking you were going to die. You know I called the hospital several times, asking after you. I didn't get much satisfaction."

"Orders," he said cryptically. "We didn't want word of how bad my injuries were to leak out. Business reasons." Neal Harper chuckled. "If you'd told them I was your husband, they might have let you in on the good news. I don't know whether they would have, but you might have stood a chance."

"Well, just as long as you're well now. Are you well?"

"Not completely. The doctors all prescribe rest and relaxation, tender care, and no worry. Especially no worry."

She eyed him dubiously. "You say that as if I were about to trouble you in some way."

"Why should you? You're my wife. By the way, I like that outfit of yours—very much."

Beth flushed a deep red and gathered the flimsy stuff of the robe about herself. She muttered, "I wasn't expecting anyone, I was just trying these things on—and you have some nerve to come barging in like this."

His eyebrows arched. "You're Mrs. Neal Harper."

"In name only. I just married you so—so you could die happy."

"How touching."

The gray eyes went on regarding her, as though examining her face feature by feature. Beth wriggled under that steady stare, which seemed to lift and weigh her on invisible scales.

Coldly she exclaimed, "If you're finished, I have half a sandwich to eat."

She stood up and felt his eyes running up and down her body. Frantically, she ran for her bedroom. She had thrown that old wool bathrobe in the dirty clothes hamper in the bathroom, and she needed it now. Desperately.

Her hands dragged it out and shook it. She slid an arm into a sleeve, and then another. Wrapping it about her, tying the cord belt, she moved back into the living room.

His face was comical in its dismay when he saw her. "What'd you go and do to yourself? You're like a frumpy housewife in that thing! Take it off."

"I will not! I don't know you from Adam."

"I've explained that I'm Neal Harper."

"So you say."

He chuckled, then reached into his hip pocket and tossed her a grained leather wallet. "Go ahead. Open it. See for yourself."

She saw the gold letters first. NKH. The wallet was filled with money—she saw the edges of the greenbacks even as she threw it back to him. "I don't pry into men's wallets."

"Funny. I thought all wives did, when it's a husband's wallet." His fingers opened the wallet, extracted a driver's license, then handed it over.

Almost against her will, Beth let her eyes drop. It was Neal Harper's driver's license, all right. She shrugged.

"So you're my husband. So what?"

"So what? I want you to get dressed and come visit my family. They're dying to meet you."

Beth didn't know whether to laugh or to cry.

Chapter Four

Her temper was close to the boiling point. This man—husband or not!—had no cause to be here in her house. Beth felt very much as if she had been tricked, in some way she could not quite understand. But the feeling persisted. As their eyes met and locked, she bit down hard on her lower lip.

Then she turned and marched, with as much dignity as the flapping bathrobe would give her, into the kitchen. Her half sandwich and the cold cocoa still rested where she had left them. She sat down, reached for the sandwich, and bit into it.

She was chewing as Neal came to the kitchen door and leaned against the jamb. A tiny smile curved his mouth.

"Whenever you're ready," he said calmly. "Though I'm sure Mother and Sis will have some sort of spread ready for us."

Beth swallowed and took a sip of cocoa. Very calmly, she turned to him. "I have no intention of going anywhere tonight. Except bed."

Neal chuckled and took off his coat, draping it over a kitchen chair. "Fine. When do we go?"

"We?" she yelped. "I sleep alone."

"But I'm your husband."

He had her there. She must be reasonable and sensible about all this. He did not look like a kook; there was a sense

38

of security, of latent power about this Neal Harper. He was a businessman. He would listen to plain old common sense.

"In the first place," she began, "I didn't want to marry you at all."

He nodded, amusement in his gray eyes. "So I understand."

"In the second place, that lawyer man you sent to see me was very persuasive."

"I pay him a very generous amount of money every year for that persuasiveness."

Beth swallowed. "I did it out of pity for you, to fulfill the last wish of a dying man."

"And I love you for it."

"Love," she sneered.

Neal Harper spread his hands, looking faintly aggrieved. "All right, I don't love you." His grin was annoying, Beth decided, very annoying. "But I figure that in time we can come to love each other dearly."

"Oh, do you?"

"Frankly, I came here tonight to see what you looked like. I told myself you couldn't possibly be as lovely as you appeared to be in that hospital room, with that white lace veil covering your pixieish face. You do have a face like a pixie, you know. A very adorable pixie."

Beth Sheldon was a woman. She reacted as any woman might react to something like that. She was pleased. She felt certain that a man like Neal Harper would not say such a thing unless he meant it. On the other hand, she was too smart to be taken in by a bit of flattery.

"That has nothing to do with it," she exclaimed irrationally.

"I think it has everything to do with it. A man likes his wife to be glamorous, adorable, pixieish. At least, I do."

"You said I looked like a frump."

He laughed. "You must admit that thing you have on wouldn't win any prizes from *Women's Wear Daily*."

Beth looked down at herself. The robe was old and worn, stained here and there. Its only value, really, was that it was warm and comfortable during cold winter nights.

She said, "I couldn't stay in that mini-nightie and negligee I had on."

"Why not? If you could have seen yourself, you would know how absolutely ravishing it made you."

She bit into what was left of her sandwich and chewed. It didn't help to have him across the table from her, staring at her so intently. It made her uneasy, nervous.

"Can't you look at something else?" she snapped, after a few moments.

"I keep finding out new things about you, the more I see. For instance, your nose is absolutely kissable. I don't know how I can go on sitting here and not do something about that."

Beth stood up so swiftly that the chair behind her skidded and toppled over. "I have to do the dishes," she said breathlessly.

"Oh, let them go. Mrs. Newton will do them in the morning."

"Who's Mrs. Newton?"

"The lady who came to clean your cottage every couple of days while you were frittering away your money in the big city. Her husband did your lawn and flowerbeds."

"How do you know where I was? Or what I was doing?"

"I kept a close eye on you. Or rather, men I hired did."

"How could you—if you were dying?"

"All right, then. Bertram Lambkin did it all, because I told him to, I didn't want anything happening to you, just in case I might get better."

Beth carried the dish, her cup and saucer to the sink and put them in, then began to run the hot water. She didn't know whether to be glad or to resent the fact that a strange woman had come in here to clean up while she was away. She washed the dishes, dried them, put them in their proper place on the shelves, all the while being very conscious of his eyes that never missed a move.

She hung up the dish towel, turned, and asked, "Well? You aren't going to stay here all night, are you?"

"It all depends. Are you coming with me to meet my folks?"

"No. Absolutely not."

"Then I'll stay. Which way's the bedroom?"

"Oooh! You're infuriating!"

His black eyebrows rose. "We're on our honeymoon, darling."

Beth reflected that there was no lock on her bedroom door. There was no reason for one. Until now, of course. Even if she could make it to the bedroom ahead of him, he would be able to force his way in, no matter what she did or said.

Her eyes studied his wide shoulders, deep chest and lean waist. There didn't appear to be an ounce of fat on his body. He looked as fit as an athlete in training. His clothes hung on that body as if they were on a clothing store dummy.

She began to sidle around the table, keeping her eyes on him. It would never do to phone Big Hank Layne. Neal Harper could always claim he was her husband, and even Beth in this almost-hysterical moment had to admit that a husband's place was with his wife.

Neal Harper rose to his feet.

Beth ran.

He caught her at the open bedroom door, pulling her back against him. "I'm in just as much of a hurry to get into bed as you are, dear—but you'll tire yourself out, running like that, and a tired wife isn't much fun."

"Ohhh! You!!!"

His arms were like steel cables, holding her helplessly. She had the uneasy feeling that he was laughing at her, and this maddened her all the more. She tried to kick his shins, but her slippers were soft and did no damage whatsoever. After a moment she desisted, and the grip of his arms relaxed a little.

When he didn't speak, she turned slightly and looked up at him. His face was white, and she could see the pain, the strain in his features, in his eyes.

"Oh, I forgot! It's your operation, isn't it?"

He nodded angrily. Typical male pride, Beth told herself. Angry because he couldn't play the big strong caveman. Still, she did feel sorry for him.

"Sit down. Yes, yes. On the bed. And lie back."

She eased him onto the bedspread.

"I'll be all right," he growled.

"Of course you will. Just lie there for a little while."

His eyes followed her as she moved toward the bathroom. "Where are you going?"

"To brush my teeth and wash my face. I'll sleep on the couch."

"Oh, no."

He made as if to rise, which brought Beth back to him, putting a hand against his chest to push him downward. His hand caught her wrist, held it with a strength that surprised her.

"You will sleep here, with me," he said firmly.

"I will not."

"Then come and see my family. They're waiting to meet you."

If she agreed, it would get him out of her cottage. Once out of it, she would find a way to keep him out, even if it meant changing locks. This marriage of theirs was a mistake. It had been a mistake from the very beginning.

"Look," she muttered. "We'll get an annulment. I'll give you back your hundred thousand dollars. This whole affair is ridiculous."

He shook his head. "The money is yours. No matter what happens."

"But I can't take all that money and not—"

Beth bit her lip. Damn him! He was always putting her in the wrong. She was his wife, and he had every right to be here in her bedroom, according to the law. But not according to her. And she certainly couldn't accept a hundred thousand dollars and not give something in return. And she was very certain that she was not going to sleep with him, no matter how much money was involved.

"All right," she exclaimed. "I'll get dressed and go with you."

"Honest Injun?"

She smiled, nodded. His grip on her wrist relaxed. There were tiny marks on her skin where he had held her, she saw. He saw them too, muttered something under his breath, and caught her hand.

He kissed her wrist where he had marred it.

Beth felt her heart flop over and caught her breath. Nobody had ever kissed her wrist like that, to take away a pain, except maybe her mother, long ago. She wanted to pull her wrist away, but the sensation was so pleasant, she let him go on holding her hand.

Then his lips trailed up her arm, to the hollow above her elbow. Now she did pull away from him, a little breathlessly.

"What'll I wear?" she almost shouted.

"Wear where?" he wondered.

"To meet your family."

"Oh. The family. Yes. Just wear anything. Anything at all."

She darted him a scornful look. Just like a man. Going to visit his family for the first time and "anything at all." She went to the clothes closet, slid back a door, and paused to stare at her neatly hung gowns and suits.

Her hand reached for the three-piece knit suit by Gino Paoli, in misty blue and gold, that had caught her eye in New York. At the time, it had been planned as part of her travel wardrobe. Hmmm! And thinking of travel, what about her travel plans now?

She glanced over her shoulder at her husband. Her husband. Ha! She could imagine the dim view he would take of her haring off on a long trip. Without him, that is. And Neal Harper played no part in any travel plans she had made.

She marched past him to her bureau drawer, extracted a black lace bra and pantie set, a garter belt, and brand-new nylons. In the bureau mirror, she saw how he had turned his head on the pillow to watch her. Ignoring him, she moved into the bathroom.

She dressed as though she were on her way to meet the Queen of England. As she did her rich brown hair in an upsweep, Beth told herself all this wasn't for Neal Harper or the Harper family. It was for Beth Sheldon. She wanted to make an excellent impression on everyone. She didn't want the Harpers to think their precious Neal had married somebody out of the nearest trash bin.

Neal gaped when she made her entrance.

"Hey wow," he murmured, sitting up.

"Just something I frittered away my money on in the big city. Your detectives told you all about it, remember?"

She could not resist a sideways glance into the bureau mirror. The Paoli really did something for her, she had to admit. It gave her an air of elegance that seemed slightly unreal. Her color was high, which set off the dark brown of her hair and eyes, and enhanced the redness of her mouth.

Suddenly Neal was beside her. "You're beautiful," he said huskily. "Breathtaking. I was right, in the hospital. You're exquisite."

"It's just the clothes," she said off-handedly.

Nevertheless, she felt pleased. At least this husband of hers reacted nicely when she made an effort to doll up.

Suddenly he was laughing with almost boyish glee. Beth regarded him with suspicion flaring in her eyes. "What's so funny?"

"I was thinking of my mother. You should have heard her sounding off about—about my marriage."

"Oh? And when was this?"

"The first day she was allowed to see me in the hospital."

Beth scowled up at him. "What did she say?"

He took her arm and brought her to the kitchen, where he slid into his coat, still chuckling. "I don't think I'd better tell you. But I can't wait to see her face when you walk in."

A horrible thought struck Beth. She asked slowly, "You aren't a mamma's boy, by any chance?"

He tilted his head at her, and his eyes narrowed. For a brief instant, Beth saw cold fury in those eyes. Then he smiled, shook his head briefly, and said, "No. Not by any stretch of the imagination."

His hand made a little motion, and Beth, shrugging, walked ahead of him, out of the kitchen, through the living room and toward the front door. Neal was at her elbow to open the door for her, ushering her out into the cool night air.

A glittering dark blue car, the likes of which Beth had never seen, stood in front of the picket fence. It was sleek and low to the ground. Almost instinctively, she knew it would go fast.

"What is it?" she asked, a little awed.

"An Iso Grifo. It'll do a hundred and sixty."

"Where?"

He laughed as he opened the door. "Not around here, that's for sure. I needed a new car when I cracked up the old one, so Bertram Lambkin got me this. Like it?"

"How much did it cost?"

"Something in the neighborhood of twenty thousand."

"Talk about frittering away your money," she muttered darkly.

She slipped onto the blue seat, stared at the padded leather dash, studied the instruments, and the steering wheel. This was something more than a mere car. It was a living luxury. It must be nice to be so rich, she thought morosely, before she remembered that she was reasonably rich in her own right, thanks to this husband of hers.

The motor throbbed to life under his touch. He eased the wheels onto the country road, then kept the speedometer needle at forty. Beth sat with her eyes straight ahead, wondering whether he liked a quiet wife or a talkative one. She decided it didn't really make any difference—she wasn't going to be his wife for very long.

"What's your mother like?" she asked.

"A snob."

She turned to him, honestly surprised, and yes, a little shocked. "How can you say that? Don't you have any feeling for her?"

"Sure, but what's that got to do with it? The woman's a snob. You asked, I told you."

"And your sister?"

"Not as bad as mother, but she's getting there."

Very quietly she asked, "And you?"

Amusement was in his voice as he said, "I'm a damn good businessman. I am also a playboy."

Bertram Lambkin had said much the same thing about Neal Harper, she recalled. Well, he was honest about it. In a subdued voice she muttered, "Swell husband material."

"I could change, you know."

She looked at him from the corners of her eyes. "Why should you?"

"I have a wife, now. Responsibilities."

She hooted laughter.

After a time he said, "I meant that, about changing. I really did. I think it's time, don't you? I'm thirty-four. Unmarried until you came along. Yes, it may be time to restructure my lifestyle."

"Don't do it on my account."

"I wouldn't have any other reason."

Something about the way he spoke stung her. She fancied she read laughter in his voice, that he was playing some sort of game with her. Tartly she snapped, "This is all one great colossal joke to you, isn't it?"

Anger surged inside her. "It's something new and different, having a wife. You've had a lot of girlfriends but you've never been married before. This is a whole new ball game. You want to see what happens, what my reactions to you are. I'm just a specimen on the pin of your curiosity."

"Hey, now . . ."

"I haven't finished. I just want you to know that I'm not going to play your stupid little game. Life's too serious to me, always has been. I've had to work hard for everything I've ever gotten. Except—except for that hundred thousand you gave me. Well, you can have it back."

"No, the money's yours," he murmured very quietly. "You did your part of the bargain. No matter what happens, I don't want it back."

"Well, I don't want it, either."

That isn't true, Beth Sheldon.

She did want the money, she needed it to get away from Rocky Cove and whatever danger faced her here. Surprise touched her mind. Ever since Neal Harper had come into her cottage, she hadn't thought about the bearded man or the hands that had pushed her into the car, or those terrible moments when she had come close to being drowned.

Beth sat huddled in the car seat, suddenly frightened. In a low voice she said, "That was a lie I told you. I do want the money."

He braked the car, stopping it. He turned and stared at her, eyes wide. She gave him a brief glance, then stubbornly looked straight ahead at the white swathe the headlights made in the road before them.

"Why?" he asked softly.

She shook her head.

He put a hand on her wrist, ran it down to her hand, clasped it. His flesh was warm and firm as he gripped her fingers. Gently he urged, "Come on, tell me. You aren't the gold-digger type, you're too independent for that. And you don't have any great lifestyle to live up to, no mink coats, no jewelry.

"Oh, yes. I checked. The first day I was allowed out of the hospital I came straight here. I walked around the cottage, opened doors, poked my nose into your fridge, into your closets. I wanted to learn a little something about this new wife of mine, you see."

She stirred, unable to feel anger or resentment. In a small voice she whispered, "And?"

"I liked what I saw. You make your own way. I took a couple of your books and read them. They're really very good."

That perked her up a trifle. "Did you really think so?"

"I did. I still do. I think it's great, creating characters, a story, plot, setting down words on paper in such a way that other people will buy them. I'm not at all creative, you know, I can analyze a market, sense business trends before they happen, that sort of thing. But make something out of nothing, not on your life."

"It isn't all that hard," she murmured.

"Not to you, perhaps."

He still held her hand, and Beth realized she liked the sensation of his flesh on hers. It gave her a sense of companionship. She shifted a little in the bucket seat, moving closer to him. When she lifted her face and looked at him, she discovered he was smiling at her—well, almost tenderly.

"Now tell me," he suggested.

"Tell you what?"

"Why you need the money."

They had been staring into each other's eyes, as though they were the only people in the world. With something like intimacy, Beth reflected uneasily. It was only the mood of the moment, she understood. Neither of them meant anything to the other. Yet it seemed to her that a closeness had sprung up suddenly between them. She tightened her fingers on his where he held her.

"I wanted the money to get away from Rocky Cove."

She felt his start of surprise. "Now why would you want to do that? Your cottage is lovely, it's in a beautiful setting with the woods around it and the sea so close you can see it from your kitchen windows. Why run away?"

"Because—well, because somebody wants to kill me."

He sat quietly, not speaking, just listening as she told him about the day she had gone scuba diving off Capstone Rock and how the hand had tightened on her ankle and pulled her down. Beth relived that frightful instant, feeling again the gray-green waters around her that seemed to conspire with the unseen hand, pushing her downward, downward.

She drew a deep breath.

"The night you had the accident. You didn't run into me, you know. Somebody pushed me forward just when you were going past. Abe Boldin and those two ambulance interns thought it was a tree branch that had shoved me when I backed into it. But it wasn't. It wasn't!"

Neal Harper was very still. She did not dare look at him, for fear of seeing doubt as to her sanity in his face. She stared down at his hand that still held hers, and gripped it tightly.

"A man's been watching my cottage, too. A bearded man, a man I've never seen and don't know. That's why I want to run away from Rocky Cove and my cottage. I'm s-scared."

"You poor kid," he breathed.

Beth felt oddly let down. He didn't say he believed her, and he didn't lash out with words, telling her she was imagining all this, either. He just sat there quietly, looking down at her, until she began to stir uncomfortably.

"Well, go ahead," she urged. "Tell me I'm a nut or something. Go ahead. But it's true, everything I've told you. And that's why I married you, if you must know. So I could get my hands on all that money and leave Rocky Cove forever. Change my name, become somebody else."

"You don't have to worry about being in danger anymore," he said at last. "You have me to protect you now."

Some protection, a guy who was so weak from his recent operation he couldn't run after her and catch her without feeling weak. Beth flushed, angry at herself. Neal couldn't help it if he was weak—he was lucky to be alive. She squeezed his fingers.

"I know," she whispered. "I'm grateful."

"Let's go get this family bit out of the way, shall we?" he asked, and let go of her fingers to put his hands on the wheel.

He still hadn't said whether he thought she was telling the

truth or whether he felt her imagination was running wild. He hadn't committed himself to anything but an exclamation of pity. Pity for her? Or pity for himself at having married a nut?

Chapter Five

Harper House was at the top of a high hill that gave an excellent view of the sea, of the little town below in the valley, of the woodlands and mountains to the west. As the Iso Grifo came into the drive that circled before the big, old-fashioned building, Beth saw that the lights were on all across the lower floor, casting a faint radiance out upon a broad lawn and rows of flowerbeds, pruned trees, and neatly clipped bushes.

She had never been this close to Harper House before. She stared now at cupolas, at gingerbread scrollwork, at a vast porch that ran almost around the entire house. It had been built in the Nineties, she guessed, and must have been a model for sheer elegance in those days. Even now, with all the modern improvements that had been added, Harper House was something of a showcase.

Lighted lanterns that were works of art gave illumination to the porch and its steps as Neal slowed the car and braked it. Beth took one fast look at the front door, of mahogany and cut glass, before she turned to the man beside her.

"You live here?" she wondered.

"Oh, no. I live in Boston. This is the old homestead, if you want to be corny about it. The family comes here in the summertime. And in winter, on occasion, when the skiing is good."

He came around to her side of the car, opened the door. As she slid out, he added, "I have a room here, of course. Or rather, we do."

She gave him a dark look. "You were right the first time. You do."

He chuckled, taking her arm and guiding her toward the porch steps. As though she couldn't find them on her own, Beth reflected. Still, it was nice to be chaperoned this way, treated like some delicate Dresden china doll. It made her feel more of a woman, suddenly.

A man came to the front door, opened it, and stood aside. He bowed his head, but Beth watched his eyes flick toward her, taking her in at one glance. He was an old man, maybe even in his eighties, but his back was ramrod straight, and there was good color in his face, below the thick white hair.

"Thank you, Benjamin," murmured Neal.

Then they were walking toward a big archway, and came to a stop. Beth raked the room with her eyes frantically, vaguely aware of blue and gold carpeting, of a great marble fireplace, oil paintings on the wall, several large sofas and chairs, and tables, lamps. But it was the people who held her stare.

A very handsome woman in her late fifties, in a simple beige dress with gold accessories, was leaning forward, a book she had been reading forgotten now on her thighs. Her hair was frosted, and her blue eyes were very sharp and penetrating. Her features were set in cold lines, and the corners of her mouth were drawn down disapprovingly. Mrs. Harper, Neal's mother, Beth told herself.

A man in a smoking jacket and slacks stood beside the mantel, pausing in the act of filling a meerschaum pipe from a tobacco humidor to run his eyes up and down her body, from her Capezios to the top of her rich brown hair. His face was creased suddenly by an admiring smile.

The momentary silence was broken by a woman who had been standing beside the rear windows, out of Beth's line of vision. She came striding forward, a faint grin on her pretty face.

"So this is the mysterious bride," she chortled, and held out her hand.

Beth took it with gratitude, glad to be doing something to

avoid, if only for the moment, the chilling stare of the older woman.

"My sister, Joan," Neal said.

Joan exclaimed, "So my little brother has finally gone and done it. Taken himself a bride." Her head tilted slightly, though her eyes were friendly. "I must say he showed uncommonly good sense."

"Indeed he did," agreed the man, pipe in one hand, the other hand outstretched as he came forward to offer his own congratulations. "I'm Joan's husband, Arthur Mason."

"Art is the sailor in the family. He handles our shipping and fishing fleet interests," Neal supplied.

Beth smiled, then turned and looked at the older woman, who had not apparently moved a muscle since her son and his new wife had appeared in the archway. There was frost in her stare, and disapproval in the set of her lips.

Beth took a few steps forward, addressing herself to Mrs. Harper. "This must have come as quite a shock to you, Neal's marriage. It came as a bit of a shock to me, as well."

The woman seemed surprised. "You surely must have known what you were doing."

"Oh, I knew very well. I didn't want a husband, Mrs. Harper. I still don't, frankly. I only married your son because I thought that by doing so, I would ease his dying minutes."

She wondered if she were being brutal, but she did not care. Something about this older woman set her teeth on edge. She went on, "I was amazed to learn that he was alive. Instead of being a widow, I'm a wife. I'm not used to the idea, yet."

Mrs. Harper said coldly, "I imagine that, in such circumstances, you would not object to a divorce or an annulment."

"I feel this is between my husband and myself, Mrs. Harper. Surely you can understand that."

"We can make it very much worth your while."

"Neal has already been more than generous. I don't want any more money, Mrs. Harper, thank you just the same."

She swung about and let her eyes roam. "It's a beautiful room, quite the loveliest I've ever seen."

The older woman was not accustomed to being dismissed. Her back straightened, her eyes narrowed, and she drew a deep breath.

"My son is a very sick man, young lady. He has only been out of the hospital a week or two. I think under such circumstances, I am entitled to speak for the family."

"But not for him," Beth murmured gently.

As though he had been quiet long enough, Neal Harper moved forward, putting his arm about Beth's middle and hugging her. Ordinarily, she might have pushed free of him, but with his mother eying her so forbiddingly, an imp of deviltry entered into her. She let herself lean against her husband, almost seductively.

She felt Neal go rigid in surprise, but he let no emotion show on his face. Beth said, "We really don't know each other at all, you see. That's why we feel we should get acquainted before we decide on any course of action."

"I never heard of any such thing," gasped Mrs. Harper.

Neal said, and Beth could sense the strength in him, "Mother, I'm married. You've always been after me to get married, so I did."

"But—but to such a—"

"Nobody?" volunteered Beth.

For once the older woman was discomfited. "I said nothing of the sort. However, you must admit that a Harper has certain obligations, not only to himself but to his family as well."

"His family seems very sane, very sensible. I doubt very much that Neal's marriage is going to shatter any of them."

Beth was aware that she was making an enemy of this woman, who was probably used to having people kowtow to her slightest whim. The cold blue eyes that regarded her so dispassionately assured her that she was. Beth didn't care. She had stood on her own two feet too long to be fearful of family disapproval.

She and Neal did not love each other, so it wasn't as if they were here to get her approval. Still, she mustn't overdo this independence.

She drew a breath. "I don't want to defy you, Mrs. Harper. I don't mean to do so. But the fact remains that Neal and I are married. I gather that you disapprove of his choice. I can't help that. He did the choosing. Why not argue with him?"

Neal chuckled as the blue eyes swiveled toward him.

"Beth's right, mother. I sent Bert Lambkin to talk her into it. She didn't want any part of me, he had to go back twice to see her, to plead the fact that I was dying, before she'd consent."

Before her mother could think up a reply, Joan asked brightly, "Could anyone use a drink? I'm absolutely parched with thirst."

"A great idea," exclaimed her husband.

Mrs. Harper picked up her book, put her reading glasses on, and settled back in her chair. Beth got the feeling that she had been dismissed for the nonce. Neal still had his arm about her waist, hugging her against him, and she tried to wriggle free.

"I don't even know what drink you prefer," Neal said to her, leaning so close his lips were touching her hair. There was laughter in his voice, and she had no doubt but that he enjoyed the feel of her body against his, and that that arm of his—despite his apparent weakness—was like steel.

Suddenly he let her go, to catch her elbow and draw her with him toward Joan and Arthur, where they were standing side by side at a portable bar overloaded with liquor bottles, glasses, and ice buckets. He was like a leech, Beth thought. He didn't seem to want to let go of her.

"I'll have a vodka martini, just one," he sang out as they moved along. "Doctor tells me I mustn't overdo so soon after the operation."

"Do you overdo?" Beth asked. "As a matter of course?"

Art Mason grinned. "Don't let that husband of yours fool you, Beth. He's no drinker. Pretends, of course, for business reasons, but I've seen him pour cocktail after cocktail into an empty water glass."

"You shatter her illusions, Art. Beth thinks me strange enough, as it is."

Joan raised her eyebrows at Beth, as her hands paused over bottles. "Just wine, if you have it."

"Claret?"

"Please."

"She wants a cool, clear head for what is to come," Neal smiled.

Beth flicked him a glance. "Oh? And what's to come?"

"Bridge with Joan and Art, if you're up to it. You do play, I hope?"

"Yes, I play. But not tonight."

His face was drawn, she thought. There was strain in his eyes. He would be better off in bed than sitting with cards in his hands until all hours. She didn't intend to remain his wife, but there was no reason why she couldn't see to his welfare. She would do the same for any human being.

"You need your sleep," she said gently.

A stubborn look touched his face. Joan nudged Art and they moved away, carrying their drinks. Neal said stiffly, "I am quite capable of deciding when I want to go to bed."

"You're just over your operation. Besides, you have to drive me home. Did you forget that?"

"Oh, you're staying here. You'll live here from now on."

Beth opened her mouth to protest loudly and vociferously, but she caught sight of Mrs. Harper in her chair and lowered her indignant yell to a fierce whisper.

"I am not staying here overnight. Absolutely not."

"Certainly you are. You're my wife, remember?"

Beth said so that everyone could hear, "Why not show me around your home, darling?"

Neal was about to protest when he changed his mind. "Stupid of me. I should have done that earlier. Come along, dear."

His arm encircled her waist, hugging her as before. But this time, as they moved into the hall, she caught his hand and pushed it away. "Look! Let's get one thing straight between us. I don't love you, you don't love me. Agreed?"

To her surprise, he hesitated. "I'm not so sure. About my not loving you, I mean. Sure, sure, I know it sounds crazy, but you do appeal to me. A lot."

"That's nice, but it isn't enough. I always told myself that when I married a man, it would be for love. If that makes me old-fashioned, so I'm old-fashioned. But it's the way I am."

He was walking as she spoke, and he drew her now into a wood-paneled den, where a television set warred with a table covered with books and magazines. He closed the door behind him.

"Okay, we can talk now," he announced.

"I'm not staying here tonight," Beth began. "This whole marriage bit is so unreal, it's fantastic. I don't feel like a married woman, and I'm not about to act like one."

She scowled at him. "If I didn't know better, I'd believe you tricked me into marrying you for some absurd reason I can't guess."

He said, "The first time I saw you was when you came leaping out in front of my car. The second time was when we were married. Beth, believe me. I had been told there wasn't much hope, I wanted to make it up to you—for hitting you with the car, that is. I know it was a nutty idea, but at the time it seemed very sensible."

"All right, all right. We got married, for whatever reasons we had. We're man and wife in the eyes of the law. But not in my eyes. And not in your eyes either!"

"Well, now. I'm not so sure of that last."

"I'm serious, Neal."

He walked up and down the room, frowning. There was a wistfulness about him that touched Beth as she stared at him. He said, "I'll make a deal with you. Stay here tonight. Act as if you really are my wife. As a matter of fact, I'd like you to stay here a month or two."

Before she could protest, he raised his hand. "You'd be safe here, don't you realize that? If what you were telling me tonight is the truth, and that someone wants you dead, don't you understand that this place will be like a haven to you?"

She had forgotten all about *that*. But as Neal spoke of it, her old fears came flooding back. He was right. Here in the Harper house, with people always around her, no one would be able to get at her. She nodded slowly.

"That makes sense. I am frightened, Neal, I admit it. But if I stay here, there's not going to be any hanky-panky. You understand that?"

"If you say so."

She frowned. "What I can't understand is why you want me here. You aren't getting anything out of it, to put it bluntly."

"If you're around to take care of me, maybe I'll get better sooner."

She eyed him suspiciously. "I wish I knew what your real reason is."

"For one thing, I like the way you stood up to my mother."

"I behaved badly, I made an enemy out of her."

"Nothing of the sort. You took the wind out of her sails, true, but she'll respect you all the more for not giving in to her. Arthur dances to her tune, and so does Joan. I'm the only one she hasn't been able to bully, so far."

He chuckled. "Now that I'm married, she won't be after me all the time about getting myself a wife. I have one."

"Such as she is."

"Adorable and pixieish."

"Oh, honestly, Neal. Come off it."

He said, so seriously that he surprised her, "I do think you adorable, Beth. You're cute, you're beautiful, and I think there's a lot of steel under all that soft skin of yours."

He was moving toward her slowly, and there was an odd light in his eyes. Beth said hastily, "I think we've been looking over the house long enough. Time we went back to your family."

This time he didn't run after her and grab her. He just got an injured look on his face as he followed her out the door. "Chicken," he whispered.

Joan and Arthur were off in a far corner of the room, sipping their drinks. Mrs. Harper was seemingly immersed in her book.

But as they entered, the older woman very carefully slid a bookmark between the pages, closed the book, and placed it on an end table. Then she gave her son an odd look.

"I don't know what Candace will say about all this nonsense," she announced.

"Who's Candace?" Beth wanted to know.

No one answered her, but Art and Joan rose from where they had been sitting and came closer. Neal had paused, regarding his mother with a blank face.

"She'll get over it," he said at last.

"It won't be all that easy, old boy," Art chimed in. "You're quite a catch, you know. Or were."

His eyes touched Beth, and beamed. Joan said drily, "Arthur doesn't like Candace."

"Too bossy by far."

Mrs. Harper turned and fastened her eyes on him, and to

58 *Lynna Cooper*

Beth it appeared that Arthur wilted. The older woman turned back and now she focused her attention on Beth.

"I've been sitting here thinking as I read, and it seems that I recall your saying that you only married my son so that he could die more easily, or words to that effect. You also said that you didn't want to marry him."

"That's true."

Mrs. Harper sat back in the chair. "Then you have no valid objection to giving him a divorce or an annulment?"

"None at all. The sooner the better."

Arthur and Joan were shocked, she saw. But she didn't care. She was tired of this whole farce. If somebody named Candace wanted Neal Harper so badly, she could have him. And with her, Beth Sheldon's, blessing

Beth murmured, "I also said that this was our affair, Neal's and mine, and nobody else's."

"And especially not mine. Still, I am making it my business. As his mother, I certainly feel I know what is best for my son."

Neal murmured, "Mother, I am not about to divorce Beth. So forget it. She's my wife, I married her with open eyes, and I haven't regretted it. Now if that's all we have to say on the subject, I'm tired. I'm going up to bed."

He caught Beth by a hand and drew her with him. He was angry, Beth knew, very angry. He was breathing heavily, and a red flush tinted his otherwise pallid cheeks.

She said gently when they were out of earshot, "I'm surprised you stay in this house, if your mother annoys you so much."

"Ordinarily, I never come here. But I had papers for her to sign in my car the night I wrecked it. Bert Lambkin got the papers from the wreckage and got her to sign them. By rights I should be back in Boston right now. But the doctors won't let me. I have to rest and relax."

They moved up the huge staircase, past the bronze statuettes on the newel posts, the thick carpeting muffling their footfalls. Beth wondered if a house such as this, with its obvious indications of great wealth, muffled as well the spirits of those inside it. Arthur certainly was affected by it, as perhaps Joan was, as well. Still, it didn't bother Mrs. Harper. Indeed it seemed only to add to her overbearing personality.

She flicked a sidewise glance at Neal. His mother's tyranny did not seem to upset him too much—it only made him angry. Or perhaps that was his reaction when he felt helpless against it.

Beth asked, as they moved along the hall, "Who's this Candace your mother mentioned?"

"A girl I know. Has a summer place not far from here. It's always been assumed—by her family and mine, and by Candace herself, I might add—that we would marry."

"She's very rich, of course?"

"I suppose so."

"Oh, come on, Neal. I'll bet you know to the penny just how wealthy she is."

He smiled as he reached to open a door. "All right, I know. Yes, she is rich. Maybe not as rich as the Harpers, but rich enough."

He put on lights. Beth saw a canopied fourposter English antique bed, draped in a cotton print and with a patchwork quilt, a big fireplace with an old-fashioned long rifle and powderhorn above it on the wall. A dresser with an ornate mirror on the wall behind it was framed by two large windows hung with floral print drapes. Scatter rugs set off the dark stain of the floor, and the chaise longue rested in a corner near a standing lamp and a small table that held a few books and magazines. On the other side of the room was a writing desk and chair, and a worn leather chair that had seen better days. Beth frowned as she saw it, it seemed to clash so much with the decor of the room.

Neal had been watching her. He said now, "Don't blame anybody but me for that old monstrosity. I insisted it be put there. It was mine when I was in college. It's the most comfortable chair I've ever known."

"I'm surprised," she finally admitted, "that your mother would let you get away with it. It's absolutely out of place, you know."

He nodded. "Right you are. But I like it."

"You're stubborn, too."

"Among other things," he chuckled.

Beth sat on the edge of the bed and looked up at him. "What's Candace going to say about this marriage of yours?"

Chapter Six

"She won't like it," he grinned.

"—and may make trouble," she added thoughtfully.

Neal seemed surprised. "Hey, now. Candace isn't like that. She won't come clawing at you. She's a good sport. She'll understand."

Beth gave him a long, slow look. "You don't know women very well, do you? If she wants you badly enough, she'll fight for you. One way or the other. The question is, ought I fight back?"

Neal Harper slid out of his coat, moved to a closet and placed it inside, on a hanger. He undid his tie, tossing it over the back of a chair. He began to unbutton his shirt. Beth watched his moves with growing concern.

"You haven't answered me," she exclaimed.

"About what? Oh, Candace."

He pulled his shirttails out of his slacks. "Forget her. I'm married, that's all there is to it."

"Is it?"

Panic rose inside Beth as he slid out of the shirt. He certainly didn't expect to sleep with her! She had no wish to make a scene, but while she might be legally wedded to this man, she was not about to play the role of loving wife.

"Where are you going to sleep?" she squeaked.

Neal let surprise touch his face. "Why, here. With you, of course."

She jumped to her feet. "No way!"

He stared at her, disbelief replacing the surprise on his features. "Oh, come on, Beth. You can't be serious."

"I most certainly am." She looked around her. "I'll sleep on the chaise, you can have the bed."

She ran for the closet and searched through it until she found a man's robe. It was of terrycloth, obviously meant for beachwear. But it would cover her when she undressed. She turned, clutching the robe, to find him shaking his head.

"I don't believe this."

"You'd better believe it," she remarked.

She sidled toward the open bathroom door, clutching the robe. Neal watched her, eyes amused. When she was a few feet beyond him, she scampered for the bathroom. She shut the door and locked it.

Her heart was thumping almost uncontrollably. What in the world was the matter with her? There for a moment, she was positive he meant to reach out and grab her, kiss her. Well, what if he had, Beth Sheldon? You've been kissed before, it isn't anything that has never happened.

She lifted off the Paoli suit, folding it carefully. She sat on a vanity stool and rolled down her stockings. She would wear her bra and panties, of course. She stood and slid into the terrycloth robe. It came to below her knees, and when she had wrapped it around her, it certainly was modest enough.

Beth found a brush, began to brush her hair as she did every night before going to bed. Staring at the reflection of her flushed face, she told herself that nothing was going to happen. She would not let it. She was not Neal Harper's wife, no matter what the law said. And if he attempted to do anything about it, on his own . . .

Well? What will you do, Beth? What can you do?

Fight him, of course. She would not scream, no. Despite her inner anxiety, she did not want the rest of his family to know the situation between them. Especially that mother of his. No. She might bite and claw, but she would not yell.

She thought about Neal's weakened state, and felt reassured. He was not strong enough to overcome her physically.

Nevertheless, her knuckles rapped on the closed bathroom door. "You decent?" she called.

"Come on, come on. You're perfectly safe."

She emerged, holding the robe around her. Neal was stretched out on the chaise longue, hands clasped behind his head, covered by a blanket. His eyes moved over the robe, her bare legs, her loose brown hair, and he made a face.

"You were a lot more glamorous earlier, in that black lace thing."

Beth ran for the bed, leaped into it, drew the covers up to her neck. Then she looked at him. He was studying her rather as an entomologist would regard a strange bug on the end of a pin, Beth thought. As though she were of a strange species of womanhood he had never seen before.

Let him. She was herself, an individual with certain very strong feelings, and the sooner he learned them and to respect them, the better for them both.

He said slowly, "Sleep well, my love."

"You too. And be sure to stay where you are."

His sigh was mock tragic. "As you wish."

He was laughing at her, she knew. So let him. Beth frowned, started to giggle, then turned over with her back to him, drawing the covers closer around her, almost as if they could shut him out of her thoughts. They could not. She found herself wondering what tomorrow would be like, here in Harper House, and how they were going to be able to carry on such a farcical marriage.

There was this Candace, too. She would make trouble . . .

Beth woke to sunlight shining in her eyes. She stirred fretfully, keeping her eyes squeezed shut. She was warm and cozy, and she did not want to stir. The room was quiet. Too quiet.

Very gently she opened one eyelid. The chaise was empty. She opened the other eye, raised her head, and stared around her. The room was empty. The clock on the nighttable told her it was close to nine o'clock.

Beth threw back the bedclothes, then ran for the bathroom. She made a face when she saw the Paoli dress. Not quite the thing for breakfast. Still, it was all she had to wear. She showered, dried herself, and dressed as swiftly as she could.

She went out into the upper hall. There were voices from below, a burst of laughter. Female laughter. Strange female laughter, at that. She was reasonably certain that Mrs. Harper would not gurgle in just that manner, with almost indecent amusement. It did not sound like Joan, either.

Beth went downstairs slowly, and moved toward the dining room. Mrs. Harper was at the head of the table, smiling coldly. Joan was to her right, and a girl with blond hair piled high on her head, and with perfect features, was to her left. Even without being told, Beth sensed who she was.

They all turned and stared at her.

Beth said brightly, "Sorry I overslept. Is there any coffee left?"

Joan exclaimed, "My goodness, yes. And don't apologize for sleeping. You have every right to, as a bride."

Beth decided not to comment. She looked brightly at the blond woman, and said, "I'm afraid I don't know you. Are you a member of the family, too?"

Even as she spoke, Beth was reproving herself. If this really was Candace, it was rather mean of her, considering. But an imp was inside her, born of the cold looks Mrs. Harper was flinging her way.

Joan gasped. "Oh, forgive me. Candace, this is Beth, Neal's wife, you know. Beth, this is Candace Thorne."

Beth murmured greetings, as did Candace, and Beth noticed that the blond never took her eyes off her as she moved to sit beside Joan. There was cool appraisal in those eyes, and more than a hint of animosity. Beth couldn't blame her. She might feel the same way if someone had married the man she loved, snatching him, as it were, right out from under her nose.

Candace let her eyes touch the Paoli dress. Beth tried to be very casual as she said, "Neal insisted on bringing me here on the spur of the moment, so I could meet his family. I hadn't time to fetch any of my other things."

"Of course, Neal is rather impetuous."

"Where is Neal?" Beth wondered, with a bright smile.

"He had business in town," Joan explained.

The coward. He knew Candace was coming here. Somehow he had found out, and run away. A maid placed a cup of steaming hot coffee before her. Beth looked down at it, wishing Neal were inside. Serve him right for abandoning her like this.

The silence was prolonged until Beth murmured, with a glance around the table, "I interrupted your talk. Please forgive me. Go right on where you left off."

Candace said, "I've brought an invitation for you and Neal to come visit my hunting lodge up at Moosehead Lake."

She sat there with a smile on her lips but a challenge in her eyes. Beth murmured cautiously, "That's very nice of you."

It wasn't only nice, it was a trap of some sort, she decided. Beth was no huntress, though she did fish. If Candace expected her to go traipsing through the Maine woods for deer or bear or whatever was in season, she was sadly mistaken. Beth knew her own limitations.

Mrs. Harper announced coldly, "I think it very nice of Candace, myself. It isn't every girl whose husband-to-be was snatched away from her by a fortune-hunter who would be so noble about it."

Joan gasped. Beth saw that even Candace was a little startled by the older woman's words. She herself heard them in sheer disbelief. Then her sense of humor came to her aid.

"Everything's fair in love and war," she stated with a smile. "Actually, it was almost like a grab bag. When we were married, I didn't see Neal's face, it was so covered by bandages. I was just taking potluck."

Candace sat up very straight, staring at her with complete disbelief in her eyes. Her right hand was clenched into a fist.

Beth went on, "So I didn't know him when he came knocking at my cottage door last night. Isn't that something? Not to know your own husband when you see him for the first time!"

Mrs. Harper asked, "Do you actually expect us to believe that?"

"I almost didn't let him in," Beth nodded.

"But—"

Candace looked so bewildered, Beth came close to feeling sorry for her.

"But if that's so, why did he marry you?"

Beth shrugged elaborately and murmured, "You'll just have

to ask him. All he tells me when I ask him is that he felt guilty about knocking me down with his car."

The blank faces staring at her told Beth better than words that Neal Harper was no blabbermouth. The marriage had been carried out in almost complete secrecy, so far as his family was concerned. Apparently Bertram Lambkin had said nothing, either.

"Well, really!" Mrs. Harper was beginning, when Neal walked into the room. Beth noted that he avoided meeting Candace Thorne's eyes.

He came to her side, bent and kissed her on the cheek. "Hallo, darling. I trust you slept well?"

His tone of voice hinted that they had held practically an orgy in the big fourposter bed before he would let her get to sleep. Beth felt color warm her cheeks. She opened her lips to deny his broad hint, but when she saw the raw fury in Candace Thorne's eyes, she closed them and leaned against the hand he put on her shoulder.

"Of course, dear," she murmured sweetly. "You saw to that, didn't you?"

She felt his hand tighten in surprise, she saw Candace scowl and glance down at the empty cup before her. Mrs. Harper sniffed, and Joan repressed a giggle.

"Candace has invited you and your wife up to her lodge at Moosehead Lake," Mrs. Harper said. "I think it's very sweet of her."

Over her head, Beth knew Neal was looking at the blond girl. What were his eyes saying to her? Her own eyes were gently chiding, reproving, faintly angry. Yet under these was a vague challenge, Beth thought. It was as if Candace were asking him to compare the two of them and then ask himself if he had made the proper choice.

Neal murmured, "It was good of her, indeed. But under the circumstances—"

Candace laughed, waved a hand. "What circumstances, Neal? The fact that you're married? I should think Windflower Lodge would be the ideal place to—to spend your honeymoon."

Beth stirred. There was something about Candace Thorne that bothered her. Oh, yes, on the surface she seemed all sweet affability, but beneath it, behind the green eyes and fair skin was something hard, like tempered steel.

It came to Beth suddenly that this woman was going to make a fight of it. She was not about to yield up Neal Harper to some unknown who had taken advantage of the man she loved at a weak moment. She was asking Beth and Neal to meet her on her own grounds, to come to Windflower Lodge where she, Candace Thorne, would be in her element.

And Beth Sheldon would be at a distinct disadvantage.

She wanted to blurt out that the blond woman could have Neal Harper, she herself certainly didn't want him as a husband. Yet something held her back. She did not know what it was—some instinct, perhaps. Or the fact that having chosen her as a wife, Neal Harper should not regret it. At least, too soon.

Neal said, "You're right, Candy. It's very generous of you." Then in a slightly different tone he added, "You'll come along, of course?"

Candace nodded. "I did have my heart set on doing some shooting." Smiling faintly, she murmured, "I won't get in your way, of course."

Not much, Beth thought.

"What do you think, darling? Ought we go?"

She could hardly stay here in Harper House with Neal, and she certainly didn't want to go back to her cottage with him. Most assuredly she was not about to return to her cottage alone, where anything might happen to her.

Beth reflected morosely that she really didn't have much choice in the matter. Aloud she found herself saying, "Whatever you say, Neal."

"You'll need clothes—you can't go into the north woods in that dress. I think a visit to our cottage is called for."

Beth didn't need any further invitation. She got to her feet, thanking Mrs. Harper and Joan for their hospitality, then moving ahead of Neal toward the hall. He opened the door for her, smiling down into her eyes.

"What did you think of Candace?"

"She still wants to marry you."

"I am married," he replied, grinning.

"That won't stop her."

He opened the car door, watching as she slid onto the seat. He waited before closing the door. "Forget Candace. I have. There's nobody for me but you."

Beth sat thinking about this as he went around the car to get behind the wheel. Then she said, "I don't quite understand you, Neal. We aren't in love, you don't love me, and I don't love you. Maybe you're just in love with the idea of marriage itself."

"That's a silly thing to say."

"What I mean is, maybe you don't want to marry Candace, you've never wanted to marry her, and this marriage between us is your way of getting out from under some sort of obligation."

The Iso Grifo was on the road heading toward the cottage before he spoke again. "If you must know, I never wanted to get married. Period. Not to anyone."

She swiveled around to stare at him. "For Pete's sake. If that's true, why in the world did you marry me?"

"Because I expected to die," he growled.

Beth began to laugh. She supposed she was slightly hysterical—last night and this morning at that house would be enough to make anyone hysterical—but she could not help herself. She laughed until she cried, and then she sobered, to open her handbag and use a tissue to wipe away her tears.

"What's so funny?" he rasped.

"You. And me. I married you because I thought you were going to die. You married me for the same reason, probably as some sort of gesture of defiance at Candace Thorne and your family."

"And now we're stuck with each other."

Beth sobered. "Neal, you can divorce me. I won't fight it. Or you can have an annulment, I won't contest it. And as I've already said, I'll give you back all that money."

"Will you forget the money? It's yours. You earned it."

"And the divorce?"

He was silent a while, then asked, "Would you insist on it?"

Neal was putting it squarely up to her. Beth frowned. Did she want to divorce this man? Yes. On the other hand, no. Beth could not decide quite how she felt, and stirred in irritation at herself. Ordinarily, she was able to make quick decisions. She did not love him, he didn't love her.

And yet she liked being with him. He was handsome and friendly, and there was a charm about him that touched a chord deep within her. Even more important, he represented security and safety to her. With a husband beside her, she need not fear that unknown danger which threatened her quite so much as she did when she was alone.

"No," she murmured at last, "I wouldn't insist on it. But I'm willing to go along with what you decide."

"Good girl. We'll stay married."

Beth settled back in the bucket seat, vaguely surprised at the relief that flooded her body. She hugged herself, smiling at her thoughts. She wouldn't have to run away from Rocky Cove, which she loved. She wouldn't be forced to move or take any of those silly trips she had planned. She could make do with a mother-in-law who despised her simply by keeping out of her way.

Neal chuckled. Beth glanced at him, eyebrows arched.

He said, "You look like the cat that just ate the pet canary."

Beth giggled. "Maybe I feel like it, too. I have a rich, handsome husband. I have peace and security. For the first time in a while, I'm able to really relax."

They rounded the bend in the road and Beth could see her cottage. At the same instant she saw movement off to one side, in among the trees, and caught a fleeting glimpse of a bearded man with long brown hair, and the flash of corduroy slacks. She cried out, straightening up and pointing.

She heard Neal say something indistinguishable under his breath. His foot hit the brake and the Iso Grifo slowed. The man was gone, suddenly, from between the trees. He would be running, dodging, and darting, using the tree boles to hide him.

"Did you see him?" she choked.

"If I hadn't believed you before, I do now. Who is that character?"

"If I knew, I'd tell Hank Layne. He's the same man I saw before. He was just standing there, looking at the cottage."

The fear was deep inside her, like a chill. She shivered.

Neal put his hand on hers, squeezing it. "I've got to get you away from here. It's a good thing we're going north."

His face was sober and grim as he regarded her. "You must know why he was there, why somebody tried to drown you, why you were pushed in front of my car."

"I don't know, Neal, honestly," she wailed.

"All right, don't get upset. We'll work it out between us."

"I can't drag you into my affairs," she quavered.

"Don't be a little idiot. I'm your husband, remember? Your troubles are my troubles, from now on."

She half laughed, half sobbed. "I'm not much of a wife to you. It's hardly worth your while."

"Let me be the judge of that," he told her gently.

When Neal emerged from the car he stood a few seconds, staring at the woods. Beth wondered if he thought he should go haring after the skulker, and came out of the car to run to him, catching him by the arm. He was still too weak for any such heroics.

"Get into the house," she pleaded.

"I'd go after him if I thought I stood a chance of catching up to him. But he's long gone by this time."

She drew him with her into the cottage, making him sit in an easy chair and relax while she packed her bags. "I'm not that much of a cripple," he assured her. "I'll give you a hand."

"All right, but only after I change."

She left him sitting there, running into her bedroom and closing the door. Deftly she slid out of the Paoli dress, hung it up, and reached for a pair of beige slacks and a thick maroon pullover sweater. When she felt she was presentable, she opened the door and invited him in.

In the bedroom, Neal was such a help that Beth found herself staring at him from time to time. He was not at all abashed, gathering up her nylons or her Olga bra and panty sets, or even the black Lastex and lace girdle which she wore upon occasions. He was much more like a husband of long standing than a recent bridegroom.

Once he held up the mini-nightie she had been wearing the night before. Beth realized she could see right through it and flushed faintly.

"I won't need that," she exclaimed hastily, trying to snatch it from his hand.

"On the contrary, it'll fit in perfectly," he grinned.

Beth scowled darkly. "I'm bringing flannel nighties and that old woolen bathrobe. It gets cold up around Moosehead Lake this time of year."

"Just don't let Candace Thorne see you in them."

She hesitated, eying Neal and the thin scantiness he was still holding. She had forgotten Candace. "On second thought, maybe you'd better pack it," she announced.

He laughed, handed it to her. "I'll go open the car trunk. Leave the bags for me to carry."

But she would not do that. She had the feeling that it might be better for Neal Harper not to lug around any weight so soon after his operation. He was making excellent progress, and she didn't want him to have a relapse.

He exclaimed angrily when she appeared, the two Ventura valises dangling from her hands. He ran to take them from her, reaching for their handles.

Beth said, "Okay, okay. I just wanted to save you the trouble."

He tossed the bags in the trunk and slammed the lid. Anger flushed his cheeks, but when he caught her looking at him worriedly, he relaxed and smiled.

"So it's male pride," he muttered.

"I'm not thinking about your pride, but your health. The doctors have patched you up inside, we don't want anything tearing loose, do we?"

"I'm not used to having anyone worry about me this way."

She sighed. "Let me put it this way. If you stay healthy, I stay healthy. Does that make more sense to you?"

He turned her and gave her a pat on her fanny. "Get in the car," he said gently. "We have a far piece to travel."

"Don't you have to pack, too?" she wondered, as she settled herself in the bucket seat.

"Oh, I have my things up at the lodge. Keep them there in case of need."

Beth digested that as he started the engine. How well did Neal know the blond woman? To keep his clothes at her place argued a pretty good amount of intimacy, to her way of thinking. Maybe it wasn't so smart of her to go traipsing north to Windflower Lodge, if Candace Thorne was going to be there.

She might have to fight to keep Neal Harper as her husband. Was she willing to do so? If her life depended on it, as it might very well, she decided she would fight—and fight hard.

Chapter Seven

The road was straight and narrow, running between heavily wooded slopes, with a glimpse of sunlight on distant blue water, the air fragrant with growing things. The dogwood was in bloom, its flowers so white they seemed like late snow clinging to the branches. The birch and oak trees were hung heavily with green leafage, and once in a while skunk cabbage or the golden yellow flowers of field mustard made its appearance.

Beth lost herself in a silent contemplation of this apparent wilderness through which they were moving. She was enchanted with the wildwood; she loved Nature in all its manifestations. This was the main reason she had finally settled at Rocky Cove, when her books had begun to sell. Rocky Cove offered her forest and seashore both, and on her long walks—before she had become too frightened to take them—she had enjoyed moving in under woodland giants and finding wild grapes to make jam or hazelnuts to munch on as she walked along.

In the hazy distance, she could make out the bulks of mountains, and grassy slopes dotted here and there with a red barn, a white house, a tall silo. A purple finch swooped low across the road, and then a meadowlark rose up from a clump of bushes beside the road.

"Hungry?"

She had forgotten food in the delight of the scenery, but now that Neal reminded her, she realized that she had only had a cup of coffee for breakfast. Her eyes glanced at the lonely road, the trees that flanked it.

"Can we get food?"

"We're in the backwoods, but there's a place I know up ahead a few miles that will be happy to serve us some fish chowder and a sandwich."

Had he and Candace eaten at that place before? Had he driven the blond woman up to her lodge, and how often? Obviously the answer was yes to all those questions, and Beth felt a tiny stab of jealousy.

But that's ridiculous, she told herself.

I have no claim on Neal. Certainly before we were married I hardly knew he existed. What he had done was his own business.

Yet the feeling persisted that she was moving steadily into what military strategists would call enemy territory. She was going to fight Candace Thorne, or felt she was, on Candace's own home ground. It didn't seem quite fair, somehow.

Where the road dipped and swerved, the trees fell away to show long meadows and a vast expanse of blue lake. Beth stared, gurgling in delight.

"You like it?" Neal asked.

"Oh, yes. It's beautiful. Breathtaking."

"You surprise me, you really do."

She swung about, eyes wide. "Surprise you?"

"You don't seem like a nature girl."

"Oh. Well, I don't know about that, all I know is I love trees and flowers, a walk in the woods, the sight of a lake like that—so virginal, so untouched. Pure. You can almost imagine an Indian in a birchbark canoe paddling lazily across it."

"Ever been in a canoe?"

"Of course." She stared scornfully. "I didn't grow up in the country for nothing, you know."

Neal was still smiling when he turned into a parking lot to one side of a long, low building with a sign hanging from a post, reading: BIRD 'N' BOTTLE. Even as she opened the door, Beth could smell the aroma of cooking meats.

The fish chowder was superb, the roast beef sandwich large

and thick. And the coffee was rich and fragrant. Beth ate until she could eat no more. As she leaned back in her chair, sighing, she felt like the proverbial new woman. Maybe she looked better, too, because Neal kept giving her admiring glances.

Too bad she didn't really love Neal, or he, her. She would give Candace Thorne some real competition, if that were the case. And the moment of truth was not far away.

Exactly two hours and fifteen minutes, to be exact.

They pulled in off the dirt road onto blacktop, catching a glimpse of what appeared to be a huge log cabin with a balcony around the upper part of the house. It was lovely with the electric lights gleaming against the dusk of early evening. It gave Beth the impression of a Swiss chalet that might have been built by Daniel Boone.

Candace was at the door to meet them, radiant in a long-skirted cocktail gown, the bodice of which was *crèpe de chine* which clung lovingly to the blond woman's contours. Beth blinked as she got a good look at her.

In her own slacks and sweater combination, she felt dirty and grimy. It didn't help when Candace said, looking coolly at Beth, "You'll want to wash up. Yes, of course you will."

A man in a heavy lumberjacket appeared out of the shadows, to take the bags from the trunk and carry them into the house. Then Neal came forward after closing the car trunk, to meet Candace.

The blond woman pressed herself against Neal, lifting her mouth to be kissed. They held their position a few seconds, and Beth thought, I might as well not be here. Why had she come, anyhow? Her earlier mood had deserted her, so that as she stood now in the shadows and watched Neal and this blond girl hug each other, she felt gloomy forebodings touch her mind.

Finally Neal got around to remembering her, she thought darkly. He turned, gave her a smile and stretched out a hand to her. "Come on inside, honey. We can't stand out here forever."

Beth was speechless. She wanted to snap, "It was you who kept us out here, not being able to let go of your girlfriend." She decided against it, giving him an answering smile instead and catching his hand, bringing it up against her body and holding it there.

Candace saw the gesture and her eyes narrowed.

Try *that* on for size, sister.

The ground floor of the lodge was astonishingly modern, Beth thought, considering that the outside was fashioned from logs. A huge, wide fireplace of white bricks covered half a wall, and beyond it was a built-in bar. Vast windows looked out onto the woods; in daylight the view must be magnificent, since the lodge itself was perched on a hill. The floor of the room was tiled, and the massive sofa and many chairs, though seemingly new, gave the illusion of great lived-in comfort.

As she walked through it, she told herself that this place must have cost a not-so-modest fortune, and then she remembered that someone had said Candace Thorne was wealthy in her own right. She had the impression of other rooms leading off this one, and a floor-to-ceiling glass wall that fronted a flagstone terrace.

Candace said, behind her, "I've given Beth a room all to herself, Neal. You, of course, shall have your old one."

Again there was that proprietary air about the blond girl that so annoyed Beth. It was as if Candace were the wife and she, an interloper. As she came in sight of the staircase, of redwood and stone, she turned and stared straight at Candace.

"It's awfully good of you," she said sweetly, "but I really think Neal and I should stay together. If you don't mind, naturally."

Candace's long blond eyelashes flickered. Beth sensed her annoyance, saw how she fought to dissemble it. "Not at all. You and Neal may sleep wherever you like. Just take any room."

Neal was watching her in something like shocked surprise. He could not believe his ears, she knew. Well, maybe she didn't blame him, but she was not about to let Candace Thorne separate them as she intended. Beth wasn't sure just how, but it would have symbolized a victory for the blond woman.

Her bags were in a large room with windows draped in ivory brocade. Twin beds were united by a single headboard that held books, a radio, a few knickknacks. Beth was admiring it in the doorway, when Neal caught up to her.

His hand took her elbow, propelling her inside the room. He closed the door and swung on her. "What was that all about?"

"What was what all about?"

"That bit about wanting me to sleep with you. You don't. Why did you tell Candace you did?"

"I wasn't about to have her tell me when and when not to sleep in the same room as my husband. I'm not about to have her separate us." She added darkly, "Where is this room that seems to be yours in her place? Right next to her bedroom?"

"Yes. Say now, you don't think——"

Her eyebrows raised. "Think what, darling?"

His face was red. "Think that she and I—you know. With you in the house and all that."

Beth patted his cheek. "Certainly not. The idea never crossed my mind. But since you mention it, I think my idea's the best one for everyone concerned."

"You certainly don't trust me."

"Neal, the world looks on us as husband and wife. The world includes Candace Thorne. We're going to act like husband and wife, publicly at least. Aren't we?"

Suddenly he chuckled. "Okay, okay. You don't want Candy to get her long red fingernails into me. I approve of it as a face-saving gesture. So we sleep in here tonight, right?"

Beth nodded at the twin beds. "There's one for each of us."

Neal walked toward the beds, studying them. He said thoughtfully, "Actually, they're wide enough so we could sleep in just one of them."

Beth scowled. "I throw myself in all directions when I sleep."

"Do you, darling?"

"I wouldn't want to disturb your dreams."

"Oh, I don't know. Might be fun."

She sniffed and turned to the wall mirror. She wasn't quite the grimy gamin she had thought herself to be downstairs, looking at the cool, lovely Candace. Of course, her hair was tousled and windblown, but it gave her a gypsy look, a sort of provocative devil-may-care appearance. A quick shower, an application of her Borghese eye cream gelee and Luminosa face powder, and she would be able to meet the world.

Her hands were reaching for the sweater hem when she remembered Neal, and glanced back at him over her shoulder. "Darling, would you mind?"

He had been standing there, studying her, and she could see the admiration, the glint of masculine desire in his gray eyes. Beth's heart began to thump alarmingly as she found her gaze caught and held by his. It was an intimate moment; she was a woman, he was a man, they were married and alone in this room.

"Candace will be impatient to talk to you," she almost whispered.

He started. "What? Oh, Candace. Yes, well, maybe I'd better go see her, make arrangements for tomorrow."

He walked toward her, however, instead of to the door. His hands came up to her shoulders. "Don't tease me too much, Beth," he murmured.

Then he was gone, closing the door gently behind him.

Beth tried to control her rapid breathing, fighting against the increased banging of her heart. What did he mean? She had no intent of teasing him. Just because circumstances had dictated that they come running up to this hunting lodge didn't mean she was throwing herself at him.

She lifted off the maroon sweater, biting her lower lip. Was she unfair to him? She was no siren, no *femme fatale* to have men swooning at her feet. She was just plain Beth Sheldon, a writer of children's books. Until very recently, she had had no interest in men whatsoever.

"I still don't have any interest in them," she muttered.

Oh, no? What about your husband?

"That's different," she breathed.

But was it? After all, they'd slept in the same room last night, and they were going to sleep in the same room tonight. And for as long as they were staying at Windflower Lodge. It really wasn't fair to the guy. Beth shrugged petulantly and marched toward the bathroom.

He was the one who had wanted to marry her. She hadn't wanted to marry him. If he suffered, he had brought it on himself.

Close to an hour later, she was again before the mirror,

clad in flaming red linen lounging pajamas, her brown hair loose and spreading about her shoulders. A simple necklace and her wedding ring were all her jewelry. She frowned as she regarded herself, wondering if the pajama jacket might be a little too revealing.

She didn't want Neal to think of her as a tease. Still, she had nothing else to wear other than this outfit. At the time she had bought it, she had planned on donning it only on the quiet evenings she spent in the cottage, reading or making research notes for her books.

She hadn't planned on having a man see her in it.

"Oh, for goodness sakes," she exclaimed. "Stop being such a prude, Beth Sheldon."

She swept from the room, conscious of the cloud of perfume that went with her. As she came down the staircase she saw Candace turn from the bar and stare, eyes wide. Almost in the same moment Neal appeared, mouth open at the sight of her.

Confidence came to Beth in that moment. Just because she was a solitary sort of person, being a writer used to working and thinking by herself, didn't mean that she couldn't turn on the charm when she wanted to. And she wanted to, right now, very desperately.

"It's just something I picked up in New York," she told the staring Candace. Beth swiveled, striking a pose with her arms out. "Like it?"

Neal came up behind her, put his arms around her, and gave her a hug. "Darling, you're absolutely radiant."

She could feel him up against her, and she knew that he could feel her, too, which was worse, because she didn't have very much on under the pajamas. Candace turned away quickly, busying herself with ice and liquor.

Beth dug an elbow in Neal, freeing herself.

As she did, she raised her eyes to his, saw the amusement in them, as well as the male admiration. She was skating on very thin ice here, she knew. It was all very well to carry on like a loving wife in front of Candace, but Neal might take her act a little too seriously.

"I don't think we should carry on in front of our hostess, dear," she said, loudly enough so Candace could not fail to hear.

Ice rattled in the glasses.

Touché!

"You're absolutely correct. We'll wait until we retire for the night," he grinned, and Beth began to worry.

How far dared she go in this performance of hers, with a man like Neal Harper? She might be announcing to Candace Thorne that Neal Harper was her husband and hands off because she loved him so much, but what about her husband? How would he take all this posturing?

In a somewhat subdued mood, Beth accepted a glass from Candace and seated herself. They made small talk for a while, concerning the spell of fair weather they were having, the chances of the Red Sox in their drive for the pennant, and the robbery of a Brinks armored truck several months ago.

"You lost money in that robbery, didn't you, Neal?" asked Candace.

"Yes, but we were insured. So we didn't suffer any loss."

It came to Beth that Candace Thorne could talk more knowingly to her husband of the things he was interested in. If she were going to play this role of wife, it might behoove her to learn something of those interests.

After a time, Candace excused herself to go see about the salad.

Neal came over, drawing a hassock along, and sat close to her feet. His eyes went all over the pajamas, and Beth, who knew very well how the linen clung to her flesh, flushed faintly.

"You're very beautiful, you know," he said softly.

"It's just the pajamas," she said hastily.

"No. It's what's inside them."

Beth hid behind her upraised glass, drinking.

When she lowered it, he was still studying her, his gray eyes moving here and there. "Stop staring at me," she hissed.

"I made a better choice than I knew, picking you for a wife," he grinned. "It's the old Neal Harper touch."

"What are we doing tomorrow?" she asked, in an attempt to turn his interest away from her.

"I know what I'd like to do."

"Neal!"

He made a face. "We'll go hunting, I suppose. Might get a

rabbit or two, or see a deer. Who knows? I'm supposed to relax, take it easy, get in light exercise, like walking."

Beth wondered whether she had the proper clothes to go hunting. Probably not. All she had in that line was the slacks and the maroon sweater she had worn today on the drive. Maybe they would do.

Candace was back then, telling them dinner was ready. There was steak and salad, and for dessert, strawberries in cream. It was a good meal, and Beth was surprised by her appetite. She complimented Candace, who shrugged.

"I really can't claim credit for the meal, outside of the salad. I have a woman who does the cooking when we come up here."

Candace paused a moment, then glanced at Neal. "Is your wife a good cook?"

"I haven't the faintest idea. Are you, dear?"

Beth said, "I can whip up enough to stay alive."

They seemed to forget her, then. They spoke of mutual friends, of times when they had gone to parties, to ski lodges, to bathing beaches, to the weddings of their closest friends. Beth sat quietly, listening, telling herself that these two had far more in common than she and Neal did.

She found herself wondering once more why in the world Neal had ever married her. It had been a quixotic gesture, granted. But had it been something more than that? A gesture of defiance as well? Against his mother and the Harper family? Even—against Candace Thorne?

As she let her eyes roam over the blond woman, she saw cool beauty, absolute confidence, a woman who was superbly groomed, never at a disadvantage. Neal Harper must be crazy not to prefer Candace Thorne to her. Or maybe he did, maybe he already regretted his hasty marriage and was showing Beth how close he was to Candace so that she would not object when he told her, some fine day, that he was getting ready to discard her.

As if she would care, when that day came.

She would give him a divorce. Very willingly. Gladly.

Wouldn't she?

She twisted a breadcrumb between forefinger and thumb, feeling oddly miserable. She didn't love Neal, so why should this idea of a divorce suddenly trouble her? She had no claim on him. She would step aside whenever he asked, whenever he grew tired of this farce.

Earlier, talking with Mrs. Harper, she had been most agreeable to leaving Neal. Why should she feel any differently now? Maybe it was because she was growing used to having him beside her. He was a great companion, always amusing, always concerned for her comfort or well-being. That must be it.

She came out of her reverie to find Neal and Candace looking at her. She straightened self-consciously, asking, "Have I missed something?"

"Candy was asking if you wanted to go hunting tomorrow, or if you'd rather stay around the lodge and loaf?"

Beth said slowly, "I'm sure I could never shoot at anything."

"Then stay here and enjoy your day," Candace smiled. "I'll take good care of Neal for you."

I'll bet you will!

"I may go for a walk, explore the woods."

"There's a canoe. Neal tells me you know how to handle one. And a rowboat. Also a Chriscraft."

Beth shook her head. "I'll probably just stroll around."

She wasn't going to tell them that she was afraid of water, since that hand had tried to pull her under, back by Capstone Rock. The memory of it still came to her, at times in dreams. It was always the same, the grayish green waters around her, the thing that held her ankle, dragging her downward, always downward. Sometimes she woke gasping for air.

Candace turned back to Neal and they began to talk again. Beth paid little heed to what they said, and since she knew none of the people they mentioned, she went back to her musings.

Perhaps she should offer to go with them, just to be on the safe side, to make certain that Candace didn't try to steal Neal away from her. But what difference did it really make, if she did? She was a wife by virtue of an accident and a medical miracle, no more.

She had no claim on Neal Harper. It was merely her pride as a woman that was involved, that was all. She would free Neal of his contract any time he asked. She didn't enjoy the idea of playing the stupid, innocent wife who didn't know what was going on right under her own nose.

A yawn constricted the muscles of her throat. She fought against it, giving a horrified glance at her companions. Neither of them noticed, they were too busy laughing together, remembering something or other out of their pasts.

Beth said, "If you don't mind, I think I'll go to bed."

Neither of them heard her. Candace, her hand on Neal's arm, was regaling him with a story about somebody named Jo. Or Joe. She wasn't sure which. Beth cleared her throat. They still paid no attention.

This time she could not fight back the yawn. She gave into it, wholeheartedly.

Neal must have seen it out of the corner of his eye. His expression changed, and he said, "We must be boring you silly, Beth. I'm sorry."

"No, no, not at all. It's very interesting." She gave him a weak smile. "But I must have had too much fresh air today. I'll go upstairs, if you two won't mind too much."

"Not at all," Candace said.

Neal was on his feet, but Beth waved him aside. "I know the way. Don't bother, I really mean it."

She moved toward the staircase, aware that they had turned and were watching her. Suddenly she was too tired to care what they thought. They were both strangers to her, really. She made her way up the redwood and stone staircase and into the bedroom.

She undressed, slid into a warm flannel nightgown, and crept between the sheets. She would not have a hard time falling asleep tonight. Her eyelids were like lead weights. She curled up, head on the pillow, and closed her eyes.

She woke in the morning to a sense of utter silence. She lay a moment, orienting herself to the room, to the fact that she was not in her cottage but in Windflower Lodge. She turned to see how Neal was.

His bed was empty. It was still as immaculate as it had been last night when she had gone to sleep.

Neal had not slept in here, after all.

Had he slept—with Candace?

Chapter Eight

Beth washed and dressed in something like ten minutes.

Her thoughts were chaotic. She had felt dismay and anger at the idea that Neal had not been in the other twin bed. He had betrayed her. He had run to the blond woman at the first opportunity he had. But slowly, as she slid into the beige slacks and maroon sweater, she told herself that she could not blame him.

She didn't want him. Candace did.

It was that simple.

Just the same . . .

She could not help the quivering of her lips, but she would not cry. She would not! Her dismay and anger faded into a sort of numb resignation. It was fated to turn out this way, ever since the beginning. She could scarcely play the role of neglected wife when he lived the role of neglected husband.

"I don't blame him, I don't," she whispered as she ran down the staircase. But in her heart, she did. Bitterly.

There was a note propped up on the kitchen table. It was from Neal.

We ran off early this morning without disturbing you. Be back around dusk—with rabbits and/or a deer. Enjoy the day. Take anything you want.

Neal

" 'We ran off early this morning'," she quoted. "Probably unable to face me after what they'd done last night."

Tears glistened in her eyes. She brushed at them furiously. What was the matter with her? How could she expect Neal to act like a monk? If he didn't have a wife who loved him, what was more natural than for him to turn to Candace Thorne? As he had turned often in the past, no doubt.

Beth was not hungry. Her eyes went around the spotless kitchen, seeing the coffeepot on the stove, the refrigerator that would hold eggs and bacon. There was bread, too, in the breadbox. She could eat as much or as little as she wanted.

Her hand turned on the gas under the coffeepot.

The smell of perking coffee made her change her mind. Why shouldn't she eat? Eat, drink and be merry, for tomorrow we get divorced. So be it, then. Her marriage had been fun while it lasted.

She cooked herself a good breakfast, sat and ate it without appetite, just as something to do. She cleaned up after her, washed and dried the dishes, put them away. She turned and walked into the big living room.

It was ten minutes past ten. She had the whole day to herself. Already, she was lonely. She picked up a magazine, flipped through the pages, tossed it aside. She turned on the radio, listened to some music, then switched it off.

She went out onto the patio. It was cold, and the day was raw, threatening rain. She shivered, went back into the house, found a fleece-lined mackinaw that probably belonged to Candace, and put it on. She stepped out the door into the gray day and bent her head to the wind that whistled past her.

Beth began to walk. She had nowhere special to go, but she found a narrow trail between some trees and followed it, discovering that it led down to a boathouse. She opened a door and peeped in.

A gleaming Chris-Craft bobbed in the lake, roped to pilings. If Neal had been here, she would have enjoyed a ride in that boat, despite her fear of water. But alone—no, thanks. She closed the boathouse door and walked down a wooden quay toward an overturned rowboat and a sleek aluminum canoe alongside it.

Paddles lay under the canoe, she saw as she bent over. She

turned and looked at the lake. It seemed sullen and angry,
under a gray sky. It would rain very soon, in all likelihood.
She did not relish the idea of paddling around in a rainstorm.

The day stretched ahead of her, empty and lonely.

What difference did it make if she went canoeing? Who
would care if the canoe overturned and she drowned?

"Oh, stop feeling so sorry for yourself," she exclaimed.

It would help her get over her fear of water if she took the
canoe out. She couldn't spend the rest of her life hiding from
lakes or oceans. Sooner or later somebody was going to ask
her to go swimming. Or there would come a hot day when a
cool dip would be most appealing.

She had to fight and overcome her fear, right now, when
no one was watching. Beth bent and turned the canoe right-
side up, then began dragging it toward the lake. It was light
and easily manageable. She grabbed the paddles and carried
them to the water's edge. Then she slid the canoe into the
water and, gripping the moldboards, stepped inside, seating
herself on a thwart.

Paddle in hand, she eased the boat out into the gray-green
waters. Despite the rawness of the day, there was a sense of
peace about the forests shutting in the lake waters, the flop of
a fish breaking the surface off toward the tangle of dead
branches where a tree had fallen. Beth breathed in the cool,
damp air, delighting in the movements of her arms and body
as she dipped the paddle, moved it, lifted it out.

The canoe responded to her motions. It shot forward, sliding quietly, with scarcely a gurgle of water at its prow. So
must the Indians have moved across this lake, long ago, before the coming of the white man. This was Nature in its
calmest mood, and for a long time Beth reveled in its
quietude, forgetting her own problems in a deep appreciation
of this wilderness beauty.

Her eyes ran over the distant trees, recognizing a balsam
fir, a white spruce. Once she saw a deer tiptoe lightly toward
the lake, pause at the sight of her, and fade back between the
trees. A raccoon, more daring than the deer, scarcely bothered to lift its head as she passed. She lost track of time,
moving so gently, so slowly, pausing every so often just to
glide soundlessly over the water, paddle suspended so that
drops fell splashing into the lake.

Only when the wind grew brisker did she shiver suddenly and come back to an awareness of how far she had traveled. She straightened and looked back. She could no longer see the boathouse or the lodge. And the water was being whipped up into tiny waves all around her.

She tried to turn the canoe and found that the wind, hitting the empty prow, was matching its strength against her own. Deep went the paddle, and her muscles strained. She bent forward and the breath hissed in her throat as she threw herself against that wind, seeking to swing the canoe about so that its narrow front would face those gusts.

In time she succeeded, but she was very tired. And her work was not yet done. She did not know how many miles she had come. Perhaps the wind had been at her back on the outward trip, and she had not noticed it. And the bite of these stiff breezes were sharper, with a remembered chill of winter lingering in their touch.

When her every bone seemed to ache, Beth turned the canoe and drove it toward a little promontory where a tree hung out above the lake. Hidden behind its branches, close in to the shore, she could wait until the wind abated.

Her hand reached out and caught a branch, and she worked the canoe in beside the fern-covered bank. She slid the paddle into the canoe and sat, breathing deeply, letting the tiredness ooze out of her. She was stranded here, she knew. Unless the blow subsided, she was marooned.

There was no hope of rescue, not for a long time. Neal and Candace were tramping the woods trails, hunting rifles across their arms. They would think her safe and secure in the lodge, probably with her feet up before a roaring fire, immersed in a book. They would never credit the fact that she was sitting huddled here, half frozen, beginning to worry.

Of course, she could step ashore, try to find her way back between the trees, but one glance at those boles and the darkness between them, told her she would never find her way. She did not know where the lodge was, except its general direction. No, it would be better to wait here.

After a time, she grew hungry.

It must be two or three in the afternoon. She had eaten a good breakfast—gratefully, she thought how she had decided to eat, despite her lack of appetite—so there was no danger of her starving to death.

"Starving to death," she giggled. "Honestly, Beth Sheldon."

But because she could not put her hand to food, she grew even hungrier. And because she wore only the slacks and sweater under the mackinaw, the wind bit more coldly against her flesh.

"All I need now is rain," she muttered.

The rain came in time, wet and cold. It drove downward as if with sadistic cruelty, having found a weak, helpless human to annoy. Beth endured it for a time, head bowed. Then she noticed that the wind had abated and was little more than a zephyr, now.

She eyed the lake, the droplets of water drumming down upon it. Dare she venture out there? She was wet and cold already, so some more water on her would make little difference. It was the wind that had balked her; the rain would not.

Beth pushed away from the shore, digging in the paddle. Out from under the protection of the tree, the rain pelted her. But her chin rose defiantly. She blinked the rain from her eyes and concentrated on her course.

The paddle rose and dipped, lifted and dipped again.

She never knew how long it took her to make that return trip. It seemed an eternity. She was drenched to the skin and shivering steadily, but she fought the canoe and the water and the steady rain with a grimness that tightened her lips and drove all thought of discomfort from her mind.

It was hard to see in the downpour, and she was never quite sure of the landmarks she had noted on her outward journey. All she could do was keep going, and hope and pray that soon now she would catch a glimpse of the boathouse and the wooden quay.

After a long time, she heard the deep throb of a motor. She squinted through the rain. Yes, over there. A speedboat with a man and woman in it, clad in sou'westers and raincoats. She yelled and waved.

The speedboat was backing out of a boathouse.

Beth recognized the Chris-Craft, and in it, Neal and Candace. She dug in the paddle, straightened, and brought the canoe surging forward. Almost at the same moment, Neal saw her.

He gunned the Chris-Craft, bringing it sweeping around and toward her. Beth went to meet it, trying to sit as straight as possible, to appear as nonchalant as the rain pouring down on her would permit.

Neal yelled, "You idiot! Didn't you know there was a storm coming? What were you trying to do?"

Her lower lip quivered, and she blinked back tears. Here she was exhausted, chilled to the bone, wet and damp and dismal, and he was yelling at her. When she realized that no one would know whether she was crying or not—her face was so wet, what did a few tears matter?—she let them go and sat there weeping, half in anger, half in relief.

Candace came to the back of the boat, reached out with a hook attached to a long cord, and dropped it over the pointed prow. Neal watched, eased in the motor, and swung around in a long arc toward the boathouse. Beth sat there, feeling very much like a naughty child who had been caught with a hand in the cookie jar.

If Neal had been alone in the boat, it would not have mattered at all that she should be found like this. But it was the presence of Candace that drove hot iron into her, that made her grit her teeth and whisper words under her breath. The blond was so cool, so self-possessed, she seemed so much at home that the sight of her only added to her own abasement.

Then the Chris-Craft was sliding into the boathouse, Neal was shutting off the motor, leaping out, coming along the catwalk to grasp the canoe and pull it forward. He was opening his mouth—probably to yell at her, Beth decided—when he glanced into her eyes.

He changed what he was about to say. He asked gently, "Are you all right?"

She nodded dumbly, unable to talk.

His hand was there, she put her own in it, he brought her up onto the catwalk and against him. His arms went around her, holding her. Under his breath he whispered, "You goose. I ought to spank you."

But he hugged her, held her so closely that Beth could hardly breathe. Yet she liked the sensation. She felt a warmth come into her blood, and for the first time she stopped her steady shivering.

"I—I'm s-sorry," she breathed.

This time she was afraid he would break her back, his hug was so strong. But he let her go, his hands still on her, as he muttered, "Let's get you out of those wet clothes."

He half-carried her, an arm about her middle, up from the boathouse and along the little trail that led to the lodge. When Beth protested that she would drip water all over the place he merely gave her a squeeze and brought her into the lodge, up the redwood staircase and into her room.

"Get undressed. Take a hot shower. I'll be up with some wine."

It was only in the light of the bedroom that she saw his face clearly for the first time. There was lipstick on his mouth.

He had been kissing Candace.

Beth stood frozen, dripping water. She watched him turn and walk out, closing the door behind him. So, then, what she had suspected, was true. He was amusing himself with Candace, right under her nose. Almost in defiance of her. Or maybe it was something more than mere amusement. Maybe he had been telling Candace what an idiot he had been, marrying a nobody when he should have married her.

All last night he had told her. His bed was not slept in. And again today, he had been assuring her of the fact. Beth was numb inside.

She had to force herself to undress, to get under the shower. She stood rooted there for a long time, her thoughts chaotic. She must let the guy go. She saw that clearly now. It wasn't fair to him, this crazy marriage.

"I don't want to let him go," she whispered to the cascading waters.

Do you love him? she asked herself.

We-ell, n-no.

So why do you want him as a husband?

I've grown accustomed to the guy, as the song says.

Angrily, she shook herself, turned off the shower, then dried herself in a fluffy Cannon. A girl can't have her cake and eat it, too. She had to face up to this fact. The sooner the better. For everybody. Yes, for her, as well.

Once she let him go, she could go back to her old life, her familiar ways. She wouldn't stay in Rocky Cove any more, she would sell the cottage, go somewhere else, away from Neal Harper, away from that somebody who had tried to kill her twice.

Wrapped in the towel, she came out of the bathroom. Neal was standing in the room, a glass filled with wine in a hand. His eyes went over her and she turned her own eyes to a mirror, to study herself as he would see her. The towel covered her modestly enough. A lot of her legs was showing, and her bare shoulders, but no more than a man would see if she were wearing a bathing suit. Indeed, not nearly as much.

Her thick brown hair was tousled, hanging down her back, and her eyes were overly bright. Her mouth seemed to pout in sullen lines. Not very attractive, all things considered.

Beth put her eyes on him. The lipstick was gone. Probably Candace had noticed it, pointed it out to him. They didn't want to hurt her too much, maybe.

He held out the wine to her. "Drink it, it'll do you good."

She sipped it, standing there before him, her eyes never leaving his face. Well? Was he going to give her the bad news now? Or was he going to wait until she was dressed, and had eaten, and was maybe in a better mood?

"Did you sleep well last night?" she asked sweetly.

His eyes darted toward his bed. Guiltily, of course.

"I didn't want to disturb you. You looked so comfortable, so sweet lying there, I just couldn't wake you up."

"Was Candace glad to see you?"

"Candace? What's she got to do with it?"

"Oh, come on, Neal."

She turned away from him suddenly, so that he would not notice the hurt in her face. Her lower lip was quivering again, dammit. For a brief moment, the room was silent.

Then he was behind her, his hands on her shoulders. He said softly, "I slept in my old room. Alone. You can believe that or not, but I did."

"I s-suppose she didn't kiss you today, either? There was lipstick on your mouth when you were in here before. Did she tell you to wipe it off so I wouldn't see it? It was good of her."

Neal was silent. The only indication he had heard was the

pressure of his hands where they lay on her shoulders. Then those hands were turning her, leaving her shoulders to go around her.

Beth was slammed against him, was lifting her face to protest this rude handling, when his lips crushed hers.

For just a moment, she was so surprised, she could not move. Then her body told her she did not want to move, that she was enjoying this kiss, it was sending bolts of savage electricity all through her flesh. Her own mouth was betraying her, and she was kissing him back, as fiercely as he was kissing her.

Suddenly she realized what she was doing.

She gasped, then sought to push him away from her. But as she made the attempt, the towel slipped and she had to grab it. Flushed and shaking, she drew back, staring up into his burning eyes.

"I was right," he whispered. "I knew it. Inside me, I knew it. There's fire inside you, in back of that icy shell."

"I—I don't know what you're talking about."

He smiled down at her. He caught one of her hands, drew it to his lips, kissed it. "I'll wait. Oh, yes. I'll wait, Beth Harper."

"You're just wasting your time. I don't love you and—and I never will. Go back to Candace. She'll kiss you and cuddle you."

"She kissed me when I got a brace of rabbits with one shot, earlier. It was an impulsive thing. It didn't mean anything."

"You can divorce me anytime you want. I won't fight it."

"Will you stop yakking about divorce? I'm very happy the way we are."

She turned away to adjust the towel. The wine was very warming inside her, and a quick glance at the mirror told her how it had heightened her color. Or had the kiss done that?

"I don't know why you're happy," she muttered.

"Aren't you happy?"

She shrugged her shoulder petulantly. Behind her, Neal laughed softly. He bent his head and kissed her bare shoulder, then moved toward the door before she could resent it.

"Dinner in an hour, cocktails before," he sang out.

The door closed behind him.

Beth stood a long time staring at her mirrored reflection. What about it, girl? You enjoyed that kiss, you sure did. Don't lie to yourself, no matter how much you may to Neal. He had you going, for a few seconds. You didn't even want to push him away, you wanted to throw your arms around him and hold onto him for dear life.

When he kissed your shoulder, you thought you'd faint. What's with you, Beth Sheldon? Have you finally gone and fallen for this guy?

She sneered, "I have not."

Liar! Liar! Liar!

She scowled at herself, muttered in vexation, and went to the clothes closet. She would wear something plain and sensible tonight, something warm and comfortable. She settled on a pair of brown slacks, a pullover sweater, and a sweater jacket in space-dyed stripes, with kimono sleeves.

When she was dressed and finished doing up her hair in an upsweep, she felt more her normal self. The emotional upheaval Neal had caused with his kiss was a thing of the past. Not exactly forgotten, but at least laid away to rest. She hesitated a little, uneasy about meeting Candace after having been rescued from that downpour.

She certainly hadn't appeared in a good light. But what had happened couldn't be helped. She could scarcely hide herself away in this room for the rest of her stay.

Determinedly, her chin lifted. What could Candace Thorne do to her, that she hadn't already done? Take her husband from their room last night and kissing him today? Nothing. She told herself gloomily that she didn't believe those excuses Neal had given her. Not one little bit.

Neal was coming up the stairs as she left the room. His face seemed worried as she glanced at it. But at sight of her, he smiled. "I was wondering how you were making out."

What he meant was: was she going to stay upstairs all night? Hide from him and Candace because of what had happened? She laughed and caught his arm.

"I just wanted to make sure I looked presentable."

"You'll always do that."

"Oh? Even the way I was in that canoe?"

"You looked adorable, even then. Wet—but adorable."

Beth laughed. "What a flatterer. Still, I will admit it was

foolish of me to go so far. I should have realized the sky was gray, that rain was coming. But it was so peaceful, so lovely out there, Neal, I—I just forgot about everything."

"When the weather clears, I'll take you for a moonlight ride, one of these nights."

Candace came striding to meet them, clad in a gray velour kaftan. Her long blond hair was loose, falling below her shoulders and caught in a golden headband. Something very expensive-looking dangled from a golden chain below her breasts. She looked like a fashion model, Beth decided morosely.

"Are you all right now?" she asked.

"Never better. I'm very comfortable. And I want to say I'm sorry to have put you to so much trouble."

Candace smiled faintly. "I'm used to rescuing people who go out on Moosehead. It's a very temperamental lake, this one. But since you came back to us, I guess it all worked out fine."

Unfortunately for you, Beth told herself. It would have made life very simple for Candace Thorne if Beth Harper had tumbled out of the canoe when a particularly fierce gust of wind had caught the frail craft. Beth shuddered. If she had fallen into the lake she would have panicked and drowned. She knew it. It was too soon after that other time she had gone swimming, when the hand had caught hold of her . . .

"Are you okay?" Neal was asking.

Beth forced herself to smile. "I'm fine. Just happened to think that if the canoe had gone over with me, I might not have been able to swim to shore."

Neal caught his breath. Ah, he understood what she meant, at any rate. He was remembering what she had told him about the time she had been out at Capstone Rock in a scuba outfit.

His hand caught her arm, drawing her toward the bar. "You need a good, stiff drink," he said quietly.

Candace Thorne was watching them from across the room, biting her lip and frowning thoughtfully. Was she, too, contemplating the fact that if the canoe had gone over with her, she would not have Mrs. Beth Harper to trouble her any more?

The idea seemed to brighten Candace. She gave Beth a

wide smile and said, "We can forget about what happened. We won't do anything so foolish again, will we?"

No, indeed. We will remain alone in the lodge, never stirring from it, so that Candace Thorne can have Neal Harper all to herself, and know that when she returns with Neal, Beth will not need to be rescued and so take Neal's interest away from Candace Thorne.

All this ran through her head as Beth returned that smile, while Neal held her arm, keeping her near his big body. She said, "I hate to be such a helpless creature. I guess I'm not used to this rough and ready life."

Neal said, "You go on long walks by yourself, back home. Why can't you come with us tomorrow? You don't have to shoot guns, you know."

Candace did not like that idea. Her eyelids flickered and she turned to hide her expression, bending over the cocktail glasses.

Beth murmured, "No, I think I'll stay close to home. Rest up, so to speak, from what happened today."

She would be giving Candace all the opportunity she might need, she thought grimly, by letting her go traipsing off through those woods with her husband. Well, so be it. If Neal wanted Candace, let him have her. She accepted a cocktail from the blond girl and began to sip it.

Dinner was pleasant enough, lamb with mint sauce and au gratin potatoes, with a salad garnished by an Italian dressing. Beth ate heartily—the exercise in the canoe had given her a good appetite. She even permitted herself a helping of the *mousse au choclat* that was so light and sweet as it melted on the tongue. She thought of her own cooking efforts, an omelet or maybe pork chops or broiled fish, and made a face.

She complimented Candace on the meal and Neal chuckled.

"Candace can't boil water," he said. "A French-Canadian woman gets these meals. She and her husband live here. Candace told you about her last night, remember?"

"Oh. Oh, yes. Of course."

Suddenly she felt a little better. She supposed she could make a chocolate mousse like this, after years of practice. If Neal liked it that much, that is. He would have to be understanding, naturally. She couldn't whip up such a dessert and make it taste this good the first time.

Whatever was she thinking? She and Neal would not be together long enough for her to cook his meals. Her daydreams were part of this life she found herself living, and just as nonsensical.

They had Irish coffee in the big family room, relaxed and indolent. Candace was tired, Beth was happy to see. All that tramping had worn her out. And Neal—well, one look at his face was enough to tell her that he, too, felt the strain of the long day.

At ten o'clock, Beth sighed and rose to her feet. "Come along, darling," she said sweetly. "You need a good night's sleep."

Neal glanced up at her in surprise. Beth went on, "Mustn't overdo, you know."

"I'm fine," he muttered.

"Of course you are. But if you're going off with Candace tomorrow, you want to be in good shape."

Neal eyed her suspiciously. Beth made her face bland, expressionless. He scowled and shrugged, "I suppose you're right. I do feel a little tired, come to think of it."

She held out her hand to him. "Then come along. Tonight you're going to get your proper rest."

Candace Thorne stared back at her, challengingly. For an instant, Beth braced herself for a fight. But Candace only gave a shrug with one shoulder and reached for her glass.

She'll have him all day tomorrow, Beth told herself gloomily. And here I am worrying about his health and his strength, after that operation. I'm helping to keep him well so he can hug that blond all day long. I must be some kind of nut.

Chapter Nine

For the next two days, Beth poked around the lodge or sat reading, curled up in a comfortable chair. When the urge moved her, she went for long, lonely walks through the woods, always making sure that she could find her way back home again. No more near-accidents for her. She would be careful, very careful.

If only she were as careful where Neal was concerned! She was practically throwing Neal into the blond girl's arms, letting them roam the woods together with rifles under their arms. She could guess what they did when they weren't hunting!

So let them. It didn't bother her. Neal had made a mistake when he had married Beth Sheldon. There was no reason to crucify the poor guy because of it. She wanted to be fair about all this. If he discovered a little too late that it was Candace Thorne he loved, it was better for both of them to know it now.

Before—

Well, before their married life got too involved.

Beth sat with her chin on her fist, staring out over Moosehead Lake, seated on a tree stump on a small bluff above the lake. Her eyes could touch the log sides of the lodge from this eminence, see also the woodlands around it. It was a beautiful spot. In other circumstances, if she and Neal really loved each other, for instance, it would have been ideal for a honeymoon.

She and Neal slept in the same room, of course. But every night when they retired, she made Neal undress in the bathroom and get into bed before she herself undressed in the bathroom. She always made sure he was comfortable, she tucked in his covers, she asked him if there was anything he wanted, before she slid between her own sheets.

It was a little game they played.

Beth kicked at a stone, sending it tumbling down the slope. A tiny part of her wished he wouldn't be so acquiescent to her wishes. Once, just once, she wished he would grab her and kiss her again, as he had that other night. At least he would be telling her she was a desirable woman.

She sat up straight, horrified. What was the matter with her? If Neal ever did what she was thinking, she would have fought him off. She knew it, deep inside her. She didn't want his kisses, his caresses. Let Candace Thorne have those.

Beth jumped to her feet, then began to walk. She was certainly giving the blond all the opportunity she needed. She was practically throwing Neal into her arms. Yet something deep within her was making her do this, almost as though she felt the need to test her husband.

Or was it that she wanted him to turn away from her, toward Candace? To set her free to lead her own life? She did not know. All she understood was that she was miserable, that she felt lonely and abandoned.

When she returned to the lodge, Neal and Candace were already there.

Neal said, "Come on, I want to show you the lake while the sun is setting."

"I'd love to," she exclaimed.

To one side, Candace was frowning, biting her lip. Was that jealousy flaring in her eyes? Or cool calculaticn? Beth could not tell. All she knew was that she was eager to be with Neal again, to sit in that canoe and be paddled across the lake waters, calm in this late afternoon of the day.

They walked down the narrow path to the boathouse. Neal slid the canoe into the water, watching as Beth deftly seated herself. Then they were gliding silently out onto the still water, Neal's paddle slowly dipping and rising. Beth stared around her at the reflection of the trees in the placid lake, at the blue bowl of sky, darkening slightly now as the sun was setting westward.

It was so quiet, so peaceful, Beth could not speak. She sat there drinking in the scenery, telling herself that the moods and emotions of people were of no concern here, that whatever problems she might have disappeared here, where nothing mattered but the land and the water.

"It's beautiful," she whispered after a long time.

When Neal did not answer she looked back over her shoulder at him. He was looking at her with tenderness in his eyes, with a muted affection that made her catch her breath. He nodded then, lifting the paddle free so they would drift.

"It's the loveliest place I know," he said at last, staring where the red ball of sun outlined the trees.

"No wonder Candace comes up here," she murmured.

"She doesn't come very often."

Beth frowned. "But I thought that—"

"That she was a huntress? An outdoors girl?"

"Something like that, yes."

"She's doing it for me, you know. Thinks the open air and exercise will get me back on my feet real soon. And maybe she's right. I'm feeling a lot stronger, the last day or two. Won't be long now."

And what then, Beth Harper?

She ran a fingertip along the moldboard. "After you get back on your feet, what are you planning?"

"To go back to Boston and my business. What else?"

"Oh. And—and what about us?"

"You'll come to Boston as my wife, of course."

Beth stared straight ahead. She did not want to go to Boston with Neal Harper. Actually, she was not his wife, not really. She hadn't thought about this angle of her marriage. In her mind it was always a perpetual being together, this marriage of hers, like a loveless honeymoon. In Boston, of course, there would be a lot of women who would be quite willing to take Neal Harper, married or unmarried, she thought gloomily.

"There will be dinner parties, theater groups. Shopping to do. You'll love it."

His voice droned on, pointing out all the pleasures in life she would have as Mrs. Neal Harper. Beth scarcely heard him, she was too deeply immersed in her thoughts. She could scarcely go on living with Neal as his wife without accepting him into her bed. She made a face. Accepting him into her bed. It sounded so cold-blooded, that phrase. As if she were paying him back for taking care of her.

She didn't want a husband on such terms.

She wanted love with her husband. A breathless, emotional turmoil of love. Maybe she was being silly, maybe there was no such thing. But it was what she wanted—no, what she demanded—of marriage.

Neal asked, "How does that appeal to you?"

"I'm sorry. I—I was thinking."

"About us, I trust."

She nodded, staring at the water as it slid past. "Yes. I was telling myself that the sooner this farce is ended, the better it will be for both of us."

She wondered if she sounded as miserable as she felt.

Neal said nothing, but went on paddling as serenely as though she had not spoken. What was he thinking? That she was some sort of spoiled brat who didn't know her own mind? She wouldn't have blamed him if he did. She dipped her hand in the lake and watched the water swirl about her fingers.

Neal turned the canoe after a long time, sending it back toward the lodge with swift, powerful strokes. Beth could feel the surge of the craft under her, and she sensed the anger that must have been in her husband. No man likes to be told that he does not attract a woman. Neal was no exception to the rule. And yet, she told herself that he did attract her, that under different circumstances she might well fall in love with Neal Harper.

As the canoe grounded, Beth stood up, meaning to leap nimbly on shore. But her foot slipped on the floorboard and she pitched sideways.

Strong arms went around her instantly, catching her. She nestled in those arms for a moment, happy to have them around her. Then his lips were on her neck, between her sweater and her hair, and he was kissing her hungrily, nuzzling her throat.

"You see?" he whispered. "I'll always be there whenever you need me, to protect you."

He set her safely on the ground, busying himself with the canoe. It was as though nothing had happened between them. He was ignoring her. Beth drew in a deep breath. Why hadn't she pulled away from him when she felt his lips at her throat? She shook her head. She just couldn't understand herself.

Candace was waiting for them in the family room, nestled into a big chair, a martini in her hand. Beth wondered if she could see the heightened color in her face and understand its cause. Probably yes. Candace was a woman too.

Neal said, "Oooops. Out of cigarettes. I'll just run down the road a ways to the general store. Be right back."

Beth turned, watching him walk from the room.

"Beth."

She turned. Candace was staring down into her glass, frowning slightly.

"Now that we're alone and have a chance to talk . . ."

Her voice drifted into silence.

Beth murmured, "You were going to tell me something."

"About Neal. The only thing is, I don't know whether I should or not." The green eyes left the glass, lifting to stare at Beth. "I know Neal a lot better than you do, you see."

I'll bet you do!

"Neal is playing a game with you, the same sort of game he plays with all the girls he knows."

Beth asked as calmly as she could, "Is he?"

Candace smiled faintly. "Oh, he married you. It was a crazy thing to do, but typically Neal Harperish. It wasn't at all fair to you."

Beth checked the reply that came bubbling to her lips. She walked across the room to the bar and poured Scotch over some ice cubes in a glass. She was not a drinker, but she told herself that she might need this.

"How not fair?" she asked.

"You aren't used to the type of man Neal is. Reckless. Whimsical. Sure of getting his own way. Charming, when he wants to be. But underneath it all, he's utterly ruthless."

Beth moved to a chair, sat down and crossed her legs. She

sipped at the amber liquid. "He told me he was a playboy," she said at last.

Candace came close to snorting. "He's out to make you fall in love with him. And he's succeeded."

"He has not! I don't love him."

Candace smiled gently. "You're head over heels in love with him, but you don't know it. I've seen the way you look at him. Oh, yes."

The blond girl finished her drink, put the glass down, sat up straight, hands together on her knees. "You may hate me for this, but I'm going to say it anyhow. Don't let him do it to you, Beth. You're a fine girl. I admire you. You don't play this game the way the rest of us do, the girls who know Neal and men like Neal. When you give of yourself, it's going to be all the way. Isn't it?"

Beth nodded.

Candace said softly, "Neal will charm the pants off you. He'll be your dream man before you know it. He'll be protective, he'll kiss you and let you go so suddenly you'll think the kiss never happened. He'll get you off balance and keep you that way—until—

"—until one fine day you'll wake up and realize that Neal Harper is your entire life, that without him you're absolutely nothing. And then Neal Harper will have won his game, and you'll be out in the cold."

Beth whispered, "He can divorce me any time he wants."

"Can he now? Level with me, Beth. No. Level with yourself. If you get a divorce, you're going to cut off your nose to spite your face. You're in love with him already, I tell you. I just don't want you to love him so much you're going to let him hurt you, and hurt you badly."

As he had hurt Candace Thorne?

Perhaps the blond girl sensed what was in her mind. "He's hurt me, and badly. And I know what he is. I don't want to see you hurt. You'll be hurt far more than I was."

Candace leaned back, crossing her legs at the ankles. "You think Neal slept with me, the first night you were here? He didn't. Yes, I kissed him the next day and left lipstick on his mouth for you to see. Not to hurt you, though. To try and warn you, to let you know what sort of guy Neal is.

"He can't help it. It's like food and drink to him, this

courting of a girl. It's relaxation from business pressures, I think. It's a different kind of activity, one he can lose himself in, and it's too damn bad for any girl he picks on."

Candace brooded at her Pappagallos. She muttered, "Go on. Hate me. I won't blame you."

Beth opened her mouth, then closed it.

Finally she murmured, "I don't hate you, Candace. I'm glad we've had this little talk. I—I just don't know what to say."

The blond girl waved her hand. "No need to say a word. Just be careful. Don't let Neal break your heart the way he has others." She put her hands on the chair arms and got to her feet. "Now I'd better go see how far along Marie is with dinner."

Left alone, Beth thought about what Candace Thorne had told her. How far could she trust this woman? Maybe this was all part of a caper Candace had thought up to get Neal back for herself. Still, she had seemed honest enough. What she had told her was little more than what Bertram Lambkin had said about Neal Harper. Or Neal himself, for that matter. He had admitted to being a playboy.

When her husband returned, Beth studied him. He was tall, lean, very athletic. There was an air about him, a confidence that had been born of continued success not only in the business world but in his affairs with women. He actually oozed charm when he smiled, as he was doing now at her, and moving toward her solicitously.

"Tired? Want to shower and lie down before dinner?"

She nodded, rising. "Yes. I think I will, Neal."

She did not add that she wanted to get away from him, from his physical presence that always had such a magnetic attraction for her. She might know him for a playboy, but that didn't mean she was indifferent to him. Alone, she could think more rationally, without his nearness to distract her.

Yet when she was in the shower, she found that she was just as mixed up as ever. Granted the truth of all that Candace said, the fact still remained that she was married to him, that he represented some sort of security to her, that with him beside her, she need not fear the danger which had threatened her in the past.

She did not know what to think. Or do. One thing was

clear: she would not be the one to divorce Neal. She would go on playing this role of unloving wife, and if he didn't like it, then let him do the divorcing.

But she would be wary of him. Oh, yes. When he grabbed and kissed her, as he would no doubt do from time to time, she must close her heart to him, bank the emotions she admitted he stirred in her. There must be no yielding to him, no entanglement of her heart. This was what Neal wanted.

Once he had gotten that, he would toss her aside. Ruthlessly, he would go on to other conquests. If she remained cool, if she refused all his advances, he would stay on with her until he got his way. Which would be never, naturally.

At the very least, he would keep her alive.

She donned a white dress and jacket outfit with blue scallops, then slid her feet into platform-heeled shoes. Turning before the mirror, she felt suddenly more confident, more able to meet these problems that had arisen. She could not change the fact of her marriage nor Neal Harper's character, but she could keep a tight control over herself.

Candace and Neal were finishing their cocktails when she came downstairs.

"Nothing for me, thanks," she smiled, waving a hand as Neal rose. "I'm not going to spoil my taste buds."

Neal said, "Our little canoe ride seemed to do you good."

The mirror had assured her that the white dress and jacket were setting off her rich brown hair and heightened skin tones superbly. When she had stared into it, Beth had wondered whether that lakeside kiss had anything to do with the color of her cheeks. As Neal was thinking now, of course.

So let him think he was the Prince Charming who would sweep her off her feet. It would only make him more agreeable. Beth gave him a radiant smile.

"Indeed it did," she answered. "I wouldn't have missed it for worlds."

Dinner was another masterpiece. Chateaubriand steak served with oyster *au poivre*, baked stuffed potato, and arugala and escarole salad was a meal Beth would long remember. Not only for the food, either. Because Neal kept flashing her glances in which she could read admiration, puzzlement, and challenge. She fed on those as much as she did the meat.

As they were about to sample the crepes suzette flamed in liqueurs, Neal announced that they were leaving in the morning. Beth caught a flicker of surprise on the blond girl's face an instant before she herself reacted.

"We've imposed on Candy enough," he stared with a wave of his hand. Then he added with a grin, "And I'm certain that Marie will be happy to see the last of us. These crepes are a specialty of hers, but they're a lot of work."

Candace said, "She enjoys cooking."

"Still, I'm afraid we have to be going. I'm feeling a lot better, much stronger. It was a brainstorm to have us, Candy. I won't forget it. But I can't hide up here for the rest of my life, much as I'd like to. I happen to be a businessman."

Candace shrugged. "Whatever you say, Neal."

Beth had the idea that this was the rule of a lot of people who knew Neal Harper. Whatever you say, Neal. Nobody ever stood up to him, apparently.

Beth murmured slowly, "I'll have to pack. But it won't take long. I'll get it out of the way so we can relax with a nightcap before bedtime."

Some hours later, when they were alone in their room, Beth asked, "Why do you want to go home tomorrow, Neal? All of a sudden, out of the blue, there it is. We go home."

"There are things I have to do."

"What sort of things?"

He gave her a big grin. "Just—things. Oh, I'm not going back to Boston. Not just yet. But I feel a lot stronger. I'm getting restless."

She had to be content with that, but Beth had the feeling that he was returning to Rocky Cove because of her. Why? What had she done or said that had caused him to decide so suddenly?

She drifted off to sleep trying to find an answer.

They were up early next morning and on the road after a hearty breakfast. Neal did not push the powerful Iso Grifo, but they seemed to cover the miles much faster than they had coming. He was silent, seemingly preoccupied, and Beth's occasional glances caught him frowning thoughtfully.

It was not until three in the afternoon that they stopped for lunch, and then it was only for sandwiches and coffee.

Neal seemed to be in a fever of impatience, as though he had a task to perform.

When he let her off at the cottage, he carried in her bags, nodded to her, and took off. Beth stared after the dark blue car with wonder in her eyes. What was so important to drag him off, away from her so suddenly? Musing, she walked back into the cottage.

Only when she was alone did the memory of her personal danger touch her mind. She shivered, standing in her bedroom, peering out at the woods. Would that bearded man be out there, after all these days when she had been gone? If he meant her harm, as he did, he might well be. Beth rushed to pull down the shades before she turned on the lights.

Tomorrow she would call a travel agency, make a reservation for a trip to England and Ireland. She would stay away three weeks to a month. While she was away, she would put the cottage up for sale. She wasn't going to get herself killed for some reason she did not know or could not guess. Thanks to Neal she had enough money to afford it.

She changed into lounging pajamas and brushed her hair, letting it fall loose about her shoulders. Her marriage was at an end—Neal's strange conduct had assured her of that. He could hardly wait to drop her off and get away.

Probably to see some girl who would welcome him with open arms. Beth stopped brushing and scowled. In Boston, no doubt. He must have a whole harem in that city. Well, it was no skin off her nose.

Just the same, she missed him.

All she had to look forward to was a lonely meal in her kitchen and a book to read. She made a face. The prospect wasn't very appealing, not any more. She had grown used to the idea of having Neal around her.

She moved at a listless pace into the kitchen, then opened the refrigerator. There wasn't very much to eat. Some cheese, a piece of dried meat, eggs, milk. First thing to do was put up a pot of coffee. After that she could make her meal.

Beth was turning the gas on under the coffeepot when the doorbell rang. She shut off the gas and moved into the living room, a cold chill running down her back.

"Who is it?" she called.

"Neal. Come on, open up."

She ran to the door, unbolted it, turned the lock, and flung it open. Neal Harper stood there, a heavy bag in one hand, a sleeping bag in the other.

"Aren't you going to invite me in?" he grinned.

Chapter Ten

Beth had never been so happy to see anyone. She reached out, caught his arm, pulled him inside. He put down the sleeping bag and the valise, and said, "I'm hungry. What's for supper?"

Beth did not move. She let her eyes rove over him, noting that his efforts with the bags had not weakened him, that he seemed filled with vitality, with energy.

"Not very much," she said slowly. "I was going to make myself an omelet. I'll make a big one. I don't have much food in the house."

"We'll go shopping tomorrow."

Beth was uneasy. "There's something you should know. I'm not the cook Marie is."

Neal chuckled. "Not very many women are. Marie's a jewel. I've tried to get her to come down here and work for me, but she likes the north woods." He sighed. "The only way I'll ever get her to work for me is to buy Windflower Lodge. And Candy's father won't sell."

He rubbed his hands together. "What about that omelet?"

Beth ran into the kitchen, aware that her heart was pounding and that she had a big, silly grin on her face. Neal was back with her, and she did not have to fear an attack by that bearded man. She could have hugged him, but decided against it. Neal had brought along a sleeping bag. No sense in tempting him too far.

She cut up chunks of cheese, broke eggs into a bowl, mixed in the cheese, and buttered the big skillet. She worked swiftly, dexterously, and was only aware that Neal was watching her when she brought bread out of the breadbox to toast.

He was sitting in a kitchen chair in his shirtsleeves, smiling faintly. Beth raised her eyebrows. Neal said, "This will be the first time you've ever cooked for me. I'm looking forward to it."

Was this part of the game that Neal found so interesting? He had a wife, new to him, she was preparing his food, also a different experience. She turned from him to the toaster, putting it before him with some bread.

"You can make the toast." She regarded him a moment. "You do know how, don't you?"

"Golden brown. Watch."

Then they were eating together, chewing and sipping coffee, smiling at one another. Just like an old married couple, Beth thought. She wondered if he was any good at drying dishes. Probably not, she decided.

Over their second cup of coffee, Beth asked, "Can't you tell me now? Why were you in such a hurry to get back here?"

"I'm closer to my field of operations."

Beth swirled that around in her mind. Was *she* his field of operations? Did he think that by being with her day and night, he would be able to break down the barriers she had thrown up against him? There was no Candace Thorne here to act as a possible deterrent to his amorous ideas. Beth started worrying.

Despite that sleeping bag, he might well try to force his way into her bedroom. There was only one bedroom in her cottage, and it held only one bed. A bed she was not about to share, not even with this husband of hers.

To her amazement, when she started washing the dishes, he began drying them. She shook her head at him, saying, "You're not my idea of a playboy at all. Or do playboys dry dishes? Maybe there's something about them I don't know."

"I'm not a playboy any more. I've given all that up. I'm a husband now, with duties and responsibilities."

Beth eyed him carefully. Was this just a ploy in a scheme he had been cooking up to break down her defenses? Actually, he was being more a playboy than ever, she reasoned, only this husband-and-wife act was very much a part of it. He must have seen that she liked it—he would use it as a wedge to make her give in to him.

Once that happened . . .

They finished with the dishes, then went into the living room.

Neal asked, "What do you usually do at night? Before you hit the sack, that is?"

"Read. Sometimes I watch a little television. What would you like to do?"

"Anything you say," he beamed.

He was being much too agreeable. Beth seated herself, settled back comfortably in the easy chair, and watched him sit down across from her. She could play this game just as well as he could. Armed by the knowledge of what he was trying to do, she was quite safe.

"Let's talk," she suggested. "I don't really know much about you. This will be a good way for us to get acquainted."

Neal began to speak, telling her stories of his boyhood and college days. He explained how his studies had prepared him to take over the Harper interests when his father had died. He was an interesting talker, and he held her spellbound. But this too, was being a playboy. A playboy was always interesting. Boredom, to such a man—or to the woman whom he was favoring at the moment—was a dirty word.

"And what are you going to do here, with me?" Beth wondered when he was done. Her hand moved to indicate the cottage. "I should think that a place like this would be very confining to a man like you."

"On the contrary. While you write, I'll work out there in your garden. Weed it, care for the flowers, for the tomatoes and eggplants, that sort of thing."

"You'll die of boredom."

His eyes went over her. "I don't think so. At least, if that man who keeps watching you sees a man around the place, he may be scared off."

Beth stiffened slightly. Was that it? Was her safety his main concern? But why should it be? After all, he was rich enough to hire round-the-clock guards to keep her cottage under surveillance. Still, it was a nice gesture.

Beth said slowly, "I won't deny I'm happy you're here. You're right, of course. With you here, I'll be safe." She hesitated, then asked, glancing at the clock over the mantel, "How about a cup of hot chocolate? I always have one before going to sleep."

They drank hot chocolate. Then Neal undid his sleeping bag in the living room, giving her a wry smile. "In case anybody tries to get in at you, I'll be here."

Beth closed her bedroom door and leaned against it. Just knowing he was out there put a warm feeling inside her. She did not have to call a travel agent or arrange to sell the cottage, with Neal here. But how long would he stay? He was an important man in the business world. How long could he afford to remain away from his varied interests?

She showered, undressed, and slipped into bed. She was too tired to read. She nestled under the covers and fell asleep.

The smell of frying bacon woke her. She scrambled into slacks and a pullover, then ran out to lend a hand. But Neal had everything under control. Scrambled eggs were simmering nicely, there was a smell of toasting bread in the morning air, and Neal pulled back her chair.

"I overslept," she wailed. "I should be the one doing the cooking."

"Maybe you'll change your mind after you've sampled mine," he chuckled.

The eggs and bacon were delicious. So was the toast. And the coffee. Beth gave him a wry look. "How are you with chateaubriand steak?" she wondered.

"Not as good as Marie. Breakfast is my specialty."

She wandered into her writing room afterward, to sit down and look at her covered typewriter. Neal was outside in the garden, and she could hear him whistling from time to time.

She ought to do something, she supposed. But she didn't have an idea for a new book in her head. She reached for a file in which she kept ideas that came to her from time to time, flipped it open and studied the scrawled notes. Nothing appealed to her, or caught her fancy.

After a two-hour struggle, she closed the file, tossed it aside, and went out to join her husband. He was putting weeds into a trash can.

"All finished? So soon?"

"Nothing would come," she muttered glumly.

"Then let's go shopping. Your car or mine?"

"Mine. It's used to carrying packages of food."

She drove into Rocky Cove, aware that they were getting stares. Word had gone the rounds by this time about their marriage, so it was only natural to expect sly looks and glances. They didn't appear to bother Neal—he was quite nonchalant about the whole thing.

She had intended to do the shopping, but it was Neal who took over, ordering steaks and roasts, slabs of veal and chops, until she had to stop him. They would never be able to eat all that food; it would go bad. She sent back half of his order and even then it was far too much. The meat alone would strain the freezing unit of her refrigerator.

Neal helped her put the things away when they came back to the cottage. It was lunchtime then, and Beth made several sandwiches and iced coffee.

Over his last sandwich, Neal said, "I have a little speedboat I keep at the marina. How about a ride in it this afternoon?"

Beth felt uneasy. Would he want to go to Capstone Rock, to see for himself where she had almost drowned? She did not want to see that rock ever again. It reminded her too vividly of the afternoon when that hand had caught her ankle and dragged her under.

"I don't think so," she murmured, staring into her empty cup.

"Sure you do. You can't hide away forever. You can't let your fear get the upper hand. Just as you do when you've tumbled off a horse, you get right back up and ride him again. Same thing with swimming. Helps you overcome your fright."

Nothing would ever do that. The fear was too deeply ingrained in her. She could not face another moment such as that other one had been. Her heart would stop beating instantly and she would die.

His hand was on hers, gripping it, squeezing. His face was tender, and there was something in his eyes that made her heart lurch. "Trust me," he breathed. "I know what I'm doing. We'll get into our bathing suits and robes, drive to the marina, take out the boat."

When she still hesitated, he added, "Oh, come on. It's sunny out, it'll be great there on the water. All you have to do is to sit in the boat, the same way you did in the canoe. What do you say?"

He made a good advocate, she decided, and found herself nodding. "All right. I'll come with you. But I reserve the right not to swim."

"Swell. Go ahead, get into your suit. We can leave these dishes, do them when we get back. I'll change in the living room."

In her bedroom, Beth lifted the Emilio Pucci floral print bikini from the drawer where she had placed it, together with a matching robe, when she had returned from the city. As she held it up now, she scowled. Whatever had possessed her to buy this skimpy thing? Oh, yes. She'd had some vague idea of sunbathing on a cruise ship, beside the pool. It would certainly show a lot of her!

Still, with the robe, it wouldn't be too bad. And she wasn't going to swim in it. Definitely not. She began to ease out of the pullover.

The mirror told her that she was not wrong. The Pucci bikini did show a lot of skin. Beth flushed, staring. She couldn't wear this, she absolutely could not. My goodness!

It did show her figure off to advantage, however. Beth turned before the mirror, slowly, all the way around. After all, Neal was her husband. It wasn't as if he were some stranger. Besides, she had the robe. Girls wore these things all over the place, where there was water to swim in. She wasn't all that old-fashioned, was she?

Of course not.

She grabbed at the robe, slid into it. It came to the tops of her thighs and gave a wonderful view of her long legs. Hmmm. She had nice legs, very good legs, as a matter of fact. And she really ought not to appear a frump, she *was* Neal Harper's wife, she guessed she had a kind of standard to live up to.

Neal gaped as she made her appearance.

"Hey, now," he breathed.

Flustered, Beth asked quaveringly, "Is it too daring?"

"Not for you it isn't. It's magnificent. Or rather, you're magnificent, in it. Yes, indeed."

He came toward her and, thinking that he was going to grab and kiss her, Beth retreated. He stopped, shook his head, then said, almost plaintively, "I was just going to turn you around so I could see you from all angles."

She turned, tingling inside her at the admiration in his eyes. One thing she had to admit about this husband of hers, he showed appreciation when she showed herself off to him.

"Now let's see you without that robe," he grinned.

Beth shook her head, flushing violently. Her hands clutched the print, holding it closer. "I couldn't."

Neal chuckled. "You're the most modest girl I've ever known."

"Is that bad?"

He regarded her, head tilted to one side. "I don't know," he said slowly, his eyes glinting with amusement. Then: "We'd better get started, right?"

Neal wore Italian stretch Lycra trunks with an Italian cotton pullover. His body was lean and well-muscled. Just by looking at him, one would never know he had been dying a few months ago. The pullover hid his chest, so that no operational scars showed, and Beth wondered if he might be sensitive about them.

They went out into the late June sunlight and walked to the Iso Grifo. Beth let her eyes roam around the woodlands on all sides. There was no sign of any bearded man, and the place was peaceful and quiet, as it always had been—until recently.

She had never been to the marina. The boats she rented came from Charley Johnson's boatyard and were used mostly by fishermen up from the cities or picnickers who wanted to skim around on the water. But as the dark blue car came to a halt, Beth found herself staring at wharves and quays where huge Flying Bridge Cruisers lay at anchor beside Chris-Craft Constellations and Wheeler Playmates.

She was hardly aware of Neal as he took her elbow, she was so busy admiring these oceangoing craft, wondering how much they had cost and who could possibly own them. Only when he chuckled did she turn her eyes from the boats to glance at him inquiringly.

"Beautiful, aren't they?" he asked.

"And expensive! Why, the cost of just one of them . . ."

She shook her head, letting her words trail off. Neal said calmly, "I own that big one, the Flying Bridge. And Art's is just two over from it, a Richardson Golden Express."

"Do you ever use it?"

"Sometimes, to take business acquaintances out for some fishing. I've made good deals on it. It's well worth its upkeep."

He did not take her to the Matthews boat, but to a smaller quay, where a sleek 21-foot Century Coronado lay glistening in the sunshine. Her eyes ran over a sleek white hull, a sliding hardtop roof, mahogany planking. The interior was upholstered in white leather. Neal caught her hand, helping her onto the forward deck.

She had never been on a boat such as this one, any more than she had been in a car like the Iso Grifo. Almost in awe, she seated herself. She watched as Neal came to sit beside her, touching controls, glancing about him to make certain everything was in working order.

The V-8 engine throbbed to life.

Then the Coronado was backing out of its slip, slowly, under wraps. Only when he turned the prow to face the open water did Neal feed power into it. There was a faint lurch and then the powerboat was sliding forward easily and effortlessly.

Sunlight glinted off the water, warming them. The shore receded swiftly, and soon there was only empty sea around them. And always Neal drove outward, the Century rocking gently to the waves, flinging them aside almost contemptuously.

"Like her?" Neal asked, grinning.

"She's unbelievable."

"Here, you take over."

He was easing out of the pilot's seat, indicating she should take his place.

"Oh, I couldn't."

"Of course you can. Just take the wheel, as if it were your car. She'll respond. Don't be nervous. There, that's right."

Before she knew it she was in back of the wheel, the water was calling to her, and the Coronado seemed to be a very part of her. Beth laughed, leaning forward, hands securely gripping the wheel. Neal watched her a moment, then nodded.

"You have to become used to it," he told her. "As my wife, this boat will be yours."

"Neal!"

"You'll have to get used to the other one, too. You'll be hostess at my parties. Maybe now that I have a wife, we'll have a lot of parties on the big one. They'll be fun."

She eyed him carefully. He wasn't looking at her, his gaze was off somewhere over water. Did he really expect them to go on being married this way? She bit her lip. There was no use trying to argue sense into this man. He had some wild notion in his head that sooner or later he would get her to fall in love with him, and be a real wife.

Then when he had won his little game, he would throw her aside. Candace had warned her. In a way, so had Bertram Lambkin. She hardened herself against him, but she said nothing.

She drove where he told her, swinging the Coronado in a wide arc north and eastward. It was such a pleasant day, the sun felt so good, the salt air so bracing, that she found herself forgetting everything but the moment.

After a long time, Neal said, "Better let me take the wheel now."

She turned it over reluctantly.

But she continued to delight in the vast sea, its surging waves that sometimes lifted the big powerboat as though it were no more than a dry leaf. Its present calmness could turn, she knew, with terrifying suddenness into a frightening storm. The Coronado rode these deep waters easily, moving steadily back toward its quay.

She could see the shoreline now, distinguish houses, trees. Far ahead a natural stone jetty extended far out. There was one big boulder with a flat rock balanced upon it—

Beth drew a deep breath. Capstone Rock.

In the waters that rose and fell about it now, she had been caught, trapped. Instinctively her muscles tensed, and her hands clenched into fists. Then she felt a hand on her thigh.

"Easy, now. Easy."

She was surprised at the tenderness, the understanding in his voice. His hand stroked her thigh a moment, and she sat there, making no move. Beth didn't know whether she wanted to push his hand off or not. Its touch was reminding her that he was here protecting her. To have thrown it off would have been to reject that protection, which she was not about to do.

"That's the place, isn't it?" When she nodded, he said softly, "I'm going to dive down, have myself an underwater swim. You want to come along?"

She shook her head vigorously, and ran her eyes along those huge gray rocks, the grayish-green waves slapping against them. Beth shivered. The sun was warm, and the water would have felt good to her, she knew. But she could not go down into it. She just couldn't.

Instead she watched as Neal slipped a Falco diving mask on his face, then eased into the straps that held an Aqua-Lung tank. He buckled the belt to hold it more firmly, then eased his feet into a pair of Scubapro jet-fins. He fitted the mouthpiece between his teeth, jerked his thumb upward, then slid backward off the side of the boat.

There was a splash and he was gone.

Beth was alone. She shivered, looked around her. There was no other boat in sight, no one appeared to be on shore, and certainly those big rocks were empty of all life. There was absolutely nothing to worry about. She rose, walked to the side, and peered down into the gray-green waters.

She could see nothing, of course. Neal was long out of sight. Yet in spirit she was down there with him, peering this way and that, seeing the bulk of the big rocks, feeling the water all around her, pressing in. The bottom was rocky here, very pebbly. There would be crabs, and maybe a lobster or two scurrying to get away from Neal, but that was all.

Beth drew a deep breath.

She must have been mistaken about that hand that had caught hold of her. But her intuition told her she had not. And certainly she had been pushed into Neal Harper's car. She still remembered the feel of the two hands, the pressure of the fingers, against her back.

The water swirled and broke. Neal was coming up the ladder, removing the breathing mouthpiece and grinning at her.

"Nothing down there. Absolutely nothing. Want to have a look?"

She hesitated. Neal was right, of course. She should go down there, get rid of this awful water-fear. Get it out of her system.

He was standing beside her, dripping water, big and strong. She could see the scars of his recent operation very clearly. He had been so near to death! Beth felt a coldness in her midsection.

"I have an extra set of lungs. Actually, they're my sister's. I borrowed them so you could use them. What do you say?"

There would be no better time than now. The sun was warm, almost hot on this summer day, and there was nobody around.

"All right," she agreed. "I'll give it a try."

She was out of the robe before she realized it, standing there in the bikini. But Neal was paying no attention to her, he was too busy lifting the Aqua-Lung, fitting its straps about her shoulders. In moments she was ready. His hand caught hers, drawing her to the moldboard.

They sat together, went over backwards.

Panic hit Beth just as she sank below the surface. She wanted frantically to claw her way upward, to the surface. She had to fight against that terror with every ounce of her willpower. Neal was beside her, bulking hugely. His hand touched her arm as he pointed downward.

She doubled up, dove, feet and legs churning. The fins gave her power, and the Aqua-Lung weighted her so that she made the descent easily. The water was cold, but not as cold as it had been that other time. She swam easily and gracefully.

The bottom, shrouded in gray, came up to meet her. She could make out a big crab scuttling under a rock overhang. Then she was moving past that overhang, skirting it. It was pleasant down here. It was a quiet world where nothing existed but water, sand, and rocks. And the creatures whose homes these were.

She swam strongly, delighting in this new element. She forgot about Neal, telling herself that she was perfectly at ease, now that she had conquered her initial fear. There was nothing or no one about to harm her. She was absolutely safe.

Her scissoring legs brought her between Capstone Rock and the next big boulder. She darted into the passageway—

Instantly she was caught by a tidal flow, a suctioning of water between those rocks. It twisted her, turned her, lifted her, and slammed her sideways. She could not call out—the mouthpiece was too firmly planted between her teeth. She could only feel the terror rise up inside her.

Metal grated on stone.

The Aqua Lung! If it got caught . . .

She fought that current, trying to swim, but she could not. Like a piece of driftwood, she was driven hard into the rock, feeling the straps tighten about her. Her hands pushed at the stone, trying to force herself free. Instead she was driven even harder against the insensate gray stone bulk.

Her head rammed into it . . .

Something was holding her, tightly. Beth moaned.

"You've got to be all right," a voice was saying. "Oh, my God—if anything happened to you, I'd never forgive myself. This is twice I've almost killed you!"

She tried to talk, to reassure this man that she was alive, that she was all right. But there was a strange paralysis about her body that touched even her tongue.

Lips were on her mouth, kissing. Beth kissed back. It was the only way she had of telling him that she was still alive. The strong arms that held her tightened even more. The kissing went on. Now his lips were on her cheeks, her closed eyes, her forehead. They came back to her mouth and lingered there.

Gradually Beth became aware that she was almost naked in the bikini, as was Neal in his swim trunks. Blood was coursing through her body, and she felt little tingles of delight, of enjoyment.

And this must not be.

She moaned again, then forced her eyes to open.

Neal was bending over her, his face very close to her own. His gray eyes were worried and frightened. She stirred slightly, but sank back into his embrace. It was so pleasant to be held, cuddled like this, she did not want it to stop.

"Does anything hurt?" he whispered.

She shook her head a little.

"You're sure? Here, see if you can stand up."

The strong arms went away, and a hand caught her arm and lifted her. She was on her feet, swaying a little, as he stared at her anxiously. She gave him a faint smile and the words, "No broken bones."

"I damn near died down there when I saw what was happening. That tidal flow is treacherous at those rocks around this time. It just caught you, drove you into those rocks as though you didn't weigh a thing."

He drew her in against him, held her tightly. Once again, Beth became aware of the fact that they had so few clothes on. She tried to push away, but only made a half-hearted effort. It was too pleasant being held this way, fussed over as Neal was fussing.

But they couldn't go on this way. Anyone who cared to look would think they were embracing. And a sneaking thought slid into her mind. Maybe this was part of his playboy charm, this anxiety, this worry.

"I—I'm all right now," she murmured against his chest. "You can let go of me."

"I don't want to let go of you. You've become very dear, very precious to me, Beth. If anything happened to you, I'd die."

She could hardly breathe, his arms were so strong. The tingling in her flesh told her she did not want to move away from him, that she absolutely reveled in the feel of his masculine body against her own.

"But we can't just stand here like this!"

"Who's to see?"

"Somebody might."

"So what if they do? We're married."

She inched away from him, not daring to look up into his eyes, contenting herself with turning, reaching for her robe, gliding into it. Beth didn't know just how she felt, right now, but an inner voice told her that if Neal had reached for her, she would have tumbled into his embrace most happily.

She did not want to admit this to herself. She did not want to be tossed aside by playboy Neal Harper. She wanted the security of their marriage to go on and on, and never end. If she did not yield to him, he would not leave her.

Beth sighed, near tears.

Chapter Eleven

Beth was making notes for her new book one morning when the front doorbell rang. Neal was in the back garden, so he could scarcely hear it. Beth put down her pen, frowned, then rose to her feet.

Candace Thorne, radiant in a scoop-neck sleeveless jersey with a long, button-front skirt, was smiling at her as she opened the door. With her blond hair worn in a fall, she was so lovely that Beth felt like a bedraggled gypsy.

"Hi," Candace exclaimed. "I've come to borrow you for a spot of shopping. If Neal isn't around, he can't object."

"I don't know. I've been working on the plot of a new book."

"Oh, that can wait. Climb into something and do come along."

She should not. She ought to finish that plot outline, or at least add a few more twists and details to it. But the sunshine and the cool breeze floating in through the door made Beth realize that working over a desk was very much like drudgery on such a day.

"Come on in. I'll just be a sec."

She ran for the bedroom, sliding out of the sleeveless shirt and jeans (both somewhat worn and ragged, but comfortable) as she fled. Her hand reached for a paisley shift with

120

white ring collar. It was loose and cool, and with white sandals, seemed summery enough. Candace gave her a long, slow look as she came into the living room, and Beth read grudging approval in the green eyes.

"I'd better tell Neal," Beth said.

"Oh? Don't you go anywhere without his approval?"

"I just don't want him to worry about me."

Candace looked vaguely puzzled, but Beth ran to the back door and out along the tiny garden path. Neal straightened at sight of her, whistled soundlessly and put down his weeder.

"Going somewhere?"

"Candace is here, she wants me to go shopping with her."

Neal said softly, "I don't believe it." When Beth looked shocked, he held up his hand, head held to one side as he smiled down at her. "I believe that's what she told you. But I don't think you're going shopping. However . . ."

He reached into his slacks, lifted out a wallet, drew a couple of fifty-dollar bills from it. "In case I'm wrong, take this."

"I have money."

"Don't be so independent. Let me think you need me."

Their eyes met. Beth drew a deep breath. "All right. Thank you."

She turned and almost ran back up the path. It had seemed to her that Neal had been pleading with her silently just then. For understanding? For love? For—what? The man had everything. There was nothing Beth had to give him.

Candace was driving a new Audi. She handled it competently and surely. But as the miles rolled away under the wheels, Beth began to wonder where the blond woman intended to shop. As she turned onto a long, winding road that led upwards, understanding came to her.

Candace Thorne glanced at her, but Beth sat quietly, saying nothing. Only when Candace braked the Audi before Harper House, did Beth stir.

"Neal was right, then," she murmured.

"Oh? What was he right about?"

"He said we weren't going shopping."

Candace looked at her hands, shrugged, and reached for the door handle. Beth got out too and stood a moment, staring up at the house. It stood like a barrier against her, she thought. Symbolic of Mrs. Harper herself. Well, here she was, the sacrificial lamb being led to the slaughter. Might as well go to meet her fate with a smile.

Candace was waiting, watching her.

Beth said, "I'll have to give Neal back his shopping money. Too bad."

She felt delighted when Candace scowled.

A maid let them into the house, disappearing almost instantly. Candace led the way into the living room where Mrs. Harper was ensconced in the blue wing chair, which seemed her favorite spot. Like a throne, Beth thought. She wanted to giggle but didn't dare.

She murmured a greeting and was fixed by the ice-cold blue eyes.

"I think it's time this whole nonsense was ended," the older woman said curtly. "I asked Candace to fetch you here so we could have a little talk."

"Ought I sit down?"

The older woman colored slightly. "I'm sorry. Of course. Please be seated."

With her handbag gripped between her hands, Beth waited. The blue eyes went on staring at her. Finally Mrs. Harper murmured, "I'm offering you a quarter of a million dollars to set Neal free of this farce of a marriage."

Beth bit her tongue, fighting back the impulse to rise and walk out of this house. She must not judge this older woman, who, she supposed, had planned on marrying off her only son to a girl of a wealthy family, somebody like Candace Thorne. Somebody like Candace? No, no. To Candace herself.

She said slowly, "I will not oppose any divorce action your son brings, Mrs. Harper. Be assured of that."

The older woman sat back in the wing chair, smiling triumphantly. Beth was aware that Candace was shifting uncomfortably in a nearby chair.

Now Candace said, "But suppose Neal won't institute divorce proceedings?"

"Then we'll go on being married, I guess."

The smile faded from Mrs. Harper's mouth. It was a thin mouth, rather grim, with tight lines around it. Beth was certain that it was the mouth of a person long used to being obeyed without question. That mouth tightened now, angrily.

"You said you would be willing to divorce Neal," it snapped.

"If he wants the divorce, I'll agree to it, yes."

"But Neal won't divorce you," Candace exclaimed.

Beth turned to her, aware that her heart was pumping away madly. Her mouth was dry, and she had to lick her lips before she could speak. "Then there isn't very much I can do, is there?"

Mrs. Harper shrilled, "You can divorce him! A quarter of a million dollars ought to be a good inducement."

If she should take the money and divorce Neal, it would be like cutting her own throat, Beth thought. The mere idea of living without him around, to watch over and cook for, was abhorrent. Had she come to love the guy? No, she didn't think so. It was just that she had grown used to his companionship. She didn't want to give it up, not even for all that money.

Beth nodded. "The money would be a most attractive inducement, Mrs. Harper, if I—if I were not in love with him."

There! She had said it.

It wasn't true of course, but neither of these women could know that. Only Neal knew the truth. And he, thank goodness, was nowhere around.

"Love," sneered the older woman. "An animal attraction, no more."

"We have very much the same interests," Beth pointed out, remembering their love of Nature, the canoe ride, their swim at Capstone rock—and especially what happened afterward—and the long hours they spent together now after supper, seated in chairs near each other and reading.

"You come from different backgrounds. There can't be the same interests, not at all. Besides," and here the older woman drew a deep breath, "my son is only playing with you. Once he knows that you love him, that you can't live without him, he'll throw you over."

This was what Candace Thorne had told her. Now his own mother was reaffirming what Candace had said. Neal Harper was not to be depended on. It was a facet of his character that she must come to accept; indeed, she had already accepted it.

"He hasn't thrown me over yet," she blurted.

Mrs. Harper gave her a chilling smile. "Give him another month, perhaps only a week."

"Then when he does, you'll get your wish."

The older woman blinked. "I want it sooner than that, young lady. I want you to give Neal his freedom." She spoke coldly, then leaned forward, eyes angry, filled partially with subdued rage. "There are ways, young lady. I could cause you a lot of trouble, you know."

If she had not been attacked long before she even knew Neal Harper, she might be inclined to believe this woman guilty of that happening, or of the hands that had shoved her almost under the wheels of Neal's car. But that could not be, certainly.

And yet, she knew very well that the menace staring at her from those icy blue eyes was just as deadly as that other menace that had struck at her twice and failed. With her money, Mrs. Harper was able to hire any number of people to drown her or get rid of her in some other way. She had the feeling it would not be a nice death, if it were up to this older woman.

"I think that's just about enough, Mother."

The older woman gasped and whirled. Beth did not know whether she or Mrs. Harper was the more surprised. But her own heart thundered at sight of Neal standing in the hall archway, still in sweatshirt and slacks, stained from kneeling in her garden. He seemed so calm, so sure of himself.

And then an idea hit her. How long had he been standing there? Had he heard her say she loved him?

Color flamed as her cheeks burned. Her eyes fell away, but he was not looking at her, he was studying his mother, meeting her eyes with gentle determination.

Neal said again, as the silence lengthened, "I didn't believe Candace was going to take Beth shopping, you know. I told her Candace had lied, but she trusted her, in her innocence."

Neal moved into the room gracefully, and again Beth was struck by his athletic poise, his strength. Something of his confidence filled her now, so that her muscles relaxed, and she sat back slightly in her chair.

"For once and for all, Mother, I'm not going to divorce Beth. And you heard her say she wasn't going to divorce me."

He turned his head and smiled at her. Her cheeks were still on fire, but she met his gaze eagerly. He had heard her, then. He had! Beth did not know whether to run or drop through the floor.

The older woman cleared her throat.

Neal forestalled her. He held out his hand to Beth who grasped it. Easily he lifted her to her feet, putting his arm about her. Beth let her weight go against him, as though telling him how much she needed and depended on him.

"We'll go home now."

Mrs. Harper found her tongue. "Neal, we mustn't part like this. I still don't like this marriage of yours, but I'm willing to accept it, if you insist."

Beth wanted to scream a warning. She did not trust this woman, she was afraid that Neal would give in to her, out of pity or perhaps from filial love. But her husband was not fooled.

He said, "I'm glad of that, Mother. Because if anything happens to Beth, I'll know whom to blame."

They walked out of the living room with his arm still around her. Only when they were out in the sunshine did she slide free of him and move toward the Iso Grifo, parked far down the drive.

Neal said, "I got here just behind you. I didn't trust Candace, as I hinted."

"You heard everything I said."

"And I'm proud of you. A quarter of a million is a lot of money."

Beth murmured as she slid into her car seat, "She could have offered me a million. It wouldn't have made any difference."

Neal still held the door open, not yet having closed it. Suddenly he leaned inside the car and kissed her on the mouth before she could pull away. She felt the pressure of his lips, her increased heartbeat.

Oh, Neal! If only I could believe in you!

Then he was moving around behind the car, having slammed the car door, leaving her alone with her tumultuous emotions. She wanted so desperately to fling her arms about him, to nestle close, to be wrapped in those strong arms and

to hear him tell her that everything she had heard were
vicious lies.

"Hungry?" he asked when the Iso Grifo was halfway back
to the cottage.

"No. How can I think of food?"

He looked at her, surprised. "Why not? It's lunchtime."

"Neal, honestly! Are all men as blind as you? Here I've
been put through the third degree by your mother and—"

"—and she's tipping her hat to you right now, mentally."

She rounded on him. "She hates me. I saw it in her eyes.
She th-threatened m-me, too. As if I weren't scared enough
al-already."

He drove more slowly. "Mother is all huff and puff. She
wouldn't hurt a fly."

"That's what you think. Where her only son is concerned,
she'll battle like a beserk Viking."

The Iso Grifo purred along the road. Beth sat looking
straight ahead, very well aware that Neal had not replied to
her accusation of his mother. Was he agreeing with her? Did
he realize how dangerous his mother might prove to be to
her?

As the cottage came into view, Neal said, "Mother just
needs time to adjust to the idea of our marriage and to the
fact that she cannot order us about as she does Joan and Arthur."

"Well, I hope you're right."

He took her in his arms as they paused before the cottage
door, smiling down at her upturned face. He made no attempt to kiss her, however.

"Just trust me. No matter what anybody else does or says,
have confidence in me."

If only I could! If only I could!

The afternoon was lovely, warm and almost hazy with
golden sunshine. Beth could not return to her notes, she
wanted nothing so much as to relax. She changed into shorts
and a shirt, then made club sandwiches and iced coffee and
brought them out onto the tiny flagstone patio.

They ate with relish, sitting side by side and staring out
across the sweep of woodlands toward the ocean. She could
not see Capstone Rock from here, but it was there. Waiting
for her, Beth thought, with a shiver. It seemed to have an in-

sensate desire to destroy her. She was too imaginative, perhaps, that went with being a writer. Still . . .

"How's the new book coming?" Neal asked.

"Not badly at all. In fact, I've outlined the first half. I just need a couple of ideas for the last."

She spoke about the book, knowing it was taking her mind off herself and her troubles. Neal had a way of doing that where she was concerned. It seemed he knew instinctively what to do or say to bring her out of herself. He had probably learned that trick from going around with so many girls, she decided morosely, being suddenly jealous of the lot of them.

They went out to dinner that night—Neal insisted on it. They had been too much in the cottage, and it was time for her to wear the low-cut black crepe evening dress by Estevez and the pink velvet coat with the white fox collar on which she had spent so much money in New York. She had had no opportunity to dress for dinner, and it was time she did.

She spent an hour getting ready. Little enough time, she thought, but she didn't want to keep Neal waiting. Her brown hair she piled high on top of her head, almost in a Nineties style. But it seemed to go with the dress and evening coat.

Neal blinked when he saw her. He himself was wearing a white formal dinner jacket with maroon trousers and a silk, ruffled-front evening shirt with butterfly bow tie. He walked around her, lips pursed, and shook his head gently.

"What's wrong?" she inquired in alarm.

"You. Me. Everything. Come on, let's go."

In the car she kept asking him the trouble, but he only fended her off with laughter, gripping her hand and holding it, telling her she was absolutely perfect and that she was much too good for him. When she denied this indignantly and accused him of putting her off, he merely chuckled.

He wheeled the dark blue car into a parking lot outside the very exclusive Lobster Claw. Beth had never been inside this restaurant, but she had heard reports of how expensive it was. Judging by the Cadillacs and Lincolns and the occasional Lamborghini or Rolls Royce in the parking lot, it was patronized exclusively by the very rich.

Heads turned when they entered. Beth could scarcely be unaware of the inquiring and admiring eyes that raked her from slippers to hairdo. A few hands were raised, then waved at Neal. Voices called out, inviting them to one table or another. Neal waved back, murmuring names, but kept a firm grip on her elbow, making her follow the maitre d' who was escorting them to a table, all smiles and rigid back.

"It is good to see you again, Signor Harper," he said as he bowed Beth into her seat.

"Good to be back again, Angelo."

Beth knew very well that Angelo was sizing her up, though he appeared not to glance at her. He would answer questions all over the big room, she knew. It suddenly struck her that this was the first time they had dined out in public as man and wife, where people would know her husband.

A waiter came with cocktails. "From the Hudsons."

A few moments later a heavy-set man and a very lovely woman, obviously his wife, came over to say hello. It was the beginning. Before long their table was surrounded, Neal was standing exchanging light talk, and Beth was the cynosure of every eye. They did not stare, they were too polite for that, but the women would know every detail of her dress, and the men would have memorized her face and figure.

When they were finally alone and Neal was able to order their meal, he had a faint smile on his lips. Beth eyed him carefully, trying to read that little grin.

Over her second pink lady, she could no longer control herself. She leaned forward and almost whispered, "Well? What's the verdict?"

"The men were madly jealous of me, the women of you."

"Come on, Neal. Be serious."

He was surprised. "I am serious. It's a total triumph for you, my love. And word of that triumph will reach Harper House inside the hour."

Beth regarded him curiously. "What does that mean?"

"That you have knocked the pins out from under Mother."

"You're mad. I always knew it."

He laughed, honestly amused. "They will be phoning mother asking who you are, wondering where Neal found such a beauty, trying to discover what's behind all this."

"Hmmmm. And your mother will tell them that—"

"—that ours was a flaming romance, that one sight of you did me in, that you are a successful novelist, that you are very much a mystery woman, or words to that effect. She will also add that we have her blessing or something like it."

When she just stared at him, speechless, he added, "She will never admit that what we have done is against her wishes. In private she may huff and puff, but mother always presents a placid face to the public."

"I don't understand her, if what you say is true."

"It's a matter of what the Japanese call 'face.' "

Beth let it go and glanced down at the menu. The prices stunned her, but Neal appeared to take them in his stride. "Lobster for both, I think?"

"Can't you see what lobsters *cost?*"

He grinned. "Thrifty, too. Yes, you're going to make me a wonderful wife, darling. But don't worry about prices. Is it lobster?"

She agreed, but told herself that if she really were his wife, with all it meant, she would never throw away their money in this reckless fashion. She could eat for a week on twenty dollars, and feed them both on forty.

Still, after she had eaten, feasting as well on strawberry shortcake and coffee, she decided that having a wealthy husband wasn't so bad, after all. Not if he took you to places such as the Lobster Claw. It was pleasant to sit here, surfeited with food, knowing that admiring glances came your way whenever anyone happened to glance at you, to understand that you were the subject of a lot of conversation. All in your favor, naturally.

"Now the bar," Neal said, as they were rising, with Angelo holding her chair and fussing over her.

"The bar?"

"The Hudsons will be waiting. And the Camerons, the Prentices, the Principes, all the others."

Horror dawned on Beth. She was not a gregarious person—she liked her solitude, her loneliness as a writer. She was never one for tablehopping, for exchanging pleasantries with people she did not know. Quaking inwardly, she let Neal guide her from the restaurant into a vast room, very dark, with a bar from one end of it to the other, and little round tables crowded together where people sat and drank.

Beth never afterward remembered much about that part of the evening. She saw a host of faces, she smiled and spoke words, she laughed and chattered, but she never could recall what she said. There were drinks, too, and she coped with these by sipping them and leaving them on the tables where they stopped, where she sank into chairs vacated by the polite gentlemen who rose to their feet at sight of her.

She could not tell how many drinks Neal had, either. He was always buying or some other man was, and they seemed to float in an alcoholic haze through the room. Beth did not protest; she felt that Neal was among his friends, that he was anxious to mingle with them, that he had been too much alone with her of late.

Eventually they found themselves beneath the stars, walking toward the Iso Grifo. It was a magnificent night. The air was cool and bracing after the heat and the closeness of the Lobster Claw, and Beth caught herself thinking that it might have been made for romance, this night. Except, of course, that there was no romance between her husband and herself.

She sat wrapped in the pink evening wrap all the way to the cottage, wondering if Neal thought the night romantic, or whether he was too full of food and liquor to think of anything but sleep. She was doing him an injustice, she knew. If he had attempted any romantic moves, she would have fought him off.

And then all thoughts of romance were driven from her head. For as the car swung toward the cottage around a little bend, the headlights picked out the figure of a man standing very still beside a tree bole. Neal saw him at the same time. He smothered a curse and stood on the brakes.

But the man had seen the car lights. He did not turn, he merely slid sideways behind the trees and ran. They could see his shadow for a few seconds, and then it was gone.

Fear came back to Beth as she shivered.

Neal said, "It was the same man, wasn't it?"

"I think so. Yes."

He had long hair and a beard, she knew that much, though the corduroy trousers and patched jacket were gone, replaced by a short-sleeved shirt and summer-weight slacks.

"This can't go on," he muttered as if to himself.

"There isn't much we can do about it."

"I'll think of something."

They walked toward the cottage with his arm about her,

and Beth leaned into him gratefully, drawing strength and courage from his size. If he had not been with her, she would never have stayed in the cottage overnight, she would have run to a motel. But she could scarcely keep running the rest of her life.

When they stood in the living room, Neal put his arms around her and held her against him. "We'll work this out, somehow. Don't worry about him. I'll be here."

He kissed her on the forehead and pushed her toward the bedroom. Oddly enough, she felt vaguely rejected. Which was silly of her, she knew. She certainly didn't want him in her bedroom. Still, he could have held her a little longer, maybe even kissed her mouth. She would not have fought him off.

"You don't know what you want, Beth Harper," she muttered under her breath.

She knew, all right. She wished Neal was a poor man with a job, without any playboy tendencies. Then she could have accepted his love, knowing he meant it, without any fear that when he had made her his wife in actual fact, he wouldn't throw her away and go on to his next conquest.

Beth undressed in a miasma of self-pity.

Chapter Twelve

When the doorbell sounded next morning, Beth was alone in the cottage. Neal had gone off on some mysterious errand of his own, taking the Iso Grifo and looking very grim. He had parried her questions, explaining that he wanted cigarettes, but when she had straightened up the living room she had found an untouched carton of Kent filters.

Beth paused in her vacuuming to brush back a tumbled lock of hair. Who could that be, ringing the bell so early? Certainly not Candace Thorne again. She doubted whether the blond woman would have the nerve to visit her so soon after driving her off to meet Neal's mother.

A man in a lightweight summer suit, an attaché case in hand, was standing there as she opened the door. He was middle-aged, with a speckle of gray in his hair and sideburns.

"Mrs. Harper? I'm Adrian Bushnell. Is Neal here?"

"I'm sorry. No. He's gone off after cigarettes. Won't you come in?"

The man was courteous, suave, and very apologetic. "I hate to intrude like this, but circumstances force me to. Neal's been away from the office for a long time, and matters have come up that demand his attention."

"He was in a car accident and was operated on . . ."

132

"But that was a long time ago, and I've been given to understand that his recovery was complete."

"Yes, he's fine now."

The man seemed puzzled. "Then why hasn't he come back to the office?" He hesitated, opened his eyes wide, and blurted, "Oh! I'm sorry. He did get married, didn't he? What an idiot you must think me."

He was so distressed, Beth felt sorry for him. "Please, I don't think any such thing. Our marriage was so—well, unusual—that I'm not at all sure I'm married myself. Come on into the kitchen, if you don't mind. I've made some coffee. It's just about ready, so you can join me in a cup."

Adrian Bushnell was a director of several corporations of which Neal Harper was chairman of the board, he explained. His various businesses needed him back in the office, since there was no one else to make decisions of great magnitude. There was a bond issue to be offered, and something had to be done about the construction details of their new offices outside Cambridge. Also the shipbuilding company they had so recently acquired needed special funding to enlarge its capacity to build oil tankers.

"All in all, we're at a standstill. You can understand that?"

Beth nodded, vaguely awed by the glimpse she had been given of Neal's importance. No wonder he was so rich! It sounded as if he owned half the Atlantic seaboard. And this puzzled her. Why should such an important man hide himself here in her cottage when he should be down there in Boston taking care of all that work?

"I'll tell him, certainly," she assured Bushnell. "I think he's healthy enough to go back to work. He walks and swims, he goes out in his motorboat."

"Oh, I know Gus Donovan did a great job on his insides, as he always does. There was no internal bleeding after Gus sewed him up, that was the one big worry. Now, of course, there's no danger of any relapse. So I just couldn't understand why he keeps staying away."

His eyes touched Beth and he flushed slightly. "What I mean is, I realize he was just married, but—I'm putting this badly, I know. Still, couldn't he have honeymooned in Boston?"

Beth sighed. "You'll have to ask Neal about that. He keeps telling me that he needs rest and relaxation."

"But he's had plenty of that," Bushnell protested.

"Yet not enough, Addie."

Neal was in the doorway, smiling faintly. He wore blue slacks and a sleeveless striped shirt. He came across to shake Adrian Bushnell by the hand and exchange amenities.

"Neal, you have to come back," the older man pressed when Neal was seated beside him, sipping the coffee Beth brought him. "There are decisions to be made. Important ones. I don't have to remind you about them, you know them. There's the Shipkey deal, the bond issue, the bank loan for those tankers, those two new corporations you want formed. We can't do anything without your okay."

"Certainly you can," Neal said quietly. "I can't leave here, not yet."

Adrian Bushnell pursed his lips. "We stand to lose millions."

"I don't see why. Bert Lambkin knows what I want, he's drawn up the papers. Get them here to me, I'll sign them. Then you can go ahead with a clear conscience."

"I still don't like it. These matters are of the utmost importance."

"But not as important as what I'm doing."

Beth saw his eyes flick toward her for a moment, and she thought: These men depend on him just as I do. But what's so important here that it can keep him away from his office? Millions of dollars are involved—Adrian Bushnell just said so. But Neal was passing that need up to stay here, with her.

Bushnell opened his attaché case. "I did bring some things for you to look over . . ."

Beth rose hurriedly. "I'll get back to my writing. I'll leave you two to talk all you want. And Mr. Bushnell, please stay for lunch. We have all sorts of goodies to tempt your appetite."

But when she came out of her room two hours later Adrian Bushnell was gone, and Neal was in the garden, picking radishes. He brought in two handsful just as she was putting bread in the toaster for sandwiches.

"Neal, are you sure you're doing the right thing?"

He began washing the radishes, cutting off the greens. He

said after a few moments, "I haven't had a vacation for three years."

Beth thought about that as she sliced chicken and watched the skillet where bacon was being fried to crispness. "He sounded so worried. As if—as if you'd lose all your money if you stayed here any longer."

"Would that bother you so much?"

"Oh, no! As a matter of fact . . ."

He turned, knife still in hand, to smile at her. "Go on. As a matter of fact—what?"

She shook her head. Neal put down the knife, wiped his hands, came to take her by the shoulders and looked down at her. "Go on. Tell me."

"It's just a silly thought."

"Silly or not, I'd like to hear it."

"It's just that sometimes I've felt—I suppose I might as well say it, you won't give me any peace until I do. I've felt that things might be better for us if you weren't so rich, if you had a job and I had my books to write."

He considered that, turning it over in his mind. "You're afraid of so much money."

"It isn't the money, it's what the money does to you."

Her face was troubled, she realized, but she just didn't care. Sooner or later, she supposed they might as well have a face-to-face confrontation like this. She'd felt it all along, but Adrian Bushnell had brought it to a head.

She plunged on, recklessly. "You warned me. Candace Thorne warned me. Your mother warned me."

"About what?" he asked grimly.

"About your—your being a playboy. Candace and your mother hinted that you would make me fall in l-love with you and then—then when I did, you'd throw me over, get a divorce and find another girl to—to work your charm on."

His hands fell away from her shoulders. He walked to the kitchen door and stood staring out at the lawn. Beth watched him with worry in her eyes. She had finally faced up to him, had come right out with it. And he had not denied it. Was he seeing the end to his hope of succeeding with her? Was he planning right now to leave her as a bad job and go back to Boston to some other girl?

When he turned, his face was relaxed and smiling. "The bacon will burn. You'd better watch it."

"Oh!" Beth wailed, and leaped.

She was aware that he was watching her every move as she built the club sandwiches and poured the hot coffee. She did not look at him. She was afraid of meeting those gray eyes.

They ate in silence. Only when they were finished eating, and she was pouring a second cup of coffee, did Neal say, "I damn near died in that hospital, you know. It was like a miracle, what Gus Donovan did to me, stitching up my insides. I never expected to live. I really mean that."

She nodded. "Nobody expected you to."

"I thought a lot, in that hospital bed, about the sort of life I had been leading. I wasn't very proud of it. It was time I settled down, got married, that sort of thing. Maybe even have kids."

"But you married me!" she blurted. "Somebody you didn't know."

"That was my first reaction to the accident, when I didn't know whether Gus Donovan would get to me in time. I'd go out with one good deed to my credit, at least. I'd marry the girl I hit, and devil take the hindmost."

Beth stared at him. "You were trying to hurt somebody," she accused.

"Yes, I was. My family. All my life I'd done everything they wanted. When my father died, I was two years out of college. I stepped into his shoes and ran all those corporations with only the family in mind—Mother, Joan, and Arthur. I did everything that was expected of me—except get married to Candace Thorne. This I would not do."

He shrugged. "Maybe a psychiatrist could explain the notion that came to me to marry you. The girl I'd injured. I'd make it up to her. I didn't expect to live, I was just about dead. It would be the one thing in my life that I would do please myself."

Beth looked into her cup. "What about those—those girls you were playboying with?" she asked in a small voice.

Neal asked softly, "Could you believe there were no girls?"

Beth stared.

"Could you believe that my being a playboy was a myth I started myself? First with my family, so I wouldn't have to nursemaiding the lot of them, then with some of my business associates?"

"B-but . . ."

Beth was bewildered, out of her depth. She felt as though someone had yanked a rug out from under her. It was only because of the fact that Neal Harper was a playboy that she had fought against the affection she felt for him. If he were not the playboy she had been led to believe he was, then . . .

"But even that lawyer, Bertram Lambkin, said you were," she protested.

"He thinks so. So does Adrian Bushnell. That's why he can't understand why I'm spending so much time down here with you. Off again, on again Harper, the man who rarely squires the same girl twice. It didn't seem natural to them." He added morosely, "It's a classic case of the biter being bit himself."

He chuckled wryly. "Well, that's that. Now I have an idea. Let's get away from this cottage, just the two of us. We'll go camping somewhere, we'll go swimming in some lake, and for canoe rides. We'll spend a week together, just the two of us. What do you say?"

"But—but why?"

She was still suspicious of him. She realized this confession of his might be just another in his bag of tricks. If he were a real playboy, to deny it to her might seem like good clean fun. If she swallowed it, all the better. She would drop into his arms like a ripe plum and he would have his fun and then forget her.

On the other hand, she did not want to disbelieve him in case he *might* be telling the truth. It wouldn't be fair.

Neal said, "Because I want to get us away from here. Far away, where nobody will suspect we've gone."

She thought about the bearded man. It made sense. Still, when they returned, the man would still be here. She thought some more. A week with Neal, alone in a tent. Canoe rides under a moon. Swims in the lake before breakfast. Maybe even moonlight swims. Eating steak cooked over a campfire. Fish, too, that they might catch.

"Old clothes?" she asked. "No glamor?"

"Old clothes and no glamor," he agreed, a twinkle in his eyes.

"All right. When do you want to go?"

"How about right now? I have a Coleman stove in the car, plus other things we'll need. A few clothes for myself, a couple of fishing rods, a gun. You go change. I'll do the dishes."

"You were pretty sure of my answer, weren't you? Is that why you had to go buy cigarettes? When you had a full carton of Kents?"

"That and certain other matters I had to see to."

"What matters?"

"You'll learn in good time."

"Mysterious, too. All right for you."

She moved into her bedroom and closed the door. Old clothes, the man had said. Okay, then. First, the woollen bathrobe. That wasn't very glamorous. She was glad now she hadn't thrown it away. And flannel pajamas slightly too large for her. Two old sweaters, some patched slacks, a couple of pairs of shorts, and some shirts. The days would be warm but the nights might grow cold. She'd better throw in an extra blanket or two, and a fleece-lined safari coat.

She was wearing bluejeans and a pullover with leather patches at the elbows. She stared at her mirrored reflection. She looked unglamorous enough, all right.

Beth began to giggle. They were nuts, the both of them.

The dishes were washed, dried and put away when she came out. Neal caught her bags and carried them to the Iso Grifo. Beth gave a last look around the cottage, then followed him, closing and locking the door behind her.

They drove through the summer day almost like a pair of conspirators, Beth thought. Neal was running away from his business duties, and she was fleeing from the bearded man. But it was more than that, she realized. They were reaching out for something, too. Beth wanted to find out if Neal was the playboy type or not. And Neal? What was he after?

Had he given her a pitch about making up that playboy lie? Was he telling the truth? Was he counting on that to wear down her resistance? Did he expect the moonlight and the campfires to help him? That must be it. She could think of no other reason why Neal Harper would want to go on a camping trip, right about now.

They drove all day, until toward dusk Neal nosed the Iso Grifo onto a dirt track that ran in under some trees. I bounced over ruts and tree roots for two miles. But when the trees fell away, Beth could see a lake and a spread of grassy knoll that ran its grass down to the water.

"I like it," she said.

"I found it years ago. It's off by itself, there's good fishing in the lake, and there's a store on the other side where we can rent a canoe. Or a rowboat."

Neal put up the tent first, then helped Beth start a fire in a ring of smoke-blackened stones to one side. Neal had put those stones there a long time ago. Nobody had ever disturbed them. In moments, red flames were throwing shadows all around them.

From somewhere at the edge of the woods, Neal found two crude wooden benches he had left here years before. A yellow tarpaulin had protected the wood from the weather; it was trailing now from the benches as Neal carried them.

"The tarp comes in handy when it rains. It protects all our gear. Now then, how about steak and salad for supper?"

Beth watched as he brought a hamper of food in dry ice from the car trunk, went to help sort it out. There was enough here for two days, she decided, lifting out a thick steak and carrying it to the grill Neal had set into the ground on iron legs above the fire.

In moments, the smell of grilling beef filled her nostrils, making her realize how hungry she was. There was salad to be prepared, and thick Roquefort dressing from a jar, and bread to be toasted over the flames.

They ate side by side on the benches, with the moon above and the stars like diamonds in the blue velvet sky. The night was pleasant, still warm from the day, but with a hint of coolness in the wind sighing gently across the lake. Her shoulder rested against Neal's and it's warmth and bulk seemed very natural to her. It was good to lean against him.

He lighted a cigarette for her, and to her surprise, lifted out a pipe and filled it with tobacco. When he caught her eye, he grinned.

"Seems fitting, somehow, for an old married man," he laughed, holding out the pipe before lighting it. "Do you object to pipe smoke?"

"I don't know," she said slowly.

"Then let's find out."

She enjoyed it, she decided, after a few sniffs. Out in the open, it was very pleasant, almost part of the scenery. Was Neal doing this to impress her, in some way? Did he really feel it made him seem less the playboy? More the married man? She could not decide.

When the fire died down, he put more wood on it, and Beth felt her gaze drawn hypnotically by the flames. They were very much by themselves here, almost as if they were the only man and woman in the world. Occasionally she could hear the faint cry of a loon, the flop of a fish breaking water in the lake, the rustle of underbrush as some furtive animal investigated their camp site.

"Nervous?" he wondered.

"Not with you here."

He regarded her with his calm gray eyes. "You're a funny sort of woman," he said after a long time.

"Oh? In what way?"

"You're equally at home here and in a place like the Lobster Claw. Not many women would be, you know. They might shine in one spot, but not in the other."

"Candace would," she murmured faintly.

He hooted. "Don't let that act of hers fool you. She's no more an outdoors girl than I am a beggar. No, Candy enjoys being pampered." His gaze went over her bluejeans and pullover. "Nor would she wear anything like that. Never."

"You agreed to old clothes," she muttered.

A stray breeze tossed hair before her eyes, so that she could not see the expression on Neal's face for a few seconds. But she could feel his arm slide about her shoulders, feel it draw her to him.

The next moment his lips were on hers, covering them.

Beth yielded to that kiss, before she realized what she was doing. It was an instinctive thing, born of their fellowship about the campfire, of the moon and the stars and the balmy July night. Her senses swirled, her heart thudded crazily, she knew a moment of heightened sensation, of pleasure amounting to rapture.

Then she eased away from him, gently, not daring to look into his eyes but staring off across the lake. "I—I think we're both t-tired," she whispered. "It's been a l-long day."

He could have pulled her back into his embrace and Beth

told herself numbly that she would have returned to his arms and his kisses without more than a token struggle. *I've really fallen for the guy!* He's used his playboy charm and I'm just like all the other girls he's ever known, willing to roll over and play dead for him.

She didn't know whether to laugh or to cry. She was all mixed up. Despite her fine resolutions, she was like a big blob of putty in his hands. Oh, sure. She loved him. There was no sense in denying the fact, especially to herself. She had even blurted it out so he could hear it.

But she mustn't give in to him!

This camping trip was just one more of his tricks, to place her in a romantic setting and then break down her resistance. If she didn't love him so much, if the idea of losing him wasn't like a knife jabbing her middle, she might well have flung herself at him.

It wasn't as if she wanted to marry the man. She was his wife, already. And that made it all the worse. She wanted to keep him and this wild, mad, accidental marriage of hers. It couldn't go on forever, she understood that. But just let it go on for as long as possible.

Neal said gently, "I'm an idiot. Of course, you're tired. Go on, you get into your things, onto whichever cot you want. I'll be in in a little while."

She turned and moved toward the tent. As she stepped inside, she paused to look back at him over her shoulder. He was sitting before the fire staring into the flames that tinted his face crimson, that highlighted the pain lines, the desperation, which she could read so clearly.

Beth undressed swiftly and crawled between the sheets.

After a time, Neal came in. She could hear him undressing in the dark. His cot creaked as he gave his weight to it.

"Neal? You asleep?" she whispered.

"Not yet. What is it?"

"Are we going fishing tomorrow?"

"If you'd like to. Would you?"

"At dawn, Neal. So—good night."

She would keep him busy, thinking of things other than his wife. She would tire him out—and herself into the bargain— so there would be no more campfire kisses. Beth was not all that sure of her resistance powers to risk very many of those.

She was up in darkness that was just giving way to light. She shivered as she eased out of her flannel pajamas, giving glances at Neal from time to time to make sure he was still asleep. Then she was outside, staring at the redness to the west where the sun was rising, feeling the cool morning air invigorate her.

She rescued the fire by getting down on hands and knees and blowing faint coals to life, by adding twigs and then a big chunk of wood. When the flames were shooting upward, she put the granite coffeepot above it, and began frying bacon in the skillet. The eggs were fluffing nicely when Neal came out and blinked at her sleepily.

"You're a peppy one," he muttered.

"An early start, remember?"

He walked to the lake, knelt on a flat rock, and splashed water on his face. Beth watched him, wondering at his thoughts. Was he telling himself this was all nonsense, this courting of a wife in a wilderness? Would he much rather be in Boston, where all he had to worry about was what girl to call up for a date that night? A date which would be more rewarding than sleeping in an empty cot in a tent?

After breakfast, Neal picked up his fishing poles, his creel, his bait-box and moved toward the car. Beth went to join him. They would rent a canoe, which Neal would paddle back to their campsite, while she drove the Iso Grifo.

It took him close to an hour to bring the canoe to shore. Beth sat on a tree trunk and watched him approach, telling herself he would be tiring himself out in grand fashion. When the canoe grounded, Beth asked him if he wanted to rest.

"No need for rest," he growled. "I'm fine."

"Maybe I ought to paddle," she suggested.

He gave her a black look.

Still, when they were out on the lake and wetting their lines—Neal had insisted on baiting her hook, despite her protests that she did it for herself all the time—she felt a little guilty. Was she overdoing it? Would he grow suspicious and realize that she was trying to tire him out? Apparently not. He seemed to thrive on activity.

Neal caught the first fish, a big bass, fighting it for several minutes before Beth could slice the net into the water and scoop it up. "Supper," Neal announced triumphantly.

Beth caught the next two fish, playing them carefully, giving them line to run, then bringing them up short and reeling in. She worked them skillfully, as her father had taught her, and from time to time heard muttered exclamations from her husband.

After he had netted her second bass, he studied her slowly. "Well done," he said at last. "You played those two fish like a real pro."

"I was my father's only child. I had to play boy for him from time to time. I know all about football, baseball, and hockey. I can fish and shoot a gun. I don't like hunting, but that's because I don't believe in killing wild animals just for fun."

"But at Windflower Lodge . . ."

She shrugged. "I thought you wanted to be alone with Candace. Besides, I didn't know you so well, then."

"And you know me now?"

"Better than I did. Now I'll paddle back."

"You will not. You'll relax and enjoy the trip."

"Whatever you say, Neal," she answered meekly.

In the afternoon they went for a long hike through the woods, along a narrow path that Neal claimed was an Indian trail, long ago. They came to a hill where the trees fell away, giving them a view of the forests and the distant lakes that were tiny blue dots glinting in the sunlight. Almost of its own will, Beth's hand fumbled for Neal's, held it.

They stood that way, looking all around them, and then Neal murmured, "It's as if we're the only man and woman in the world."

"A modern-day Adam and Eve."

Neal *was* the only man in the world as far as she was concerned, she reflected. If only she were his only woman! A woman he could cling to, to have and to hold, as the saying went, forever.

But Neal Harper was not like that. He looked on a woman as a challenge, as someone to overcome with his charm, and when she was firmly hooked—like those bass they had caught—he would free her and toss her aside.

Beth sighed, saying, "Time we were getting back. I have fish to cook. And I'll admit, I'm hungry."

She was tired, too. All this crisp air and steady activity was putting a lassitude into her limbs. From the glances she gave Neal as they walked along, she decided he seemed tired, too. They would get a good night's sleep, be up at dawn, and throw themselves into more fishing and more hiking.

Their supper was an intimate experience. While she fried the fish, Neal busied himself washing the wild blackberries they had picked earlier, on the way back to camp. These would be the dessert, served in tiny tin bowls with milk on them. They ate side by side on the bench, shoulders touching, and later shared their tin mugs of coffee as Beth smoked cigarettes and Neal his pipe.

They watched the sun set beyond the woods on the other side of the lake, studied its reflection in the waters. The world was calm, quiet around them, as though it were sinking slowly into slumber.

"Tomorrow we'll fish the far end," Neal said at last.

"Up at dawn," Beth nodded sleepily.

"Then it's time you went to bed."

"What about you? Aren't you tired too?"

"I'll be in later, after you're tucked in."

She nodded, rose to her feet. He made no attempt to stop her but sat staring down into the campfire as he had done last night. What thoughts were running through his head? There was again that half-sad look on his face she had glimpsed before.

Beth almost turned back to him. He seemed so alone, so despairing, with his shoulders rounding and that hurt look in his eyes. But she went into the tent, undressed swiftly, slid under the covers. She was asleep before he entered.

The next day was much like their first, fishing and hiking. Neal was seemingly inexhaustible, using the paddle with the ease of long practice, hiking without breaking stride except to let her rest, at times. They went a different way through the woods, until they came to a height of jagged rocks, where they could look down into a tiny gorge, the bottom of which was covered with jagged boulders.

"The Abenakis, the Indians who used to live in these parts, had a legend about this place." Neal said slowly. "There was a girl who loved an Abenaki brave. Nobody today knows her name, or his. But the story goes that they were very much in love but that the girl did not quite trust him. He had a reputation as a lady-killer."

Beth shot him a suspicious glance. "Are you making this up?"

"No, no. It seems a lot of the Abenaki girls set their caps for him, or whatever the Indian expression for that might be. Our maiden couldn't make up her mind to marry him. She was afraid that—"

"—that as soon as they were married, he would be out fooling around with the other maidens, I suppose?"

"Exactly. And so the brave went off to war, where he performed incredible feats of bravery, helped win a great battle—and was killed."

Neal paused, picked up a pebble, and tossed it into the gorge. "They brought his body back for burial. When the maiden saw it, she realized what she had lost. Two days after the burial, she came up here and leaped down on those rocks."

Beth sighed. "You're trying to tell me something, I know."

"Am I, Beth?"

Something in his voice made her glance up at him. She could not be mistaken. Love for her was there in his eyes, with tenderness and adoration. If only she could be sure of him, not tortured with doubts! Why then, she would throw herself into his arms, tell him she loved him, too, and wanted to be his wife in all ways.

"I suppose every place like this has a legend about it," she whispered.

"I guess so."

"As a man, you can't know how that girl felt."

"Perhaps not."

They were still staring at each other. It was an intimate moment. One word from her and he would take her in his arms, devour her with kisses. She could read all that in his eyes. All she had to do was take one little step toward him.

Yet she could not. It was as if she were paralyzed.

She found herself saying, "It's getting cold. We'd better be heading back."

As she turned away, Beth felt a cold premonition that such a moment would never come again. In some way she had made a decision and was going to be bound by it. Forever.

Chapter Thirteen

Something was gone from between them.

There was nothing said, nothing done, that gave her this impression, but she sensed it, as a woman will. Neal was outwardly courteous, attentive, but a spark seemed to have died inside him.

Perhaps he had put too much importance on this camping trip. In some way he had hoped, had expected, that these days of wilderness living would beat down the barriers she had erected against him. And they almost had, Beth admitted to herself. Several times she had almost yielded to him.

On the rock above the gorge, it had been a near thing. Earlier, over those campfires, once when he had kissed her, and again when she had seen his face as he stared into the flames, she had come very close. Just a word, a glance, even an outstretched hand, would have brought her into his arms.

But it was over now.

They stayed three more days, but they were more like brother and sister than man and woman. They did their chores, they went out onto the lake in the canoe, they fished and hiked as before. But they did not reach out hands to the other, and there was never another time when they might have picked up the pieces and resumed their old companionship.

146

When she was alone on the morning of their last day, before getting into the Iso Grifo and going to get Neal who had taken the canoe across the lake to its owner, Beth felt tears come into her eyes. She paused in her packing to brush them away angrily.

This was what she wanted, wasn't it?

She had exactly what she had been working toward, a marriage relationship without love, even without affection. And Beth was discovering that it was a very barren thing. There was an emptiness in her, a helplessness about her every move that told her that somewhere along the line she had made a bad mistake.

Better to have fallen into Neal's arms long ago, better to have known a few wild moments of ecstatic bliss, than this abandonment of spirit. So what if Neal threw her over? This sort of marriage was worse than none at all.

Listlessly she walked to the Iso Grifo.

She drove to the other side of the lake slowly, trying to muster her thoughts, her emotions. Was it too late for her to offer herself to Neal? How could she do that now? It was next to impossible.

If only he would make some move, some gesture!

She watched him as he walked toward the car, away from the little shed that served as office for the man who rented the canoes and rowboats. Something seemed to have gone out of Neal, too. His step had lost its elasticity, his face its usual tenderness.

There was a heaviness about him, a sadness, almost a sense of defeat. Or was she, with her vivid imagination, imagining all of this? Certainly he was tired. After the week of activity, it was only normal for him not to have his usual energy.

She slid over to make room for him.

"Everything's packed, we're ready to leave," she said in a small voice.

He nodded. There was no smile, no reaching out to touch her. She felt like a stranger to him. As a result, she huddled into a small ball on her seat and stared out the car window as he drove. Tears hung in her eyes, ready to spill over at a word or glance. She had never been so miserable.

The day was no help, either. The sky was gray, lowering, it threatened rain. A leaden heaviness to the air pressed in on her, dampening whatever spirit she had left. It was affecting Neal as well, as he stared straight ahead at the road with a grim set to his features that told her, when she glanced at him, that he was in no mood for easy conversation.

After a time the rain came, beating against the windshield, making the wipers all but useless. Twice Neal had to pull over to the side of the road and wait until the downpour eased. When this happened they sat in a tiny pall of gloom, neither speaking.

The silence became unbearable to Beth. No matter what they said to each other, it would be better than this dead stillness, where the only sound was the drumming of the raindrops on the car roof.

"Are you going back to Boston when we get home?" she asked softly.

"I'm not sure. I think so. Adrian was right, I've been away too long."

"You've neglected your work on account of me."

"Oh, not entirely. I needed the rest. I really did."

She ran a fingertip up and down her bluejeaned thigh. "Are you sorry you married me, Neal?"

He was quiet so long she looked at him sideways, out of the corners of her eyes, past a spill of brown hair. He was regarding her, she thought, with dazed astonishment.

"Aren't you?" he asked at last.

She shook her head. "No. No, I'm not. I'm—glad."

There! She had made the first advance. The rest was up to him. If he moved over a little, drew her sideways—though bucket seats were never made for cuddling—she would topple into his arms.

He made no move at all. Maybe she had scared the guy silly. He looked on her as a frozen turnip, and she didn't blame him. How could she tell him that she loved him, needed him, in a way that would make him believe her?

She was hoist on her own petard. Just as he claimed never to have been a playboy, that it was something he had made up and could not now live down, so she herself had no way of convincing him that she meant what she said. Outside of flinging herself at him like a wild woman, and that was something she just couldn't bring herself to do, she could do nothing at all.

She sighed. The rain had eased. Neal slid the Iso Grifo into gear and moved out onto the road. He drove as silently now as he had before, ignoring her, paying her no attention at all.

They did not stop for lunch; it was as if Neal had forgotten all about food. Her own stomach told her she could eat, but she decided to say nothing.

The weather cleared slightly, the further south they traveled. The rain stopped, the wind freshened, and the sky brightened. If she had felt at all differently, Beth might have taken this for some sort of happy omen. As it was, she was so steeped in gloom, even a touch of sunlight on the edge of a cloud did nothing for her.

The cottage would be a welcome sight, she told herself. At least, there she could busy herself with her writing, lose herself with words. Forget Neal and this dull ache in her heart. He would be going away soon, back to Boston.

Ah, and when that happened—what about her?

She didn't dare stay in Rocky Cove. She would leave, too, maybe go back to her original plan to sell the cottage and take a trip.

She sat up, her back rigid.

"Neal, over there—look!"

The bearded man was lounging against a tree bole. He wore a slicker but his head was bare. He turned his head casually at the sound of the car motor, came away from the tree in one fluid move, and began to run.

Neal swore. He braked, leaped out, and went racing after the man. Beth opened her own door and sped after them.

"Neal, no!" she cried. "Let him go, let him go."

He did not listen, but went pounding on, through wet underbrush and tree branches drooping with wet leaves. She could see him, fifty to sixty yards ahead of her and moving further away. Beth ran as fast as she could, scrambling over big boulders and fallen tree trunks that Neal took with one jump. Her eyes scanned the woods, seeking to keep track of his broad back.

But in short moments, he was out of sight.

Beth staggered to a halt and leaned against a tree bole. She drew in breaths of cool air gratefully, letting the tiredness seep out of her.

Then her eyes went around her slowly. She was all alone in these woodlands. There was no sign either of Neal or the bearded stranger. Ah, but suppose that man circled around behind her, caught her when Neal was out of earshot? Warily, she stood erect, fists clenched at her sides.

The moment she had dreaded for the past few months was here. She was alone, vulnerable to attack. The bearded man might be behind any of these trees, listening for Neal, waiting to leap out at her, hands going for her throat.

Beth whimpered. All her worry about Neal and herself went up in smoke. What good was anything if she was caught here alone and choked to death? Her tongue came out, moistening her lips.

Very carefully she began to move away from there, back toward the cottage. She placed her feet where the fallen pine needles would cushion them, trying to avoid the pokeberry and bunchlily bushes, the arrowheads and Indian Pipes for fear of making them rustle. She must make no sound, none at all. And she must be sure that she did not move until there was no one to see her.

After a while, she could stand the suspense no longer. She ran and ran, along the way she had come, throwing quick glances over her shoulder to be sure no one was following. When she came to the road she sped past the dark blue car toward the cottage door, fumbling in her jeans pocket for her keys.

She inserted the keys and threw open the door.

And paused, stricken.

Someone had broken in, had searched the cottage. Her books lay scattered on the floor, tumbled from the bookcases built alongside the fireplace. Chair pillows and cushions were tossed here and there, and a few of them had been slit open. Beth ran into the room where she worked.

Her books had been tossed about in here, too. They lay helter-skelter, everywhere. Her heart was in her mouth as she stared at her desk. The manuscript she had begun was not torn up, as she had feared, but the pages had been thrown about. Every drawer of her desk had been pulled out, the contents scattered.

Beth sank into a chair, put her hands together, and burst into tears. It was too much. She could not stand up against all this. Her relations with Neal, the bearded man in the woods, the searching of her home, were like blows her heart and body had taken.

She was still sobbing when she heard Neal come in the front door, pause to mutter something, and then listened to his footsteps approaching the doorway. Beth tried to wipe the tears from her cheeks with a piece of tissue, but he saw them, clearly enough.

"I'm sorry about this—I'd give anything for it not to have happened," he murmured, kneeling beside her.

"That m-man thinks I ha-have something. He s-searched the place when we were gone."

"Did he take anything?"

"I d-don't know. I ha-haven't looked."

She sobbed some more, unable to control her emotions. Neal knelt beside her, saying nothing, doing nothing. At any other time, he would have taken her in his arms, comforted her. But the breach between them was too wide, now.

Beth rose to her feet. "I—I'd better straighten up, put things to rights."

"I'll give you a hand."

They worked together for two hours, and then Beth slumped into an easy chair and stared at Neal. Nothing had been stolen. Even the few dollars she had put in a kitchen bowl for food money had not been touched.

"What was he after?" she asked wearily.

"You must know," he said.

"I don't. I haven't the faintest idea. It's just as much a mystery to me now as it was the day that hand grabbed my ankle near Capstone Rock."

Neal shook his head. "Well, it beats me. We've swum near the rock, I searched the bottom, didn't see a thing."

He walked around the room restlessly, frowning.

"I can't leave you like this, all alone," he said at last, almost as if to himself.

She felt obliged to say something. "You've done all you can, Neal. I'm grateful. And you can't stay here forever, protecting me. I understand that."

"I'm glad you do," he nodded.

Something in his voice caused her to lift her head sharply, stare at him wonderingly. He paced up and down, not looking at her but staring at the walls, the fireplace, out the windows at the darkening dusk.

"You can divorce me whenever you want," he said slowly. "I won't contest it. I'll pay your attorneys' fees, any legal fees, and settle a lot of money on you."

Beth felt a vague surprise. Here he was throwing her aside and she had never given herself to him. It didn't make sense. This wasn't Neal Harper the playboy against whom everyone had warned her. This was an empty, helpless man who stood in her cottage, a man who looked almost broken. Defeated, certainly.

Beth murmured, "I don't want to divorce you, Neal."

He turned and this time his eyes met hers. "What do you mean, you don't want a divorce? I've heard you tell Mother you'd give me a divorce willingly, without hesitation."

She nodded, staring at her clenched hands. "I know I did. But you have to be the one to institute the action."

"Scruples?"

Again her head shook. "No. But I don't want a divorce. I want you as a husband."

He drew a deep breath, still regarding her with his cold gray eyes. "You want a protector, not a husband."

"That isn't true," she whispered.

Neal threw up his hands. He walked to the front door, opened it, went out into the dusk. He reappeared with her bags. But not with his own, she noted.

"Aren't you going to stay?" she whispered.

"What for?" he asked bluntly.

Her eyes dropped. Almost under her breath she murmured, "You must be hungry. Let me get something for you to eat."

"We're good at that," he nodded. "I always seem to be eating great meals with you. But that's as far as it goes."

"Please," she whispered.

Neal sighed. "All right. I guess I don't blame you. I can't just ride off and leave you here alone with that bearded man somewhere out there in those woods. Okay, okay. I'll stay the night. But tomorrow I'm leaving, I'm going back to Boston."

"And file for divorce?"

"And file for divorce."

It was the end, then, between them. Beth felt as if her heart was a leaden ball in her rib cage, weighting her down

All along, she had been hoping for some miracle that would convince her beyond any doubt that Neal Harper was not the playboy she feared, but was solid, substantial husband material, who would love her for herself, who would want to spend the rest of his life with her, who wouldn't toss her aside to go looking for other girls.

There was no miracle.

The cold truth was that she had failed, in some manner she couldn't quite understand. Or maybe she did understand. She should have taken him on trust. When he had told her that he had made up that playboy bit to keep people off his back, she should have believed him.

The trouble was, she wasn't sure of him, even now.

But—

She could make one last try, couldn't she? Even now, it might not be too late. Forget about his being a playboy, accept him for what he seemed to be, for what he had proven himself to be with her.

He had been gentle, understanding, and sympathetic. He had not tried to force himself on her at their little camp, he had contented himself with hints and innuendos. He had offered her chances to respond to him, chances she had ignored or rebuffed.

Beth said now, "I'll start dinner. You bring your things in."

She turned and moved into the kitchen. It would keep her mind off Neal, busying herself with pots and pans. She prepared a pot of coffee, took lamb chops out of the refrigerator, and mixed a salad.

She forgot Neal, forgot time.

When everything was ready, she called, "Come and get it."

There was only silence.

Wondering, she went into the living room and peeped into her workroom. There was no sign of Neal. A stifled feeling came up into her throat. He had run out on her! He was giving her no chance to set matters right between them, no chance at all.

Numb, she went back into the kitchen, turned off burners, stared down at the salad. She had no appetite. The mere idea of food repelled her.

Beth wandered back into the living room. The cottage was very quiet, as empty as herself. She seated herself in an easy chair, but she was too tense to relax. Her nerves were at the breaking point. She bit her lower lip and clenched her hands until her nails drove painfully into the flesh.

An idea touched her mind. Maybe he was having trouble with the car, with the things he was to bring in. Or maybe he had fallen, hurt himself.

The thought of that brought her running to the front door, speeding out of it. She slid to a halt on the flagstone path. The Iso Grifo was gone.

She was certain, now. Neal had let her think he was coming back to her, then had fled as though she had the plague. She turned, moved toward the cottage, slowly at first then more swiftly as she remembered the bearded man. She closed and locked the door behind her.

She was alone at last, finally. All her bridges were burned. She had gotten what she wanted. Neal Harper had not tossed her over because she had yielded to him. Oh, no. He had thrown her aside without making one final effort to break down her defences.

Tears brimmed at her eyelids.

She gave way to them, sobbing unashamedly, feeling her cheeks grow wet. Huddled in as small a corner of the easy chair that she could occupy, she let the tears and the sobs take hold of her, making no attempt to check them. Utter misery ran through her like a flood.

Briiiing

She did not hear the bell, she was too deeply immersed in her sorrow. But it must have touched a chord of understanding, for she straightened, brushed the tears from her cheeks, and muttered, "I despise weeping women."

Briiiing

This time she heard it. Her head turned, her heart gave a great leap. She whirled from the chair, ran toward the door. At the last moment, caution touched her mind.

"Who—who is it?"

"Neal. Come on, let me in."

For a moment she couldn't move. Her legs were rubbery, it took all her willpower to make them work, to carry her to the door so she could unlock it and throw it open.

Neal grinned down at her.

Beth threw herself at him. Her arms went around him, she held him as tightly as she could.

"Hey, what's all this?" he laughed.

"I thought you'd left me," she whispered against his chest.

His arms came up, went around her. She nestled into them, comforted. It was the first time since they had stood together on that rock above Indian Leap that he had held her this way. She leaned her weight on him and relaxed.

One hand went from her side to tilt her chin up so he could look down into her eyes. They were tear-stained, red, but Beth did not care. She didn't care about anything except that Neal was here with her again.

He kissed her closed eyes, her wet cheeks. Finally his lips went to her mouth. She kissed him hungrily, with all her yearning in her quivering mouth. They held that kiss a long time.

Neal whispered, "I don't believe this."

"It's true. I'm an idiot."

"I'm a playboy, remember?"

"I don't care, Neal. I just don't. You've won. I love you. I love you, do you understand?"

He kissed her again. His lips moved against hers when he spoke, "And I love you, you goose. I always have, ever since the day I came to this cottage. Or maybe when I saw you behind that little veil, the day we got married in the hospital."

"You couldn't have," she half-laughed, half-sobbed.

"It's true, though." He paused briefly, then murmured, "Hey, don't I smell something cooking?"

"Forget food," she whispered, cuddling closer.

"But I'm hungry."

She drew away to stare up at him. His eyes were filled with all the tenderness and love she had ever imagined could be in those dear gray eyes of his. His hands still held her hips, where his fingers seemed almost to caress.

"How can you think of food at a time like this? Don't you understand what I mean? I love you. I want you the way a wife wants a husband."

She flushed as she spoke, half angry at his obtuseness. He drew her to him again, kissing her throat. "And I want you. But not yet. Not yet."

Beth gaped. What kind of playboy was this, to turn down a

woman he wanted when she was throwing herself at him? What kind of *man* was he? Perhaps it was her fault. A man could scarcely find a woman ravishing with her eyes red and her cheeks still damp with tears. She must do something about that.

But not until after she had fed him.

She nodded, caught him by the hand, and drew him into the kitchen. Beth said, "You sit. I'll take care of everything."

When they were finished, Beth whispered, "Let the dishes go. Go back into the living room and sit down. I—I have a surprise for you."

She fled into the bedroom, closing the door. She grasped her sweater, slid out of it, and wriggled free of the skirt. She ran for the shower, her heart humming a tune. She was going to be the *femme fatale* who would be utterly irresistible, this night. She had put away all doubts of Neal Harper. Indeed, she did not care whether he was a playboy or not. It was up to her as a woman to keep him so interested that he would never be able to toss her aside in favor of another.

Why hadn't she understood that before, instead of playing the ninny who expected him to perform some sort of miracle to convince her she was the only woman he loved? Her very femininity ought to have told her that! But she had been too much in love with him, desperately afraid that once she let down her guard, he would run away from her. As she thought he had done, tonight.

She spent a long time under the cascading shower waters. Then she found an open bottle of Joy perfume and used it liberally. She slid into the black lace mini-gown that was little more than ebony mist.

The mirror confirmed her decision. In this bit of seductive fluff, she would finally prove to him that she loved him. Her hand went automatically to the matching robe, but she decided against it. If she were going to prove to him that she was ready to be his wife, this mini-nightie was absolutely right.

Flushing, she came out into the living room. Neal was seated in a chair, reading. He put down the book and stared at her. His eyes went up and down, then reached her face.

"There's a bottle of wine in the fridge," she whispered. "Shall I go and get it?"

He shook his head.

"Go to bed," he told her gently.

"Wha-at?" she gasped.

He put the book down, came toward her. His hands touched her bare shoulders, held her. "You think I've been a playboy. That I've been waiting to bed you and then walk out on you. What changed your mind?"

"I don't want you to leave me," she whispered.

"Is this your bribe to keep me beside you?"

It was, of course, the way he would think. She had been so standoffish in the past, no wonder he was so suspicious of her now. Beth shook her head.

"No. I didn't mean it as a bribe. I—I've been a little fool. I know that, now. I should have taken you at your word and not listened to Candace Thorne or your mother. I should have realized they had axes to grind."

His grin was infectious; it made her smile. "Good. Now I'm going to prove to you that I'm not a playboy. I'm going to let you sleep by yourself while I stay out here. Alone. A real playboy wouldn't do that, would he?"

"N—no."

He caught her, kissed her on the lips. Gently, without any hint of male ardor. And yet—she sensed that he was holding himself in check, the trembling of his hands on her shoulders told her he wanted nothing so much as to sweep her up into his arms and carry her into her bedroom. As she wanted him to do.

Those hands turned her toward her bedroom door. He gave her a little push.

"Get a good night's sleep," he called. "We have a lot to do tomorrow."

That brought her up short. She turned, unconscious of the picture she made in the doorway, with the bedroom lamp on behind her. "What are we going to do tomorrow?"

"You'll see."

Beth sighed. "Neal, you're infuriating. I ought to be raging like the proverbial woman scorned—"

"You know better than that."

His eyes glowed and she realized how he must see her, with the nighttable lamp framing her in a golden halo. She flushed, dropped her gaze, then muttered, "And now you tell me you have plans for us tomorrow I don't know about."

"You will."

He blew her a kiss. He was still watching her as she closed the door and leaned against it. She ought to be wild, furious at him for ignoring her invitation to share her bed. Instead, she was leaning against her bedroom door in a happy glow.

He had proved he loved her, hadn't he, paradoxical as that might sound? If he had been the playboy Candace Thorne and Mrs. Harper had warned her about, he would have been in here with her, instead of sleeping out there, by himself.

Beth danced around the room, hugging herself.

Chapter Fourteen

A butterfly brushed her lips and clung there.

She felt warmth fill her, knew a contentment that made her stir and lift her hands to catch that butterfly. Her palms touched freshly shaven cheeks, and her eyes sprang open.

Neal knelt beside the bed, smiling down at her.

She put her sleep-warmed arms about his neck, drew his mouth to hers once again. She kissed him as she had never kissed anyone in all her life, before now. Her heart banged away, her pulses drummed, she tightened the clasp of her arms until her muscles ached.

Now his arms were around her as well, holding her as she had wanted him to hold her for a long time. His kisses roved across her face, her closed eyes, her forehead, her throat.

"We can't," he whispered hoarsely. "We have things to do."

"What's more important than this—to us?" she breathed.

"We have to exorcise the last ghost."

As she stared, he reached out, caught up her woollen bathrobe, and put it into her hand. "Put that on," he told her. "I can't think with you the way you are."

"Good," she giggled. "I don't want you to be able to think."

He turned away as she came out of bed to wriggle into the robe.

"Chicken?" she asked softly, belting the garment.

"Something like that," he nodded, turning. "But today we're going out to Capstone Rock. We're going to find out what it is out there that's been causing you all this trouble. When we find that out, I think we can forget about that bearded man."

Beth felt her heart leap. "Is that the ghost you want to exorcise?"

"It is. Then you'll be a whole woman. You won't need me as a protector."

"But—"

He caught her hands, held them. "I want you to want me for myself, as a lover. Does that strike you as being silly? All my life I've had to go it alone, I never thought there could be anyone who would mean as much to me as you do.

"Is that selfish of me? To want you to know I want you—and you alone—forever? To want you to want me not just as someone to keep that bearded man from you but as the one man you want and need?"

He was so wistful, she came toward him, putting her arms about him. For the first time since that hand had seized her under Capstone Rock, she was really anxious to go there. If by solving her problem she could prove to Neal that she wanted him for himself, she was ready.

She dressed in her bikini with the matching jacket. Neal was putting the diving gear in the car trunk. When she stepped outside to join him, the sun bit into her flesh. It was going to be a scorcher of a day, and the water would be invigorating.

There was a man in the Century Coronado, clad in stained fatigues with a sea cap on his head. He turned as they came down the quay, nodding his head at Neal and gathering up some dirty rags.

"Everything's shipshape, Mr. Harper. You leaving now?"

"In just a couple of minutes."

The man sprang from the Coronado to the quay as Neal helped Beth on board. In his blue fatigues, the man seemed out of place, somehow. There was an air to him that reminded Beth of the military. Well, maybe he was retired from active service or something like that.

"Who was he?" she wondered out loud.

"A man I pay to keep an eye on the boat."

Beth shrugged, seated herself on the whitely upholstered seat beside Neal. He checked the instruments, touched the starter. The big engine rumbled to life. Almost instantly, the Century was backing out of its slip.

Neal did not offer to let her take the wheel today. He sat crouched over it, face intent, in utter silence. Only from time to time did he glance behind him at the receding shoreline, or to the south. Beth watched the waves form before them, break as the sharp prow sliced into them, sometimes lifting the Coronado, sometimes letting it drop into a trough.

Yet the wind was sweet with salt, a touch of spray now and then was bracing to her sun-warmed flesh. It was good to be here with Neal, sharing this moment with him. She did not mind even when he began the big swing that would bring the boat inward toward Capstone Rock.

Soon she would be swimming down in those gray-green depths. But Neal would be with her. Soon now, she hoped, all her troubles would be at an end. On impulse she reached out to touch him. He turned, smiled at her, pressed her fingers.

"It won't be long. You okay?"

She nodded. She was okay, sitting here serenely, as if without a worry in the world. Whatever was down there by Capstone Rock they would find today. And with that find, her own personal torment was going to end. She was sure of it.

Neal shut off the engine, the Coronado drifted until he went forward to drop two anchors. Then he turned and came back along the mahogany deck, to step down beside her, where she was gathering their gear.

He helped her into her Aqua Lung and buckled the straps. Then he was sliding into his own, fitting his feet into rubber fins.

They sat on the moldboard, then went backwards. The sea reached up to catch and cradle them as they sank into a grayish green world. A fish darted past them, terrified. Beth doubled up, kicked downward. She saw the bulk of Capstone Rock to one side, avoided it and the tidal flow that had caught her the last time she was here.

Her eyes scanned the sea bottom. It was pebbly in spots, sandy in others. A jellyfish moved lazily to her left, while below her a crab scuttled out of sight. Neal waved, pointed ahead, and side by side, legs kicking, they began their search of the rocks.

It was a strange world where they moved, the silence was almost like a physical force around them. To one side the rocks were humped and jagged, tossed and tumbled as though flung carelessly by a gigantic hand. Barnacles protruded from their sides, and here and there Beth could glimpse a China-man's-hat limpet clinging to the stone.

They swam on past the rocks, then swung back to approach Capstone Rock. Neal waved a hand, urging Beth to stay away from the gap between the foremost rock and the others, where the tidal flow was at its worst. They moved outward, then came back on the other side of the rock.

Irish moss seaweed, growing seemingly from the rocks themselves, floated lazily in the gray-green water. Beth made out a bed of mussels and a starfish crawling toward it.

Then a hand caught her wrist.

For a moment she forgot the mouthpiece, then started to open her lips and yell. But Neal was there, pulling at her, pointing ahead and downward. She stared where he pointed, saw a dark bulk resting under a rock overhang. Neal went down, with Beth close behind.

It was a large metal box, she saw, with a lock. At first she had thought it an iron-bound chest, something a pirate may have left there, centuries ago. But the box was modern, machine-tooled. Neal tried to budge it and could not.

His hand jerked upward. Beth nodded, kicked with her finned legs.

She came out of the water close to the big boulders, with Neal beside her. He put a hand on the stone, hung there as he removed the mouthpiece.

"Neal! What was it?"

"A sort of treasure chest, unless I miss my guess."

"Treasure chest? But——"

Neal chuckled. "Not the pirate kind. At least, not the sort of pirates we're accustomed to think about, Captain Kidd and Bluebeard, men like that. No, these are latter-day pirates."

He replaced his mouthpiece, then gestured her to do the

same. Then they dove and swam around Capstone Rock back toward the Coronado. They moved easily, without hurry, with no sense of danger threatening.

They came to the surface together.

And this time, Beth did scream.

A boat bobbed close by the Century, and five men were leaning over its starboard gunwale, grinning at them. Two of the men had rifles. One of the men was bearded, with long brown hair. Instinctively, she knew he was the man who had kept her cottage under surveillance.

One of the men said, "You were right, Monk. She found the chest, all right."

The bearded man snarled, "I knew I should have finished her off, instead of just trying to scare her."

A rifleman put his .458 Winchester to a shoulder. "I can take care of that, easy enough."

Neal said, "It won't do you any good. You see—"

The rifleman laughed, bent his head, his finger tightening around the trigger. Beth stared at him, horrified, unable to move. All she had to do was double up, drop beneath the surface. Yet she could not stir a muscle.

Neal lunged at her just as the man fired.

Beth saw his body in front of her, watched him jerk as a bullet ploughed into him. She woke to life, caught him in her arms, held him. He lay heavy as a leaden weight against her. There was no life in him at all.

The rifleman laughed harshly. "I missed her, but I got him. Well, it don't matter. I can pick her off now, just as easy as—"

The man with the Winchester dropped it from suddenly nerveless hands. His eyes opened wide. He began to turn, very slowly and sat down. Beth saw blood at his shoulder. She was vaguely aware that she was hearing other gunfire, now.

The boat with the five men in it began to move.

"Stop engines," a voice roared.

Beth went under then, still hanging onto Neal, trying to lift his head upward, above water. The Aqua Lungs were weighing her down; with a deft twist she slid free of hers, got Neal out of his. Then she turned him on his back, cupped him under his jaw, swam upward with him to the surface.

She gave no thought to the men in the boat, all she was intent upon doing was getting Neal onto the Coronado. She put out a hand, caught hold of the ladder, clung to it, still with an arm about his chest.

He was dead!

She felt like death, herself. This was the end of everything, this body she held in her arms was leaden, without life. Never again would Neal give her that faint, almost wistful smile, never would he reach out suddenly to grab and kiss her. She sobbed, tears stinging her eyes like drops of acid.

Beth rubbed her face against his, whimpering.

"Neal, Neal—come back to me. Oh my dear, don't leave me. Don't go away from me. I can't live without you, darling. You mean the world to me."

Was that her imagination—or did his eyelids flutter?

Was he—alive?

Beth stared down at that face so close to her own. Yes! His eyelids were moving, opening slowly. So slowly. But then—ah! His gray eyes smiled into hers, his lips curved into a grin.

"Are we dead?" he asked.

"No. Oh, no, darling. We're alive. But you've been wounded. You jumped in front of me, to take the bullet that man aimed at me."

"Sure. I remember."

He stirred, but Beth wailed, "Don't move! Don't hurt yourself. Just relax. Wait!"

She turned, scanned the sea waves. The boat with the five men in it was close, bobbing up and down near a sleek gray Coast Guard cutter. The men were being taken aboard the cutter, even as a tender came through the waves toward the Coronado.

A uniformed man stood in the prow. He shouted, "Is he badly hurt?"

"He's been shot. Can—can you help him?"

The boat swept alongside. The lieutenant with two other men reached out for Neal, caught him, lifted him as gently as possible into the tender. Beth climbed the ladder into the Coronado, head turned to watch as they placed Neal on the deck and a man knelt over him with a first aid kit close to hand.

The lieutenant called to Beth, "He's wounded in the shoulder. I don't think it's too bad, but we've sent for a helicopter and we'll fly him to a hospital."

Beth shivered. Her eyes closed and she whispered, "Please God, let him live. Let him live so I can make it up to him, all the things he's done for me."

She watched as the tender turned, churned its path through the choppy seas toward the cutter. In a few moments she heard the drone of a whirlybird. Her eyes followed it to the cutter, saw it drop downward. A stretcher on a cable was lowered to the deck. Gentle hands lifted Neal, set him into the cradle, buckled straps, covered him with blankets.

The helicopter rose, veered sideways, was off with its burden dangling helplessly at the end of the cable. Beth watched until it was out of sight behind the shoreline. Then she reached for her wrap and put it around her.

She would have to take the Coronado back to the quay. By herself. She went forward to the anchors, tried to drag them free of the bottom.

A voice said, "Here, let me help."

The lieutenant was back, leaping from the tender onto the Coronado, giving her a reassuring smile. He joined her, drew up the anchors. When they were in place, he asked, "Can you take her in?"

"I think so. I'm not sure."

The lieutenant waved to the tender. "Follow me," he shouted.

He went behind the wheel, touched the starter, listened as the engine roared. "A good boat, this one," he muttered, and put his hands on the wheel.

As the Century slid through the waves, Beth asked, "Is he—is he badly hurt?"

"A flesh wound, mostly. The bullet took him in the shoulder and I think it went out the other side. That was a high-powered rifle the man was using, and he fired it from up close."

"I thought Neal was dead."

"A bullet like that will knock a man out when it hits. Shock. Luckily, he—your husband?—yes, your husband was moving as he fired. Then too, the boat the guy was shooting from was bobbing in the waves. With any luck he would have missed him entirely."

"He leaped in front of me. He took the bullet that was meant for me."

The lieutenant gave her a hard glance. "For you?"

"There's a box down there under one of those rocks."

"I know."

Beth stared. "You *know?*"

He smiled. "Your husband's been to see us, Mrs. Harper. Does that surprise you?"

"It certainly does. Why in the world should he do that?"

"Because he suspected something of the sort. He told us how you have been attacked, twice. How a man kept his eye on your cottage. Nobody does that who doesn't have some good reason. The obvious answer was that you'd unwittingly stumbled across something that somebody wanted kept secret."

"But we dove down there before, and didn't see anything."

"You didn't have time. Wasn't there something about a tidal flow that caught you, jammed you up against those rocks?"

"Yes. I didn't want to swim, not after that experience I had. When that tidal flow caught me, Neal must have felt I wouldn't want to dive again. And—and he didn't want to leave me to dive himself, knowing I might not be safe in the cottage alone."

Neal had done all that for her. He had given up his business interests just to stay with her, to keep her safe. She owed so much to him.

The lieutenant was talking. "So he came to us, put his suspicions on the line. We could have sent our own divers, but he thought it might be better if you and he went, with us in the background, waiting to see if anyone appeared, to attack you."

His face was concerned as he looked at her. "I hope you don't mind that you and he were the bait for our trap."

"No, of course not. It had to be that way, if you wanted to catch the men who owned that box."

"Mmmmm. I wouldn't say they owned it, exactly. Your husband thought it was the loot from a Brinks robbery."

Beth remembered the night at Windflower Lodge when Candace Thorne and Neal had talked about that robbery. She hadn't paid too much attention, she was too wrapped up in

her personal problems at the time. But they had spoken about
it. Neal or Candace, she couldn't remember exactly which,
had said something about some of that stolen money belong-
ing to Neal, or to one of his businesses. And he had replied
that it had been insured. Yes, that was it.

"Will you dive for it now?"

"Right now. We have divers on the cutter. By nightfall
we'll have the box and know its contents."

It was over, then. All the dangers she had faced were at an
end. There would be no more bearded man, no more hands
to push her into the paths of speeding cars, nobody to drag
her under when she went swimming. A vast relief flooded
through her.

Beth looked around at the waves, that seemed merrier,
somehow, at the cloudless sky which appeared almost to
smile at her. The sun was hot on her body, the air was clear
and salty. She had so much to be grateful for. Neal would
live, she was his wife, and—

She caught her breath.

Last night he had made it quite clear to her that he did not
want her as a wife! She had put on her most seductive garment (if one could call that black lace fluff a garment), and
he had sent her off to bed. Alone.

Maybe he didn't want her any more.

The idea appalled her.

Now wait a minute, Beth Harper! The guy leaped in front
of that bullet, to save your life. That means he loves you,
doesn't it? Of course it does. She had to pull all these doubts
about Neal right out of her mind.

Did she want him as a husband? Did she ever!

Did he want her as a wife? If he didn't, he soon would.
She would see to that. There would be no more sending her
off to a lonely bed. From now on, Beth Harper was going to
be the sort of wife Neal had dreamed of all his life. She was
going all out, with nothing held back.

The Coronado slid into its slip. The lieutenant shut off the
engine, sighed and leaned back. His eyes went up and down
the boat, glistening in admiration.

"Some day I'm going to own a boat like this," he said
softly. Then he came back to the present. "Ooops. Sorry. For-

got about you and your troubles. Do you have a car? I'll drive you home."

"I'm not going home. I'm heading for the hospital. May I drop you off somewhere?"

His eyes touched her bare legs, the bikini, the open robe. He sighed again. "Some day I'm going to have a wife like you, too."

Beth laughed. Some wife she had proved to be! But all that was changed, now. She rose, gathered up towels and Neal's robe, let the young lieutenant help her onto the quay. A man came forward from the shadows, saluted the Coast Guard officer. Beth recognized him as the man who had been in the Coronado when they had come aboard.

"Everything work out, sir?" he asked.

The lieutenant grinned, "Perfectly. Except that Harper was shot. But he'll be all right." He turned to Beth. "Coggins here reported to us when you left. That way we were able to be on time to prevent any more shooting."

Beth nodded gratefully. Coggins grinned.

"Now let me drive you where you want to go. After that, I'm off to see my husband."

"No need for that. Coggins and I have transportation."

His hand waved and Beth saw the Coast Guard tender in the water, almost rubbing prow to stern with the Coronado. Several men were watching them, grinning. She had forgotten about the tender.

"Oh, well, in that case."

The lieutenant and Coggins shook her hand, stepped across the Coronado to leap lightly aboard the tender. Beth stood and watched them, waving a hand, feeling the sea breeze ruffle her wrap, toss her hair about. Those men would be going back to the cutter that was anchored off Capstone Rock as divers went down for the metal box.

Beth sighed, turned toward the Iso Grifo.

She drove swiftly, surely, wanting to see Neal and take him in her arms. She needed very much to tell him how much she loved him. Anything that interfered with that must be pushed aside as swiftly as possible, as the dark blue car was pushing aside the miles that lay between them.

Her foot pushed down even harder on the accelerator. Faster she went, still faster, with the motor humming powerfully the dark blue body of the car like some magic carpet carrying her to her heart's desire.

When she came to the hospital, she hesitated. She was still in the bikini and beach robe, hardly fit clothing to wear to visit a hospital sickbed. Still! She was not going to waste time by going back to the cottage and changing her clothes.

She ran to the desk, asked after Neal.

"I'm Mrs. Harper. He was shot, the Coast Guard brought him here."

The receptionist gave her a quick glance, consulted the card file.

"We don't have him listed, he's not in any room."

Beth felt her heart sink. "But he has to be! This is the nearest hospital. They wouldn't take him anywhere else."

"It's about time you got here," said a voice.

Beth whirled. Neal was moving along the corridor in a wheelchair, conducted by a nurse. She ran to him, seeing the bandage on his shoulder, the hospital gown thrown about him.

"You're all right. Thank Heaven! Neal, I've been so worried."

"The bullet went right through, cleanly. The doctor patched me up, put a bandage around me, and let me go."

"Let you go? You can come home?"

The nurse smiled. "He'll be fine, Mrs. Harper. No need to keep him here. All he needs is some rest, he's not to use that arm for a while, then he'll be as good as new."

Beth closed her eyes, her lips trembled. She opened her eyes, caught Neal's hand and held it all the way to the Iso Grifo, walking beside the wheelchair. She lifted out the terrycloth robe from the car, put it around Neal as he stood up, then thanked the nurse.

She fussed over him, making certain that he would not injure himself as he slid into the car, then came around to get behind the wheel.

"The last time I was here was when we were married," she said softly. "It seems like an eternity. So much has happened since then."

She started the motor, backed up and turned. From time to time she glanced at him, wondering if his wound were hurting, but she could detect no signs of pain on his face.

"Did you really know that metal box was down there? Or that it was from that Brinks robbery?" she asked.

"I guessed. It had to be something like that. Those attempts on your life weren't undertaken out of sheer caprice. This meant someone was trying to keep a very important secret. It had to be money."

"It might have been pirate treasure."

Neal chuckled. "That's your imagination at work. No, if it had been pirate treasure, they could have produced it, laid claim to it, there was no need for all the hush-hush."

Beth thought for a few minutes. "Why didn't they move it, if they suspected I had seen it?"

"Because someone else, even a whole lot of people, might have noticed them and asked embarrassing questions. It was perfectly safe where it was, as long as you didn't say anything."

"I couldn't, Neal. I didn't see the box that first time I went swimming there, when that hand grabbed me."

"They didn't know that."

"I'm surprised they just didn't kill me and have it over with."

"Killing you—say, with a bullet—would have brought the police. The police might have stumbled onto something. For instance, if you had written down that you had seen a metal box there by Capstone Rock—"

"That was why the cottage was searched!"

"Yes, they were after some hint to tell them whether you really knew about it. Since nothing happened after a time, they grew more relaxed. But one of them was told to keep an eye on you and your cottage."

"Well," Beth sighed. "It's all over now, thanks to you." She frowned. "You might have let me in on what you planned, having the Coast Guard there, and all."

"You'd have given the show away."

"I would not," she flared.

His hand caught hers on the wheel, squeezed it. "I didn't want you there, as a matter of fact, when I dove for that box. But the Coast Guard and the police thought it would be better, more natural. Besides, sight of you would bring the men there so the Coast Guard could round them up."

"I'm glad you did," she murmured. "A wife's place is with her husband at a time like that."

"I think so. What about—other times?"

"At all times."

"Hmmmmm."

She glanced at him, flushed, then laughed.

As she pulled into the cottage driveway, there was a tiny glow inside her. The day was warm and pleasant, the little cottage seemed bathed in a golden splendor from the sunshine. All her troubles were over, now she could devote herself to taking care of this husband of hers.

"I'll open the door," she cried.

As he slid from the seat, she said, "Lean on me. I'll support you."

His arm went around her shoulders, he hugged her to him but did not lean his full weight on her. They moved up the path and to the front door. Beth fumbled in her tote bag for the key.

"You'll have to get out of that swimsuit and into your pajamas," she told him. "Then it's into bed for you."

"Into bed?" he asked wonderingly.

"Into bed," she nodded. "That nurse told me you needed rest, you're going to get it."

"But what about you?"

"I'll be there to see you get it."

His eyes touched her face, ran down her body. The light wrap she was wearing had fallen open. In the tiny bikini, there wasn't much of her that wasn't on display. She met his eyes and gave him a slow smile.

Neal shook his head. "With you around, it won't be very restful."

"Is that meant for a compliment?"

With his good arm, he drew her closer. "What about my being a playboy? Are you still afraid I'm going to toss you aside once I've—ah—enjoyed your favors?"

"You're no playboy," she murmured. "I know that now."

"Oh? How do you know it?"

"You wouldn't have sent me to bed last night the way you did. You'd have taken what I—offered."

"You have a point there," he smiled.

She leaned to kiss him on the mouth, gently. "Chicken soup coming up. And maybe hot tea."

Neal made a face. "I'm not an invalid. My arm doesn't hurt that much."

"That's another reason," she said, turning to move toward the kitchen. "You took that bullet that was meant for me. No mere playboy would do that, either."

She was almost at the stove when he called, "I'll probably need help dressing."

Beth halted, walked back to him. "Of course you will. How silly of me. Come along. I'll get your pajamas and robe."

He blinked in surprise. Beth caught his reaction, giggled. She said, "Didn't you think I'd help you? Do you think I'm such a prude? Or so cold that I have no feelings for you?"

She went up to him, caught his face between her palms, pulled it down so she could kiss him. His one good arm came around her, to hold her close.

"I don't believe this," he said dazedly, after a while.

Beth pointed. "The bedroom, darling."

He grinned and went where she ordered. But when it came time to slide out of his swim trunks, Neal muttered, "I can handle this. Just put my pajamas and robe on the bed."

Beth stared at him. "You *are* shy."

Neal scowled and she laughed, clapping her hands. "Some playboy," she jeered happily.

"If you ever say anything about that to anyone, I'll deny it," he growled. "Candace Thorne believes it. If she hadn't, I'd have had her in my hair even more than she has been. And my mother, as well. She was always after me to get married, so I had to make it appear that I wasn't the marrying type."

"Oh, I'll keep your secret. It's my secret, now."

Beth danced into the kitchen, began heating chicken soup with rice in a pan. Happiness was a muted explosion in her, she could hardly stand still at the stove. Neal was her husband, he loved her, she loved him. They had all their lives ahead of them in which to prove that love to each other.

Neal came into the kitchen, looking rather sheepish. Beth beamed at him, brought him a bowl of steaming chicken soup and rolls, insisted he eat it all. She herself had a chicken sandwich with hot coffee.

She said then, impishly, "You'll have to go back to work one of these days, I suppose. But not yet. For the next few days you're going to be an invalid and let me take care of you."

"Oh?"

Beth nodded emphatically. "Yes. Now you're going to take a nap."

"I don't feel sleepy."

"You will. Come on now."

"What about the dishes?"

"They can wait. We can't."

He stared at her. Dazedly he asked, "Am I hearing correctly?"

"Once you said, after you'd kissed me, that I had a fire in me. Well, I do, Neal Harper. I've been saving that fire for the right man. You're the one."

She caught his hand, drew him unresistingly with her. She made him get between the sheets and cover up. Then she snatched up the mini-gown and walked into the bathroom.

"I'll change and be with you in a sec."

When she came out, she felt no embarrassment. This was right and proper, with this man who was her husband. As he eyed her, she slipped between the sheets on his unwounded side.

"How can you expect me to take a nap with you here—like that?"

"I didn't say exactly when you had to take the nap, darling."

Neal paused, grinned, gave a shout and reached out for her. She went into his arms happily, slightly delirious. She may have been an accidental bride, but she wasn't going to be an accidental wife. This was one marriage that was going to last forever.

"If I hurt you," she whispered, "let me know."

"I won't even feel it," he laughed. "I'll have other things on my mind."

And from this day on, Beth thought, as she began to kiss him.

SIGNET Books You'll Want to Read

Buy them at your local

bookstore or use coupon

on next page for ordering.

SIGNET Books by Glenna Finley

☐	THE MARRIAGE MERGER	(#E8391—$1.75)*
☐	WILDFIRE OF LOVE	(#E8602—$1.75)*
☐	BRIDAL AFFAIR	(#E9058—$1.75)
☐	THE CAPTURED HEART	(#W8310—$1.50)
☐	DARE TO LOVE	(#E8992—$1.75)
☐	HOLIDAY FOR LOVE	(#E9093—$1.75)
☐	KISS A STRANGER	(#W8308—$1.50)
☐	LOVE FOR A ROGUE	(#E8741—$1.75)
☐	LOVE IN DANGER	(#Y7590—$1.25)
☐	LOVE'S HIDDEN FIRE	(#W7989—$1.50)
☐	LOVE LIES NORTH	(#E8740—$1.75)
☐	LOVE'S MAGIC SPELL	(#W7849—$1.50)
☐	A PROMISING AFFAIR	(#W7917—$1.50)
☐	THE RELUCTANT MAIDEN	(#Y6781—$1.25)
☐	THE ROMANTIC SPIRIT	(#E8780—$1.75)
☐	STORM OF DESIRE	(#E8777—$1.75)
☐	SURRENDER MY LOVE	(#Y7916—$1.50)
☐	TO CATCH A BRIDE	(#W7742—$1.50)
☐	TREASURE OF THE HEART	(#Y7324—$1.25)
☐	WHEN LOVE SPEAKS	(#Y7597—$1.25)

* Price slightly higher in Canada

Buy them at your local bookstore or use this convenient coupon for ordering.

THE NEW AMERICAN LIBRARY, INC.,
P.O. Box 999, Bergenfield, New Jersey 07621

Please send me the SIGNET BOOKS I have checked above. I am enclosing
$_____ (please add 50¢ to this order to cover postage and handling).
Send check or money order—no cash. or C.O.D.'s. Prices and numbers are
subject to change without notice.

Name _____

Address _____

City_____ State_____ Zip Code_____
Allow 4-6 weeks for delivery.
This offer is subject to withdrawal without notice.

𝒪

Big Bestsellers from SIGNET

- [ ] MADAM TUDOR by Constance Gluyas. (#J8953—$1.95)*
- [ ] THE HOUSE ON TWYFORD STREET by Constance Gluyas. (#E8924—2.25)*
- [ ] FLAME OF THE SOUTH by Constance Gluyas. (#E8648—$2.50)
- [ ] ROGUE'S MISTRESS by Constance Gluyas. (#E8339—$2.25)
- [ ] SAVAGE EDEN by Constance Gluyas. (#E8338—$2.25)
- [ ] WOMAN OF FURY by Constance Gluyas. (#E8075—$2.25)*
- [ ] HARVEST OF DESTINY by Erica Lindley. (#J8919—$1.95)*
- [ ] TIMES OF TRIUMPH by Charlotte Vale Allen. (#E8955—$2.50)*
- [ ] THE HOUSE OF KINGSLEY MERRICK by Deborah Hill. (#E8918—$2.50)*
- [ ] THIS IS THE HOUSE by Deborah Hill. (#E8877—$2.50)
- [ ] BELOVED CAPTIVE by Catherine Dillon. (#E8921—$2.25)*
- [ ] REAP THE BITTER WINDS by June Lund Shiplett. (#E8884—$2.25)*
- [ ] THE RAGING WINDS OF HEAVEN by June Lund Shiplett. (#E8981—$2.25)
- [ ] ALADALE by Shaun Herron. (#E8882—$2.50)*
- [ ] THE SAVAGE by Tom Ryan. (#E8887—$2.25)*

  * Price slightly higher in Canada

More Bestsellers from SIGNET

Recommended Reading from SIGNET